UNDER THE
BLADE

Also by Matt Serafini

Feral

Devil's Row

Island Red

All-Night Terror (with Adam Cesare)

UNDER THE BLADE

Matt Serafini

Sign Up for Matt Serafini's
These Dark Woods Mailing List
at mattserafini.com and
receive an exclusive ebook

 **One**

The killer was coming back.

Melanie heard impatient footfalls pacing just beyond the cabin wall.

Across the room, Bill's body lay sprawled across the floor, face down in a thousand glass fragments—hurled through the casement window five minutes earlier.

Melanie had thought fast, leaving her seat beside the fireplace and pushing two bookcases in front of the shattered sill, reinforcing them with all the furniture in the cabin's living room—a crude blockade of couches, chairs, and lamps. Forcing through it would require more strength than she hoped the killer had.

She pulled her head closer to her knees and winced each time the madman's fists fell on the door. He grunted like an animal as he pounded.

The corner of the room was a sea of spilled cassette tapes and smashed boombox pieces that surrounded her. They'd fallen from the shelves during her impromptu barricade. Across the way, Bill stared indifferently—his one visible eye vacant and popped wide. A hammer buried so deep in his neck that only half the handle jutted up through the torn flesh and broken cartilage.

He wasn't the only victim. Melanie stumbled across the

first bodies an hour ago. Once everyone had failed to show up for their nightly poker roundtable, she'd gone walking down to the female counselor bunk and found Jennifer there—strung up on the inside of the door like a rabbit and suspended off the floor with thick manila rope, rugged gashes sliced into her neck. A thick pool of blood grew at her feet, gathering every drop from her leaking body.

During Melanie's sprint back to the main cabin, Jennifer's killer had presented himself. A misshapen silhouette of a man, marked by an unnatural form, pulled open the door and filled the frame. Melanie about-faced and bolted up the trail toward Mr. Dugan's office, screaming for help the whole way. Fast and heavy steps gave chase at her back.

Mr. Dugan's office hadn't been locked. Melanie slammed the door shut and bolted it. The camp owner failed to respond to her frantic pleas. Lightning flashes rinsed the dark in quick bursts and she timed her movements with them.

There was a phone on the kitchen wall. She lifted it and found no dial tone.

At that point in the evening, only Jennifer was gone for sure and there hadn't been time to mourn the loss of her best friend. Instead, she hoped Bill, Lindsey, Tyler, and Becky were out there somewhere.

But they weren't.

While scrambling for a weapon, she'd discovered Lindsey and Tyler's naked bodies impaled together atop Mr. Dugan's bed. A pitchfork went straight down into Tyler's back and pushed through Lindsey's chest. In those sporadic lightning crashes, she noticed Tyler's head wet with blood, the back half of his skull completely recessed.

The grisly set piece carried with it the realization that everyone else had been butchered.

And the man responsible was outside, looking to come in.

The door had burst open, raining splinters across the room. In another eruption of lightning, the not-quite human lumbered in from the pouring rain. Melanie retreated to the rear of the cabin and pushed through the back door that had thankfully been there. She ran hard through the mud. Her feet felt like they sloshed through molasses on the way to the main cabin.

And here she was—fishing a small hunting knife out from beneath a pile of tapes as the doorknob jiggled.

Melanie brushed a strand of her curly red hair aside and pressed her fingers against her palms, hoping to steady her nerves. It was pointless because flashes of death stormed her thoughts with every blink. Her blood rushed with equal parts panic and adrenaline.

Time slowed to a crawl as she willed Mr. Dugan's return. The camp's owner would be marked for death the second his Jeep lights broke the dark. And if she unlocked the door, or moved the barricade aside to get out through the window to warn him, all the killer needed to do was choose which of them died first.

The cabin was safe for the time being. The remaining windows were either too small to fit through or so awkwardly sized that squeezing in would create one hell of a struggle. If the killer tried doing that, she'd have plenty of time to bury a knife in his skull.

The front door was shut and reinforced with a buntline hitch sailor's knot tied from the knob to the cabin's rafter. Melanie hadn't recalled her sleepaway camp know-how in years, but it rushed back on instinct the second it was needed. To prevent a breach of the back door, she'd spent the last of her energy sliding the kitchen's old lead refrigerator across the floor to block it.

At last, the damn doorknob stopped jittering and the

footfalls slipped away into the night, out of earshot. She brushed aside a Winger cassette as she stretched out, trying to shake away the crippling tension.

The maniac's retreat might've brought momentary relief, but her apprehension worsened. Where had he gone and why? Was Mr. Dugan back? Had someone come out here to check on them? That was doubtful, considering they'd spent the last two months fixing this place up without a single person happening through. If anything, the killer could wait her out, knowing full well she would cave before he did. She strained her ears, but there was only the rain.

If Mr. Dugan was back, he needed to be warned. She got to her feet and hoped to hear his Jeep's familiar axle squeak approaching. Without it, she had no intention of rushing out there.

These woods belonged to *him*, and she wouldn't stand a chance on unfamiliar terrain and in a torrential downpour. She didn't think she stood a chance at all, really. How could a seventeen-year-old fend off a mammoth-sized psycho?

Melanie walked around the cabin and pushed aside just enough of each curtain to look for arrival signs. Water sluiced against the glass, limiting her visibility to almost nothing. Mr. Dugan never came. Her hopes fell on Becky next. Hers was the only body still unfound. It was a big campground and she might've been hiding somewhere out there.

It was likely that she had been in the mess hall when the power was cut. Girl was a phenomenal cook—always experimenting in her off time. Just this afternoon, Bill had pulled three trout from the lake and Becky put them on the grill with some parsley, basil, and rosemary. Simple, but her decision to improvise some lemon/Worcestershire butter sauce made it one of the best things Melanie had ever eaten.

Over that lunch, Becky had announced to the group her

admission to Johnson and Wales' College of Culinary Arts. A prideful smile beamed across her face as they congratulated her, brainstorming all the possibilities at the end of that path. If there was even a chance she was still there—

I can't go outside. I won't.

Melanie felt ashamed of that cowardice, but had no trouble justifying it. For all she knew, the killer was waiting just beyond the door, ready to pounce. Did it make sense to try and get to the mess because Becky might be alive? And if she was, he might've been on his way there now.

I'm not moving from here, goddammit.

"I'm sorry, Bill," Melanie said. Her pitch was frail. Her hands tugged at his ankles, dragging him across the room. A trail of dark crimson followed them into the corner. His Motley Crüe *Girls, Girls, Girls* shirt had been torn to shreds from multiple stab wounds to the stomach. She hadn't noticed them before, suddenly remembering their plans to catch the Crüe next time they were in the area.

She shook off the memory and told herself that she could grieve only at the end of this. For now, Bill needed to be out of sight for sanity's sake. Only way to survive was to keep calm.

With a whimper, she turned him over and pushed his body as far into the corner as it would go, draping a heavy blanket over his length. Her eyes were wet and it was getting tougher to breathe.

"You're going to be fine," she whispered, not believing her own encouragement.

The place was locked down nice and tight. And Mr. Dugan would be back at some point. Maybe he decided to stay at Sherry Peterson's—a local widower who ran the town diner. Word around Forest Grove was that they had been carrying on for the last few years. But Mr. Dugan seemed to like Becky's company, too. On more than one occasion, she'd offered him a private home cooked meal in his own cabin. It happened so often that Bill had been sure they were sleeping together.

Men and their need for variety, Melanie remembered thinking, wondering if Bill had ever fantasized about the other girls. As if any of that mattered now. Her eyes drifted to the limp, red-stained sheet in the corner.

She dropped to her knees, the knife clanging beside her, crying.

They were gone. Jen—her best friend and confidant. Theirs was the kind of friendship at seventeen that already offered a lifetime of great memories. And Bill—her summer steady. An innocent fling in bloom. Their desire to go all the way was challenged by mutual reticence. She had been surprised to learn that Bill hadn't ever done it before. He was okay with that, too, saying that he wanted it to be with someone special. This was right before he took her hand and said, "You're special." Cheeseball sincerity had been his specialty.

The floor groaned beneath her pale thighs and a sharp click snapped through the cabin's silence. Behind her, steady creaking. She didn't want to look but turned around anyway. The throw rug rose up off the floor and then slipped away to reveal a cellar trapdoor lifting upward—a dirty, blood-caked hand pushed up on the square latch.

The killer rose from the darkness and, for the first time, she saw him against the dancing firelight.

It's him, she thought with wide, bulging eyes. *He can't be real!*

He was a campfire tale in the flesh, but no one had really bought the stories. The town drunk once accosted them outside of the gas station, swearing they'd meet their ends at the hands of Cyrus Hoyt. *"Hoyt'll hack you up. That's what he does."*

A surreptitious campfire fable recounted Hoyt's modus operandi. Melanie had found it scrawled in graffiti on the side of the boy's bunk one morning and barely had time to read it before

Dugan barked orders for a prime and re-paint:

> *Cyrus Hoyt haunts these woods, ready to attack*
> *He comes by firelight but you won't see him*
> *Don't know you're dead until he hacks*
> *His axe through your bone will please him*

Bill had asked Mr. Dugan about it at dinner once. "Don't worry about that bullshit," he said. "That's just a story some of the townspeople came up with to justify two kids who disappeared years back. Mothers and fathers didn't want to take responsibility for their piss-poor parenting, so they invented a story instead."

The story took a heavy step forward. His head was obscured by a welder's mask, a featureless steel plate covering his face. The dark and dirtied lens shade hid his eyes, while his breathing was both muffled and amplified beneath it.

He wore what looked like military garb: a thick and tattered surplus coat along with pants that were either black or caked with so much filth that it was impossible to tell otherwise. A gigantic hunting knife with lots of hungry, serrated teeth on one side was tucked into a fist. He studied her, cocking his head from side to side.

He lifted his head upward, almost daring her to make the first move.

Melanie felt like a cornered animal. Her hands fumbled for the knife as she was struck by a sudden realization: *I've trapped myself in here.*

There was absolutely no time to undo any of the barricades and the front door taunted her from over the killer's shoulder.

His heavy work boots inched forward and Melanie got to her feet, knife loose in her wobbling hand.

The killer raised the blade high above his mask. He was much taller—well over six feet—and wouldn't have a problem landing the stab.

Melanie realized she'd been backing up and felt the cabin wall against her. Nowhere to run.

He was close and there were wet bloodstains on his jacket—runny remnants of her friends. Even the welder's mask was stained with streaks of them. A few hardened chunks of gore clung to the steel. He reeked of perspiration, refuse, and rot.

The urge to vomit was powerful, but she stifled it while the fireplace lit an actual fire under her ass. Then she remembered the poker. It should still be atop the burning log she'd thrown onto the blaze earlier.

He was a few feet away and his breathing sounded excitable. The blade danced in the firelight, hanging high overhead.

Melanie flung her own knife outward, straight at his face. It bounced off the killer's mask but caught him with enough surprise to halt his approach. Momentarily. All the time she needed to drop to the floor, her arm fanning out and pulling the poker from the fire.

The killer came forward, his knife threatening to cut through her pastel "Camp Forest Grove" t-shirt on its way to her innards.

She had a split second's worth of advantage and used it to stab his thigh. The poker sizzled and slipped through his leg. He let out a muffled wail and tumbled back, covering his smoldering wound with a shaky hand.

Then she scrambled to her feet, scooping up the knife and running for the door. The little blade cut sharp and tore through the rope on the knob as she pushed through and into the rain, too scared to look over her shoulder.

No chance of escaping in a car, since Bill's keys were likely still in his pocket. She could've kicked herself for forgetting to check. Jen's keys were in the girls' cabin, but she wasn't going back there, either. There wasn't any time to search. Not with a killer on the loose.

The entire campground was mud, making it impossible to conceal her tracks. The only thing to do was make erratic movements and hope that Cyrus Hoyt lost her trail.

She trudged across the hostile terrain until the kitchen was close, and then debated her next move between gasps of air. It wasn't worth the risk of being trapped inside another cabin, especially if there were more secret entrances she didn't know about.

Instead, she snaked around the building and moved to the forest's edge, just enough to lead her tracks in that direction. Then she skirted the muddied grounds while doubling back toward the lake. He might come across her trail to the water, but if he searched the kitchen or forest first, it would buy her all the time she needed.

The waterfront was quiet and a thin layer of fog rose up off Lake Forest Grove like strands of white wool. Three canoes sat grounded on the shore. She dropped the knife into the nearest one before setting the others adrift. She waded back to the straggler and got inside, paddling for deeper water.

Melanie didn't stop until the camp was out of sight, and even then, she kept going. The waterfront disappeared in the foggy shroud. As the rain stopped, she breathed a cautious sigh of relief.

It was easy to imagine him rampaging from building to building, rage mounting along with the realization that he'd been outsmarted. Eventually, he would check the beach. And what would he think upon discovering all three canoes missing?

Her heart sank with that realization. She'd taken away his ability to give chase, but by drawing an arrow in the sand.

Now she watched the other side of the lake in depression. Hoyt knew the area well and could already be on his way to the other side. What if he drove? Or, at least, knew where to wait. She wiped tears from her eyes and half-expected to see him suddenly standing among the watery fronds, waiting with open arms drenched in her friends' blood.

Melanie felt more exposed than ever. Every paddle dip felt like a radar ping. And it was only a matter of time before Hoyt locked on. Her best bet was to get to shore and run. The killer might've been wounded, but that wasn't going to keep him away. And if he figured out that she'd escaped in a canoe, he'd be guessing as to where she'd gone.

The fog was good for that, at least.

She decided to change direction slightly, banking to the right and cutting a swath diagonally across the lake.

That's when she spotted one of the other canoes.

Impossible! How did it drift out this far?

It was floating off to her right, just a few yards behind her. Moving closer somehow.

Melanie pushed the oar down through the water, but the errant canoe continued drifting forward. Her biceps tightened and she paddled harder.

The empty canoe slammed against hers, knocking her forward. The oar slipped from her grip and she shrieked. Her hands launched toward the water, reaching for it. But it was already gone.

"Shit," she said, and thought about swimming the rest of the way.

The hull exploded beneath her feet.

The canoe's side splintered to pieces as an axe swiped across the floor. Melanie was fast, kicking her legs up to avoid the slice. The boat filled with water almost instantly, and Melanie's off-kilter body sent it capsizing into the blue.

Into the arms of the killer.

Olive-drab sleeves wrapped around her waist and pulled her deep into the cold.

She cried out and choked on the sudden intake of water. Her arms flailed and her hand gripped the bottom of the welder's plate, yanking the mask off his head.

His bear-grip tightened into a squeeze and the mask fell from her hand, slipping away into the gloom. Melanie's mouth was clamped and that meant inevitable drowning as soon as she needed to breathe. Her stomach and chest constricted, giving way to crushing pain beneath his flexing forearms. She felt the rough and misshapen features of his face while he struggled to choke her out.

She jammed her thumb straight into his eye.

He screamed out—a soggy and high-pitched yowl—before releasing her.

Melanie floated to the surface and gulped for air as soon as she broke through. Then she swam. Land wasn't far—maybe ten feet—and she managed to pull herself ashore, crawling through the mud like an animal. Too tired to stand.

Without a weapon, all she could do was hope the killer wasn't following. That he'd been wounded enough to abandon pursuit. Town was probably five miles away and she could clear that in an hour, if only she could stand.

Have to get up.

Two hands launched straight out of the water and clamped down on her ankles like wrenches. They were pulling her back toward the murk.

She used her last breath to scream, one final cry for help. One of his hands let go long enough to punch down on the back of her skull. Her eyesight became a blur as another punch landed, and then another—each of them accompanied by an inhuman grunt.

She kicked at him with her free leg, but he brushed it aside and pulled her closer still. Hoyt rolled her onto her back and climbed out of the muck, pinning her against uprooted branches with a knee to her belly. A strand of puss dangled from his bloodied eye socket, plopping onto her cheek while he slapped her endlessly, giggling in demented glee.

Her hands fought his face, clawing and scratching to no avail. He merely brushed them aside. Somehow, his blows landed harder. Hurt more.

She did the only thing left to do—launched up and attached her teeth to the tip of his nose. She'd been going for his neck but had miscalculated the trajectory. Without a second thought, she bit down with a wild growl.

Her teeth sunk into flesh and filled her mouth with the stranger's blood. Undeterred, she tightened her jaw and chomped through the flimsy slice of upper cartilage with as much ease as chewing through a chicken bone. The nose collapsed with a crunch and the killer recoiled, whimpering.

He crawled backwards and dropped into the mud, covering his face with open palms.

Melanie pulled a broken branch out of the moistened earth at her feet. It slipped from the mud with a plop and she fastened it in her grip like a baseball bat.

The killer had only now lifted his head up out of his hands and the branch connected against his skull, breaking the wood off in shards. Melanie swung a second time. And then a third, not stopping until his face looked like crumbled meatloaf. The branch connected against his flesh with wet smacks that rained blood down on the muddy bank. At last, he slumped over with only a faint wheeze slipping past his mangled mouth.

Satisfied that he wasn't getting up, Melanie made a clumsy retreat. It was hard to know how much time had passed, but at last, the overgrown foliage gave way to pavement. Her head was heavy and her survivor's adrenaline was almost depleted.

She shuffled down the tarmac, the soles of her sneakers scraping along. Her brain was nearly as exhausted as her body, and the only thing that propelled her forward was the thought that she wasn't yet far enough away from that monster.

Someone would happen by any minute now.

But that minute stretched into many. Ten, then twenty. The night was as silent as the road was empty, and her mind began wandering into hopeless places. She was lost and would die out here.

The explosion of red and blue lights was startling, but she calmed once she saw that it was a police cruiser slowing to a stop in her path.

"You okay, young lady?"

Melanie dropped to all fours and sobbed uncontrollably. "They're all dead," she cried as the police officer made his way over.

"It's okay," he said. "Let's just get you over to my car and you can tell me what happened."

And just like that, she was saved.

 **Two**

Melanie Holden awoke to the sound of the house alarm and lifted her head up off the pillow. An artificial voice alerted her to an opened patio door. It spoke with the kind of unnerving indifference that made her heart hurt.

She climbed out of bed wishing she'd taken those firearm lessons. The prospect of owning a gun was repulsive. Not that she objected to their existence—she held no stance on the issue—but she didn't trust herself to handle them responsibly.

An aluminum baseball bat was clenched in her palm as she made her way into the hallway. The house was dark, with only the faint glow from the cat's nightlight showing the way. Her steps were plunged in muted orange glow as she moved forward, chewing the inside of her cheek to stay composed.

She flicked on every light in the house as she walked, sweeping the kitchen and bathrooms. The spare bedroom was clean and the office was empty.

The alarm hub crackled to life, "Ms. Holden, is everything okay?"

She was reluctant to wave their assistance away. The patio door off the kitchen was ajar—as though someone had almost gotten inside and was startled by the alarm.

Melanie stared at it through watery eyes as the dispatcher tried again. "Ms. Holden, would you like for us to send the police?"

She pushed the door back into its jamb and threw the deadbolt. Her heart pumped so fast that she felt the blood streaming. Somewhere, the alarm voice was talking, but she couldn't focus enough to hear it.

Was this the night *he* finally found her? Nobody was in here and they couldn't have gone down to the cellar because that door had its own sensor. If it had been opened, the system would've detected it the same as the patio door.

The alarm company wasn't taking any chances, though. The voice called out again, stating that the police have been dispatched to her location. She might've saved them a trip, but her confidence was nonexistent. It was best they came out here.

She kind of needed that peace of mind.

Melanie ran a hand through her straight blonde hair, remembering how red and curly it used to be. It wasn't long after Forest Grove that she changed it, hoping she could stop thinking of herself as a victim by physically altering the person she'd been.

She tapped quick-bitten nails against the kitchen countertop and counted the minutes until the police arrived. These feelings of violation were as infuriating as they were terrifying. And that dream. With it on the brain, it was no wonder she thought Cyrus Hoyt had come back to finish the job.

He's. Dead.

That mantra had been repeated enough throughout the years. But in twenty-five of them, she wasn't sure she ever really believed it. Her psychiatrist insisted that the ongoing feelings of vulnerability were normal because of the way she escaped. That killing Hoyt in self-defense had been necessary and she should never feel guilty about it. She never had. The problem was that Melanie never saw him die.

In that last glimpse of him, bashed and bloodied on the

shore of Lake Forest Grove, the bastard had been breathing.

She went back into her room and grabbed her phone. It was 3:47 am and there was no getting back to sleep now. Lacey, her eighteen-year-old half-Siamese, half-Burmese cat lifted up off her paws and surveyed the situation. When she saw that Melanie wasn't coming back to bed, she folded her head back down against her chest and went back to sleep.

Charmed life, you little shit, she thought.

She brewed a cup of coffee and dropped into a chair, fiddling with some new apps on her phone while her mind was back in 1988. Details of that night ran through her head, rehashing all kinds of bloody imagery that she had never truly escaped.

The police showed up twenty minutes later and gave the place a once-over. They were quick about it, telling her about some downtown punks who enjoyed trying their luck in the suburbs every now and again. It was likely that they wouldn't be back, because they usually just moved onto their next mark. That assurance was empty and brought little comfort.

By the time things were squared away and her heart rate returned to normal, it was close to seven and that meant she had class in just over an hour. The *would've-been* thieves hadn't left behind any traces, although they *had* succeeded in picking the deadbolt. Even the officers thought this showed more skill than evidenced in local break-ins. That was all she needed to hear, making a mental note to add additional locks to the patio door this afternoon.

After a quicker shower than she would've liked, she dropped a can of Fancy Feast into Lacey's purple dish, scratched the kitty on the head, and grabbed her professor's satchel. The cat meowed an audible approval as Melanie headed out the door.

The faculty parking lot was always filled, no matter the time. Since there were no classes before eight, Melanie had no idea why her colleagues got here so early, but getting a good parking spot probably had everything to do with it.

She found one among the student cars on a side street and parallel parked her cherry LaCrosse. She had five minutes to reach the library's fourth floor or those enthusiastic learners would be quick to assume they were getting the day off.

This was the last class before finals, and Melanie couldn't wait for this semester to be over. Her days of teaching *Introduction to Journalism* were finally at an end, and they would not be missed. It had never been her forte and she never wanted to teach kids how to be muckrakers. Instead, she'd stepped in for the English department when another professor went sick. Turned out to be cancer and watching it eat away a woman of fifty-six was a hell of a thing.

Melanie was only fourteen years away from that age and didn't want to think about fighting for her life again anytime soon.

The campus library was all but abandoned at this hour. A volunteer student sat behind the front desk, scrolling his Instagram feed. She skipped past the elevator to opt for the stairs. Anything to get the heart rate up, if only for a few seconds.

"Sorry I'm late," she announced on her way in. The students offered no visible reaction, but there was disappointment in the air as she dropped everything onto the desk and climbed atop it. Her business skirt clung to her thighs, putting her in complete discomfort as she took quick attendance.

She concluded the course with a lecture on libel and a few of the kids appeared genuinely stunned to learn they couldn't slander people or businesses on a whim.

"Why not, Professor Holden? That's just, like, my opinion,

you know?"

A very twenty-first century mindset, she thought.

But the kids were mostly concerned with the grading of their final assignments and found creative ways of asking for them over the course of her lesson. When she admitted that she hadn't yet graded any, a wave of audible displeasure rewarded her honesty.

"I need to make sure I have you all back here on Thursday, yes?" she said. "That's when finals technically begin, and that's when you'll get your papers." She dismissed them fifteen minutes early because she was anxious to get down to her office and make an appointment with the locksmith.

Melanie walked past two straggler students—scruffy-looking teenage boys in long-sleeve t-shirts—and flashed a polite smile. Once she rounded the corner they remarked how "nice and juicy" her ass looked in that skirt, their voices bubbling with more lusty excitement than she was comfortable hearing.

I'm never wearing this thing again.

Riley flagged her down as she walked past his door on the way to her office. Melanie thought he smelled faintly of patchouli and weed. Unsurprising, considering he occasionally wore bellbottoms without a trace of irony.

"Can it wait, Riley?" she said. "I've got to set up an appointment for this afternoon. Kinda important."

"Nada, professor." He tossed Melanie a doorknob hangar that read: *Out to lunch—back in one hour.* "Put that on there and shut the door. Trust me, you want to hear what I've got to say."

When she was seated, he fished a sheet of paper out from the bottom of a stack. "You remember when I agreed to play the role of part-time admin in this department? Something about doing more with less?"

She did. It was that same mantra that brought her into the folds of journalism. In a sluggish economy, everyone in the department was putting in more labor to fill the gaps.

"Look, Mel, I'm just going to blurt this out, okay? Even though it, like, totally goes against my energy. Negative feelings and all that."

Melanie thought her eyes would burst if she widened them any further. There was a point to be made here, and she wished Riley would hurry up and make it.

He pushed the paper across the desk and pointed to it. "That's a list of all the summer courses."

Her heart skipped a beat when she realized where this was going. Morton, that bastard, had cut *Dissection of the Epic* off the curriculum, hadn't he? The course she'd been developing and planning for the better part of two years was, at last, gearing up for a trial run next month. The course that had reached its max number of registrations in one afternoon wasn't ready for collegiate prime time, apparently.

Melanie held the printout with wobbly hands. *Dissection of the Epic* was listed there among the other summer courses.

Riley must've noticed her confounded expression. He shook his head and avoided her eyes. "It's still there," he said, "but you're not teaching it."

Melanie followed the line across the page to where the corresponding professor was listed. It didn't read HOLDEN. According to this, Jill Woreley was teaching her course.

"This is wrong, right?"

Riley's face was blank.

"How can you be sure?" she said.

"Because Morton was in here this morning with Woreley. Said he was confident that she was up to the task of running a narrow course like that and it would lead to bigger and better things at this college. His words exactly."

Melanie felt like she'd been punched in the gut. Jill Woreley was an assistant professor, same as her. They started here together six years back—with Melanie beating her to seniority by three months. The only difference being that Jill had been fished right out of college. Word was that her father had worked on the mayor's re-election campaign. Once that happened—successfully—the green graduate became a professor.

Melanie paid her dues, working twelve years in the public school system as a high school teacher. A gig with many lows and only a handful of highs. It gave her the proficiency that she needed to step onto the college circuit and offer her students a compelling experience. Far too many of her peers failed to grasp the concept of an enjoyable academic lecture and it was easy to spot them. Theirs were the classes that never filled and always thinned as the semester wore on.

Melanie prided herself on being better than that, working hard to keep her students interested. She couldn't cope with the misery of being branded a "boring teacher" and fought to avoid that stigma every second she spent inside a classroom.

She even checked herself compulsively on RateMyProfessors.com to make sure she was succeeding. If she wasn't good at this, after all, what else was there?

"Where is Morton?"

Riley frowned. "Taking Woreley to lunch."

"Son of a bitch," she said. "He gave me permission to build this course. Told me I had carte blanche. Said it would be my stepping-stone to tenure. And he hands it to the girl who tried teaching *Beowulf* off that CGI cartoon?"

"I helped grade some of those papers," Riley said. "Not one, but two essays absolving the title character's sin of sleeping with Angelina Jolie."

Melanie cupped a palm over her mouth. She snickered, but only at the absurdity. "I can't believe she'll have tenure before me."

"Not even Dennis Morton can keep that from you.

Numbers don't lie. The students love you. Attendance is high, feedback is great. Semester after semester. Probably doesn't hurt that you're cute as hell. I play for the other team and even I've thought about what it would be like to take you for a roll in the hay."

Riley attempted a seductive grin that made Melanie burst out laughing.

"Well," he said. "I'm glad I never waited around for you, Melanie Holden, you never took my advances seriously."

"Oh stop it. Unless you want me to tell your husband you've been sexually harassing me again."

"Point taken." Riley reached out and took Melanie's hand in his. "This is bureaucratic nonsense. Just keep showing this college how much of a rock star you are. That's all you can do, and it'll be enough."

"I don't know how many more papers I have to publish. How many more conferences I have to attend. I would've thought six years of bringing my A-game would've been plenty. Apparently, I just need to be younger and better connected. What the hell does Woreley even know about epic poetry? Her concentration was Women's Studies."

Melanie's face was flushed. Having a naturally pale tone, she never bothered to perfect a poker face. No point when her complexion went rose red the second she got upset or angry. Her body temperature was an unavoidable tell and she had grown to accept it.

"Don't worry about it," Riley said. "We're going to get the last laugh."

Melanie appreciated Riley's supportive outlook, although it was far too optimistic for what was happening. She went down the cramped hallway, ducked into her office, and slammed a fist down on her desk. Jill Woreley had somehow snaked her baby out from underneath her. That twenty-eight-year-old tart, with constant Facebook status updates (*Partying with my bitches all night long!*) that proved more dedication to eroding her liver than honing her craft. Once, she even bemoaned the process of reading entirely, longing for the day when it was obsolete.

Your professor of Dissection of the Epic, ladies and gentlemen.

There wasn't much to be done until Dennis got back from lunch. So she went online and got her locksmith's phone number. When the appointment was made, she got to thinking about outdoor cameras, warming to the idea of monitoring her yard.

She closed her eyes but saw *him* there, with the gore-stained mask and hungry blade. She felt that rotten blood seeping into her mouth, staining her tongue like it happened only yesterday.

He's dead. Don't do this to yourself.

Melanie wanted to be sure of that. But the way she'd left things—there wasn't any way to know for certain. It was absurd to think that Cyrus Hoyt had been outside her door last night, but the thought filled her with dread all the same. It was just too easy to imagine him in her back yard. The army jacket, jagged knife, dirty mask—everything.

An ugly thought.

She pushed it away, knowing it would always come back. Just like it had every day for the last twenty-five years.

It was a little after four when Melanie got home. Her locksmith was waiting in the driveway. While he went to work, she sat down with the intention of grading those damn journalism finals, but her mind wandered and soon she was shopping for outdoor surveillance equipment.

After an hour of clicking through customer reviews and over-confident product descriptions, she settled on a sleek-looking DVR unit that recorded a week's worth of reconnaissance. A high-end device just shy of a grand—a small price to pay for a better night's sleep.

She cut the locksmith a check and added an extra fifty bucks for the speedy service, showing him out once she was satisfied. It was nearly six and time to start thinking about dinner. A salad was looking like the best option when the doorbell rang.

Melanie was startled. Through the living room's bay window, she saw her neighbor slouched into a riding mower with a beer clenched in his fist. He was a mere stone's throw away— further proof that there was nothing to be scared of.

Cyrus came at night.

"Shut up," she whispered and went to the front door, eager to get her mind off that boogeyman.

Riley stood there, a box of wine and a bag of subs in his arms. He came in and pressed a scruffy cheek to hers. "I kept thinking about your day and knew you needed company. I brought wine."

It was exactly what she needed right now. "Boxed wine," she said. "Guaranteed hangover."

"Yep, and I have a night off from the hubby. So let's cut loose."

They sat at the kitchen bar and noshed vegetarian subs while the wine flowed. Dialogue was casual and it reduced the day's devastating events to insignificant background noise.

Riley's eyes were glossy when he pulled out a bag of weed and asked if it was cool to roll and toke.

"Go right ahead," Melanie said. "I might even join you."

The conversation shifted back to the day's problems once they ran out of casual topics. Riley nodded his approval when she got to the part about the kids checking out her "juicy" ass.

"They're lookin' and that's a problem for you? Take solace in the fact that you've still got things that teenagers want to see."

"They're kids. I'm old enough to be their mother."

"MILF fantasies," Riley said and lit the joint. The kitchen was rife with haze in a second. "What's hotter to a bunch of coddled adolescents than a mature older woman with a rockin' body who also has the world-experience to keep on coddling right where mommy left off?"

"Cynical."

"We work with twenty-year-old children, Mel. How many times a semester do you get calls from these *adults'* parents asking for them to be excused from whatever assignment they didn't do."

"And yet I'm supposed to be flattered that a bunch of six-year-olds trapped inside the bodies of young men find me attractive?"

"Why not?"

"Let's not go there tonight. Didn't you come here to try and cheer me up?"

Riley put an arm around Melanie's shoulder and tugged her close. His aftershave was the right amount of pleasant and leaning on his shoulder felt restful after the day's events.

"I was thinking about something, Mel, and hear me out. Since Dennis is a douche and took you off *Dissection of the Epic*, I was wondering what your plans are for the summer."

She hadn't thought about it very much. That class was going to be the bulk of her June and July. Now she had three months wide-open and without a clue what to do.

"Okay, totally spit-balling here, but...why not go to Forest Grove?"

Melanie's stomach sunk so far it felt like it was in the basement.

"I know it sounds nutty," Riley said. "But this was Aaron's idea, and while I think my husband errs on the insensitive side sometimes, he does have a connection to a literary agent in New York. And you sort of came up over dinner last weekend. The agent is interested in the material and guarantees he can sell your story for a generous dollar amount."

"I told you, Riley, a hundred times…"

"I know," he said. "You have. You've said that you were lucky to get out of Camp Forest Grove. And that you can't be sure Cyrus Hoyt is really dead. Except that he's been buried—"

"At Eternal Walk Cemetery," she said, nodding. She might've checked and then confirmed that a few dozen times throughout the years. Didn't help much.

"You're haunted by the ghost of a lunatic that you killed, girl. Forest Grove has moved on, but you haven't. What better way to do that than through a little soul searching and dirt digging? Profit off your misfortune. This is America. Everybody does it."

"I'm not haunted," Melanie said, but her words were without fight. Riley was correct and it stung like hell to hear it.

The prospect of returning to the grove was not appealing. It might've been safe but her memories were vivid: the light wood panel décor of the cabins, the graffiti in the outhouse that assured, *He who writes on bathroom walls, eats their shit in little balls,* and the picturesque waterfront with its false sense of security.

Beyond that, there were the bodies: Jennifer's corpse strung up inside the girl's cabin. Her hot pink Victoria's Secret bra torn and spattered with blood. They'd taken a trip just a few days before leaving for Forest Grove to get that thing. All because Jen wanted to look her best for *"them country boys."* Then there was Bill's body, hurled through the cabin window—Hoyt's attempt at psychological warfare.

Painful memories that would only strengthen once back in Connecticut.

Maybe Riley was right about playing the part of victim on a loop, but how was she supposed to feel? Not a day slogged by where she didn't wonder what Jen might've gone on to do with her life. That girl always had a way of getting what she wanted and it had never been a question of if she made it in the world of NYC fashion, but rather when.

And Bill—good-looking, strong, and with one of the most obnoxious senses of humor ever. The kind of guy who made you laugh even if you were fixing to smack his mouth. She liked picturing them together every once in a while, settled into suburban life with three kids. Arguments over who was bringing the youngest to soccer practice. Coordinating the oldest child's football schedule so that they never missed a game. Saturday date nights, Sunday sleep-ins, and drinks with the neighbors.

The things life was supposed to pony up.

For a while, it looked as though she could've had those things with Reggie Nolan. Her ex-husband. An assistant football coach with deep-rooted anger issues tied directly to his own inadequacies. Melanie found his obscenity-laden approach to coaching reprehensible, but stayed out of it for a long time. Reggie always kept his discontent out of their relationship.

Until the day he didn't.

Even now, Melanie felt responsible. Maybe if she found a better way to breach the issue, things would've gone differently. He might've deserved more than a midnight ambush on the drive home from a faculty party. Of course, she hadn't deserved the reaction it provoked.

She remembered her head smacking against the window as he barreled across the two-lane street, pulling into a turnoff and striking her with a backhand. She'd never been called a "cunt" before, and that had hurt the most, even as the muscles in her face stung like winter's frost from the brutal blow.

Melanie filed for divorce the very next day, and Reggie was gone from the house by the time she got home. She only saw him a few more times throughout the rest of that school year and he did not return to the position of assistant coach. Or maybe he wasn't asked back. His absence was all she cared about. Better to be alone than to go through that kind of misery.

Riley rubbed the top of her hand and eased her out of the daydream. "I didn't mention this to make you feel bad," he said, "but you're far too gorgeous and brilliant to live out your years as a prisoner in your own home. You should be carving a new life for yourself. Not clinging to the one that was taken from you."

"You can't know what you're asking me to do."

"You're right," he said, "I'm going to drop this. But think on it. You've got a story to tell, and people want to hear it. Remember the EMT who treated you that night?"

She did. He was a true crime author out in California now. And Riley was right about this. Breaking out from beneath Dennis Morton's thumb was a powerful motivator. Chronicling that long night at Camp Forest Grove was not appealing, but the idea of gaining leverage over that worm certainly was. Especially if the book was a success. Any school would be glad to have her then, and the board of trustees would likely put a little pressure on Morton to make their resident author happy. It was a hell of a hoop to have to jump through to get her class back, and she resented the fact that she had to do it.

"Just give it a thought," he smiled. "The option is there for you if you want it."

"Can't hurt to think about it," she said.

Melanie spent all of Wednesday barricaded in her office, grading papers with the ferocity of an academic psychopath. Four classes worth of material, two general *English Lits* and two iterations of *Intro to Journalism*, wrapped up in less than six hours, and another two to process and input final grades.

The likelihood of Dennis' possible backstab increased with

every passing hour. He usually made himself available to all his professors as part of his end-of-semester shtick. Wanted to know how things were wrapping up, if there were problems with any students, and/or potential grade controversies—thinking it best to be forearmed in the event of enraged parents. But he was a phantom today, and his closed office door spoke volumes about the situation at hand.

Riley floated word that *Dissection of the Epic* had been yanked from Melanie's control, resulting in a stream of sympathetic faces to her office. Colleagues offered consolations that made her feel liked and respected, even if nothing changed. She lost the most important gig of her career and her boss couldn't be bothered to tell her about it.

Once the final grade was in, she decided that she couldn't stay in the office another second. Dennis was still MIA at four-thirty. As far as he knew, Melanie was still acting on the assumption that the class was hers—unless he counted on Riley seeing the schedule and breaking the news.

That sounds about right.

She ducked out and drove home. Lacey was curled up on the couch, looking like she hadn't moved since this morning. She meowed a few times as Melanie stripped off her clothes and tossed them into the laundry room. The cat hopped off the couch and followed her down the hall to the bathroom, only to hightail it back the way she came once Melanie turned on the shower. The little animal was still scarred from the time she rolled in the mud and found her fur so matted that she needed an actual bath.

There was a text from Riley when she got out. *Dennis just showed up on campus. Saw him pull into the parking lot as I was leaving. Get him! Be fierce! :P*

She threw on a pair of khaki shorts and a sleeveless tee. There wasn't a lot of time, so she pulled her hair into a bun and slipped a navy blue Red Sox hat over her still-damp head.

It was almost six by the time she got back to campus and the place had cleared out. The small parking lot behind the English building was wide-open as she slipped into the spot beside Dennis' car. Her door might've dinged the silver body of his Lexus, but she didn't stop to check.

He was combing his mustache in a tabletop vanity when Melanie came in. The startled look on his face, coupled with a noticeable jolt through his body, indicated surprise.

"What can I do for you, Melanie?" he asked, his vowels shaky.

"You know what," she said. This kind of thing had never been easy. Her body felt awkward and her words sounded thick and alien. *Just grit your teeth and keep going.*

He sighed and tugged his coat tighter across his beer belly. "This wasn't an easy decision, Melanie."

"Enlighten me, please," she said. "You're the one who told me to build this course from the ground up. I spent two years refreshing my knowledge of it. Deep-diving into Homer, Virgil, and Hesiod. Researching them. Writing about them. Nobody at this school knows that stuff better."

"Do you know which course you've had the most success with throughout your career?"

She was tempted to say all of them, not out of arrogance, but because she recognized her worth. As Riley said, the proof was in the proverbial pudding of consistently overloaded classes. She chose to bite her tongue and shrug instead of answering the question.

"*Intro to Journalism,* wouldn't you know?" he said. "And the most interesting thing about that? You came here as a literary professor. But you, being a team player, stepped into those journalism shoes when this college needed you. Your accomplishment has been unbridled. Packed rosters, gigantic success rates, and top-notch results. It seems you found your strength. Your…niche. Whether you want to admit it or not, I think we know where you belong."

"Dennis, that's not fair. I'm glad to have done that. And I'm glad that people like what I do. But you swore to me that teaching the journalism tract wouldn't be a permanent thing. You gave me the go-ahead to develop *Dissection of the Epic* as a means of placating me. I know that. But now you're stealing it out from under me. Let me have it back. Please."

Dennis poured two scotches but Melanie refused to acknowledge hers. She waited for his answer, realizing at once her mistake of begging.

"I'm giving the course to Miss Woreley because I want to see how she thrives outside her comfort zone. Like you with journalism. She will be the first one to tackle the curriculum."

"And that's bullshit." Her blood was boiling. "You want her to *thrive outside her comfort zone* then let her talk about journalism ethics for two years. Reward me for having done that by letting me teach the class I created."

"My mind has been made up. I'm evaluating Miss Woreley this way, and I apologize if that upsets you. Being the team player that you are, I know you can respect it."

She stewed in anger while her milk-white skin baked. Morton probably saw her cheeks stained a dozen shades of red. And worse, her eyes welled up just enough to make her uncomfortable. "The least you can do is tell me that I got my tenure."

He lifted the glass to his hairy lip. She could've sworn it was to stifle a laugh. "I'm afraid that you are not yet tenured at this college."

"Dennis."

"With the budget being as tight as it is, I could only grant tenure to one professor this year. The panel was unanimous in their push for Jill Woreley as a long-term investment." He finished his drink and then went to the door and opened it. "I will be more than happy to discuss this further during my normal office hours."

Melanie felt dazed. Her heart pounded and she stormed out without another word. At least she knew, although it didn't make her feel any better. Walking back to her car, she was sick to her stomach. Like she might keel over and vomit.

Not because Dennis had passed her over for tenure.

And not because a stupid girl was suddenly more valuable to this school than she was.

But because she knew what she had to do.

The next day Melanie could think only about concluding her business and getting the hell off campus. She handed out corrected papers like her life depended on it and dismissed her classes once no one had any lingering issues.

Small miracles…

Being here was almost impossible to stomach. It was a bitter reminder of her professional failure. There was no other way to take it, considering her career was the only thing she had in life.

She was packing up her office when Jill Woreley, of all faces, knocked on her door and stepped inside.

"Not a good time, Jill…"

"When is it ever? Word around here is that you're leaving town for the summer. I just want to talk to you for a few." The girl wasted no time in sliding into a chair. Her white shorts rode up in the seat as she crossed her legs, thick bronze thighs rubbing obnoxiously against one another as if to flaunt.

Melanie felt her face heating up as she jammed her laptop into her bag. "Fine," she huffed. "You can walk me down to my car." She hadn't planned on leaving yet, but since Jill insisted on making herself at home, her office felt like a den of ill repute.

"Don't be pissed off at me, Mel."

The approach was blunt and it landed that way. Before Melanie could recover from her astonishment, the girl was already off on a tangent.

"For whatever reason, Dennis gave me *Dissection of the Epic*, right? It isn't my fault, so how about dropping the sour grapes?"

Melanie couldn't believe what she was hearing. It wasn't cowardice preventing her words, but utter shock.

Jill went on, unabated. "The council liked my dissertation on Greek Gods as the externalization of human thought. So don't act as though this subject matter is beyond me. I got to tenure before you, fair and square. With a fresh perspective and some new ideas. You're not going to create a hostile work environment for me now, are you?"

The urge to smack her upside the head grew, but Melanie said nothing. They walked the rest of the way in silence, at least until they were outside. Then Jill took her by the shoulder.

"So here's the thing, Mel," she said. "I got no beef with you. And you best have no issue with me. The decent thing for you to do would be to hand over the curriculum you've been developing for that class so I don't have to start from scratch. That way I can tell Dennis you've been mint in helping me. That would benefit the students, help me out, and look good on you next time tenure talk comes around."

Melanie glanced at her shoulder. The girl's hand remained palmed over it. Jill seemed surprised this was the case and let go, clearing her throat as they resumed their walk.

They went down to the corner of the street where Melanie was parked. She tossed her bag in the back seat of her car and slammed the door, displaying more of a tantrum than intended. Without another word, she got behind the wheel and tried shutting the door. Jill grabbed the top of it and tugged it back open.

"You don't have anything to say?"

"Nothing," Melanie said. "Good luck with that class, Jill. You're teaching it on your own."

"Come on, Mel. Let me have those notes. It will make life so much easier on the both of us."

"I'm curious to hear how you fare, but I'm not giving you anything. That's my work, and I'll use it once the time comes."

"Your time already came, and then it went. Talk about holding it against someone. Take some fucking responsibility for your own failures, you bitch."

Melanie could only grin, finding a strange justification in a wobbly decision. "I am," she said. And couldn't wait to get the hell out of town.

 **Three**

Forest Grove was a four-hour drive.

Melanie headed down I-290 though Worcester until it became I-84.

As her return became a reality, so developed the inescapable feeling that she was making a mistake.

She already missed Lacey. The kitty was staying with Riley and his husband, despite the latter's allergies. The little old lady wouldn't care much about being displaced. She was positively mercenary as long as there was a warm lap to curl up in. Cyrus Hoyt could break in and stick a bowie knife through her skull and as long as he dropped a can of Friskies on the floor, the cat wouldn't mind one bit.

The comfortable anxieties of urban life—unnecessary traffic, frantic lane changes, and unprovoked honking—became a stillborn country row of isolated houses, sporadic vehicles, and occasional businesses. The onset of dread this brought her was unavoidable.

Melanie hated summer. Its inevitable return always set her on edge as she wondered: *Will this be the year he returns to finish the job?* Outdoor activities in balmy weather were unappealing and she much preferred crowded sidewalks to countryside trails for vacation getaways.

As a teenager, the town of Forest Grove felt so much

further away. An isolated dream place hidden away from the word, where its inhabitants sat, susceptible to unspeakable terrors, and outside help was impossible. Today, it grew closer with every passing mile.

A winding right off the highway spilled onto a rural road of potholes and wooded overgrowth. She drove past a collapsed barn set several feet off the thoroughfare. All that remained of it was a pile of smashed and broken beams. An ancient pick-up truck, its flatbed loaded with flapping chicken cages, puttered past in the opposite direction and blared its horn for no discernible reason.

Her own personal welcome wagon, perhaps.

Melanie tried to think of the generous amount of money the publishing company was offering as a means of combating the rising trepidation. It was hard to believe that anyone would be interested in her story. Who even remembered Forest Grove after all these years save for those whose lives were altered by it?

Melanie guessed the town remembered all too well. Its reaction to Hoyt's killing spree was a bizarre one. The town council came together in the wake of the murders to ban every activity that brought kids together in sizable groups. Dances were off limits, parties were punishable by hefty fines, and sporting events were monitored as though it was life behind the Berlin Wall.

The idea that something she was involved in produced a kind of gestapo police state sat raw with her. From the sound of things, modern day Forest Grove wasn't any different. It remained the town from *Footloose* on steroids.

What she didn't like about the publisher's deal was their insistence on using this trip as a means of drumming up interest for the book. They wanted to arrange a day with a photographer for some "authentic" publicity shots, and the thought of that made her feel dirty.

Everything about it sounded incredibly self-important, and Melanie hated the spotlight. A trip back to Forest Grove was bad enough, but to market it? It wasn't okay to use the deaths of Jennifer and Bill—or the rest of the victims—for publicity. Their deaths meant more than that. She was adamant that her memoir respect their memories, though the need to spite Dennis had somehow taken precedence over both her morals and mental well-being.

With assurances that this was a surefire bestseller waiting in the wings, it was easy to be seduced by that certainty. Especially when used against Dennis. Living well despite his best efforts was a powerful motivator.

The GPS put her arrival in Forest Grove at forty minutes out, meaning there was a lot of countryside to see between now and there. The road was uneventful. Lots of pastures and corn stalks. Not much else.

Completely deceiving.

Dancing red and blue lights lit up her rearview, followed by the adjoined siren's wail. One of Forest Grove's finest was on her bumper, close enough that Melanie saw the driver's aviators leering without expression.

Her foot had gone a little too heavy on the gas, zipping along at 60 mph in a mad rush to start the homecoming. Only thirty over the speed limit.

Melanie eased off the pedal and pulled off the road. Overgrown fronds slipped off her bumper and bent beneath the hood as she stopped. A trembling hand reached for the glove box to retrieve her registration.

The cop appeared window side, his knuckles rapping the glass as she fumbled around inside the overstuffed everything-but-gloves box.

A flick of the window switch brought the glass partition down, and she looked everywhere but at the officer's face.

"Going a little fast, ma'am. Mind if I ask where the fire is?"

"I'm so sorry," she said. "No fire...just getting lost in my own thoughts."

The officer pulled the aviators from his face and stuffed one of the temples into his breast pocket, leaving them dangling off his chest. He clamped his large hands over the door and knelt down to get eye-level. It was a bit too invasive of her personal space, but hardly the time to complain.

"Miss...Holden," he said. "Am I right?"

She could only imagine what a mess she looked. Skittish and probably more than a little confused. Her face felt hot and she didn't need a mirror to know her cheeks were the color of fresh-picked cherries.

The officer continued speaking, lightening his expression as he went. "We've been expecting you is all. I'm Chief Brady. Nathan Brady. That publishing house in New York contacted the bed & breakfast you'll be staying at to arrange billing. Didn't take long for word to spread of Miss Holden's return to our little corner of the world."

"Makes sense." Melanie breathed easier with that explanation, but there was still the matter of speeding back into town. Caught by the chief of police, no less. "I'm kind of a mess about this trip. I think my jitters turned me into a speed demon."

"Got it, miss. And, uh, welcome back. Hopefully our town gets a pleasant write-up in your book. Although, given the subject matter, I'm guessing that might not be the case."

"Is that going to be a problem, chief?"

"Not for me." He motioned toward the open road with his chin. "For some of them? Maybe. I'm sure you understand that your homecoming doesn't excite the lot. Lots of good folks living there, though, I can promise you that. They just want to forget about what happened in their little town."

"Can they do that?" she said. "I would think it difficult to forget with so many rules and regulations born out of what happened."

"A lot of us are doing our part to try and reduce the reach of those regulations. Off the record, I don't think it does much except punish kids for being born here."

The chief seemed honest and Melanie appreciated that. He looked a bit too young to be the authority in Forest Grove, though—couldn't be much over thirty. Maybe that wasn't so abnormal, though. She wasn't well versed in small town law enforcement and decided that a younger guy was probably better for the situation at hand. Preferable to some old *stuck in his ways* codger escorting her to the edge of town, at least.

Besides, he was handsome, and just acknowledging that made her feel like one of her hopeless students. He couldn't be more All-American if he tried with his piercing brown eyes and a cropped crew cut. And his chiseled jawbone and thick forearms said he worked out. No doubt he walked the walk, too.

"Just so you know, I *was* going to ticket you. I don't tolerate people doing ten over the speed limit out here, let alone thirty. But, as I said, we're all doing our part. And since I won't be able to apologize for the less than enthusiastic reception you're bound to get from some, the least I can do is cut you a break. That way, your second first impression of our town might not be so terrible."

Melanie was glad to see him back out of her personal space. "I appreciate the leniency," she said with a dopey smile. "I won't be a problem. Staying long enough to jog my memory. Then, I'm gone."

"Take as much time as you'd like, ma'am." He offered a welcoming grin and then turned to go. "Nice meeting you," he said and kept walking.

With a sigh, Melanie started the engine and eased onto the

road, careful to stay at 30 mph. Brady didn't bother following, but the damage was already done. Whether or not it had been his intent, he'd succeeded in making her feel worse about this. Now she had to worry about annoying the locals with her presence.

Did I expect them to roll out the red carpet?

Melanie felt like cutting her losses and turning back. Her heart hadn't stopped pounding all day and now she was heading to a place that didn't want her. If Forest Grove had ever felt guilty about its part in the massacre, it traded remorse for resentment long ago.

Did it matter to them that a seventeen-year-old's life was irrevocably changed? Or that others had lost their lives to a deranged lunatic they knew was out there?

What could she expect from a town that chose to immortalize him in a campfire yarn, rather than deal with the problem? Of course they would view her as an exploiter and nothing more.

It maddened her to know that people already thought of her like that. If Melanie had any intention of cashing in, she could've written about it years ago. There had been an invite to do Oprah back in 1989, but that had been during the worst of it: sleepless nights, images of dirty welder's masks seared into her brain, and uncontrollable hysterics. Survivor's guilt. Therapy sessions. Off-and-on institutionalization.

She'd desperately needed to forget back then.

That wasn't untrue now, either. Only the need to spite Dennis Morton was a dramatic counterweight against decades of anxiety. Her career was the only distraction she had. It filled her days with thoughts and worries of something other than the ghosts of murdered friends and crazed killers. She was going to fight like hell to keep it.

Her GPS said Forest Grove was six miles away. Well past the point of no return. She swallowed and pushed down on the gas, anxious to get this over with.

Brady watched the Buick LaCrosse pull away.

At least she buys American, he thought.

No reason for such a chilly disposition, though. There was tragedy in Melanie Holden's life, sure, but she allowed herself to be defined by what happened all those summers back. The skittishness and trembling inflections as she spoke—she was a woman scared of her own shadow. You had to accept and then drop that baggage.

Though he supposed it was easier said than done when it came to the hell that poor girl had endured. He'd seen people traumatized over a lot less in his line of work.

Brady grabbed for the thin two-way radio sitting beside the cab computer and flipped it to the car-to-car frequency, pausing at the stream of chatter he hadn't been expecting to catch.

"I was just talking to Lloyd this morning. Said we're in for a full-on happy hour discount on pitchers. All we have to do is go out to his house and tell those asshole renters across the street to shut their goddamn mouths at night."

The voice belonged to Alex Johnson, his youngest officer. Brady couldn't wait to hear with whom he was speaking.

"Already did that twice. Nasty bitch just sits in her screened in porch, guzzling Budweiser, sucking on Newports, and swearing at her kids on the phone. Figure we'll have to step up the intimidation some if Lloyd's willing to give us a generous price on frosty ones. Hell, I'll arrest her if Lloyd'll throw in a plate of buffalo wings."

That was Sergeant Steve Maylam. What a disappointment. The kind of guy who acted like your best friend when you were in the room. Apparently, also the kind of guy who thought having a small town badge meant you could barter for better services. Coming into this gig, things were always going to be tense. Maylam had technically been in line to secede the old chief, but that meant he should know better than to act like a first year rookie.

Brady's personal cell phone buzzed on the dash. He ignored it.

"I like where your head's at," Johnson laughed. "Whatever we do, we gotta figure it out over the next few months. I want to spend my Sundays at Lloyd's Bar once the Pats come back. And if I can do that without blowing half my paycheck, that'd be even better."

Brady's fist tightened around the radio. "I wouldn't expect to see much of this season. Not only won't you be doing any extra favors for Lloyd Henderson, you've also bought yourselves Sunday afternoon shifts effective September 1st. How would this look if a civilian got on this frequency and heard about your little racket?"

"Sorry, chief." Johnson's voice was quick and apologetic. "I know that didn't sound good but—"

"Sounded terrible, officer. I'll take it up with you once I get back into town."

"Yes, sir." Johnson went radio silent.

Maylam said nothing and only fell off the channel.

Brady dropped the radio into the empty seat beside him and glanced at the cell phone text. Trish wanted to know if he was coming home for dinner. He tossed the phone aside with a groan. Wasn't like he didn't love and worship his wife, but why in the hell was she so thick when it came to understanding the way things needed to be?

He wasn't used to Forest Grove yet, and the arrival of Little Miss Book Deal only complicated things further. This was a juggling act. On one hand, he had to prove to the grove that he was a worthy successor to their beloved Ronald Sleighton. The other hand required him to please the woman who could potentially drag this town's reputation through the muck for a second time.

Guilt ate at him as he threw the car into drive and headed back. Trish's question would have to go unanswered until he knew for certain.

Christ, he thought. One of his guys was supposed to play the welcoming committee and meet Miss Holden at Desiree's Bed & Breakfast, but after the stunt he just eavesdropped, he wasn't sure which of them could be relied upon. Trish said—repeatedly—that he needed to be more authoritative, like her father had been. True words, but things only got done right when he did them himself.

Brady struggled with the idea of delegation—even when he had been a sergeant detective in the city. There were men under his command then, too, but he always had the urge to street it himself.

Today was no different. He wanted to drive out to Desiree's but decided that wouldn't work. Not after making Miss Holden so uneasy. Still, Forest Grove couldn't stand to be massacred in her book. The mayor had been very clear about that. Brady didn't know why it fell upon his shoulders to give the woman a wholesome impression of the town, but it wasn't his place to question it. Not after Mayor Cobb had been so accommodating when it came to sliding him into this position.

Poke your head in once she's settled. Apologize for today and see what else you can do, he thought. *That's how you get Melanie Holden to come around on Forest Grove.*

"Dammit," he muttered, thinking of the full plate before him. Trish should probably know sooner rather than later that this wasn't going to be an early day at the office. For now, the best place to be was back at the station. He ground his teeth as he drove. There were two idiotic officers that needed chewing out.

Trish Brady read the text and tried not to feel disappointment: *No can do. Home late. Duty calls. And calls. And calls…*

Another day all alone, she thought and dumped the frozen chicken back into the icebox.

This was starting to feel like the high school summers of her teenage years. Waiting for a boyfriend to get off work by occupying her time with a little grass and whatever movies the video store hadn't deemed "morally questionable." The grove's think tank had done away with most of the violent and sexual films on the shelves, but failed to understand how fucked up kids movies were in the 80s. Trish argued that *Garbage Pail Kids: The Movie* had done more damage to her than any horror flick—and she was grateful for it. Even the smallest thing, like a video store rental, felt like an act of rebellion in a place so quick to pass judgment.

There wasn't much else to do back then and times had scarcely changed. She pitied the kids of Forest Grove for having the misfortune of growing up in this oppressive environment, but they had it a little better. At least the Internet made the world a smaller place and the yokels around here lacked the *know how* to censor it.

In her day—she laughed at the thought of sounding like a senior citizen at thirty—libraries destroyed F. Scott Fitzgerald and George Orwell while refusing to carry any Richard Matheson for fear that literature might create another summer camp killing spree. And Trish had lived three decades without having gone to a dance because the denizens here thought it promoted debauchery. In their minds, it was practically daring another Cyrus Hoyt to make a move.

It was all so fucking puritanical.

If you asked Trish Brady a few years ago if she'd rather live out her years in Forest Grove or go to an early grave, she would've been first in line for a ride down the river Styx. The people who lived here weren't actually living—not in her estimation.

But love makes you do all kinds of crazy shit...

She had come down into the basement to get tonight's dinner out of the freezer and found herself staring at the sea of as-of-yet-unpacked boxes. They were going on four months in the grove, but she couldn't bring herself to settle in. The minute that these boxes got unpacked was admission that this place was now her tomb. She preferred to think of Forest Grove as a temporary stop, even if that wasn't realistic. She had caved on the issue and agreed to come back. It was Nate's decision now.

Dinner was off the table for tonight, so the cellar wasn't a place she wanted to be. Unpacking could wait another month or six. She went back upstairs, unable to shake the feeling of being a zoo animal. The house was clean—the least she could do since Nate was at work all day (and night, most of the time), but she resented the housewife label. The problem was that there just wasn't anything else to do. You couldn't even take a ride with the radio blasting without offending this town.

On her first day back, she had been doing a little bit of house cleaning while rocking out to Black Flag. Nate hadn't been gone for half an hour when his cruiser pulled back into the driveway. The new chief of police's first order of business in town was a noise complaint leveled against his own house. Not one, but *three* of their neighbors had called to report an "ungodly racket."

Talk about settling in on the wrong foot.

Trish jogged up the cellar stairs that led into the dining

room. Her father was waiting at the table.

"I swear you've got worse hearing than I do, girly," he said. "I'm up here calling out your name and you just go about your day. Told you it was only a matter of time before that racket you listen to blows your eardrums out."

"What a great time for a lecture, daddy." There was mockery in her tone. As much as she loved him, being in such close proximity was a disaster. He had a knack for making her feel like a child whenever they spoke. Effortless condescension. Besides, she was startled to see him—or anyone—inside her house. Dad was of the mind that he was entitled to go wherever he pleased in Forest Grove, especially his own daughter's house.

"Didn't come here for a lecture. I came to look in on you."

"I don't need a checkup. I'm fine."

"What happened yesterday wasn't fine," he said. "Christ, you scared me half to death. I ain't ready to lose the only other woman in my life, ya know."

"Chill," she said and sprung to the tips of her toes to kiss his forehead. He stunk of cigars and beer. It was only a few minutes passed noon.

"I'll *chill* when I know you're okay."

"What's to know? I went for a walk in the woods and you're acting like I need an intervention."

"You passed out." He must've noticed her irritation because he stopped talking and took a second to reshuffle his delivery—a deep breath followed by a sigh. "Just tell me I don't have to worry about you. You haven't always made the best choices…"

"Hah, I learned from the best then, haven't I? You're going to lecture me about choices after what happened with mom? Just cut the crap and ask me if I'm using again, dad. I know that's what you're getting at."

"I can't think of any other reason you might've lost

consciousness while out hiking."

Trish couldn't either. That was the problem. She'd driven out to the trails around Lake Forest Grove yesterday to do some soul searching. There was a stigma around those woods that stretched back as far as she could remember, but her own personal associations with it were always positive. For the graduating class of 2002, it was a place where they could escape the town's oppression. Beneath that canopy of trees, they smoked a little dope, listened to popular music, and yes, surrendered their virginities.

On the night she lost hers to Chase Prescott, she had to stifle an urge to lather city hall in declarative graffiti. Thinking about the rebellious scrawl even now made her smile: *I popped my cherry without getting popped! Fuck off Cyrus Hoyt!* Chase had begged her to reconsider since it was senior year and he wasn't about to risk his scholarship over something so trivial. He was almost out of this place and wasn't ever coming back. She agreed to let it go, but her mercy was more about sparing her father potential embarrassment and not placating some boy toy jock she hadn't liked much in the first place. Their attraction was purely physical and screwing him that night felt like the last opportunity to rebel against a place that did its best to asphyxiate their hormones.

That was what Forest Grove meant to her. It wasn't about unfortunate killings or whatever ruckus had occurred before them. Something *had* happened here long before she was born, but even Dad would only talk about it in whispers and never in her presence. None of that mattered though, because this was a town that wanted to prevent kids from being kids. Curious exploration and artistic expression were frowned upon, producing a community where high school graduates fled like thieves in the night. Those who stayed—Trish recognized very few people from her class—resembled Stepford zombies.

I was right to run.

So nostalgia had taken hold of her yesterday. She had driven out to the forest and followed the flow of memories around those woods. Each recollection was like visiting old friends. It was the best she'd felt since moving back until she blacked out and collapsed on the trail. Booze wasn't involved, and she was six years off everything harder than liquor, so the experience was baffling to no one more than herself.

Two teenagers had found her. They were kids out looking for the same experiences that had defined Trish's high school career, and were so nervous that she wouldn't wake up they called an ambulance.

Dad and Nate wasted no time coming hard at her with questions as soon as she came to in the hospital. If only she remembered anything. Her old drug habit was a topic of interest, one that she adamantly denied. The men tiptoed around the subject while making accusations with their eyes. She expected it from Dad, but to see Nate's doubt was like a knife through the heart.

"Your concern is noted, Dad. Thanks for stopping by." It was time to bring this inquiry to a close and get him the hell out. She'd rather be unpacking.

"Hold on a second," he said. "You know that I'm glad to have you back. Wasn't easy to see my baby girl leave town in a hurry. You always said you would visit me and that turned into what? A few holidays each year?"

"Nate and I were always trying to get you into the city," Trish said. "And the one time we did get you out there…"

Dad rolled his eyes. "I hate that place. Know what New York City is? Bunch of assholes in a great big hurry to get nowhere."

She laughed and hated herself for it. It meant she was letting him off the hook. But maybe that was okay. The old man had done his best with raising a little hellion and now that he was no longer chief of police, he didn't have much to worry about—except his daughter.

Lucky me.

Retired Ron Sleighton was a jarring sight, almost unrecognizable when matched against her memory. His back arched like a bell curve and weeklong stubble poked out from pink jowls. A Hawaiian shirt was misbuttoned and he tugged constantly at the cramped shorts. The near-militant public servant who had lorded over her formative years was a ghost now, leaving a newly minted Medicare beneficiary in his wake.

"We don't have to do this dance again. I'm a city girl at heart and that'll never change. I'm here because…well, because I'm being a dutiful wife."

Dad wiped beads of sweat from his brow as Trish went to the kitchen and pulled a pitcher of homemade iced tea from the fridge.

"Too damn dutiful," he said. "Still don't see why Nate couldn't work for those private firm guys. Real money's there with much less red tape. He'd be the pick of the liter with them. Out here though…"

Trish handed him an ice-cold glass and took a seat at the table, kicking out the chair across the way. Instead, he turned toward the window and looked out on their quiet dead-end road.

"I thought Nate was doing fine," she said. "That's what you told me."

"It's all about perspective. Yesterday, your husband pulls Robbie Carmoody over for doing 55 downtown. We all know that Carmoody's been out of work for a few years—ever since those sons of bitches at the plant favored cheap overseas labor. Who's going to hire a sixty-year-old middle manager asking for 80k, right? Still, that's no excuse to act like an asshole. Your husband lets him off with a verbal warning. Carmoody's down at Lloyd's right now, half in the bag and two pitchers deep."

"So Nate's building a little goodwill with his people."

"Goodwill? You know what that will get him? A big old pile of dogshit dropped on his doorstep."

"I hope not, Dad, 'cause that would mean shit on my doorstep, too."

"Laugh. Be a smartass, girly. I'll tell you this, if your husband wants to act like a pushover, it won't be long before that's the word on our new chief. Everyone respects the badge at first, but once they discover the man behind it is weak…"

"Nate is not weak. Just because he let Carmoody off with a warning doesn't make him an easy mark."

"You want an easy mark?" he said with a tone that rose to meet her challenge. "Try this. Earl Bishop's kid just moved into town last month…takes over his father's store now that Earl's on dialysis. Earl never sold alcohol on Sunday, on account of it being the Sabbath. A practice that we appreciated."

"A practice *some* of you appreciated, maybe. Nate was in disbelief when he couldn't get a six of Blue Moon before a Sunday Sox game."

"That explains it." Dad's eyes narrowed and Trish recognized the look. It was the same one he'd given after she and Jerrica were caught shoplifting at the outlets in Westbrook.

Disappointment.

"What does that explain, exactly?"

"Earl's boy, Scotty, just decides *screw it*. Starts leaving the iron bars up above the liquor and alcohol cases on Sundays, available to any and all. There were complaints and Brady came down on the side of Scotty. *In this economy, every dollar earned is make or break.* That's what he told me."

"Dad, this is stupid."

"Stupid? You have to get your man in line. Hell, both of you could use a little shaping up. After your stunt yesterday, people are wondering what's going on with you as well as your husband."

"Let them wonder. Fuck, I hate small towns. Everything is everyone's business. I'm waiting for Ken Hammond across the street to tell me that something's gotta be done about the weeds in my front yard."

"Things are the way they are around here for a good goddamn reason."

"Some things change, and it's never the harbinger of doom you make it out to be. Of all the problems in this town, and around the world, selling alcohol on Sundays is the least of 'em. If Scotty wants to sell booze on the Lord's Day, God bless him! Hallelujah!"

"How did you get to be so damn liberal? I thought all those tattoos and piercings were a phase."

"Look at it another way, then," she said, ignoring the crack about her appearance. "Lloyd's dive bar isn't the only place to get drinks on a Sunday. Now we've got a competitive economy. Hey, it's a start. And if our state decides it's not kosher for us to have a drink, they'll put it to a vote. Your dedication to some outdated way of life isn't something I can relate to. Just because Nate isn't adhering to every dumb unwritten law of the land doesn't mean he's doing anything wrong."

"That's exactly what it means to some of them."

"It can't be easy to live up to the legacy of Chief Ronald Sleighton, Lord Protector of Forest Grove. Nate wants to give this place a modern day facelift. He doesn't have a choice if he wants me to pop a kid out in this place."

"I know how it looks to you kids, but people here are a fickle bunch. I want my son-in-law to prosper, so maybe you mention something to him."

She laughed. "This is why you dropped by? So that your daughter can do a little heavy lifting? Help mold Nate Brady in your image?"

"Wouldn't hurt," he said.

"Well, save it. Nate is so concerned with this town that he hardly comes home 'cept to sleep. I haven't talked to my husband face-to-face in a week. And when we do talk, it's never about anything except the fucking Grove. The place I tried so hard to escape."

Sleighton's eyes were heavy. "That's how I feel every day."

And then he left.

Melanie hoped she would be as spry as Desiree Rosemott when she was eighty.

That's in less than forty years…

The elderly owner of Desiree's Bed & Breakfast didn't look a day past sixty-five and her spring-loaded step suggested she could've passed for even younger. She'd insisted upon carrying Melanie's bags up to the third floor suite and wouldn't take no for an answer. Melanie's adamant refusal only irked her.

"Okay, dear," Desiree said with pointed acquiescence. "But I'm not thrilled about my guest trudging up two flights of stairs lugging her own bags. What kind of customer service is that?"

"It's no problem, Ms. Rosemott, really," Melanie said. "Glad to be doing something after four hours in my car." She followed the woman up the skinny stairwell, tugging a suitcase as two shoulder bags dangled off her arm.

The bed and breakfast was quaint, outfitted entirely in old rustic charm. The walls were lined with black and white photos of downtown Forest Grove, from the year it was founded to a modern day shot that accented the town's reluctant march through time. The hallway was equipped with wall-mounted candlesticks, each of them showing melted wear and tear, suggesting that Desiree lit them nightly. Floors were heavy hardwood and the eyesore wallpaper (baby blue, with white, pearl-shaped designs) suggested it hadn't been updated since Desiree was little.

"Up these last few steps," Desiree said between heavy and determined breaths. "And you'll find yourself in the best room we have." The woman pressed a hand to the small of her back and grimaced. "Just give me one minute to rest and…"

"Ms. Rosemott, please don't go through the trouble. I can manage."

"Horsepucky!" she snapped with a smile. "Don't go giving me that kind of pity. This place is my responsibility until I'm in the ground."

Melanie took point on the first step. "Please, Ms. Rosemott, go back downstairs. I don't want to be any more of a bother for you…"

"You're sweet." The old woman brushed her aside with a gentle arm. "But I have my way of doing things. In the fifty years that I've owned this bed & breakfast, I have always brought my guests to their room. A touch of arthritis ain't stopping me now."

She resumed the climb and flung the heavy door inward, stepping aside to allow her guest a view.

Melanie placed the suitcase at her feet. The room spanned the floor's entire length. In front of them was a kitchenette furnished with a stove, a refrigerator, and cupboards. A round breakfast table sat against the far window overlooking the rear parking lot. The carpeted living area sported a sitting area fashioned around a tube television. On the far end of the suite were two rooms: a spacious bedroom furnished with a queen size bed, closet, and two dressers. The other was a spotless bathroom.

"Wow," she said. It was the only word she could manage.

"You're going to be happy here, dear. Unfortunately, this suite doesn't get much use these days. But I like to keep up with the cleaning. Keeps me busy, you know?" She walked to the bathroom and stepped inside, motioning for her with the wag of an emaciated finger.

Melanie gasped as she entered. In the corner was a sparkling bathtub shaped like a curved slipper. It was off-white and the bottom rim was onyx black. It reached down onto the marble floor with thick pearl legs. Vintage, but expertly maintained and outfitted with a few modern attachments. It overlooked the quiet country road, but a folded room divider leaned against the far wall in case one got mindful of peeping toms.

"Just added a few of those detachable heads last year," Desiree said. "Ain't ever used it myself, you'll be happy to know, but it gets nothing but raves."

It promised more comfort than Melanie wanted. This wasn't a vacation and she would feel guilty if she wound up enjoying any of her time here.

"You might be happy to know that we're completely set up for wireless Internet, too. Wasn't crazy about adding it, but apparently rustic country living is only desirable when modern amenities aren't too far behind."

"I hadn't thought about that, but that's great."

"Well, I'll let you get settled. You're a bit too late for breakfast, but I'm happy to make you a sandwich if you would like some lunch."

"I think I can wait until dinner," Melanie said. "I'd rather get unpacked."

"Well, I'll give you a knock around four and see what you feel like. You're my only tenant, so let me see what I got in the kitchen and I'll cook you up something special. How would that be?"

"That would be wonderful."

Melanie saw her to the door and waited a moment, making sure the old woman got down the steep stairs without falling.

Then she unpacked, taking full advantage of the bedroom's walk-in closet. It was great to be able to splay her wardrobe out and see exactly what she had with her. It suddenly seemed like she hadn't brought enough, though the plan was still to get the hell out of here in a few days.

She stripped off her clothes, deciding on a jog before dinner. Melanie ran a palm over her toned stomach, making sure she hadn't added any unwanted poundage to her physique. She'd fallen out of her routine this week and decided it was time to get back into it. It wasn't like she needed to look good for the man who wasn't in her life, but she enjoyed keeping up with herself. Even when sleazy little students made untoward comments about her ass behind her back—it was flattering in the most degrading way.

The loose t-shirt dangled off her shoulders and Melanie slid a pair of black running shorts up over her thighs. She laced her Asics and fitted her iPod to its arm holster, jacking in the earphones as she trotted down the steps. Hitting the open parking lot, she cranked up Kylie Minogue's *Light Years* and banked a left toward Forest Grove.

This place was awash in the kind of tranquility that small town champions always sang of. Stu's Gas Station still offered a welcome ding whenever a new car pulled up to the pump, and an attendant in overalls came jogging out of the garage not only to pump the gas, but to check the oil and wash the windows as well. Last time she was here, Jennifer had insisted on stopping there for a carton of Marlboros—the night before her murder. It hadn't changed much in the twenty-five years since.

The road bent to the right, leading into the town proper. A grassy park centered by a giant white gazebo split traffic two ways, incoming to the right and outgoing to the left. A two-story middle school evoked a quaint academic feeling with its perfectly groomed lawn and rows of loaded bike racks.

She passed a local credit union that looked jockeyed by female retirees, a post office with white sandblasted steps and gleaming titanium railings, a pizza and sub place called THE SHACK, and a general store simply called EARL'S.

On the left, a tiny strip mall of local businesses was anchored by a used book swap. The walkway up to city hall was lined with circular stone slabs nestled in between waist-high shrubbery. The library was tiny and looked all but abandoned. Beside it, an Italian restaurant boasted about being family-run for five generations. A few homes sat scattered throughout, all of them updated to vinyl siding and satellite dishes.

Forest Grove had grown since her last visit.

Then she saw the sign. At the outskirts of town, staked into the ground and isolated from everything else. Somewhat faded, slightly crooked, and somehow perfectly readable: CAMP FOREST GROVE—5 MILES.

An illustrated lake zigzagged through a painted canopy of trees, leading to a log cabin that was bathed in an overly orange glow of sunshine. Graffiti looked to have been whited out and painted over a few times. One scrawl, *a nice place to die*, was a visible scar beneath a hastily brushed-on crown of hemlock leaves.

Melanie stared at it through wide eyes. Panic took her as that night came screaming back. Again. The multiple gashes that had torn Jennifer's neck open, the wide-eyed realization of imminent death etched in Lindsey's eyes—

Stop it.

But she couldn't. Unpleasant memories assaulted her from every recess of her mind: the swarm of mosquitoes as she pushed the canoes into Lake Forest Grove, Hoyt's repulsive odor, and his coarse skin on her fingertips as she tried fighting him off. His blood on her hands and inside her body when she swallowed it.

I never saw that bastard die.

Yes, he was dead. That's what they said, at least. But she hadn't seen it.

Drenched in sweat, Melanie decided she'd had enough of a workout for today and did a U-turn, crossing the street and jogging back the other way.

It was close to three by the time she got back to Desiree's. She stumbled in and climbed to her room on wobbly knees, heading directly to the bathroom and cranking the tub's hot water. Her clothes were drenched and sweaty as she pulled them off, leaving a scattered trail across the floor. Desiree had stocked an assortment of bubble baths and oils in the cabinet and Melanie could hardly believe her dumb luck. This was far too high maintenance for a country bumpkin-y bed and breakfast. And yet, here it was.

When piping hot steam was lifting up off the water, she slipped beneath the bubbly foam and cradled her neck into the padded crevice. She arched her back and stretched her legs outward, kicking up a puff of foamy soap while resting the balls of her heels against the bath's rim. Then she draped a moist facecloth over her eyes and tried desperately to starve off the enduring panic attack.

An hour slipped past, possibly more. Her fingers looked like raisins when she climbed out, but her breathing was regulated and her muscles had loosened. She toweled off and lathered her body in moisturizer, walking over to the closet and deciding on a tank top and sweats to cover goosebumped flesh.

She climbed onto the bed and folded her legs Indian-style in front of her laptop. The words didn't come easy, but she jotted the stream-of-consciousness blather down anyway—an effort to capture every thought that had spilled from her mind during this afternoon's flashback marathon.

Desiree's knock yanked her from the rabbit hole of despair she was documenting, saying something about dinner. It didn't fully register and Melanie just wanted to get back to her notes, agreeing to be downstairs at 5:30 to help set the dinner table.

Once she was certain the old woman had again made it down the stairwell, she returned her attention to the memoir. Everything on the page now felt distant and foreign, as if she had written none of it. The moment had passed for the night, but this was a good enough start. The whole book didn't need to be planned out during this trip. This was about jogging her memory, and she'd done enough of that for one day.

Pushing her work off to the bed's edge, Melanie got up and collected her scattered clothes off the floor when her eyes widened and her heart jumped into her throat.

In front of the door, on the linoleum, she stared at the outline of a naked and watery footprint.

Brady hadn't planned on being home this early.

Judging by Trish's reaction, she hadn't planned for it either. Her green eyes were flecked with traces of hazel and they watched him with something approaching disdain.

"Hi." Brady smirked and unbuttoned his uniform, tugging at the sweltering cotton tee beneath.

She came up through the cellar door wearing an old Cure t-shirt that exposed her colorless midriff with every motion. Tiny sweat shorts hung lopsided off her waist. With arms folded across her chest and her head tilted to the side, she said, "I didn't make supper. Not after your text."

"Wasn't expecting you to." Brady moved to kiss her and it was like planting lips on a marble slab. "I don't know what kind of hours I'm keeping these days. I thought I'd be later, but Donnelley decided he'd rather shuffle papers than go to his kid's year-end musical. But hey, whatever gets me home by eight.

Anyway, how was your day?"

"A waste."

"Sorry," Brady said. "What were you doing down there? Unpacking?"

"Sort of. I was looking for something. My, uh, yearbook."

"Nostalgic for an old boyfriend?"

"Not funny." She threw him a look that chilled his blood.

"I know." Brady knew better than to poke her when she was upset, but sometimes he couldn't resist. Teasing was how he diffused the tension between them. Yesterday's blackout was worrisome and Trish took to lectures like cats took to discipline, so he couldn't force the issue. There was no choice but to take her at her word when she said she wasn't using again.

Even though he suspected she might be using again.

He called the hospital this morning but they still didn't have the damn toxicology report. It was hard to believe they wouldn't find something in her system to explain the blackout, not to mention her skittishness.

Or maybe you can give your wife the benefit of the doubt.

Cynicism was a side effect in this line of work.

"What's in the yearbook, anyway?" He thought it best to come at this from a different angle. "I'd like to see it, you know. Considering that I've never seen your graduation photo."

"And you never will." The corners of her mouth hinted at a bashful grin. "There's nothing in it, save for some memories that I'd long forgotten."

"Does this mean you're warming to the idea of being here?"

Her laugh was spiteful, the smirk was gone, and her eyes offered a non-verbal way of telling him to fuck off.

Brady inched past her with his arms up. Touching her now might illicit one of those buzzes like in the game of Operation, and he'd had enough grief for one day.

She headed back for the cellar.

"Hey," he called.

She cocked her head.

"I haven't seen you in a few days," he said. "Was hoping we could maybe spend the night doing something."

"Like what?"

"Whatever you want."

"I want to get unpacked."

"Okay," Brady said and shrugged his shoulders. That sounded like a terrible thing to do after twelve hours on the job, but he wanted to spend some time with her. "Let's do that."

"I'll do it," she said. "Alone."

Brady didn't know what to say. Trish had been distant—annoyed—since the move. This wasn't something she wanted, and he had sort of forced it on her. But after yesterday's incident in the forest, he was starting to think that something else was wrong—something that went beyond her small town allergy.

He had hoped that her negative attitude would recede once they got into the swing of things. Admittedly, the Grove still carried a bit of an old world element. Some of the townspeople could barely handle the idea of Scott Bishop was running the general store now, expanding the beer and alcohol section beyond what Earl had envisioned. A gateway to debauchery, obviously.

Brady wasn't crazy about the fact that his neighbors had called to register a noise complaint on their first full day of residence. Trish's taste in music was questionable, sure. Most of her bands were obnoxious and tone-deaf, but she'd been blasting it in the middle of the day when she was well within her right to do so. He'd forced her to turn it down as a show of solidarity—even if it meant the people across the street shouldn't hold their breaths for an invite to the next Brady BBQ.

Yes, there were some setbacks here, but nothing they

couldn't adjust to. He just needed Trish to fight for it, not against. She shut down at nearly every conversation, from yard work, dinner plans or, God forbid, eventual children.

"Why don't I help you out?" he said.

Trish smiled and her eyes softened, revealing a glimpse of the woman he'd fallen for. "I don't think so," she said. "I'll unpack a few boxes and that will make me feel better. I don't need your brawn to help me bring anything upstairs."

He brushed the sarcasm off. Her independence had been an accelerant to their romantic blaze back when she waitressed an Irish dive pub in lower Manhattan. Brady used to go there at the end of his patrolman's shift, compelled by a thirst for cheap pitchers and endless mozzarella sticks.

"This should help destroy that physique" were the first words she'd spoken as she plopped a greasy plate down before him. Only the corners of her mouth hinted at a smile and Brady knew instantly that he liked her. She wasn't his type, and he obviously was not hers, but polarity could be a powerful thing. Her jet-black hair was cropped short, bangs curled down over a few inches of forehead. Tiny ears poked out beneath her hair and were just awkward enough to be an adorable characteristic. The girl might've been a vampire—with chalky white skin, black nail polish, and matching lipstick—but damn if she didn't rock the look. Her jeans were torn and Brady could see dark lace underwear when the shreds moved just right.

He watched her that night, seeing flashes of quick wit and confidence that built into serious attraction—untoward compliments broke upon her like ships on lighthouse rocks. You didn't get through to Trish Sleighton unless she let you in.

Brady dropped into a kitchen chair with a sigh and fumbled with the home-stitched placemat as memories of simpler days ebbed to harsh realities. "My men are still behaving like a bunch of supermarket bagboys," he said. "Fine to my face, but it's open season every time I turn my back."

"Dad says you gotta put the fear of God into them."

"Took away their Sunday football-watching privileges, isn't that worse? Got Steve Maylam working Monday nights, too. Effective immediately and until football season ends. I feel like that's a good start."

"I like Maylam's wife," Trish said. "Missy is the only person I'd call a friend in this wonderful little berg. The only desperate housewife I know who'll talk David Lynch instead of potato salad recipes."

"When'd you talk to your dad, anyway?"

"He came by the house today. Told me that you've got to be more like him and that people are starting to wonder about us."

"That guy—"

"Got you a job."

"And so I've got be his clone?"

"No," she said. "I actually told him that was absurd. You know how he is, though. Hates to see things change. Doesn't know what he should be doing now that he's out of the picture. If anything, you're sweet to let him come around and help out as much as you do."

"There's a whole lot of process and culture to get used to," he said. "Your dad just wants to make sure that he leaves his town in good hands. And I don't worry about him. I worry about you."

"You're such a dork."

"And you're rusty. Girl I fell in love with would've told me to worry about my cholesterol instead, then send me packing."

"Yeah," she said. "Well, you kind of live here so I can't exactly throw you out."

"When you're in a mood there's no getting through to you."

Trish came around the table and clasped her smooth hands over his shoulders. "I know I'm a terrible wife, okay? Selfish. Bitchy. Probably a little conceited, too. And I know you're having issues at the new gig. But you wanted this. I'm trying to be patient and I'm waiting for things to click."

"Maybe that's the problem. You're sitting around waiting for life to make sense instead of doing something about it."

"It's not easy, Nate. You know what you want and you have it. But me? I'm a long way from chic bars, gallery exhibits, and indie movies. This place sucks for me."

"You know what sucks? When your career goes so far south that your wife's father has to pull strings to land you a job. We agreed this was the best option for us—as a family. There's upward mobility in this, a lot more than in private security consulting."

"Not as much money, though."

Brady felt his anger boiling. Trish kept cutting wherever she could. And once his wounds were open, she was ready with the salt. "Dammit. Again? Do I really have to explain why I want to stay in law enforcement as opposed to consulting?"

"Sorry I brought it up," Trish threw her arms up on her way back down into the basement. "You definitely do not have to remind me…of anything. Why don't you trot back out on those mean streets and let me get some fucking work done."

"Work? Ha!" he screamed out as the door slammed. Her footsteps froze just beyond the door and he knew at once that he'd touched a nerve. If she was hurt at all, he was glad for it. Trish wasn't curing cancer in that cellar; instead, she was finding out that she wasn't in her twenties anymore, learning that there was more to life than belonging to some fucking social scene.

Brady's momentary triumph reshuffled and turned to guilt. That was a card he never intended to play. This move hadn't been easy on her, but she didn't understand how good they had it: a great house, fantastic job security and, most importantly, a great place to start a family. Country living at its finest. Good schools. Safe neighborhoods. A strong sense of community. Forest Grove had it all and he served its citizens with pride. Yeah, they were a little too old-fashioned in some respects, but the world was changing and that wouldn't last forever.

Brady's stomach rumbled with the expectancy of dinner. He'd be supporting one of the local places tonight. Loved the huge slices at Walt's Pizzeria, but they were all he ever ate. Tonight felt like a good night for a steak tips sub, or maybe a Mexican cheesesteak since all his guys raved about it.

And maybe another ride through town after that. He was still trying to get a sense of routine in the grove. Who should be where and when. Learning that meant it would be easier to spot things out of the ordinary.

Brady got up to leave, thought about telling Trish where he was going and decided against it.

She doesn't give a shit, he thought. And left without another word.

Marcy was feeling good. Better than good, actually. Her head swam with so much Kentucky bourbon that even wrong decisions felt like the right ones. Like leaving the bar with two guys because she couldn't make up her mind. And then agreeing to go for a ride.

Vince was driving. The sideways glances he threw in her direction were absolutely ravenous, but he stayed quiet and kept his eyes on the road. He'd been doing shots of Kettle One all night, but assured her that he could keep his shit together on the road no matter how much he had to drink.

"Everyone's good at something," he'd smirked. "I'm the

world's greatest drunk driver."

The absurdity of that statement might not have charmed her under normal circumstances. Even now, she recognized it as completely irresponsible and asinine, but her alcohol-soaked skull seemed to giggle at everything Vince had to say. That he'd slipped his shirt off at her request probably had a little something to do with that, too. Only time she took her eyes off his chiseled swimmer's physique was to make sure Caleb remained as interested as Vince. He sat in the back—his arms sprawled out across the seat tops like the Audi was a lounge. He watched her silently from the shadows with narrow eyes and a wolfish grin.

I'm totally going to let both of them have me at once. The thought of it alone was enough to make her wet. All that attention on her and her alone. Two men competing for her affections. Both of them trying to provoke the bigger reaction. They looked ready to bring their A games and so it was only fair she brought hers, too.

"Tell me again." Her words sound like mush. "Why we're driving all the way out here when we could've gone back to Caleb's empty dorm. We might've been having fun already."

"We used to come out here all the time in high school," Vince said. "All the local kids did. Some old campground. We can do whatever we want out there and we don't have to worry about…interruptions."

Interruptions. Like girlfriends. These idiots shouldn't flatter themselves. Marcy had her own complicated relationship waiting for her back at school. And if Kev wasn't such a sleazebag, she wouldn't have gone trolling for revenge sex tonight. That man whore thought she wouldn't find out he'd been banging all his co-workers at the video store. She figured this would be enough payback to call it even.

"Here's the turnoff," Vince said, squinting through the pitch darkness outside the car's headlights. "Just a quick hike from here."

"An old camp?" Marcy said, airing her displeasure.

"Better than a hotel. And don't worry, there's beds." Caleb said, as if that made it preferable.

Vince pulled the Audi onto the dirt turnoff and killed the engine. Marcy got out on her side and instantly slipped a palm over the bulge in Caleb's shorts. "We *could* walk all that way."

Caleb clamped a hand down on her ass and squeezed, planting his lips on the nape of her neck.

Marcy pulled her top off and dropped it, ruffling Caleb's hair as he kissed her breasts. "But I don't think we're going to get that far."

"Works for me," Vince said, unbuckling his pants and shimmying out of them as he approached.

Marcy pushed his head to her free breast and moaned gently as both guys kissed and fondled them.

A beam of light sliced through the night on the path at their backs. Marcy noticed it right off, pushing the boys from her bosom. They struggled like hungry calves, leaning into her the more she resisted.

"Cut the shit," she said at last and broke away, fondling the darkness beneath for her discarded shirt. "Someone's there."

The guys turned toward the light.

"Hey buddy," Caleb grunted, "Quit shining that fucking thing in my face."

Marcy was still crouched and fumbling for her top when a pop erupted from behind the flashlight, accompanied by a cracking splat somewhere above. Caleb dropped from the air, crashing onto her back like a ton of bricks. She yelped as Caleb rolled off her bare back, collapsing to the dirt with a thud. She got upright in time for another pop. A skull exploded and slapped her cheek as Vince dropped next. His body twitched and writhed at her feet as blood left his body in eager pumps.

Marcy went to scream as the killer lurched forward,

hurling the flashlight down at her feet. She jumped back and glanced at the bodies: bloodied holes in their heads and lazy drifts of smoke rising up out of broken skulls.

Before she could say anything, the gun barrel glinted in the moonlight, followed by a thunderous boom and a blinding muzzle flash.

 **Four**

In the evening's latest hours, just before the day burned out the night, he found himself awake and walking.

His eye adjusted to the world around him as he stepped back into his shelter, focusing on the structural beams that ran across a stone ceiling. His hand shot up over his face and he rubbed the torn and jagged flesh where his nose had once been—and was again.

I'm...healing...

He'd managed to catch a glimpse of himself in the mirror back there while watching the blonde woman bathe. The desire to kill her was great, but his appearance was worse. It wasn't the way he remembered himself and stared at the reflection feeling disbelief and confusion.

Why am I alive?

A lingering piece of him knew enough to contemplate this.

He put his boot down on the dirty mattress and jiggled it. It squished and water seeped out—too soaked to sleep on.

Lumbering out from beneath the lean-to while embracing the cold and cavernous air around him, his heart pounded with excitement as his attention fell upon a stack of broken remains. Dirty bones and spotted skulls in a discarded pile stacked to his knees. His work carried out a long time ago. At least, it felt like a long time ago. He didn't know much about keeping time and only vaguely acknowledged its passing.

Hunting was the only thing that brought him any joy. It was both thrilling and necessary. When he didn't protect his domain, terrible things happened.

He wondered how long it had been between murders. There must've been tools down here, but he couldn't find any. His bones began to ache and his temples throbbed as he searched. His body felt snug and uncomfortable, like slipping into a shirt two sizes too small. He thought of things he didn't understand and suffered visions of those he couldn't recognize. Was this what it was like to get older?

His brain scattered like cockroaches at the flip of a light switch. The impulse to kill gnawed at him, turning over in his mind despite the confusion.

Last time he'd killed, it had been so easy. Wandering through the woods, protecting his wilderness, there had been a glimpse of her through the trees. He saw her moving down the country road, walking faster than they usually did. His eye caught sight of her and, at that moment, she was as good as dead. He ghosted her, using the habitat for coverage while maintaining distance. All he could think about was ripping her to shreds beneath his blade—his heart leaping into his throat as he stalked.

The hunting knife had slipped from its sheath, rendering him the most powerful predator that ever lived. He kept pace while fantasizing about all the ways to kill her. A forceful jab through the top of her skull. The knife's hungry teeth sawed across her throat. Multiple stabs in the back. Hands wrapped around her neck. He preferred to look them in the eyes as he did it—that wide-eyed look of horror and disbelief never failed to excite.

He had remained indecisive right up until that final moment. Every option on the table. The whole thing almost collapsed when a car pulled over, a male voice offering a ride.

There hadn't been any way of knowing what was said, but she stormed off in a huff and the car peeled away in much the same fashion.

Giving him the break he'd been waiting for.

The hitchhiker had stepped well off the road and dropped her backpack into the dirt. Her back was to him as she sat down on top of it, sighing. He came for her with purpose, closing the gap in seconds. His eye wide with anticipation, transfixed by the sliver of exposed black flesh between her waistband and ruffled top.

Flesh that needed cutting.

He had decided that the knife wasn't necessary. It dropped from his grip as he lurched out from behind the last tree and brought both hands down around her neck. She yelped and struggled, but he yanked her off the pack and hurled her into the forest. She tried screaming but all he had to do was flex his arm tighter and her protests became crumpled gags. She fought for air while they retreated from the road.

The girl had been barely conscious by the time he released her. She dropped onto the dirt with a soft thud and he threw his weight atop her as he liked to do—the best view of the dying game. Her eyes popped, but it was much too late. His hands, thick and with broken nails on all fingers, pushed up on both sides of her face. With one simple motion, he jerked her head to the left and closed his eye.

The neck snap was always an orgasm to his ears, and he remembered the drool falling from his lips, and plopping onto her dead flesh.

Her body had gone limp and she stared up at the chirping birds with unblinking eyes. Their song oblivious to the barbaric murder it had just scored. He remembered staying there for a moment or two, watching her corpse with a hunter's satisfaction. Then he took a contented walk to the roadside in order to retrieve her bag and his discarded weapon.

That girl, his victim, had been beautiful once. The memory was old now and certain details were lost to time, but he never forgot those beautiful, bulging eyes of horror. He loved it because it made him feel strong.

He remembered dragging her corpse back home, overwhelmed with disappointment and sadness that they didn't stay pretty for very long.

Now she was disgusting. Just bones he could no longer find—lost in a pile of a dozen others. Again, he wondered why he was awake, certain he shouldn't be. It must have been because of *her*.

The one who got away.

The one who hurt him.

He often dreamt of the things he would do if he ever saw her again. The need for revenge was instinctual, as automatic as a reflex. And yet, he had scurried off tonight like a frightened animal.

Things had changed and he was out of practice. Before he could take his revenge, he was going to have to get used to the fact that he wasn't young anymore.

Though he still had the urge.

He wondered how many had grown comfortable with passing through these woods in the time he was away. This made him anxious and angry as he pulled a black parka over his shivering body. The coat wasn't as warm as his old one.

Tonight was sloppy. His body felt weak and he knew that he was going to have to act quickly to kill her.

She can't escape again.

He wanted to tear her blonde hair (it had been red the last time) from her scalp in fistfuls. Her eyes, bluer than Lake Forest Grove, begged for his thumbs to gouge them. Long and lanky legs—how easy they'd break. Pasty white flesh needed to be repainted with her life's blood.

A second later, he knew her name.

Melanie Holden.

She wasn't going to leave Forest Grove alive this time. But before he could kill her, he needed a mask. Weapons.

And practice.

Tanya pulled up to Rafe's house at a quarter to nine and honked the horn. She thought about going to the door to retrieve her boyfriend, but Mr. Hanscom was a creep who couldn't keep his eyes off her. It was worse on summery days like this, when all she wore was a pair of low-rise denim shorts and a tank top.

No, today the car horn would have to suffice.

Rafe must've been waiting by the window because he came right out, jogging down the stone path with a dopey smile on his face.

He should've been the one to drive, but the moron totaled his car last night while racing his buddy across the Grocery Basket parking lot—his Oldsmobile hopped an island medium at fifty miles per hour, leaving the undercarriage a busted mess of oily wires. The loser didn't see so well at night, apparently, and failed to stomp the brakes until it was too late.

Today she was forcing him to go to an eye appointment, after which they'd hit the highway in search of something fun to do. The one benefit of growing up in Forest Grove was that everywhere else was more interesting. They could sit in a rest area, drinking sodas and cranking classic Eminem, and it would be better than whatever they could come up with around here.

"I can't believe you're not grounded," she said as he got in and kissed her cheek.

"Like anyone could keep me away from you." He jerked

his thumb toward the house. "Especially them. Mom's just happy I'm alive. And she rules the roost, so…"

"The crazy unconscious woman from the other day texted me. Wants to meet up and have a chat."

"I figured she'd be checked into a methadone clinic by now."

"Do you even know what that means?"

"Uh, sure."

"Yeah, well, she's married to the chief. And she didn't look like a krunkhead to me."

"Because you've seen so many of them?"

"I just feel bad because everyone's talking like she's some kind of junkie. My parents don't want me to have anything to do with her. Yours?"

Rafe shrugged. "I didn't mention it to them."

It was no wonder Rafe kept his parents at an arm's length. Everything was an overreaction for them. Tanya had eaten dinner there once and forgot to inform them of her gluten allergy beforehand. Mrs. Hanscom looked at her with the kind of disdain that better suited a pregnancy confession.

They drove downtown and Rafe decided he wanted an iced coffee from Dunkins.

"We're going to the diner, you can get one there."

He was actually pouting when they pulled into the restaurant's parking lot.

The chief's wife waited for them on one of the picnic tables outside. Rafe volunteered to go in and place an order while Tanya walked over and took a seat across from Mrs. Brady.

"I, uh, never got the opportunity to thank you two for the other day." Trish wore dark jeans and a faded tee representing some band Tanya had never heard of—probably a hundred years old and long forgotten. "Got your phone number off your Facebook…you really should tweak those privacy settings."

Unlike most of the kids her age, Tanya didn't live and die by social media. Something about it seemed incredibly sad and she wasn't self-absorbed enough to believe her every thought needed documenting. No one was that deep or interesting—especially people from this yawner of a hometown.

Rafe interrupted when he returned with double fists of coffee. "Are you doing better?" He dropped beside Tanya.

The answer to his question was obvious, if only because Trish looked alive now. She hadn't two days ago. They had snuck out for an afternoon on the lake, the perfect place to get stoned and mess around. Instead, they found a woman facedown in the dirt, completely unresponsive.

"Much better, thank you." Trish put her hand out and Rafe shook it. "I'm sure you're both wondering why I'm wasting your time, right?"

Tanya wrapped her lips around her straw and sucked up a mouthful of mocha almond coffee.

"Alright," Trish said. "I grew up in this town. I see that it hasn't changed much. You guys are going to be, what? Seniors next year?"

"Thankfully," Tanya said.

Trish laughed. Her cheery white grin an odd contrast against the onyx lip color that surrounded her mouth. "Well then, you've got a vested interest in this."

"In what?" Rafe asked.

"In this town. I hated going to school here because of the way they treated us. Home before nine, in bed by eleven. Don't listen to loud music, don't read the wrong books, and whatever you do, don't fucking drink or you'll turn into a whore."

Tanya and Rafe exchanged mutual glances that said, *hey, maybe she isn't so bad.* True, she was a little strange, but her boots were really cool and she proved that the alt look worked beyond high school. Trish didn't seem to care that most of the people in town—according to her parents—were uncomfortable around her. That was pretty badass.

"It is kinda lame here," Tanya said. "But, hey, one more year until college."

"Yeah," Trish said. "But what if you didn't have to spend the next year waiting for it to be over?"

Tanya jiggled the ice around in her coffee cup, losing interest.

"I'm saying that maybe we push back a little. Maybe the juniors and seniors organize a summer dance. Something that will stomp the superstition out of this town once and for all."

"I didn't even know Cyrus Hoyt was real until last year," Rafe said. "Figured he was just an urban legend. I mean, I know that stupid rhyme like everyone else, but…"

"It was the same when I was in high school," Trish said. "And since I'm going to be living here again, settling down, it's worth my time to get involved. Kids are going to be kids and this place is all about sheltering them from the world. That needs to stop."

This was making a certain kind of sense. Tanya had been pulled over by Officer Johnson last week and he wasted no time giving her hell. All she'd done was drive through the downtown strip blasting deadmau5 and caught a lecture on *irresponsibility* as if she'd been speeding.

She was still a little sore about it.

Trish grinned. "Do you want to set something up?"

"Why are you so concerned with helping us?" Tanya asked.

"If I ever have kids, I refuse to bring them into this kind of fucking bourgeois community."

"I dig that," Rafe said, slurping the very bottom of his coffee cup for the remnants of syrupy caramel.

Tanya did, too. Her imagination was already running wild

with possibilities. If the grove were to have a dance, wouldn't the girl responsible for delivering it be a shoe-in for homecoming queen?

My gift to the class of 2014.

She'd be a hero to everyone.

Yeah, she was definitely warming to the idea.

Trish must've noticed the look on her face, because now she was grinning, too. "So, does this mean you're in?"

"We are," Tanya said. Rafe would follow because that's what a good boyfriend did. Besides, he only stood to gain from this—he had the pleasure of walking into these potential dances with a total babe on his arm.

"Beautiful," Trish said. "Just think of what we can do for future classes. And telling the establishment to fuck itself won't be all that bad, either."

"I like it," Tanya said. "What do you need us to do?"

Melanie wasn't doing any better today. Sitting in front of her laptop, the words refused to come.

She decided last night the soggy footprint was too small to be Cyrus Hoyt's. Remembering that night at camp, they way his giant boots stomped toward her, shaking the walls and floors as he readied an attack. No way could his feet be so…dainty.

After finding that watery outline, she'd hurried downstairs to interrogate Desiree. The only possible explanation being that the old woman had come into her room for one reason or another while she'd been asleep in the tub. Melanie was currently the only guest, so there was no other suspect.

To make matters worse, the old woman had denied everything: "Once my guest is settled in, it's their room. Not mine. Last thing I would do is violate your privacy, hon."

The incident had cast a cloud over an expertly prepared supper of seared chicken in apricot sauce with basmati rice on the side. Melanie simply did not believe Desiree, however adamant her denial. What felt more likely was that the old woman had snuck in for some reason and was embarrassed to be caught.

Melanie had never felt more vulnerable than after that dinner, slinking back to her room feeling isolated and betrayed. There was no alarm system to detect intruders and only a simple deadbolt to keep the world locked out of her room. Every wind wisp gave her gooseflesh, while each branch tussle sent her imagination hurdling into overdrive. She imagined Cyrus Hoyt's muddy welder's visor and tattered army coat creeping through the cover of night, his remaining eye leering up at the third floor window with fantasies of murder on his mind.

This morning brought a continuation of those feelings, so she'd packed her things and was all set to leave when an image of Jill Woreley stopped her dead in her tracks. The girl was standing in front of what should've been her class, gum smacking while explaining the significance of the first line in epic poetry. "You guys, like, have to understand the first line is a succinct explanation for the poem at large..."

Of course Jill would use that nugget. Melanie had offered it up once while listening to her complain that deciphering Homer was too difficult.

That one thought was enough to get her to drop her bags at the door and rub the jamb in contemplation. Going home empty-handed would be a mistake. Skulking back to campus, tail between her legs, would signal the complete and utter destruction of her professional life. And it wasn't like she had a personal one to fall back on. She would be a teacher who couldn't see a developed curriculum to fruition any more than she could move beyond the widespread shadow of Cyrus Hoyt. At forty-two, how much time was left to make a professional mark before she became just another purveyor of broad and boring syllabi?

No. This has to work.

So she stayed.

Tired of today's fruitless keyboard daydreaming, she took a quick shower and dressed. It was just past nine. What better time to get out and see the old campground? There was plenty of daylight hanging in the sky to expose every nook and cranny of that awful place, enough for a quick walk around and then she'd be gone before the sun even thought about setting.

Desiree was sweeping up around the front desk when she got down to the lobby. "You don't want breakfast, dear? Was just about to climb up there and give your door a knock. How do blueberry pancakes and Belgian waffles sound?"

"Like extra calories I don't need." Melanie patted her flat but rumbling stomach. There was another reason though. An encroaching unease that gnawed at her innards. "I've got to be somewhere this morning, anyway."

The ride to camp might've been pleasant under normal circumstances. Endless rows of trees lined the roadside as she passed the downtown area. Birches towered high and stretched toward the bright blue overhead while branches swayed in the late spring breeze.

She passed an old run-down gas station and market on the right and remembered that camp wasn't much further. The turnoff was marked by a totem pole on each side and an arched CAMP FOREST GROVE sign that connected them. Melanie's fingers tightened around the steering wheel as her throat closed with what felt like an allergic swell.

Brown haze kicked up as she drove the road, accompanied by a glut of long-forgotten memories. Melanie reached for her phone and talked quickly into its voice recorder, desperate to capture the estranged thoughts as they wandered back home:

Jennifer jogging this cow path every morning, no matter what she drank the night before. Lindsey's drunken effort to chop down a hemlock at 3 AM with nothing more than a hatchet. "We need the firewood!" she screamed (and they didn't). Mr. Dugan's inexplicable mishandling of the camp tractor, driving it into a ditch while offloading uprooted shrubbery. Bill and Tyler having to pry it back onto the road with a wench from Bill's pickup.

Melanie felt tears forming, spilling onto her tract of early crow's feet. The sun was shining, birds were chirping, and everything about Camp Forest Grove, save for the memories, seemed innocuous.

I. Never. Saw. Him. Die.

On her most rational days, Melanie knew that Cyrus Hoyt was dead and buried. Things had been quiet for far too long for him still to be out there. But even on those days, she went to bed scared and uncertain.

Maybe I should've done this years ago.

Once, her psychiatrist had instructed her to do exactly that: "Go there and you'll see that everything you're afraid of stems from that one tragic evening. Doesn't mean Camp Forest Grove is still a malevolent place. Face it down. See how it can't hurt you. And then you'll be surprised by how free you feel."

Hackneyed advice, she thought at the time, changing doctors instead of heeding it.

The trees fell away from the road as the turnoff widened into a clearing that overlooked placid lake waters. No canoes in sight as she drove to the edge of grass where the campground began.

There she parked and steadied her nerves with a row of deep breaths. This was a perfectly safe thing to do, and she repeated that thought until she supposed she believed it. When it failed to motivate her enough to get out of the car, she imagined Dennis Morton and Jill Woreley having a good laugh at her expense over a box of cheap wine.

That did the trick.

Her feet touched down and she lumbered over dirt like an astronaut on the moon. Her legs were heavy, as if trudging through Jell-O. Birds overhead greeted her with welcome back squawks.

The cabins still stood, having suffered smashed windows, crooked shutters, and broken drainage ruts over the last twenty-five years. The grounds looked to be more reasonably kept. Cut grass, trimmed hedges, and tidy trails. From what she'd read about Forest Grove in the last few days, no one had ever tried reopening the place after Mr. Dugan was killed.

Numerous broken beer bottles and crushed cans of Coors Light lined the cabin interiors as she peered through jagged windows. Stubbed cigarette butts were crushed out everywhere she went. How many kids had been out here in the years following the incident? Seclusion like this was a powerful lure for teenagers looking to drink and screw. An oddly reassuring perspective, meaning that if this place had become a haven for teenage promiscuity, then Cyrus Hoyt probably wasn't still alive.

She relaxed as she considered this.

What used to be the counselor's cabin loomed ahead. It had seen better days. The roof's shingles were noticeably frayed and torn, and the runoff drain was broken apart in several spots. Splintered wood stretched across all four walls and it was warped in the spots where it wasn't fractured. The sun-beaten front door had been dark brown, but it was lighter now, and discolored in several spots. Almost completely rotted and soft to the touch.

She twisted the knob, pulling it open and stepping inside onto creaking wood. The cabin smelled of must and her eyes watered after mere seconds of being in it. Her breaths grew more restricted with every step forward. The bay window that Bill had shattered remained busted. Broken glass bordered the frame and several 2x4s had been hammered across its length. Twenty-five years later and it still hadn't been fixed. Or condemned.

The floor was stained with what looked to be dried blood.

Bill.

She knelt and patted a hand over the darkest crimson splotch.

In 1988, she had known better than to put too much faith in a serious relationship. She was still in high school and he was a year graduated—two very different life stations. They were both sharp enough to recognize this challenge, though neither of them seemed to care. Things were simpler then.

The night before Cyrus Hoyt descended had been one of the simplest. She snuck into the boy's bunk while Tyler was off screwing Lindsey. The place was theirs for a while and Bill had been nothing if not the perfect gentleman. Didn't so much as cop a feel. Instead, they lay so close that she could smell that night's dinner—roasted wieners and baked beans—on his breath. They spoke in whispers and the future they discussed was laughably optimistic.

Bill wasn't the college type and swore that he could land a job in the hardware store of whatever town academia led her to. The plan was to find a little off-campus apartment for the two of them and start their joint life as early as humanly possible.

Melanie wasn't sure how that would've worked out and wondered if their ambitious life plan wasn't just an angsty dream.

I'll never know because some sicko buried a hammer claw in his neck.

The floorboard was rough on her fingertips as she traced the dark stain, hoping Bill might somehow feel it, wherever he was. She found it comforting to imagine that he could.

The shadow of a man passed by the boarded window.

Melanie saw the hulking outline creep past without a sound and her jaw dropped low enough to scrape broken glass. She shook the paralysis off and got to her feet. Somewhere in the cabin's gloom, floorboards creaked beneath shifting weight. She knew the sound well and dreamt of it often: someone was inside.

In a minute, there was a rattling sound that she recognized as the kitchen drawers.

He was opening them. Looking for a weapon.

The back door.

He'd come in that way and was fumbling for a knife. Had to be it. Across the way, the front door hung open, filling the decomposing building with natural light. Beyond it, a car door slammed.

Bats out of hell flew slower than her run for the exit, leaving shifting floorboards at her back.

"What the hell are you doing out here?"

She yelped and her teeth slammed into Chief Brady's shoulder.

The policeman grabbed her and gave a gentle shake. "Ms. Holden. Why are you here?"

Melanie couldn't organize her thoughts. They raced through her mind like fragmented images in a music video: Bill, bloodstains, creaking floorboards, Cyrus Hoyt, kitchen drawers, Morton, Woreley—

"What happened?"

"Someone's inside," she gasped. "Right now!" Her voice was piercing and she pointed toward the cabin.

Brady looked more annoyed than concerned as he unholstered his weapon and headed for the door. "Stay here," he said without looking back.

Melanie was groggy. Crawling back into bed and sleeping for the rest of the day felt like the only solution, provided her heart didn't explode in panic before she could get there.

Brady reappeared less than a minute later, gun by his side. He shook his head and motioned toward their cars. "It's clear," he said as they walked.

"Then he must've gone out the back door as soon as he heard you."

Brady kept walking forward, but his gait fanned outward so that he could see the other side of the cabin as they went. "If there was someone in there with you, my men are likely to pick him up."

"How's that?"

"Training exercise," he said. "They're in those woods." He lifted the two-way radio and ordered his guys to converge on the old campground. Gave specific instructions to watch for anyone who wasn't supposed to be here. "Now, can I trust you to get back in your car and get out of here? I know you need to see this place and I'll take you out myself once we're finished."

"Did I do something wrong?" she asked. "I didn't think I was breaking any laws."

The chief looked distracted. His eyes were everywhere but on her. "Of course not. Like I said, I'm running an exercise right now that requires my attention."

"More than chasing down a trespasser?"

She hadn't been trying to get his attention but she had it. He looked at her the way she looked at her students when they tried sneaking into class once it was half way over.

"You know how often we're chasing people off this eyesore?" he said. "Horny kids looking for a little alone time. Horny adults looking for a little thrill. Last month I caught a transient from New Haven living in that building there." He pointed to one of the far off bunks. "Running people off this property is as common as a morning cup of coffee."

"So that's it, then? I'm crazy and I shouldn't worry?"

"That someone was inside a cabin with you? No."

She debated telling him about the watery footprint in her room as a means of justifying herself, but didn't think it would work. This guy had his mind made up and in it she was nuts.

"And I never said you were crazy, ma'am."

She didn't know what to say so she just said, "terrific" and clapped her hands against her thighs.

"This place isn't safe is all I'm saying. By now, you've likely seen that for yourself. Been trying to have it condemned since I took this job, but it doesn't belong to Forest Grove. No one wants to give it much thought because of that. Until, of course, it's *their* kid who slices his hand open on broken glass. Then they'll be asking me why I didn't do anything about this demilitarized zone."

"I had to come see it again," Melanie said. "And someone walked right past that window while I was in there. I heard them fanning through the drawers."

"Yeah." The chief nodded. "And if it wasn't one of my men, we'll find whoever it was."

"You're a dedicated professional." It was more sarcasm than necessary, but the chief's dismissiveness was insulting.

"Thank you, ma'am. As I was saying…I'm happy to be your personal escort on another day. After the way we, uh, met yesterday, I wanted to give you a little bit of space…which is why I didn't drop by your place last night. Didn't want you to think I was harassing you on your vacation."

"This isn't a vacation."

"Right. Of course it's not. I'm just extending a hospitable olive branch, Miss Holden. Wouldn't take much to collapse these buildings, so I don't want you creeping around on your own."

"Creeping?"

"Figure of speech. There's nothing creepy about you." He gave her an awkward once-over that made her squirm. Once their eyes synced up, his widened like a kid caught cheating on his final.

"I did hear someone," she said. "And I don't think it was a cop."

"I'll check it out." Brady extended an arm in the direction of her car. "Now please…next time you want to come out here, I'll take you myself. Day or night. Your choice."

"But you're making me leave now?"

"Yes, well, this *is* private property. And, again…training exercise."

"Fair enough," Melanie said. She had seen enough of this place to last the rest of her life.

"Thank you for understanding. I'll swing by Desiree's a little later on to see if there's anything else I can help with."

The idea of spending more time with Chief Brady wasn't something to relish, but if he could help then it would be stupid to refuse him. The less time spent in the grove, the better.

The chief watched her go as she headed back to the car.

He was lying about the training exercise—that much was obvious. First Desiree, now Brady. Was the whole town bullshitting her?

Brady watched the Holden woman drive off for the second time in as many days. Then he took his Glock out and pulled open the dilapidated cabin door while radioing his men.

"Maylam, Johnson, Donnelley, Galeberg," he said into the handheld. "I thought I told you to get your asses to the campground. Double time it."

A few crackling affirmations barked back as he belted the radio and swept the rooms for a second time. No way of knowing what the Holden woman had heard while she was poking around, but it wasn't one of his men.

The jury was still out on her, anyway.

The cabin had been empty the first time he checked and there still wasn't so much as a hint that anyone else had been inside. Satisfied, Brady walked out into the morning air and glanced at his watch. Wasn't even ten yet and it had been one hell of a day. And it wasn't getting better anytime soon.

After last night's debacle with Trish, he'd gone for a drive. If she couldn't be pleased, he could at least be of service to the residents he served. Show them that their new chief was a real *Johnny on the Spot*.

Like clockwork, the town lapsed into nightly catatonia around 11. Businesses closed and the streets cleared, leaving only cricket chirps and interrogative owls to fill the evening air. He drove to the outskirts, checking for parking kids, stranded motorists, or sleeping truckers.

That's where he found the car.

An Audi. Completely abandoned. No sign of the driver. Traced it to one Vincent Robson of New Haven, Connecticut—70 miles southeast of here. It should've been an easy answer but, unfortunately for Forest Grove P.D., Robson's parents were deceased and he was an only child. As much as Brady didn't want to admit it, he had a missing college kid who withdrew two hundred dollars from the ATM at the store near his house yesterday afternoon. There were no signs of foul play around the vehicle, but it was strange enough to qualify as a suspicious circumstance.

So he called New Haven P.D. to report one, but they weren't so sure it qualified as an AT RISK case. All the same, he sent the information over to their office and hoped they might be able to connect him with any other people who might've gone missing over the same time frame.

He had yet to receive a response, though he hoped that meant they were conducting an investigation of their own: checking Robson's apartment, reviewing ATM footage, and safeguarding his computer for a possible future analysis.

Textbook things.

He was going to have to check back with that office to make sure they were pulling their weight. In all probability, the idiot came to take a peak at the infamous Camp Forest Grove and lost himself in the woods. That's why his guys had been canvasing out here all night—Brady was certain they'd find a half-drunken dipshit shivering on a bed of pines.

While his men played forest rangers, Brady had combed every square inch of the campground. Twice. There wasn't as much as a used condom wrapper or bit of fresh paraphernalia to confirm that Robson had been here.

He'd moved on to checking the woods when Melanie Holden pulled up. He should've been expecting her arrival and kicked himself for that oversight. A visit to this damn campground was the sole reason for her trip. He was batting a thousand when it came to her. It wasn't enough that he'd made her feel uncomfortable twice, but he was certain he'd insulted her today with that creeping comment.

"Sometimes there's no winning," he mumbled.

Sergeant Maylam pushed his way out of the forest and called for Brady.

"You find something, chief?" he asked.

"Not sure," Brady said. "Just had a visit from that Holden woman. She thinks someone was in there just before I pulled up. Let's hit this place again."

"Know what it could've been?" Johnson stepped heavy from the brush, rubbing brambles off his sleeve. "I ran into Henny Yurick while trawling our little piece of paradise. Old man had a handful of old and rusted cutlery."

Brady laughed. Henny Yurick's old three-room cabin sat right against the camp's property line and the old coot had been caught pillaging the buildings for everything that wasn't smashed beyond recognition. The guy found his way onto eBay about ten years back and started selling pieces of the camp as 'Cyrus Hoyt memorabilia.'

Former Chief Sleighton had spoken to him countless times, but it sounded like Yurick was trying his luck with the new management.

"You bring the knives back?"

Now it was Johnson's turn to laugh. "Sure didn't, chief. Told the old man to enjoy his one last plunder, 'cause we're going to start cataloging that shit."

"No way. This is private property. Yurick can have as much of this junk as he wants. Sleighton tells me the owners haven't been out here in ten years. Tired of looking at this god-awful place. Anyway, coordinate with Maylam, I want you all to give these cabins another look."

The officers stalked off and Brady went back to his car. Dispatch radioed over saying that Mayor Cobb wanted his ear at his earliest convenience. Playing politics was a downside of this gig—one he didn't think he was built for.

Trish was always telling him to "suck it up" and "play the game," but he couldn't. His plate was too full to worry about that nonsense. There was an abandoned car on the outskirts of town—a driver missing and potentially dead—at the same time that the grove's most notorious tourist was looking to get a handle on her life. These problems required his attention.

He was going to have to find a way to make this up to Melanie Holden before she slammed the grove in whatever damn book she was writing.

"I hate this job," he sighed and headed for his cruiser.

Melanie wasn't to the end of the road when the fuel light blinked.

"Shit," she mumbled. Yesterday's encounter with Brady

had left her so flustered that refilling the tank as soon as she reached town had slipped her mind.

Another reason to hate that jerk.

Then she remembered passing the ramshackle gas station on the way out here.

The wooden sign out front read LAST MILE GAS and it might've been in worse shape than the cabins at camp. The pumps were about to be swallowed by encroaching foliage and the garage might've been outdated twenty-five years ago.

But the prices were indicative of modern America—gouged beyond reason. An elderly man waddled out from the office as she rolled in. He rubbed his hands off on his grease-slicked one-piece jumpsuit and offered a haggard grin. His name was scrawled in cursive on a patch across his breast: JED.

"Lost or passing through?" Jed said.

"I need gas."

"Sure you do. But for my benefit, tell me straight…lost or passing through?"

"Uh, neither?"

"The hell else is there? You ain't from around here, that's plain to see. If you were, you wouldn't be here."

"Just visiting," Melanie said.

"Passing through, then."

"I suppose. Now can you fill it with regular?"

The old man shuffled to the rear of the car to pop the gas cap off.

Melanie decided she'd had enough of the third degree and wandered into the store for a bottle of water. Her nerves weren't yet balanced from the incident at camp and her tongue felt dry. A rusted kettle bell announced her arrival as she pulled open the door and the old man started shouting.

"Our shelves are as bare as a baby's balls," he said. "So I hope you weren't planning on doing yer grocery shopping." He thought this was hilarious, doubling over in a guffaw as the door swung shut.

A rolled up Hustler magazine lay coiled on the countertop, an indicator that business wasn't just slow, but terminal. The place stunk of mildew and neglect and only the two shelves nearest the counter were stocked with any groceries. A paltry collection of offerings: Twinkies, local potato chips, a few bags of jerky and Slim Jims, and two or three rolls of paper towels.

The rear cooler was as abandoned as the rest of the store—one row of bottled water and two rows of Coke products. Melanie grabbed a Dasani and headed for the counter as Jed made his way back inside.

"Don't take this the wrong way," he said and resumed his place behind the counter on a wobbly stool. He pushed a tobacco pipe into his mouth and chewed the tip. "I'm just lucky if I get two or three customers a week. And I've had them already. So I was surprised when you came pulling in. Figured you must've got off the highway and got all turned around out here. But that happens less and less these days on account of those goddamn cell phones everyone's so afraid to take out of their fists."

"No worries," she said, her eyes falling to the porno mag as he brushed it aside.

"Ain't trying to be uncouth," Jed said. "I sometimes forget my manners now that I'm on my own."

"It's fine," she pushed the water forward hoping it would be enough of a hint.

It wasn't. "I do know you, don't I? You're that Holden girl, right? All grown up? One of the town's finest was out here yesterday and he might've mentioned your visit."

"In the flesh." Melanie wasn't prepared to offer further explanation.

"Didn't make the connection until just now," Jed said, looking at her like he saw a piece of his past in her eyes. "Of course. Who else would you be?" He continued on without ringing her in. "Truckers are keeping me in business at this point. Bunch of them fill up here a few times a week. If you're wondering why I don't keep up on stock it's 'cause no one bothers patronizing us these days. Me and my wife…we've run this shop since 1963. Lost her to cancer back in '99 and I've been muddling through ever since. Most people go shopping these days, they do it downtown. Biggest assholes drive out to the CVS on the edge of Litchfield County. Don't see what's so convenient about that drive, but there you have it."

"Just the water, please." Melanie offered a faint smile while digging through her purse for a couple of dollar bills. Anything to avoid looking him in the eye. Anything to discourage more conversation.

"Oh, the water." Jed pressed a scanner to the barcode and pushed the bottle back. "You just came from the camp, am I right?"

Melanie wasn't sure her façade of manners could last.

"Your eyes are tellin' me I touched a nerve," Jed said. "So I'll leave it be. I only mention it as a courtesy because Camp Forest Grove isn't fit for you to go traipsing around. Not these days."

Melanie threw two bills across the counter. "I know that. If you know who I am, you know that I know that."

"Mind my business, right? Last thing a young woman wants is some old curmudgeon to start in with life lessons. I know that I'm a bag of wind. All the same, I hate seeing people messing with that place. After all these years, I don't trust it worth a damn."

"Makes two of us, Jed."

"More than two," Jed said, glancing around as if worried that another set of ears might overhear.

Melanie did her own uncertain slow pan over her shoulder,

but there was only an empty store. She returned her confused eyes to the front counter, to where the old man was suddenly leaned in close and whispering.

"Bad mojo in those woods," he said. "And it was there long before your friends got killed."

It was the first Melanie had heard of it. Her hostility cooled, recognizing the value in the old man's knowledge. She flashed a fake grin and put the water back on the counter. "What are you afraid of?"

"Watched cancer cut my wife down to the bone," Jed said, his old and tired eyes hardened like fresh poured concrete. "Nothing left to fear. But all the same, the grove used to be a nice place to live. You know that cliché about how your parents never had to lock their doors at night 'cause things were just *that* safe? I remember those days if I try hard enough. Good memories have a way of being bullied out of your brain by nastier ones. Guess we're sensitive things, ain't we?"

Melanie eyed Jed, trying to decide whether this was the real deal. The shoulders of his jumper were covered in dandruff and his chapped lips looked like they'd bleed the next time he parted them—a lonely old guy punished by his own limited devices. But the way he spoke—his words held authority on the subject the same as hers when she taught. It meant he knew what he was talking about.

She'd done her due diligence on Forest Grove and never heard a thing about prior tragedy. No. This was something else.

The Forest Grove murders were the subject of countless books and television specials over the years and Melanie had declined to participate in every one. Hell, some German filmmaker—Ulli something—had even taken the gist of Hoyt's killing spree and turned it into an incredibly tasteless direct-to-DVD slasher movie called *Maniac Murders of Forest Grove*.

Gross.

"Am I bothering you, with this stuff?" Jed said. "I really shouldn't be saying anything but when you get to be my age, you stop giving a shit about what others think. Trust me, it'll happen to you, too. I'm 87 and ain't got much use for tact anymore. Especially for a goddamn town that was content to let our business die on the vine."

"You're not bothering me at all," Melanie said. "I'm just surprised to hear this."

"Expect you are," Jed said. "Normally I wouldn't mention it, but I hate to see you stick around here any longer than you have to. You got out once and good for you. You need to do that again. This place's got blood on its hands and it's the kind they don't talk about."

"I'm listening."

"The grove tried hushing up some real ugly business back in '69. No one wanted to talk about what happened because they figured it'd go away and that would be that."

"That's enough." Someone stood at the back of the shop. Melanie leapt out of her skin, turning to see a younger man coming in from the garage, the connecting door swinging behind him. He looked to be her age, maybe five years older, with dark gray hair cropped against his skull. The scar on his chin rendered his features more severe, though his eyes found traces of kindness as he strode forward, like an actor settling into character. "You'll excuse my father," he said. "He tells a tale."

"Tale or not," Melanie said. "I'd very much like to hear the rest of it."

Jed's son never took his eyes off his father. "Nothing more to tell. Some people died on the lake, blame was thrown around back then as it continues to be today. They say some of our southernmost states are still fighting the Civil War. A similar sentiment applies to Forest Grove. It was a tragedy for our community and like all tragedies, it has left its mark upon our collective soul."

"Horseshit," Jed said as his son's words trampled the profanity. The old man lapsed into silence, as if trained.

"No charge for the gasoline, miss. Please allow me to walk you back to your car and I will explain."

"I think I'd really rather hear what Jed has to say." Melanie glanced at the old man but his attention had fallen away. He gazed down at the barren countertop.

"I'm afraid that is impossible." The son smiled and pushed the door open. Overhead, the kettle bell rang. "My father is an old man. He gets confused from time-to-time and when that happens, he needs his rest."

Jed fished the Hustler up off the floor as if Melanie had never been there.

"At least let me pay for the gas," Melanie said. "I know Jed doesn't get many customers so…"

"Another exaggeration." The son smiled again. "If you would please…"

"I'm coming," she said, her heart fluttering as she brushed past the stranger. He was at her side the second she was out the door, keeping pace with her hurried steps.

"I realize this is uncomfortable," he said. "You have my apology."

"I'd rather have your father's information."

"There is no deep secret here, miss. Just sympathy and respect for those who have lost loved ones."

"I lost loved ones." She looked across the street. "Out there. Years ago." Melanie hoped this type of solidarity would start him talking, but she knew he was going to be a tough nut to crack.

"And I would never infringe on your privacy. Please, let's not make things unpleasant for those who suffered prior."

"You're Jed's son?"

"Sam," he said and offered his hand.

"Your father didn't mention you."

They reached her car and Sam pulled the driver's door open. Once Melanie was inside, he slammed it and smiled. "My father is a broken man. Alzheimer's. He has good days and bad, but we keep this place open as a courtesy to him. Nothing more. Believe it or not, it has helped give his golden years some purpose and structure."

"And you help out?"

"I play the good son when I have to. Now you'd best be on your way, miss. I do not recommend sticking around here—not for one more night."

Jed was barely visible in the window as she rolled past, his head angled down at the counter—attuned to the skin rag, most likely.

Melanie was eager to get back to her room. The errant footprint at Desiree's was bad, but it was no match for the barrage of hostility and creepiness that the grove was offering today.

In the rearview, Sam stood in her dust, calmly waving goodbye with tight lips and cold eyes.

Jed doesn't have Alzheimer's.

He'd been far too sharp and responsive for that. This encounter left her feeling all kinds of wrong, but there was nothing to be done.

This was the second place she'd been chased out of in as many stops today.

Going home was beginning to feel like the best option.

Sam went back inside to find Jed missing.

Shit.

He couldn't have gotten far, though. Not at his age.

He gave the store a once-over and went to the window, looking at the old man's house in the backyard. He was nowhere to be seen.

"Let's go, Jed," he called and opened the connecting door, stepping into the garage. Oil and grease smells were pungent and the bathroom door was ajar. But the light was off, meaning it was unoccupied.

This was going to be a problem. Sam was to make sure the bitter old bastard didn't sound off like that to random passersby. They weren't going to be happy no matter how he tried spinning this, because the bottom line was that the blonde had walked out of here with knowledge she'd didn't have before. True, Jed hadn't said anything definitive, but this would register as his failure.

And that scared the shit out of Sam.

"Come on, Jed, you know I have to tell them." The garage's two bays were empty, save for Sam's pickup. The hydraulic lift in bay two was fully extended into the air, as it had been for decades. It felt like a waste to repair it, because Last Mile Gas wasn't long for this world. It would die the second Jed did.

Sam was on his way outside to continue his search when the shuffling and scraping sound of metal on metal stopped him dead.

Someone else was in the room.

"Come on, Jed. Let's shut 'er down for the day and head to Lloyd's." He followed the sound around his vehicle and a ring of chains dropped down in front of his face. Something heavy struck Sam's head and knocked him back—a harsh spike of pain ignited behind his eyes.

It was the old man dangling from a chain noose, eyes popped wide. Jed's body suddenly swayed in the stagnating garage, bodily secretions mixed with oily air.

Sam screamed, but an electric whir drowned his startled cries. Something that sounded like a dentist's drill erupted from inside the unlit bathroom. The darkness there shifted and moved until a shadow came to life and stepped free.

Sam tried to run, but a hand fell on his shoulder and spun him back the other way. The electric ratchet's LED light flicked on in the shadow's hand and Sam squinted, seeing only a drill bit attachment whirling forward and tearing through his protesting tongue.

With a grunt, the ratchet reached deeper into his mouth, shattering his front teeth like glass before it ripped through the fleshy roof and tore into his skull.

Hoyt squinted through the sprays of blood as the machine buzzed.

This—*thing*—did so much damage. It cracked the bones behind his victim's face so that his features collapsed inward, ejecting a reservoir of blood through broken orifices. The crumpled head reminded him of a popped balloon—stretched and limp.

He let the body drop beside the hanging man, studying his work with deep, satisfied breaths.

Melanie had been here, but he wasn't convinced that he was ready for the prize. Instead, he allowed her to leave in order to focus on the men. This was an isolated place and the wealth of weaponry here encouraged creativity.

Killing them had been easy, and now that it was over, he knew it was time to resume the hunt. The bodies couldn't stay, though. Someone might eventually come looking for them. Might find out what happened.

That was always the way. That was how the trouble always

started.

He stacked the bodies by the back door and planned to take them into the woods at nightfall. Then he cleaned the mess as best he could, passing the muddy garage windows in time to catch sight of a police car rolling in from the direction of camp. It sat idling in front of the gas pumps while Hoyt fished a single key out of Jed's jumper and moved into the store, crouch-walking up the far aisle with his eye fixed permanently on the vehicle.

He had to reach the front door in time.

Hoyt took slow steps across the main aisle, hoping it would make him more difficult to detect. It wasn't until he reached the door and slipped the key inside the lock that he heard a car door slam.

It was a race against time now, because the policeman would be here in a second. If the door was open he would come inside and that would be how this ended. Not at first, because what was one more man after he'd killed two? But dead police meant more would follow and the game jumped ahead too far then.

The lock was stubborn and he jiggled the key as much as he dared, keeping the noise to a minimum. There was a click as it slid into place, but he was sure it had been too loud to go unnoticed. Hoyt had just one second to hide against the space between the door and the large window front as the policeman's shadow fell large across the floor.

The knob jiggled a few times and was followed by a knock. Hoyt didn't dare breathe for as long as the cop was there, just a few wood frames and glass panes were all that separated them. When the man finally turned and headed away, Hoyt watched him go and felt the tightness in his throat withdraw. He hoped the officer wouldn't decide now to snoop around.

The man he somehow recognized as Chief Brady started his car and drove slowly past, eyes scanning the desolate aisles before finally accelerating and driving off.

Hoyt considered this an exciting success. He headed back to the garage feeling ready while thinking that sunset couldn't come fast enough.

 **Repent & Submit**

1967

Zohra sat looking out at the lake, her arms crossed over her knees and tucked against her chest. The breeze was cool, bristling her tunic and hair every which way. Her bones were glazed in a brisk chill because of the cold spring air, but inside she burned with a kind of love she never imagined possible.

She had everything she needed. Right here.

Everyone in the commune shared this sentiment. The Elder spoke often of shedding material possessions as a way of unshackling from society. Before one could join their fellowship, they were expected to understand this. Then, after a few months, they needed to practice it.

It wasn't just life's accumulations that were tossed, but former identities went into the garbage along with them. She hadn't always been Zohra, but now it was the only name she knew. The only life she remembered. There remained vague recollections of earlier days—youthful binges of drugs and sex— haunted her like waking nightmares. The Elder stressed that past mistakes were ghosts and could not hurt them anymore, and that felt true on most days.

"This is not just an opportunity to better ourselves," the Elder had said. "But to better the world. We are the ones God has enlightened. Now we go forth and offer examples of the love given to us. Repent and submit!"

That was the hook that had grabbed her at the end of her last life. She was bottomed out then, bathing in a puddle of her own drug-laced vomit. No one else was offering a prosperous path forward, so she rushed headlong into God's arms. At first, it seemed like an easy way to get back on her feet, because unconditional love and acceptance were powerful motivators.

Soon she agreed that the mission *was* Christ. The Elder imbued in them an urgency to spread that love and that's what she did.

"You must," he'd said. "Before it is too late."

Jessica sat beside her on the waterfront. Her blonde strands tussled in the winds coming off the lake. She was just as grateful to be here. And while they never spoke of yesterday's lives, Zohra recognized the torment lines etched into her face like wood carvings. Signs of a tough walk on a long road. Signs of the needle.

The Elder had been patient with Jessica. She'd needed more time than most. The girl struggled with the notion of abandoning her former life, mostly because her mom was cancer-stricken and without much time remaining. Jessica wanted to send a letter home during those final days, thinking her mother should not spend her 11th hour worrying about her missing daughter. The Elder forbade it and stressed that her previous life was gone.

"The battle for her flesh is lost," he'd said. "But the war for her soul has yet to be waged."

Zohra sympathized because she remembered a similar transition, and that understanding came to anchor their friendship. Every so often, her eyes would catch Jessica's and they'd nod—an unspoken acknowledgment of that long walk through life. The one that brought them both here.

"It makes me worry," Jessica said as she looked out across the rippling water. "They look at us like we're monsters. Why do they not believe the hour draws near? That we only want to save them?"

Zohra smiled. It could never be that easy. God gave man free will. And with it, man made many poor choices. He had to embrace the Lord because he wanted to, not because he was told it was necessary. Man's hubris often prevented him from acknowledging the wrong choices.

And Forest Grove was swimming in hubris.

The Elder liked to send Zohra and Jessica into town together. Pretty, young, and personable harbingers were harder to curse out and berate. Still, in her earliest days, Zohra had shared Jessica's frustrations, speaking often to the Elder about the townspeople and their hesitation.

"We are not some silly cult," she'd said, offended by the frequent suggestion.

"We provide the only achievable path to salvation," the Elder responded. "Surely you understand how this might upset some. They do not hate us so much as they hate themselves for their inability to embrace the proper path. The important thing, dear Zohra, is never to hate them back. Understand them instead. Only then can you hope to change their minds."

Zohra understood this and spent her days breaching the topic of faith with any who would listen. The Elder asked only one thing of her, of them—go forth and convert. Make them repent and submit.

That meant long walks into town, searching for open ears. The first couple of treks were the easiest. Forest Grove had never been especially receptive, but its hostility increased with time. *"Oh, that's really interesting, but no thank you,"* gradually became, *"Didn't I tell you fucking lunatics to stay off my doorstep?"*

Words could not hurt, but sometimes they stung.

Occasionally, there were urges: a flutter in the loins when the cute (and strangely single) patrolman glanced her way, or the need to belt the most condescending heretics across their mouths. She hated these penchants and would never admit to having them. The Elder would almost certainly deem her unworthy if he found out, and life here was too beautiful to sacrifice it to temperament.

There was nowhere to go anyway. Acceptance here meant friends and family were nothing more than affixes to a miserable old way—anchors that threatened to keep you afloat in a sea of misery.

It had been strange at first, leaving behind everyone she had ever known, but the Elder had anticipated this trepidation and supplemented his dogma with God's word. She knew these verses by heart, because adjusting to this life had been something of a challenge. Whenever she lapsed into doubt, she had only to look to the Good Book to alleviate her concerns.

Matthew 10:34-37: Think not that I am come to send peace on earth: I came not to send peace, but a sword. For I am come to set a man at variance against his father, and the daughter against her mother, and the daughter in law against her mother in law. And a man's foes shall be they of his own household. He that loveth father or mother more than me is not worthy of me: and he that loveth son or daughter more than me is not worthy of me.

Luke 14:26: If any man come to me, and hate not his father, and mother, and wife, and children, and brethren, and sisters, yea, and his own life also, he cannot be my disciple.

These words reinforced their ideals and purged the unease. This *was* right.

"What I would not give for one hour more on this beach,"

Jessica yawned. "To forego tonight's duties just this once."

They were fresh from Forest Grove where they had sermonized any who would hear. Their audience was just a few nomadic truckers in the early morning hours—overly caffeinated men who craved a temporary distraction from the road. They were more interested in having the attention of a few pretty girls—didn't matter if it was an extolment of virtues or a recipe for quiche Lorraine.

After them, there remained only uncomfortable glances as they walked the sunny streets searching out the open minded. They were sitting on a picnic table outside of Pittman Pharmacy, watching local children scurry inside for ten-cent soda floats when that young (and single) police officer approached. He shifted from one foot to the other as he explained that loitering anywhere in town was prohibited. And if they didn't have business here, they needed to go elsewhere. His eyes remained kind, even as he enforced the law.

"Folks are scared of you all," he'd said and looked down at their bare feet.

"Why should they be?" Zohra said. "We have given them no reason to fear us."

"You ladies don't look like you'd harm a gnat." He didn't take his attention off Zohra once. "And you're much too pretty to be footing it all over creation. But the law's the law, so I gotta insist."

The girls exchanged stunned glances and agreed to leave. To linger would only hurt their cause and credibility, and there was no reason to provoke additional feelings of fear and mistrust. The kind-eyed policeman had offered a ride back to the lake, but the Elder would not have wanted that.

"You're going to walk back like *that*?" He sounded offended. "Your feet will be mush by the time you get home."

Zohra thanked the man for his concern, but refused his

offer. The Elder wanted them to live as the apostles had. That meant enduring the hardships of the day. Some of the men in the compound wore sandals, but there were not enough to go around and chivalry was a foreign concept. This bothered her in her quietest moments, but who was she to question it?

Her feet did ache as they took the long way back, circling through some of the outskirt neighborhoods on the off chance that someone, anyone, might hear them out. How could everyone remain ignorant of impending oblivion?

Jessica looked tired now as she stretched out in the sand, arching her back and kicking her legs into the air. In the sunlight, the outline of her nude body was visible beneath the transparent gown. Zohra might've been aroused by this in an earlier life, but now looked only with an admiration for God's creation.

"I am so happy to see that you have returned to us, my sisters." The Elder approached, arms outstretched and a joyous smile spread across bearded lips. There was genuine warmth and delight there. "How did your journey find you?"

"No one wanted to hear us," Jessica said, her words loaded with shame. "They will never receive us."

The Elder took a seat in the sand between them and propped his palms upward. The girls clasped their hands into his and he squeezed. "While it is not our place to judge, I cannot ignore what you and the others have told me. Forest Grove is not ready for the truth. And so we shall wait."

"For how long?" Zohra said. "The end is coming. Are we to burn in hellfire because *they* will not listen?"

"We already are saved," he said. "Our mission is to help as many as we can between now and the end."

"Then why can't we save our families?" Jessica asked. "I miss my mom. If she's still alive…"

The Elder squeezed their hands again, harder this time. "They are no longer your mothers and fathers. If the day ever comes when someone from your former life is to be recruited, a brother or sister shall do it. Not you, for how could I expect them to hear our message when it's delivered from the mouth of a phantom? A vestige of their former life?"

"Yes," the girls spoke in quick unison. "Thank you, Elder."

"Amen," he smiled, stood, and strode off.

After some time passed, Zohra sprung to her feet and helped Jessica to hers. They started for the small cabin at the edge of the forest. Sister Mary was inside seasoning a gigantic cauldron of steaming water. She had them grab a batch of onions, peppers, and carrots from the storage pantry. They chopped the vegetables, dropping handfuls into now-boiling broth. Mary continued seasoning the soup and reduced the heat. When it was ready, Zohra went outside and struck the dinner bell.

The men came shuffling out of the prayer bunk with the Elder and the four children bringing up the rear. They approached Mary with wooden dinner bowls in hand. She ladled the soup to the brim and placed a torn piece of freshly baked bread into their free hands. Once the men were served, the women were allowed to take a bowl for themselves. They sat in the grass beside the picnic tables that housed the men and children.

Dinnertime conversation was the most spontaneous part of the day. There were no sermons, only bonding. Supper was a time to reflect, and the Elder had a brother retreat into the bunkhouse to retrieve four flagons of wine.

Once everyone was well supped, the Elder cleared his throat and rose from his seat. Casual conversations faded into silence as he looked at the faces of every brother and sister to ensure attention.

"Forest Grove does not want the Obviate," he said. "That is okay. People won't adapt when they are content, which explains why that little hamlet would like nothing more than to be left alone. We will abide. We were itinerants by design when I started this brotherhood. Just as Christ's apostles journeyed forth with his word, so do we. We must continue to grow our ranks but we shall do this away from here. Tomorrow, I will take what money remains and obtain a vehicle. Just like today, you will continue to be paired in twos, only Joseph will drive you to various corners of nearby states where you will do your best to search out the willing. You will find them on college campuses, in veteran hospitals, and homeless shelters. They will listen. They will understand."

The table erupted into enthusiastic growls and even the women looked at one another with excitement.

"There is more," the Elder continued. "It is true that the apostles did not have any use for churches and neither does the Obviate. We will continue to teach in small groups wherever people will listen. But we shall have our own place of worship right here. For you, and for the willing ones you bring back. Whoever does not go forth on the first journey will instead help us expand our assembly here. We will make this into a hub for worship, where our brothers and sisters may come and go as they please while always knowing they have a home."

When dinner was over, Zohra and Jessica helped the other women clean up, scrubbing bowls and spoons until the lake glowed orange in the final moments of sunset. They went out and watched nature's show with several others.

"Do you ever feel like you're trapped?" Jessica said in a whisper.

Zohra hadn't entertained such a thought since the beginning. She shook her head without answering.

"What about your son?" Jessica continued. "He cannot be happy here. You don't even get to see him. He's conditioned by our brothers without any input from his mother."

"He has no mother," Zohra said. "And if it weren't for the Elder, he might not have a life. He's safe here. That's more than I deserve."

"Is this all there is?" Jessica pressed the issue. "Sermons? Cooking? Sewing? Praying?"

"Our lot in a greater purpose," Zohra reminded her.

"Right," Jessica said with more than a little defeat. "Repent and submit."

"Repent and submit," Zohra agreed.

 **Five**

Melanie worked through the afternoon and into the evening. The creative high was such that she buzzed down to the front desk and told Desiree not to bother her for dinner. This wasn't a time to be disturbed.

The old woman had insisted upon fixing her a plate and said it would be in the refrigerator whenever she wanted it.

It was closing in on ten and the only light in the suite was from her laptop's glow. Melanie sat entranced, rapping on the keyboard while her thoughts stretched like elastic. This morning's conversation with Jed and his creepy son was a motivator and her document was 30k words deep as a result. It was loaded with recollections, ruminations, and reservations. At the top of the page sat two bolded questions:

1. Who was Cyrus Hoyt?

The question had been asked numerous times. Why, then, didn't anyone know the answer? Melanie knew. Sort of. Hoyt was a backwoods lunatic who snapped one day, hunting and murdering people like animals. A better question might've been why, but there weren't many people who could answer that one.

2. What happened in 1969?

Two hours of Googling the darkest corners of the Internet refused to yield anything that she didn't already know. If Sam had been telling the truth and a few people died on Lake Forest

Grove, Brady might be able to help find some names. But why hadn't she been allowed to hear the rest of Jed's story? What were they hiding?

Her suspicious fires were doused as fast as they could be stoked: Sam was probably trying to spare someone from unnecessary grief. Melanie was a writer after all, and the whole town seemed to know it. So Sam didn't want some long past incident to end up a chapter in a book. That was understandable, even if it piqued her curiosity even more. Conspiracy theories didn't hold much weight in her mind because people were too insecure to keep things hush-hush.

And still, there's something here I'm not supposed to know.

Melanie's fingers paused mid-sentence as the stairwell creaked. She tensed up, realizing the room was bathed in black. Another creak as her hand crawled across the bed to search out the phone. It was on the end table, charging.

Outside the room, another step shifted beneath someone's weight.

Melanie fumbled in the dark, arms flailing for the light switch. Her hand coiled around the lamp's neck and pushed on the button.

In the hall, footsteps reached the third floor landing.

She pulled a silken robe over her eveningwear and cinched it around her waist to feel less vulnerable. There had to be something she could use to defend herself.

The hall went silent.

So did she, watching the door from across the room while her eyes drowned in their refusal to blink. She brushed at them with the back of her hand while praying the doorknob wouldn't move. Someone stood right outside and Melanie was certain she heard deep, agitated breathing. Maybe Desiree was spying on her before hitting the sack and didn't want to be obvious about it. That might've been the case, but Melanie wasn't about to call out—because what if it was someone else?

Her gaze was locked but her hands roamed the night table, feeling for the phone. If Brady wanted to be anything more than a hindrance, he needed to get out here right now.

Her car alarm screamed out—a crash of noise that jolted her. She forgot about the doorway for a moment, rushing toward the open window and staring down into the night. The darkness beyond her line of sight was thick and showed nothing.

Only silence hung in the hallway beyond the door.

Wobbly fingers mis-tapped the phone, prompting the launch of several useless apps. She might've screamed in frustration if she wasn't so terrified.

Outside, the car alarm continued to assault the evening's peace, echoing through the forest like a pinball.

At last, she keyed in a search for Forest Grove P.D. and clicked CALL. The female voice on the other line was unsympathetic but her presence remained comforting. She assured Melanie that a car would be by in a few minutes, even offering to stay on the line until they arrived.

It felt like a long time to wait.

Melanie sighed and fished her keys out of the Guess bag beside the bed. They jangled in the palm of her hand as she aimed the alarm device outside, deactivating the cries with a double beep.

Then she was alone in the room. Her posture was frozen, as if moving might tip the lurker to her presence.

Someone knocked at the door.

She pushed a hand to her mouth, expressing disbelief. The door wasn't that sturdy by any means and if it was *him*, then he had probably already killed Desiree, leaving her alone in here.

Trapped.

The knocks intensified, morphing from casual inquiries to aggressive hammers. It wasn't someone asking to come in. It was someone looking to freak her out. And it was working.

Her trusty baseball bat was a few hundred miles away at home and it didn't look as if Desiree stocked a suitable replacement. If anyone broke inside in the next few minutes, she was going to have to use her hands to fend them off.

The knocks grew and the door bounced up and down in the frame. Behind it, an aggravated growl that was more animal than human. It wasn't even someone knocking anymore, arms and legs slapped the wood in complete tantrum.

Careful steps took her into the bathroom. Her legs shook and her mouth fluttered as cold title stung her feet. Two-inches of wood separated her from a maniac. She scanned the room for a weapon while imagining the hulking monster out there.

An onset of panic was coming. Her breath tightened beneath her ribs and unfulfilling bursts of air filtered into her lungs. Pins and needles stabbed her fingers as she realized there was no way to fight him off. She wondered if Desiree really was dead and felt sick because that meant it was her fault. Things had been quiet here for years.

Did I somehow will this bastard back into existence?

The battering stopped and the room went mute.

The dispatcher asked if Melanie was still there and she responded by asking the police to hurry.

Then her car alarm went off again.

She tore across the room and aimed her keychain like a craven gunfighter. The alarm beeped another acknowledgement before ending.

"Get ahold of yourself," she whispered in between breaths.

There was a knock at the door. This one accompanied by a familiar voice. "Melanie, are you okay in there?"

Melanie's cheeks were flushed and completely soaked. She didn't bother to wipe the tears away, and instead, stared with confusion. Her first instinct was to scream for Desiree to get away. To warn her about Hoyt. But the woman was in her eighties and wouldn't be able to outrun a brick.

The frail knocks continued. Melanie crossed the suite and cracked the door. When everything looked clear, she opened it wide and peered into the hall. It was just the two of them, and Desiree looked absolutely miserable. Over her shoulder, the landing window was open, leaving curtains fluttering in the air.

"I thought it was raining hammers and nails up here, hon. And what's going on with your car?"

"You weren't knocking a minute ago, Desiree?"

The old woman patted herself across the chest of her formless nightgown. "You mean the racket? I couldn't make that if I tried."

"Someone was beating the hell out of this door." Melanie remembered the watery footprint. "It wasn't you?"

"I was working up the muster to get out of bed on account of it," the old woman said.

"It was just before that. Someone climbed up these steps and…"

"And what?"

"Well, nothing, I guess. My alarm went off. Twice."

"Animals? Wouldn't be the first time I've heard it happen."

Melanie shook her head. There were way too many coincidences of late. "I called the police so I guess we're waiting for them. Do you want a cup of coffee? No way I'm getting to sleep tonight."

"Let's have some." Desiree smiled and shuffled inside. Melanie felt her nerves steady in her presence. Any kind of company felt good, and maybe it was time to let her off the hook for the footprint.

She hated to consider what that meant.

Melanie closed the door and wedged the back of a chair beneath the knob. Her cell phone buzzed to life in the palm of her hand. She turned it over and saw a text from an unrecognized number. With a swipe of her finger, the phone unlocked in order to see the whole thing. The words broke over her as she read them again and again.

YOU DIED WITH YOUR FREINDS.

Brady got home just before ten and was loosening his uniform as he walked across the driveway. All he wanted was some sleep. He hadn't had any in over twenty-four hours and tomorrow was going to be another stressful one.

As would be every day until this missing person case was solved.

There wasn't anyone in his command that he trusted with staying on top of the abandoned Audi. He was taking point because the mayor hated the idea that a New Haven college boy might've died in his backyard. The unofficial line was that Brady should try to make it seem like it happened outside town limits—provided anything had happened at all.

Brady had been around long enough to know that a missing car wasn't good news, and New Haven P.D. was doing its due diligence in working with Forest Grove. There was nothing to report yet, but he had to check back in the morning, which was great since he owed the mayor a status report first thing.

If I wanted to be micromanaged, I would've taken a corporate job.

For now, all he wanted was sleep.

"I'm home," he called out and removed his police shirt, draping it over the kitchen chair. He unbuckled his kit belt, sprawled it across the table, and then stripped down to his boxers. He was careful not to crease the slacks as he hung them over the shirt.

Trish didn't respond. She was rarely asleep this early so she must've been in the basement unpacking.

A good sign. Maybe she's finally settling in.

He pulled the cellar door open and listened. The furnace's hum was the only sound to greet him.

He went to the kitchen and pulled the one remaining beer from the top shelf of the fridge. He twisted the cap and waited for the inevitable nag. Even on nights when Trish wanted nothing to do with him, she rarely missed an opportunity to get in a really good barb. That was one of the things he loved most about her—fighting spirit was incredibly sexy to him, even if it meant being a receptacle for her frustration.

Brady took a few more sips once the coast was clear and made his way upstairs.

Trish was in front of the bathroom's vanity mirror, dressed in a tiny t-shirt that ended well above her midriff. A small pair of purple striped panties covered her lower half. She stared at herself—through herself—with pained eyes and rubbed her stomach with an open palm.

"What are you doing?" Brady asked and slipped a hand across the small of her back. Her milky flesh was soft, smooth, and pleasing to touch. He loved the feel of his wife and lamented how much he missed her. To his surprise, she didn't resist his tiny massage, so he pushed against her cheek with a long and hard kiss.

Maybe tonight won't be so awful, he thought.

"Flossing, genius," she pulled a dental sick from her mouth and shook her head. She pecked him back and her eyes fell to the bottle in his fist. "And beer? I thought we were going to make ourselves sexy again. By cutting out carbs. ALL carbs."

"After the kind of day I had, this won't hurt me."

"Right." She rolled her eyes. "Don't pull your usual, *Jeez, I don't know what happened* once the beer gut comes back."

A stupid concern—Brady was on his feet for at least half

the workday and usually more. When he wasn't bolstering the flow of bureaucracy by shuffling papers, he stayed active. He took walks on the downtown strip to increase his presence and responded to all emails through an iPad while on his feet. A beer or two wasn't going to resurrect the beer gut that had poked out over his belt while he was between jobs.

Trish was determined to slim down, although she always looked perfect. Her hips were curvy and her stomach was trim. Her tiny breasts were a nice shape and always perky. He never missed an opportunity to remind her of her beauty, but his words seemed to ring hollow in her mind. Her response was usually a wrinkled brow, and an uncomfortable *yeah, sure* gesture.

Maddening, since confidence had always been her strongest suit.

Brady patted his own stomach beneath his tee. "No gut here, I think you'll agree. And I missed you," he said. "Tried getting out at a decent hour today but that damn car…"

"Still nothing?"

"We know who it belonged to. No trace of him."

"Maybe you should go and see dad," she said. "Pick his brain."

Brady shook her suggestion away and he went into the bedroom. He dropped onto the bed and fished around for the TV remote while Trish came in and flicked the lights off. Her back to him, she pulled off her top and cast it aside. Her skin glowed gentle blue in the television's light, revealing just a hint of breast as she turned.

Brady thought of one way to cap this evening and set the beer aside. He got to his knees and crossed to her side of the bed, pulling her close.

"Nate, no." Trish wriggled free and crossed her arms over her breasts as though he were a stranger.

"You've got to be kidding, Trish."

"I do? Why's that, oh darling husband—because I might not be in the mood?"

"Tonight? Try the last two months."

"Awww, you backed up?"

Trish crossed the room to her bureau mirror and brushed her cropped black hair. "It hasn't been that long," she said at last.

It had. He'd been counting. Their sex life, raucous and healthy while in NYC, had taken a beating following their relocation. Trish used to wake him up in the middle of the night sometimes—half asleep, but horny as hell. She'd growl, shout expletives, and demand to be satisfied. Brady had zero qualms with that kind of assertiveness, especially because she never stopped until he was equally fulfilled. A confident partner was the only kind worth having and it felt like a lifetime since he'd had one.

"Just ask yourself if you can remember the last time we did it, and let me know what you come up with." Brady didn't want to argue. He was too tired for it and would rather spend the night making love to the only woman he ever loved. He crawled back to his side of the bed and climbed beneath a thin sheet.

"Could you make me feel any fucking worse, Nate? I mean, honestly."

"How am I doing that? By trying to have you? What a terrible husband I've become, huh?"

"You said it."

"Jesus Christ, you've been an insufferable bitch—"

"There it is." She snapped her fingers. "How long have you been waiting to say that? Last night you mocked me, and now you decide to tell me what a terrible person I've become. All because I'm unhappy about living here again."

"I never said you were a bad person. Christ, I married you. I *love* you. But lately—"

"Alright, since you're convinced I'm a bitch let me tell you about my idea. I figured out something to do around here…short term."

Brady paused. This sounded promising.

"I'm going to get Forest Grove to lift its ban on high school dances. I want to help those kids who found me in the woods throw a party."

He didn't know what to make of this. How was Trish this selfish? If he positioned that question to her, he was going to be the selfish one. No winning here. Not in the kind of mood he was in—tired, horny, and now, irritable.

"I can tell you're not happy, Nate. Why?"

"Are you forgetting my part in this little drama? As the new chief of police, I'm trying to keep the balance between your father's old regime and my new one. How is it going to look when my wife starts trying to strike down a twenty-five year old law?"

"I don't give a shit how it looks, Nate. This town wants to hide behind this law and complain about my music while making the lives of those kids miserable…the whole thing sucks. And if I have to live here, I'm not going to sit around and let it continue. It impacts me, and it's going to impact our kids…if we ever decide to have them."

This was the first time since moving here that Trish had acknowledged a desire to start a family, and Brady wasn't going to press that issue any further. It could've been a calculated move to bring him over to her team, and it might've worked.

He motioned for her to get into bed. Her steps were reluctant but she came at last, slipping beneath the covers.

"For the first time in my adult life, I feel like I can do something good."

"And this is for the good of the town?"

"Hell no. This is for me. It's revenge. That the kids in this town are going to benefit is just a welcome side effect."

"If you're serious about this…"

"I am."

Brady remembered how supportive Trish had been in NYC on the day he came home from the hearing—once he was no longer with the NYPD. They drove thirty-three blocks in silence, and as soon as they got home, she threw herself at him. Kisses up and down his face while whispering assurances in his ear: *"Everything will be fine. We'll be fine…"*

"Okay," he said. She deserved the same encouragement, if not more. "What do you have to do?"

"Collect signatures. I start tomorrow. Get enough of them so I can drop it on Cobb's desk and ask that the city council vote be overturned."

"Then I support you."

She rose up and kissed his forehead, but retreated back to her side of the bed before anything else could happen.

"One more thing, Trish."

Her eyes flickered in the TV light.

"What happened the other day, out in the woods?"

"I have no idea. I guess I blacked out?"

"I know your father already asked, but I gotta do the same. You're not…using again, are you?"

Trish took a few breaths, each of them more frustrated than the last. "Because you're my husband I know that you have to ask that. So I'm not going to freak out. Instead, I'm going to tell you what I told him. I haven't done a bump since 2007."

"Never seen you black out, though. I'm just worried that—"

"That it'll happen again? I don't know what to tell you, Nate. Maybe I was hungry, or dehydrated."

"Doctor said it wasn't dehydration. He had no idea what the hell was wrong with you."

She shook her head. "MRI found nothing."

"You know that if you slipped off the wagon…" he reached for her, but Trish recoiled. Any further and she'd fall off the bed.

"Nate, you don't get to treat me like a child. I made mistakes when I was younger and I've been paying for them ever since. I'm clean. I know you're trying to be the supportive husband now. It's just that, this damn town…"

"I get it."

"You don't. Life is hard when you're struggling to find your place."

"Your place is here," he said. "With your husband."

"I'm not a fucking housewife. And I'm more than your woman. Maybe I'm floundering around trying to find my own thing, and I'm pissed that I can't even listen to loud music in my own home. I'm stressed that this is going to be my teenage years all over again."

"Stress? We've all got it. Only mine's worse now because I can't spend a night in bed with my gorgeous wife without her acting like I'm a creep when I try and touch her."

"Creep? I'm not in the mood. Sorry our disagreements don't get me all hot and bothered."

He rolled over and took a long pull on his beer. No sense in talking about this now. Tension was palpable and he guessed she felt it as well. They could've been fucking it away, but she apparently wanted to prolong the misery.

They laid in silence until his phone buzzed. There was a problem with the Holden woman.

He was almost relieved he didn't have to spend another second here.

"Can I be frank with you, Chief Brady?" Melanie felt scared. But more than that, she was pissed off about feeling scared.

The police chief had taken her up to her room, away from everyone else so that they could talk.

Desiree insisted upon brewing more fresh coffee and handed the chief two mugs on their way up. He placed them carefully on the table and closed the door so that it was just the two of them.

"Please," he said. "Be as frank as you want."

"I know how this sounds," she said, "but I think it's pretty clear that someone out there wants me to leave town. You can think I'm crazy all you want, but I never saw Cyrus Hoyt die."

"If Hoyt were alive, he wouldn't know how to send you a text." Brady reached out and tapped the screen of her phone.

"I was scared to death about coming here," Melanie said. "When you pulled me over the other day, you probably noticed my jitters. This morning at the camp, someone was in the cabin with me. Now there's pounding at my door, my car alarm goes off, and then that." She batted the phone across the table. "Someone doesn't like me being here. And who am I to tempt fate?"

"Let me do my job," Brady said. "For starters, that little incident in the woods today...case closed. It was a local guy named Henny Yurick. He steals rusted cutlery from the camp to sell on the Internet. Sadly. Now that text you got tonight, I have a feeling I'm going to find out it was sent from a disposable phone, but this department is going to find whoever's bothering you, ma'am."

Because you've done well, so far, she thought. "Thanks."

"I get your apprehension," he said. "But you're safe here."

Melanie stifled a laugh over the absurdity of that comment. "I am? No offense, Chief Brady, but just because you say something doesn't make it so."

Brady lifted the coffee mug and sniffed the rim before

taking a sip. "When I was younger, my family and I took off to Disney World for a week. My dad had been saving up for the trip for an eternity. My brother and I, well, we were a little too old to feel the magic of the place, but we didn't have the heart to say we weren't interested.

"Pop had a rough go of things and couldn't give us as much as he'd wanted to when we were kids, and it wasn't until we were in junior high that the Bradys could afford the trip. So my brother and me figured *what the hell.* Riding the rollercoasters, hoping for glimpses of wet t-shirts in the aftermath of Splash Mountain. Teenagers, ya know?"

Melanie offered a polite smile but her mind was miles away. That text message had chilled her and she couldn't stop thinking about who would send something like that. Or why.

The chief continued unabated. "Turned out to be a great trip. We had fun and dad seemed so…proud. Looking back, I see what a triumph it was for the guy. But the victory was short-lived because we got home only to find it broken into. We had a walkout basement and someone had slashed the screen door open and jimmied the lock. Nabbed all my mom's jewelry, my lifelong collection of baseball cards, and whatever electronics could be smuggled out. My Sega Genesis for one. That burned the most because I hadn't yet beaten *Sonic the Hedgehog 3.*"

The chief must've noticed her marked impatience because he stuttered to get his words out quicker. "I'm long-winded, right? My point is the terrible feeling you have when something like this happens. We felt violated. Vulnerable. Every time we left the house for the rest of that summer, we wondered if the thieves were coming back. It's common. People in car accidents are terrified to get behind the wheel for fear of another mishap. The worse the accident, the greater the reluctance."

"I know the violation you're referring to, Chief Brady. I wish it was simply because someone had stolen my jewelry."

Brady went quiet, looking everywhere but at her. Hopefully, because he understood how patronizing his story was. Melanie realized it was intended to quell her fears, but it was a gross simplification. One that did not make her feel any better. She wasn't about to ask for an epilogue.

"Ma'am." Brady paused, as if collecting his thoughts. "I see now that I misspoke. I'm sorry about that. All I mean is that I understand why you feel the way you do, but you *will* be safe here."

"I shouldn't worry about someone trying to scare me to death?" she said. "After Hoyt killed my friends? Jesus Christ, why am I here?"

"Cyrus Hoyt is dead and buried, that's why. I've been to his grave many times, ma'am, so I can attest to that. If you want to leave town, I get it. But you've got twenty-four/seven protection from me and mine for as long as you stay."

"That's not necessary, chief. Jeez, I'm already a disruption. Not sure I can handle being a drain on your resources, too."

"Believe me, my guys could stand a little more to do around here."

"Why do you care if I stay, chief?"

Brady went to the nearest window and looked down at the yellow parking lot glow. He sipped the steaming mug with loud smacks of his tongue and Melanie watched curiously. He was an attractive guy on the surface and had no trouble filling out that uniform. His tanned pants were tight, accentuating shapely buns, while bulging arms made her chew her lip. The real tragedy in all this was that there didn't seem to be much happening above those wide shoulders.

His radio crackled.

"All set down here, chief. Want us to leave a man behind like we talked about?"

"No," Brady said. "Take off. I've got first watch." When

he was finished, he went to the door and opened it. "I'll give you the whole of it, Miss Holden. I just wonder if you wouldn't accompany me downstairs so I can set up shop."

"Why not," she said. After the scare, she wasn't going to do any more writing tonight. It was better to be in the company of a buffoon than to lie up here alone.

They went downstairs in time to catch the last of Forest Grove P.D.'s taillights disappearing down the country road. She followed him to his patrol car, dragging her feet in the gravel. Brady popped the trunk and looked back with a lopsided grin. "Drink?" he smiled—obviously pleased with himself.

"What?"

He slid the top off a Styrofoam cooler, revealing twelve bottles of Blue Moon. "The wife seems to get agitated when I crack a beer so I've no choice but to keep my stash here."

"So you're an alcoholic chief of police? Great." Melanie wasn't sure why she said it. Brady looked far too healthy to be suffering in the throes of alcoholism. For some reason, she couldn't bring herself to let the guy off the hook, despite his obvious efforts to put her at ease.

"No, that's not it at all. I just keep 'em hidden 'cause my wife bitches."

"And you don't bitch back?"

"You haven't met my wife."

"Ah," she said. "One of *those*."

"Not really. I guess I'm just a kid gloves kind of guy…avoid marital conflict wherever possible, ya know? Trish grew up here. She wasn't thrilled with returning. You two have that in common. Her mom died when she was real young, and her dad did this gig before me. So all the important men in her life have juggled her with their responsibility to the grove."

"And did her father teach you the cooler trick?"

"Okay, forget the beer."

"Let's not do that," she said and stepped closer, feeling guilty about berating him. "A beer sounds like the first good thing that's happened to me today."

He watched her suspiciously and Melanie eyed him back with newfound confidence that surprised her. She extended an expectant hand. "Let's have it."

Brady cracked one and passed it along. "If you haven't been able to tell, I'm pretty new to this chief thing."

"I wouldn't have guessed," she said. It was true. Brady was a little awkward but he looked the part and acted it even more. His tone was friendly but authoritative.

"That's kind of you, ma'am…"

"Okay," she said. "That's enough of that. My name's Melanie. Call me Melanie."

"Melanie. Alright. Well I'm glad to hear that. I was a city cop—New York City—for almost all of my twenties. Four years in the corps right out of high school led straight to law enforcement—like my father before me and his father before him. Made detective four years after that. Two years later, I got the bug for small town living. Wanted to start a family behind white picket fences…all that good stuff."

Melanie took a sip of the Belgian ale. It was light and surprisingly tasty. She couldn't even remember the last time she had a beer.

"Anyway, I got this job. Only been at it a few months and it's been…challenging. The politics of it, man, I swear to God it's a full-time job before you even consider the policing."

That comment was like a knife to her gut. Melanie should've assumed every career was bogged down in political mire, but the grass never failed to look greener on the other side. The fact that Chief Brady had his own Dennis Morton both depressed and relieved her. If everyone had one, maybe she had no right to feel so miserable about hers.

"I know you didn't come here for my life story," he said. "So onto yours. We get a steady stream of crime enthusiasts out here and the mayor thinks we should discourage people from visiting for that purpose. We can always spot them from the second they land in town: twenty-somethings stop at the gas station asking for rolling papers and directions to the camp. Mayor Cobb's worried that your book'll cement that reputation once and for all. Now, we understand what happened to you, and to be honest ma'a—*Melanie,* I think you should write whatever the hell you want if it helps."

"And you're supposed to keep me happy. That it?"

Brady shrugged and took what looked to be a nervous swig.

"I can appreciate that," she said. If only he'd leveled with her right off, she might've toned down the ice princess act. Brady was being a team player. It was a song Melanie knew all too well.

"Now that we understand one another, how about calling me Nate?"

"Very well. *Nate.* I'll tell you what. Answer a few questions about Forest Grove and I'll make sure my book has only flattering things to say about this town's finest."

"Done."

Melanie smiled. As shaken as she was, as much as she didn't want to be alone, she wasn't going to let Dennis Morton see her fail. "Thank you, Nate," she said. "Now why don't we have another beer?"

The night was deep and he moved through it with confidence.

From where he stood, the streets of Forest Grove had not changed much since his last visit. Things were cleaner and looked newer. He didn't care for the feeling that the town had moved on.

It used to fear him. Now, did it even remember?

Hoyt saw the downtown strip from the forest and when he was certain there were no prying eyes, he stepped from cover and continued on. The walk from home was quicker than it used to be because he was faster now. Stronger. Finally, he controlled his body again.

Main Street was quiet, although he avoided the road just to be safe. He walked across rear parking lots, keeping to the shadows whenever possible, determined to stay secret.

Because once he killed *her*, everyone would know he had come home.

When he found the shop, he knew that he was going to have to slip around to the front and risk being seen. The alleyway between buildings was so narrow that he had to turn and shuffle his way to the sidewalk. The hardware storefront offered a bunch of tools that he did not recognize, much like the electric device he had used back at the garage, but knew they would have what he needed.

When he was much younger, he recalled sneaking into a home to prepare for the coming winter. The resident, some kind of solider just returned home from a war, put up a real struggle. Hoyt had barely managed to get the better of him, and only because a corkscrew had spilled onto the floor during their fight. He jammed it up through the bottom of his jaw while throwing all his weight to keep him pinned against the wall.

Once the killing was done, he had a coat, some knives, a pair of boots, and a welder's mask. The later was to protect his face while on the hunt, because occasionally, his prey fought back.

So he needed one now. The last time he tried killing Melanie Holden, she fought back. He remembered collapsing into the mud on that riverbank, certain that he was going to his grave.

But somehow, I'm alive.

He knew he was going to have to be fast about this. These buildings rang loud when the glass broke, unleashing a startling noise. He much preferred the sights and sounds of the forest. He was in control out there.

Nowhere to hide here, he thought as his hands curled around the iron bar he had fished from the dumpster. He watched the nearest buildings from alley shelter until satisfied that he was alone—that the town had packed it in for the day and crawled back to their suburban dwellings for the evening.

The window glass shattered as the bar flew through the pane. Fragments dotted the sidewalk as he stepped up and over. The alarm was already blaring and he was halfway down the aisle before the glass stopped falling.

The welder's masks dangled on a hook at the back of the store. He grabbed one and headed off, a glint catching his eye as he passed a row of steel knives.

He snatched the nearest blade by the hilt and gripped it against his palm, punching the depressor on the back door and running into the parking lot.

Hoyt was in the safety of the forest by the time he heard the siren's wail—the second time he avoided the policemen today. A thought that made him smile. He really was getting back to his old self.

He pulled the mask over his head. It was an awkward fit as he slipped it over ruffled hair, adjusting it against his face. It covered his features, giving him the confidence he needed. That's all that mattered.

A much better face than the one underneath.

He was on his way to thank Melanie for that.

 **Six**

It was raining when Melanie got into town.

She zipped her sweatshirt and pulled the hood over her frizzy blonde matte in an effort to shake the morning chill. The door-to-door investigation wasn't going well.

Six stops, ranging from the local diner to the town clerk's office, and no one much wanted to discuss Cyrus Hoyt. Certainly not Ennis, the grizzled cook whose breath was rancid with stale cigarettes when he huffed, "Forget about that psycho."

From the diner, it was a brisk walk to City Hall. Her conversation with Cindy, the clerk office administrator, had been a carbon copy of the Ennis exchange. The middle-aged woman's hands were clasped neatly on the counter, offering a wide-mouthed smile until Cyrus Hoyt came to topic. Melanie asked if Hoyt had any living relatives and Cindy's tone became irritated. "Why don't you let those demons be? No one wants to live that hell again."

The rest of the local businesses weren't any chattier. Tom the barber and Cosgrove Real Estate weren't interested in speaking. The guy behind the register at Earl's general store laughed at the question and tried selling her some schnapps in a truly baffling non sequitur.

There was trouble at the hardware store as she continued her walk. Two officers stood in front of a busted window front speaking to the harried owner.

One of the cops followed her with a slow turn of his head as she crossed the street. He was the one who'd been stationed outside of Desiree's that morning. She thought his name might've been Alex Johnson and he looked young enough to be one of her students. He had offered her a ride while she was leaving on her jog, but Melanie declined, preferring a rush of fresh country air to forced conversation. So he rolled behind her in his cruiser like he was protecting the First Lady, until he sped off to answer some call of duty.

A break-in at the hardware store, apparently.

The rain got thick and heavy as she thrust her hands inside her pockets. Her sweatshirt was soaked through and the flimsy tee underneath retained no warmth. To get out of the downpour, she ducked beneath the closest awning and realized it belonged to the used bookstore she wanted to check out. Not a bad way to kill some time while waiting for the storm to pass.

It was dead inside, filled with musty air and thick silence. Melanie inhaled it, savoring the joy delivered by that irreplaceable book smell. The clerk was a heavyset man whose hair was styled into loose and oily strands. He spoke to a younger woman in raven dark lipstick and with a clothespin piercing jutting out from the corner of her mouth.

It looked like a cold sore from where Melanie stood.

"Sure, I'll sign it," the clerk laughed and scribbled something on a sheet of paper. "The hell I care if the kids around here throw a dance? What else are they going to do?"

"Nothing," the outcast girl said. "That's the problem. I wish everyone had your outlook."

"Whatever you say," the counter jockey said, burying his nose in a paperback that showed a burning earth and some squid like mechanical creatures hovering over it.

Melanie headed past the register and the girl's eyes bugged.

They looked far too large for her tiny head. "No way," she said and stuffed the sheet of signatures into her side satchel. "Melanie Holden?"

Melanie gave an uncomfortable smile and averted her eyes. She didn't need any more passive-aggressive taunts today, especially not in the sanctity of a bookstore. There were few places that relaxed her as much as these.

"You here to do some research? To get a feel for how the other writers did it?"

"Trying to get out of the rain," Melanie said.

"I hear that. Heard you're back here to set the record straight or some shit."

"Some shit," Melanie agreed and stepped past the girl. "Excuse me."

But the younger woman wasn't having it. She took a few steps back and raised her arms in mock surrender. "Aw shit, I probably came off wrong. Look, I'm not like the rest of them. I think they've all got chips on their shoulders, too."

The bookstore clerk cleared his throat without lifting his attention from the book.

"No offense," the girl said, smirking at Melanie. "He's cool. Signed my petition and everything."

"Petition?"

"Yeah, I'm collecting signatures on behalf of the high school. Hoping the city council will reverse its decision to prohibit dances and gatherings. Been that way since—"

"Right," Melanie said. She should've been uncomfortable with the topic, but there was nothing accusatory in the girl's words. Her attitude was actually sort of refreshing in the same way a cold shower hits your body on a humid summer's day. She didn't seem to belong here any more than Melanie did, which practically made them friends. "You live here in town?" She asked.

"Unfortunately," the girl said. "Grew up here. Got out for my twenties and then got pulled back kicking and screaming." She held up her hand and wiggled her wedding ring with her thumb. "Hard place to leave, no matter how far away you get."

The girl watched Melanie with raised eyebrows—a curious expression that asked *what's your excuse?* "I thought coming back would jog some old memories," Melanie said.

"And how's that working out for you?"

"Terrible," she sighed.

"You feel like grabbing a little breakfast? Not often I come across someone who hates this town as much as me. I feel like we're already kindred spirits."

Melanie wasn't especially hungry and the prospect of greasy diner food was more repelling than comforting, but here was someone willing to talk. Someone who grew up here. She had to know something.

They trotted out into the rain and walked toward the diner. Melanie got a sinking feeling from seeing Ennis again so soon and was desperate to fill the uncomfortable silence. "I just realized I don't know your name."

"It's Trish," she said. "I think you know my husband. Chief of police? Real stickler for the rules?"

Melanie stammered and wound up nodding. She only just met Trish, but it was hard to believe that Brady was married to— *this*. It wasn't fair to judge, but she was at least thirty years old and her alternative Goth-chic style felt more appropriate for high school than real life. No wonder she worked so closely with Forest Grove's teenagers, she obviously considered herself one.

How are you doing on that whole "not judging" thing?

Okay, it wasn't fair to make assessments, but Trish's black eye liner and matching fingernails fit a rebellious coffee barista more than it did a married woman living in a small town.

They stepped into the diner and Ennis scowled while

glancing between them. It was hard to tell which of them he wanted to see less. That made her trust the chief's wife more.

They took a booth right up front. Melanie ordered a glass of orange juice and an egg white omelet. Trish ate like she dressed—in defiance. You'd have to be a rebel to order a side of bacon with a plate of sausage and hash topped with runny eggs. It was enough sodium to give the entire town gout. Then again, there wasn't an ounce of fat on this little thing, so maybe she knew exactly what she was doing.

The waitress took their order without a smile. She hurried off and Trish slapped a palm down. "Thing I hate most about this place is the judging," she said. "I feel eyes on the back of my neck when I'm at the convenience store buying milk. Like people are wishing me away—as if this is such a nice place to live."

"It's not?"

"I don't think so, do you? People get cross when you let your grass grow too long. I like leaving it long…hoping it'll bring ticks to the neighborhood."

Melanie liked this one for sure. "How is the signature collection going?"

"Oh, it's all over the place. Some folks are happy to sign… probably those who've got kids in high school. Can you imagine what a nightmare it is having to explain to them why they don't have dances like every other town in America?"

Melanie was at least partially responsible for that. It was the one thing she had in common with Forest Grove. Both she, and it, had been scarred by Cyrus Hoyt. Only there was no solidarity between them.

"Some of them look at me like I'm trying to host an orgy for the kids," Trish said. "They tell me to hit the bricks. One woman, I don't know if you've met Mrs. Maxwell yet, but she took me by the arm and asked how I could betray my hometown like this. Hope they don't find out I'll be buying them a keg as another act of disobedience."

"Your husband okay with that?"

"Define okay," she said. "He's supportive. I'm hoping he doesn't read my newfound activism as a betrayal. I'm not a culture warrior or any shit like that, but if I gotta live here, then it has to be a place I'm comfortable with."

Melanie knew what betrayal felt like. Dennis Morton wasn't exactly a friend, but their relationship had been pleasantly professional from the beginning. He trusted her and refused to micromanage. That counted for a lot in this day and age and it was mostly why she never saw the blindside coming.

"Okay, enough about my shit." Trish took a mouthful of bacon but kept talking. "What's going on with you? You look as unhappy as I am."

Melanie laughed out loud and couldn't remember the last time that happened. "These people hate me," she said. "They think I'm out for a scandal, but I've really just reached a point in my life where I need to get my story out."

That was her official motivation. No one needed to know that she had become work's whipping post and was doing this for equal parts spite and catharsis.

"Doesn't take much to get these bumpkins on edge," Trish said.

"I don't think this place has moved on any more than I have."

Trish rolled her eyes in a way that said *ain't that the truth*. "That shit left scars," she said. "Take it from a native. In junior high, you couldn't go into the backyard of your friend's house for a little necking without hearing nervous chatter about Cyrus Hoyt. He became the celibacy boogeyman. *Don't fuck, kids, or Cyrus Hoyt will kill you*. The PTA thought they could stomp out teenage promiscuity by propagating that myth. Opportunistic pricks."

They talked around the topic of Hoyt for a while. Melanie tried getting Trish's thoughts on the possibility that he was alive without asking, but it became clear that Mrs. Brady wouldn't be coerced into volunteering her thoughts on the matter. So she asked again about the impact of Hoyt's killing spree, thinking she could at least use that in the book.

"It got worse as I went through high school," Trish said. "And I don't mean any disrespect, but everyone talked about Hoyt the same way they do Santa Claus. It wasn't real anymore. Just a cheap ploy used by teachers and community leaders to keep us puritanical. In our rebellion, we laughed about it. We're not supposed to do drugs, great. Pass that joint. Sex is the devil's tool, and Hoyt is his instrument of punishment? Cool, I think I'll go all the way tonight."

It was hard for Melanie to hear how her own trauma was marginalized, but it was to be expected.

"It's not like we lived in a den of debauchery," Trish continued. "We were just kids. Drinking and mischief." She took a swig of coffee and winked. "And a drop of promiscuity for good measure. What Hoyt means to you is very different than what he was to us."

He ruined my life. "Makes sense," Melanie said.

"But this town feels more uptight than ever."

"How so?"

Trish shrugged. "I spent my twenties in New York City, so maybe it's just me having a hard time acclimating to the 'burbs. But it just feels…different."

"No one seems to want to talk much about Hoyt these days."

"Yeah," she said. "They probably saw how well their scare tactics worked on my class and dropped the spiel entirely. But a part of me thinks they've got to be more scared than ever, if they're not even willing to address his existence anymore."

"Do you know anything about this town that I might not?" Melanie asked. It wasn't the most tactful segue, but Trish wasn't likely to mind.

"Nothing really," she said. "By the time I was old enough, Camp Forest Grove was already our own personal urban legend." She repeated the old campfire rhyme with a twitching grin that suggested mockery, or at least disbelief.

"One of the old timers at Last Mile Gas told me about some trouble on the lake before Hoyt. Wouldn't say anything more, though."

"I've heard the same," Trish said. "And don't know any more than that...even with my father as a career lawman."

They made small talk through the rest of breakfast. Trish eventually tried recruiting her to collect signatures, but Melanie explained that her involvement would only hinder the cause.

"I don't care," Trish said through a grin that could only be described as shit-eating. "Having you involved would ruffle some additional feathers."

Melanie declined, saying she did not expect to be in town that long, and once she was gone, she wouldn't be back again.

The rest of the conversation was about trivialities. At some point, the rain stopped and Melanie offered to put the whole bill on her credit card—the least she could do for the background information Trish had supplied.

They stepped outside beneath a sunny sky and it was already too hot to keep her sweatshirt on.

"Great talking to you," Trish said. "I hope you find what you're looking for here. Don't let anyone stop you."

I won't, Melanie thought and watched her disappear down the street.

"Are you going to be wanting a ride back to your place now?"

Melanie turned and saw the officer from the hardware

store walking toward her. His nameplate indeed read JOHNSON and his eyes were glued to the chief's wife, who now crossed the street and disappeared around the other side of the bookstore.

She was about to decline the offer, but Johnson didn't give her the chance to. "You know Mrs. Brady?"

"Just met her, actually."

"Hope she wasn't trying to recruit you," he said. "Between you and me, the chief isn't exactly thrilled that his wife has become so…controversial."

"I'm doing just fine with drumming up controversy on my own," Melanie said. "Besides, the whole door-to-door thing isn't for me. I'm not a violent person, but one time there was a Jehovah's Witness that would not stop coming to my house…"

"Smart lady," Johnson said. "Definitely not the kind of girl you want to go hitchin' your wagon to. Had a nasty bout with drugs a few years back, and some of us think she's back at it. A little worried about having to deal with that kind of thing on the streets of the grove. It shouldn't happen here."

"'I'm sure Chief Brady won't let it," Melanie said and tried stepping around the young officer. This conversation had gone as far as she wanted it to go.

But Johnson stepped into her path. "He has a lot to worry about. Just last night some kids got bored and vandalized the hardware store."

"Then it sounds like Trish has the right idea?" Melanie said. "Give them something else to focus their energies on?"

"Not for me to decide," he said. "Now what about that ride?"

"No thanks, Officer Johnson."

"Alex," he said.

"No thanks, *officer*. Now that the rain has cleared, I think I'll take my time getting back."

"Suit yourself," he said. "You know where to find me if you

144   *Matt Serafini*

change your mind."

"All I need to do is look over my shoulder, right?"

"More or less," he said and turned back toward his car.

Across town, Brady hit a dead end of his own.

His brow was damp with a mix of sweat and water. "At least the rain stopped," he mumbled. "Feels like we've been out here all day."

"We have." Captain Ernie Oviedo of the Connecticut State Police fished a cigarette out of his breast pocket and lit up. "Nothing's here, chief. Let's call it."

Brady had received word from New Haven P.D. this morning. Their missing person, Vincent Robson, was with two other people the night of his disappearance. Turns out all three were MIA, and Mayor Cobb was shitting a brick over the idea that they might've been killed on the outskirts of Forest Grove.

"This better not go national, Brady" was the last thing Cobb had said at this morning's briefing. Captain Oviedo was called in to help coordinate a search on the mayor's wishes and he didn't subscribe to the theory that these kids were lost any more than Brady did.

"You're right, captain." Brady pulled his foot out of a puddle of mud, suddenly envying his guys who got to answer the break-in call at the hardware store.

The site around Robson's car was clean. Too clean. No fingerprints on the door, zero shuffle marks in the dirt around it. As if the whole area had been wiped. They pulled a few hair fibers out of the interior and prayed the follicles were attached—anything that might give them a suspect.

While waiting for lab analysis, they searched. And searched.

"Two of my men are in Sharon by now," Oviedo said. "That town ain't exactly close. I'm pulling them in."

Brady assumed their missing persons came out to Camp Forest Grove to party for some ungodly reason. His original assumption, that the kid got himself wounded while trying to find the camp, was preferable to the likelihoods turning over in his mind now.

Someone in your town killed them.

It was especially likely when he considered what was happening to Melanie Holden. Someone wanted her gone—or worse—and three college kids were dead.

"I doubt they're animal chow," Oviedo said. "But I'd prefer to go with that over what you're thinking."

"Don't have much choice," Brady said. "An abandoned car that still runs and not so much as a footprint out here." He mentioned to the state trooper how they'd searched the woods once already. The rain might've washed away some of the evidence today, but the trail had been every bit as cold yesterday.

Oviedo took a long drag off his cigarette. "You know about these woods, right?"

Brady nodded. He heard about Cyrus Hoyt more times than he could stand.

"Ron Sleighton didn't tell you anything?" the captain asked.

We're not exactly fishing buddies, Brady thought before saying, "I know about Hoyt."

"I'm sorry that this is in your neck of the woods," Oviedo said. "Been a blight on the state for as long as I can remember."

"The woods?"

"The woods. That camp. All of it. It arouses superstition. Been that way ever since I was a trooper. My predecessor, Tom Lawson, takes me aside the night of his retirement party. Guy's eyes are glossy from a dozen brandy doubles as he leans in and says, '*It's your problem now.*' Told me to pray that I never have to deal with Forest Grove. No clue what he was getting at."

"You asked, I assume?" Brady said.

"Yep, and he wouldn't say. He didn't have to. I was out here that night in '88—a rookie then. They had us combing these woods just like this, pulling dead people—kids, mostly—from every bunk. Found a girl hanging upside down all the way out here. Half her head missing, animals lapping her brains like melted ice cream. I'll never forget it as long as I live."

"Cyrus Hoyt's dead," Brady said, impatience showing.

"Ain't sayin' it's Hoyt." The trooper tossed his cigarette to the ground and crushed it out. "But standing here now gives me those same feelings. Miserable feelings. Emptiness. Bad shit happened out here and the ground feels tainted because of it."

Brady nodded but his brain wandered away from the fantasy of undead killers and lingering ghosts. He thought about the very real and threatening text message sent to Melanie and wondered who might break into a hardware store. Someone in town was doing this and that idea passed through his stomach like spoiled meat.

"I think I stumbled across the car while the killer was cleaning up," Brady said.

"Cobb isn't going to want to hear that you've gone right to a murder theory."

"What's the alternative?" Brady asked. "Three lost college kids? We'd have tracks if that were true. Someone cleaned up after that car. Our boy was off hiding bodies when I rolled up. I interrupted him."

"If you start suspecting murder, people's minds are going to wander back to what happened out here."

"They're already wandering," Brady said. "I've heard it all. Some think Hoyt's still out there, even more powerful somehow. My first night on the job, Henny Yurick tells me he saw Hoyt walking through the forest, bloody axe draped over his shoulder like Paul Bunyan. I knew I was inheriting a town with some history when I took this job, but I wasn't expecting so much delusion to come with it."

Oviedo called his men off the hunt and started back toward the cars. "Lawson did have one other thing to say the night of his retirement."

"What's that?"

"Said they ought to burn this whole place to the ground, woods and all, and just be done with it."

Last Mile Gas looked like it was on its last mile.

Melanie knew she shouldn't be back. Not after yesterday. But this morning's conversation with Trish had her eager for more information. And Jed seemed like the only other person in town willing to speak.

She hoped Sam wouldn't be here. Or that he would be busy. Whatever it took to pry a little more history off the old man's tongue.

It was a little after four and the place looked done for the day. She had expected to see Officer Johnson's cruiser in her rearview when she pulled in, but the road behind her was desolate.

Considering what Jed had said about his business, it shouldn't come as any surprise that the gas station packed up shop early some days. The garage door was drawn and a CLOSED sign hung in the office window, dangling over old and crusted blinds. The convenience store was locked also. She peered through the glass and saw only darkness.

Melanie walked the building's perimeter and worried that the old man might've fallen. Or worse. A dumpster buzzed with fervent flies as she passed, and the backyard was a minor scrap yard of rusted car parts. Glancing beyond, there was a house—a ranch consumed by the tall grass around it.

The brush jutted past her knees and she envisioned an army of ticks scaling her thighs. She pushed on with determination and wished she'd asked Trish to come along for the company. Knowing that someone in town shared her thoughts gave her more confidence than expected.

Kindred spirits indeed.

Rickety steps led to a rickety porch and even the railings wobbled as she stepped onto soft and unstable wood. She called for Jed while knocking. A minute passed and she wrapped again, this time with the back of her hand. She pressed her ear against the door hoping to hear some bustle.

Deafening silence greeted her back.

Concern grew—along with a feeling of missed opportunity. Melanie hated to quantify the situation that way, but Jed knew a lot about this town. And maybe somebody didn't want her to learn anything else about it.

Then again, maybe Sam had taken him out for the day—a doctor's appointment or a fishing trip, perhaps? She glanced around the neglected property. It looked like Sam didn't do a lot for his *father*.

She leaned against the brittle rail and chewed her lip in frustration. The sky overhead darkened and the temperature dropped. At her back, a flash of lightning blotted the sky. It was raining again.

Her mind floated the idea of breaking in, but timidity had held her hostage for more than forty years. She didn't speak up when neighbors fired up their leaf blowers on an early Saturday morning and never protested her miscast role as journalism professor. She let things happen because it was easier just to cope.

So breaking into Jed's home was far outside her comfort

zone. Attempts to rationalize his absence were at odds with logic. It couldn't be a coincidence that the one person in Forest Grove willing to talk about its history was suddenly missing.

"Who says he's missing," she mumbled.

Glass shattered at her back. Before she could turn, there was a loud bang that broke in the air like thunder, followed by more shattering.

A figure walked out from behind the front of the garage with what resembled a tire iron dangling from a hand. From here, it looked like a man, though she could not be certain. He moved casually, with rain pelting off his steel mask.

No. It can't be.

There was purpose in his steps. He gripped the tool like a weapon.

The figure walked toward the tree line and Melanie could only watch, standing slack-jawed and lightheaded. After twenty-five years of nightmares, here moved Cyrus Hoyt in the flesh. Alive, as she had always known, and no more than five hundred feet away. Her vision was hazy, but she didn't dare flinch.

He hadn't seen her yet.

Hoyt was a step away from the trees, one foot in the brush, when he stopped. He turned toward her and his visor plate flashed in a burst of lightning.

Melanie couldn't breathe, let alone move. Her cheeks were flushed with fear as her hand fished the cell phone from her pocket.

The killer dashed into the trees and was gone in an instant. Melanie stared, struggling to comprehend the sight. She dialed Brady with a frantic finger and his voice was muffled in the palm of her hand. She blurted something about Last Mile Gas, about seeing *him*. Before she could finish, the chief interrupted.

"I'm right there. Give me two minutes."

Melanie exhaled and struggled to reclaim her jilted breath.

If she moved, Hoyt might somehow change his mind and come stalking back. He had been so close. Why hadn't he come after her?

Brady's cruiser barreled in off the road and kicked up a mini sandstorm. He leapt from the car with his pistol drawn and bounded forward.

Melanie felt lightheaded. She dropped to her knees, engulfed in a wave of relief.

"Are you hurt?" He demanded, looking in every direction but hers.

"No." She was breathless. "Just scared. It was Hoyt."

Brady frowned at the revelation. "I caught a glimpse of your car on the way in here. It's smashed to hell."

"He doesn't want me to leave," she said with newfound realization. It made perfect sense and her fingertips went numb as the killer's strategy fell into place. She told Brady the whole story.

"And he ran through there?" Brady looked at the forest.

Melanie could only nod.

"I'm not leaving you until my guys get here," he said. "They were right behind me. Been goose chasing these woods all day. Sounds like we're going right back in to find this sicko."

"Jed," she said, "I think Hoyt killed him. Maybe his son, too."

"Jed? A son? Never had one as far as I know…"

Two more patrol cars skidded in and Brady motioned to the forest. He ran over to talk with them. They drew their guns and disappeared into the woods. He barked something authoritative into his radio before making his way back over.

"Let's get you out of here."

Melanie took one last glance through Jed's window, but there was nothing. She hated Forest Grove. This was never going to be an easy trip, but now that she knew Hoyt was alive, she was ready to call it a day.

They walked to Brady's car, both of them soaking in the afternoon shower. His arm slipped firm around her upper waist, a gentle grip that melted away some of the day's tension. Melanie hadn't been this close to a man since marriage and hadn't enjoyed the company of one for a lot longer.

This felt nice, even as pangs of guilt nibbled at her. Brady was married and Melanie quite liked her. But this gentlemanly display made her feel safe—like nothing in this damn town could hurt her. Sure, she might've been enjoying it a little too much, but she needed it.

It was stupid to feel this way, but Melanie refused to scold herself today. Instead, she put her head against his shoulder as they walked, her shoes dragging in the mud as they went.

The impulse to kill ate him like a cancer.

He wanted to exterminate her back there, but there would not be enough time to savor it. Out in the open, with the police so close. That was a risk. Instead, he knew he could funnel her back here.

He watched the building from the safety of his woods, knowing full well no one could find him here. His jaw clenched, a gesture that normally angered his rotten teeth, provoking inflamed gums that bled into a pool on his tongue. He was accustomed to the bitter and stale taste that resulted and was long used to swallowing it down. But everything was different since waking up. His mouth didn't hurt. It no longer bled.

Again, he wondered why he was alive. Why he was healing.

All was quiet across the street and his patience flaked away by the hour. Any minute now, she was going to be back. And that's when the fun would really begin.

The only problem was the police car sitting at the far side of the bed & breakfast. He knew enough to avoid *them*. They brought trouble. He closed his eye and shook his head, trying not to think about it. Sometimes, he couldn't help but remember the bad things, although there was death on the brain to distract him now.

He cultivated it with further fantasy, thinking of the ways in which Melanie Holden could die. Her pretty white flesh falling into ribbons beneath his slashes, blood bubbling up from her wounds like sliced meat. He liked to improvise, though, and that meant there was no way of knowing for sure how she was going to end.

He might not have recognized Melanie Holden as the one who fought back all those years ago. To see her today, she might've been the mother of the girl he tried drowning in Lake Forest Grove. But it wasn't. It was *her*.

That face stained his mind like an inkblot, piercing blue eyes burned with a melding of anger and madness he would never forget. Her startling desire to survive.

He was tracing a finger through the muddy dirt, bidding time, when the police car roared and sped off. The siren's wail eddied in the sky, lingering in his ears like a fisher cat's scream. They would be looking for him in the woods behind the gas station, exactly as planned. None of them would figure out that he doubled back the other way.

He rose up off the forest floor but caught himself in time, pausing like a cautious animal.

What if this is a trap?

Behind the welder's visor, he eyed his surroundings. Once satisfied, he lumbered from the tree line and crossed the desolate blacktop. His boots stepped softly onto the porch and the screen pulled away from the jamb with a near-silent yawn.

To his left was the kitchen. An elderly woman loaded a

baking dish into an oven while old time music blared through a static-laden radio. He ignored her and stalked to the rear of the house. The basement was the last door on the left. He pried it open and descended into the dank cellar—wooden stairs cracking beneath his weight.

The fuse box sat on the far wall. He crossed the stone floor and pulled open the lid, hammering switches with his chapped and rotted hands.

Overhead, the oldies station was severed and he knew he had the woman's attention. His eye searched for a weapon in the clutter of old patio furniture, paint cans, and damaged headboards. He smiled as he noticed a dulled pair of garden shears resting against the stairwell.

He took them in his hands just as the cellar door creaked open, settling into position beneath the stairs, watching for her feet to land on the step that was level with his eye.

Above him, the woman mumbled something about "too many darn steps in this place."

He slid his jaw back and forth with excitement as he separated the shears and slid them into position, the blade tips resting on the stair's edge.

Another step down.

Then another.

He waited.

At last, a sandal landed on his step. Then another.

He pushed the shears around her ankle and slammed the hilts together with a grunt. The blades sliced all the way through, cracking bone. Blood smacked his mask and her throat barked as she spun off balance and dropped the rest of the way. Her severed foot remained on the step, oozing blood.

He came around to face his victim, but his smile faded upon discovery of a corpse—her neck craned all the way around, despite having fallen on her chest. Wide eyes stared up at the ceiling and her tongue flapped against her cheek, dangling from one lone strand of torn muscle.

He took her by the hair and flung the body into the corner like a ragdoll. All that remained was keeping it out of sight until he could finish things. Now there was no one here to interrupt his fun. He took the errant foot and threw it beside the corpse, leaning the old headboards over the body.

A flick of the fuse box restored power to upstairs. The oldies station buzzed back to life with a song he recognized from his youth. Something about Cracklin' Rosie.

This woman's car was parked outside. He would've hidden it somewhere, but he didn't know how to drive and making the effort brought the potential for more trouble. Melanie would be long dead before a parked car could tip anyone off.

Three people were dead by his hands over the last two days. He felt better than he had in a long time. His hands were shaky with anticipation while he relocated paint cans to either side of the headboards, obscuring the body from any curious eyes. Then he splashed a little across the stairs to conceal the bloodstains, dipping the bloodied shears into the dark blue color to do the same. Things didn't have to be perfect. They only needed to pass someone's first glance. This was about preserving the illusion of normalcy.

Satisfied, he climbed the stairs and sidestepped fresh paint splats as he went.

The front desk's ledger was empty, save for one cursive signature he couldn't read, but somehow recognized. Fumbling beneath the countertop, he retrieved the room key marked with a 5.

The top floor.

The key slipped into the hole and the door swung into darkness. He stepped through the threshold and closed it behind him.

His lips were dry and his heart raced. He felt her presence all over this room. Smelled it through his damaged nose.

I can't wait to kill her.

Then he searched out the perfect place to wait.

Somewhere she would not expect.

Melanie watched Brady pace back and forth across the cramped confines of his office. The shades behind him were drawn, but lightning flashes lit the spaces around them in brilliant white bursts. Torrential rain pelted the glass like balls of sleet.

The chair was torture on her back, sending aches right down to the small of it. She adjusted herself and listened to the chief speak on the phone.

"That guy is a person of interest," he said. "At the very least, he's responsible for vandalizing a car. Thing is bashed to hell. Slashed tires, broken windows. And I want him in connection to our missing New Haven kids."

She couldn't hear the mayor on the other end but judging from Brady's expression, he wanted nothing more than to hang up.

"As of yet, sir, I do not have any bodies. If this guy is dressing up like Cyrus Hoyt to scare off Miss Holden, there's no telling how far he'll go to bring the legend back to life."

Melanie didn't like Brady's dismissal of the real Hoyt. But they were looking for the person making her life hell and that would have to be enough for now.

Brady took a deep breath once he put the phone down. "Now that we know where your stalker went, we'll find him. On the plus side, you've got even more material for your book, right?"

Melanie wanted to tell him to hold the champagne, but he had such a nice white smile that she could get used to seeing it. She caught herself reciprocating a look as her skin flushed red. "I, uh, I'm leaving anyway," she said, embarrassed to be flirting with a married man. His wedding band seemed to harness all the light in the room, glinting loud. *Don't get any ideas*, it seemed to suggest.

"Probably for the best," Brady said. "You're a lightning rod for our maniac."

Maniac. That word landed hard, bringing a certain degree of satisfaction with it. Two-and-a-half decades of paranoia were suddenly justified. She was no longer the crazy one. Because, yes folks, there *was* a maniac out there. As terrified as she was, it was impossible to circumvent the validation.

"Once we catch him, it'll be a different story of course," Brady said.

"You don't have to tell me again, chief. I'm going."

"Nate."

"Okay, *Nate.*" They'd been on a first name basis ever since sharing a cooler of beer. It only felt right being this casual after drinking Belgian ale from the trunk of a married man's car. "I was an idiot for thinking this would work," she said. "You can catch that freak show in the next ten minutes and it wouldn't matter in the slightest. I've had more than enough excitement for one life."

"Wouldn't call it idiocy," Brady said. "It takes…something to come back after what happened to you."

"*Something*, huh? How comforting."

"Was going to say balls," he said. "Then I remembered I wasn't talking to one of my men. Comfort isn't exactly my wheelhouse, so that's all you're getting from me."

"That, and a ride back to Desiree's, right?"

"Of course. And I'll be in touch with the details I'm

allowed to release once we find our suspect. I want to ease your mind as much as I can."

"What about Jed? He's missing."

Nate nodded. "We'll find him. Johnson's at his place now, confirms he isn't there. Not going to worry yet, though. It's possible he's with the man that you thought was his son."

"Sam," she said. "The guy who introduced himself as his son. The old man never refuted it..."

"I checked into it," Brady said. "He doesn't have a son. Not a biological one, at least."

Melanie slapped her thigh in frustration. She was done arguing. Heading back to the bed & breakfast sounded like a great idea. If by some miracle she could fall asleep tonight, tomorrow would come early. Nate talked to Stu's garage and they assured him that her car would be in drivable condition by first light. Once she got home, she'd take it to a body shop to have the dents fixed.

Desiree's seemed peaceful as they pulled into the parking lot. The rain receded on the drive over, leaving breezy air in its wake. Both of them climbed out of the cruiser and stared up at the evening sky.

"You going to be okay?" Brady asked.

"Sure," Melanie said. "I mean, I guess. Knowing that someone wants me out of town isn't going to get me to sleep any easier." She tried shaking off these feelings, trying instead to enjoy Nate's company. They stood in silence for a while and when it became clear that Nate was lost in his own thoughts, she nudged him with a smile. "Any more beer?"

"Might have one or two left. Should've refilled my stash, but this town is holding my spare time hostage."

"I know," she said. "Your poor wife." Melanie shouldn't have said that. Just thinking about Trish made her feel like a terrible person. She had more in common with her than anyone else in the grove, and yet, here she was making eyes at her husband like some oversexed teenager. It was just flirtation, though, and more for her benefit than his. It couldn't hurt and wouldn't go any further—no matter how much she wanted it to.

Nate responded to the topic of Trish with a violent headshake. He said nothing and only stared up into the onyx sky.

Melanie wasn't sure how to react. She leaned against the cruiser's hood, forgetting about the earlier downpour. Water soaked through her shorts. She leapt off with a squeak and felt her pasty skin glaze over with embarrassed crimson. Good thing the parking lot was dark.

Nate laughed. She felt uneasy about the way he watched her, but couldn't look away. And the longer their eyes stayed, the more flushed she felt.

The cruiser's radio crackled and Sergeant Maylam offered a status update. He was en route to relieve Nate. Officers Johnson and Galeberg were coordinating the foot search with the state police, while Donnelley was dialed into a status update meeting with New Haven P.D.

"I want you to set up shop inside tonight, sergeant. In the lobby. Have Desiree brew you some coffee 'cause you'll be there until the morning rays. No one comes in without a good goddamn reason."

"Right as rain, chief." Maylam dropped off and Melanie felt Brady's eyes on her again. She rubbed her forearms to quell the goose bumps while her nipples stiffened beneath the loose top.

"Every so often I feel like you," he said. "People see me as an outsider. I keep thinking that if I stick around long enough, I'll become one of them. Part of me knows that isn't the truth, though."

"Forest Grove doesn't like you unless you were born and bred here, I guess."

"Yeah, and even then…not always. I practically forced my wife to move back. She was living in New York City, so imagine the culture shock. She fits in less than I do. I might have bullied her into relocating, but now I want to tell her that she was right. I should've just taken a private security job in the city."

"Why couldn't you be a police chief in the city?"

"I was bucking for that but…" He looked reluctant to continue.

"Sorry." Melanie searched for a quick way to shift topics, but he was quicker.

"It's fine," he said. "I was a New York cop for nearly ten years. Worked my way up to sergeant in 2010 and my command was a bunch of detective investigators on the terrorism beat. We were looking into two college students from Qatar—little bastards were planning to make a statement by detonating explosives on their campus."

Hearing that freaked her out and she wondered if she was any safer at work than in Forest Grove. Evil was everywhere and it had probably always been that way.

"These guys were tied to a failed subway bombing in Brooklyn a year earlier and their names showed up on a list of prospective bomb material buyers. Because of that, we knew it was time to catch 'em in the act. I went along with a few of my men…always liked having a handle on how they operated. Anyway, someone in the building must've tipped them off, 'cause they ran like hell before we could scale nine stories.

"The sellers fled and our suspects did the same. We pursued and I found myself on the tenth floor with one of them. He drew on me and shots were fired…his aim went high and I wasn't going to give him another chance to miss. I returned fire and sent two rounds into the door he was ducking behind. Only I didn't just hit him."

Nate's face twisted and he turned toward the forest.

Melanie searched for something with which to fill the awkward silence, but everything she could offer felt moot and selfish.

The chief cleared his throat and continued. "His, uh, thirteen year old sister had wedged herself between him and the door. She was trying to tug him into their apartment, scared because strange men were trying to harm her brother. Didn't know a goddamn thing about any of it. I didn't know she was there, and when I fired back in self-defense, one of my rounds got her right in the head. She was dead instantly and the same shot nailed him in the throat. He bled out looking at his sister's frozen face."

"If he hadn't run, hadn't shot at you from his doorway…"

"Doesn't make it any easier to live with. I see those terrified brown eyes in my sleep. A child's eyes. Kid with a future I snuffed out. Couldn't think about lifting a weapon for months. It went to trial and the jury agreed that it was a tragic accident, but the political blowback was too much. The official word was that I was stepping down. Unofficially, it was either that or waste away on shit details for the next 30 years."

Nate's eyes were moist and Melanie resisted the urge to step close and wipe them. It wasn't her place, though his body language welcomed it. He might've welcomed more, too, and Melanie wanted badly to pull him close and hold him.

She needed this reminder that life gave raw deals to others as well. It wasn't that she couldn't empathize, just that she'd been on her own and out of practice for a long time. Her own pain wasn't a concern right now, only Nate's.

"I don't mention this for your sympathy, Melanie. Shit, I never mention it at all. I just want you to know I understand. It's easy to let your life be ruined by the past."

The shadow of Hoyt loomed large over hers, but that was preferable to having the blood of an innocent child on your hands.

"Nate, I—"

"Sorry," he said. "I know you probably don't want to hear about my problems."

"You've listened to more whining than anyone should have to stand," she said. "I owe you a lot more than just my ear." It was more forward than Melanie intended, although she let it ride, curious to see how he might react.

"That's my job," he said and ignored all other implications. "Yours isn't to play therapist to a damaged police chief."

"I still want to hear more about you, Nate." Her eyes fell to his wedding band and she remembered Trish again.

Dammit.

"I should go." She didn't want to, but knew she would hate herself if this continued. She started for the door when he called after her.

"Why don't we wait until my guy gets here, okay?"

"It's fine," she said. "Desiree will be up…I didn't get home in time for dinner so she's bound to be annoyed with me."

"She'll get over it. And I would feel better if you waited. Didn't you want a beer to take that edge off?"

Tempting. Nate was good company, and at the very least, made her feel safe. She hated having to depend on him but what else could she do in this situation? Besides, she liked him a lot, even if that admission made her feel like a terrible person.

He's not happily married…

Another thought that brought guilt. Where was this ridiculous confidence coming from and why would she think that Nate was interested? He was doing a job, nothing more. And Cyrus Hoyt was still out there, so why was she acting like a love-struck teenager?

Nate hurried to the cruiser's trunk and popped it. "It's a hell of a thing," he said, taking two bottles out of sloshing ice and handing one off.

"What is?"

"You think you know the people in this town…hard to get far in this line of work if you're not a good judge of character. There's bad apples everywhere, sure, but I can't imagine why anyone would promote the façade of Cyrus Hoyt."

"Like you said, a few bad apples." She ignored the façade comment. Hoyt was real and they would learn that soon enough.

"More than just him, though. My wife hasn't been honest with me since we moved here."

Melanie saw he regretted the sentence as soon as he spoke it.

"Shit," he grumbled. "Forget I said anything."

"It's fine. If you need someone to talk to—"

"Probably for the best we drop it," he said. "I've already blurred the line, haven't I?"

"I don't mind." She put her beer down on the cruiser's trunk and wrapped a trembling hand around his arm. "You can talk to me."

Brady moved close and Melanie held her ground. They stood face-to-face while her heart raged and belly fluttered. This was wrong, but she wanted it. Nate had to want it too—desire raged behind his brown eyes and he looked like a man about to take what he needed.

Only this couldn't happen. She wasn't a villain or home wrecker. She repeated those assurances in her head like a mantra. No way could she do this to Trish. Hell, she wouldn't even do this to Dennis Morton.

Both she and Nate stepped away and it was hard to tell who made the first move. It was as if their consciences reached the same conclusion at once, deciding mutually to reject the magnetism.

Nate cleared his throat as another cruiser roared into the parking lot. Sergeant Maylam climbed out, a riot shotgun cradled in his arms like a small child. He was almost Brady's size, though he looked a bit older.

"Figured this is going to be a long night," he said. "With our guy still out there, I thought I'd come prepared."

Melanie headed for the front steps, ashamed of what nearly happened. Things were complicated enough without this. She had exactly two friends in this town and nearly became the wedge between them.

"I should go sync up with the boys," Brady said.

"Real sorry this is happening, miss," Maylam said. "I'll be right in. You need anything, you just open your door and holler."

"I'll do that," Melanie said before escaping. She stumbled into the lobby and the lights were off. She started for the steps, thinking all that remained was to crawl beneath the covers and die of embarrassment.

But not before taking an ice cold shower.

She didn't trust herself not to fall in the dark, so she fumbled for the switch and flicked it. Thought about apologizing to Desiree for skipping out on today's meal, but it was late and the old woman was probably asleep. No point in waking her for something that could wait until check out.

Melanie started up the stairs when the floorboards overhead creaked.

"Desiree?" she called out.

Calm footsteps continued to thump, but there was no response.

Outside, the departing sound of Brady's cruiser.

More creaks.

Her heart felt primed to explode when the curling wood became aggressive footfalls. She ran, hoping to reach Maylam. The screen door was wobbly as she darted into the parking lot.

The cruiser was empty.

She called for him but there was only her echo.

The parking was shadows and dead silence. Melanie ran to the far side of the house, but there was no sign of her supposed guardian.

Inside, footsteps crashed down the main stairs.

Melanie bolted for the cruiser and pulled at the driver's door like her life depended on it, stubbing her fingers against the handle in a clumsy grip. She pulled them back in recoil, waving off the numbness.

At her back, the screen broke open with a thunderous crack.

She whipped around to face the assailant.

No one there.

The door fell against the jamb and the porch was as empty as the parking lot.

She sprinted for the road. Another car would happen by before long.

An arm shot out from behind the nearest tree and took hold of her. With a pull, she stumbled back as Maylam lurched forward from the brush. He knocked her off balance and to the ground, blood falling on her face like the day's rain.

Then he dropped onto her.

In the moonlight, she saw his throat torn wide. She wiggled out from under him as his slicked fingers touched his wound, pressing it shut while desperate eyes begged for help. There was nothing to be done. Melanie struggled to her feet as the sergeant writhed in death spasms, leaving a bleeding sack of flesh to leak into the dirt.

Before Melanie could process this, a blade slashed forward and someone lunged for her. The knife fell through the air with an empty *woosh* that brushed past her cheek.

It didn't deter the attacker. His ski mask-covered head smashed her nose.

Melanie swung a balled fist and landed a blow just

above the outline of his ear. He doubled over and created an opportunity to inflict more damage. One she wasn't going to waste. She brought her knee up into his jaw. There was a grunt before he dropped to the dirt beside Maylam.

Her eye caught the dirty blade resting on the ground. She squeezed the hilt in her fist and lifted it high.

The killer glanced up and his eyes winced in the moonlight.

She stabbed it through his shoulder with a loaded scream.

His cry was shrill, like a baby's, as the knife tore into him with a slurp. He rolled onto his back and scurried away in a frantic crab-walk that might've been funny in any other situation. Once there was some distance between them, he scrambled to his feet and bolted into the trees. His whimpers trailed like vapor streams.

Melanie watched in disbelief. She fished her phone out of her pocket and fumbled for Brady's number.

He answered on the first ring. Again.

Then she dropped into the dirt and lost consciousness.

A flash of lightning turned the darkened living room to brilliant white. It happened again and this time his eyelids fluttered. He was awake now and there were questions.

Like what the hell time is it?

Ron Sleighton flung the afghan off his lap. Even in the summer, he got chilly at night. He shivered as he rose from the recliner.

His back ached from being in the same position for half the night and his senses fought to adjust to the rude awakening. That's right, he'd fallen asleep to an On Demand movie, leaving only the repetitive preview guide to run its mini programming over and over on the other side of the room.

Full consciousness came back—a feat in and of itself at sixty-six years. It wasn't the lightning that had woken him.

The phone was ringing.

"Chief Sleighton." The voice was quiet and raspy. Nothing about it was identifiable. "Make your kin understand…so that she knows."

The words passed through him like a frozen zephyr. In all his years here, *they* never spoke to him, and he knew enough to leave things be. Whatever business they were up to happened outside the grove. That had always been the understanding. He never would've allowed his baby girl to come back, otherwise.

When Trish floated the idea of moving out of the city, and back home, it didn't sit right. But her husband had gotten himself in some shit, forcing him to do the fatherly thing and help out where he could. He was a lonely old man, after all, and the idea of seeing his daughter more than twice a year was a powerful lure.

Now these bastards were threatening her.

"That won't be necessary," Sleighton said. It wouldn't be enough for Trish to back down on her stupid crusade. Not now. No, she was going to have to leave this place for good.

It was his fault for ever letting her come back.

"Speak to her, Chief Sleighton. If you do not, she will be forced to repent and submit."

The line clicked dead, leaving him alone. This was what he deserved for thinking things could've been any different.

 **Seven**

There are woods and a path. She walks it with familiarity. There's frustration inside of her, but she does not remember the root cause. Only that she needs to come here. Almost as if she's done this before. The trail winds toward the mouth of a cavern so impossibly dark she thinks something's wrong with her eyes. Staring into the nether, she sees nothing.

But no, there is a man inside. She doesn't know him and can't at all see him. She only knows he's there. She squints for a better view. When nothing comes of it, she begins to move on. Fingers crawl her neck sticking and stinging like ice cubes. Rancid breath sprays hot air in a gust down her back. Her flesh stands on end.

She realizes she's naked. Turning around, so is he. And now that he has crawled outside the cavern, she finds the simple practice of looking at him a challenge. His flesh is scabbed and rotten. Both nipples are gone, sliced away with indiscriminate precision. Vertical gashes rake across his abdomen—wounds that have long since dried. His penis hangs flaccid, barely noticeable, and the enthusiasm on his hideous face invokes disgust as he stares through her like an object to be played with.

His lips part to reveal inflamed and bloody gingiva that overlaps his remaining teeth with swollen bubbles. The center of his face is a recessed cavity lined with sharp stabs of flesh where his nose had been. One of his eyes is a rotted socket while the other loops gleefully around. He takes hold of her in an embrace that's almost...loving.

Before anything more can happen, before she realizes that she has *returned the gesture, the void slips from the cave and floats in the air around them, fleeing darkness that swallows nature whole until everything's engulfed in nothing. He dissolves into shadows and it takes a moment for her to realize that she has gone with him.*

Trish sprung awake lacquered in cold sweat. Nightmares—two nights running. The details never changed, though. Like replaying a scene from a movie, they remained constant.

She stretched and felt Nate's side of the bed. It was cold. He wasn't around much these days and the way their marriage was going, she wasn't sure she blamed him.

Rain lashed against the bedroom windows like splashes from a hose. She shook off the unease and sat up, cradling her head in outturned palms. Behind her breastbone, her heart hammered so heavy that it almost hurt.

The last two days had been empowering, so why was she drowning in fright? The signature collection was coming along nicely, with nearly two hundred and fifty votes against the dance ban. Rafe, Tanya, and their friends were going door-to-door tomorrow to collect even more and she expected it wouldn't be long before she could take all of it to the city council.

And yet she couldn't shake the feelings of despair and hopelessness that lingered after those dreams.

An empty bottle of Maker's Mark sat on her bed table. Trish smacked her lips together, realizing that her mouth was drier than sandpaper. Nate hated when she turned to the bottle. It was a holdover from her punk rock days, and old habits maybe slept, but they never died. The plan had been to suppress the nightmare with copious amounts of whiskey. It was worth shredding her liver if it meant avoiding that rotted face and those fucking woods.

Her head throbbed with pain that pushed against her skull. She went downstairs wearing nothing but panties—too much effort to fumble for a shirt when all she was after was ice water and Aleve.

Not that she was in a rush to get back to sleep with dreams like that.

Trish guessed they were manifestations of recent frustrations: the forest where she passed out, the suppression of a murderous local resident—the truths were easy to identify. And she had certainly felt the urge to stick some of the locals with a hunting knife this morning. There were only so many condescending glares she could stand and the scariest thing was realizing how much she meant it.

Well, kind of.

She chased the aspirin with a huge gulp of water and went back upstairs, sliding her thong down her thighs before stepping into the shower. The nozzle sprayed away the glossy sweat and lingering tension. She felt more relaxed once she stepped back into room temperature. In the bedroom, her cell phone vibrated against the wooden bed table.

It was Dad, calling at a quarter to three in the morning. She picked up.

"You okay?" he said.

"I'm fine," she said. "And somehow awake. Why are you calling in the middle of the night? What happened?"

"Just making sure my baby girl's okay. One of the boys went down in the line of duty tonight."

"My God, who?"

"Steve…"

She gasped and took a seat on the bed. Steve Maylam, gone? Poor Missy. Their son, Jack, wasn't seven months yet. Just last week, Trish had offered a Saturday drive out to the Danbury Fair Mall for an all-day shopping extravaganza—a break from newfound motherhood. Steve was going to spend some quality alone time with his son while finally learning how to change a diaper.

This news hurt.

Steve Maylam had struck her as an honest guy who genuinely enjoyed his life as a public servant. Just like Nate. Steve had never forgiven Dad for slipping Nate into the position of chief, and there had been plenty of tension between the two men as a result. Despite that resentment, Steve was a good cop. Now he was gone and Missy was alone. A single mother at thirty-two.

It could've just as easily been Nate. Trish swallowed that awful thought, determined never to admit she felt a sick pang of gratitude that it wasn't.

"Some sicko went after the Holden woman," Dad said. "Whoever it was, he was waiting for her at Desiree Rosemott's place. Guess Maylam got in the way and died for it."

"Melanie?" Trish said. "Is she okay?"

"She's fine. But you should—"

"Did they catch him?"

"No, but we will."

"Dad…let Nate take care of this—"

"Steve was one of mine before he was one of his. No way I'm sitting this one out, girly. You just make sure your place is locked tight."

It always was. Nate had equipped it with state-of-the-art motion sensors. She glanced up at the control hub on the bedroom wall. The solid red light indicated that everything was locked tight, exactly as it should be.

She hung up and found herself more shaken and depressed than ever. In dire need of comfort, she swallowed her pride and dialed Nate.

The hospital waiting room was empty, save for Brady and the mayor.

Mayor Cobb looked haggard in these early hours. His three-piece suit was tattered at the shoulder blade, like he'd outgrown the tailoring years ago. The white button-down beneath the coat was littered with coffee stains and his belt cinched his pants without being properly looped through all the holes. His thinning hair receded to the point where there was nothing atop his skull save for a few greasy strands of sole survivors.

On top of everything else, his breath was like skunk spray. Halitosis didn't quite cover it. Something must've died in his mouth and was still rotting beneath his tongue.

Mayor of Forest Grove, Brady thought as he continued to grit his teeth through the official lecture.

"This town is coming apart at the seams on your watch," Cobb said. "You've got a man down, a wounded girl, and three missing college kids. I'm real sorry about Maylam, but unless you convince me that you're able to get a handle on this situation, I'll look elsewhere for resolution."

Brady felt as he had back in New York right after the shooting: responsible. There wasn't a trigger to pull this time, but Steve's death was on him all the same. He wasn't a half-mile away when his man got his throat slashed. It meant the killer was in the woods right outside Desiree's and had probably heard he and Melanie speaking. If he'd been more attentive, this could've been averted.

Brady had driven to the Maylam residence to break the news to Missy. It was the sort of thing he never expected to have to do here—look a young wife square in the eye and tell her that she was a widow. The onslaught of hysterics was devastating and he sympathized as best he could. He tried making assurances that she and her family would want for nothing, but it felt futile in the wake of her loss. And there was something in her eyes that he would never forget. In between the sniffles, he saw it. Disdain.

A glance that said, *why wasn't it you?*

A fair question.

"You're not wowing me with your problem solving skills so far, kid," Cobb barked. "Unless you're trying to tell me that nothing is what you've got."

"We're going to crucify this guy, mayor. He's wounded, according to Holden. We've got law from six towns, plus the sheriff and the staties. There's a perimeter around Forest Grove and my guys are right in the thick of it."

Brady's personal cell phone buzzed. He glanced at the screen and ignored Trish's call.

"Someone attacked our star tourist," Cobb said. "Bet your ass that goes in her book. Our town doesn't come back from this. No matter what we do, we're bloodstained. I've got to go clean up and start talking to the goddamn press. As you can see, I don't do so good when I'm pulled from my beauty sleep. Ripped my goddamn suit trying to put it on in the dark. Now, resolve this today, Nate, and maybe it's not too late to save some face."

Brady didn't give a shit about the town's long-term reception. Not now. "I'm going to say this once, Barney. This is my town. What happened today was my responsibility and I'm handling it. If you even think of going over my head—"

"Know what, Brady? You're a punk. When your father-in-law put in a good word for you, I knew I should've said no. Christ, when a man like Ron Sleighton tells me his son-in-law needs a gig, and that he's got his shit together, I trust him. So I grease some wheels and bring you in. Then you drop the ball all over the place. No wonder New York didn't want spit to do with you."

Brady might've knocked the mayor flat, but chose to leave him spinning his wheels alone and grumbling obscenities.

He walked the quiet hall and asked the duty nurse where to find Melanie Holden. The African American woman flashed a far more pleasant smile than 3 AM deserved as she keyed the name into the computer.

Melanie was in a room right around the corner.

Brady headed for it, wondering when everything went so wrong. Forest Grove was supposed to be a new beginning for the Bradys. A quiet place to start a family. At thirty-one years old, it was high time to begin growing one. He would be happy with any child as long as it was healthy, but in his quietest thoughts, he imagined a son. Someone to share in his mutual love of football and video games. That way he could enjoy both in the name of bonding.

But the dream was getting away from him. The continental divide between he and Trish was growing, and Forest Grove wasn't the picture perfect place he once imagined it to be. Some bad shit happened here and the town was defined by it. Almost by choice.

And then there's her...

Melanie was awake when he poked his head in. Her blue eyes lit up and she propped herself against the pillows.

Brady couldn't help but cross the room's threshold when he saw that smile. "I'm not sure what to say." He didn't know if he was referring to the almost-kiss or her attack. Either way, he felt like an asshole.

"Not your fault," she said. Her voice was quiet and a little croaky.

"I talked to the doctor and you're getting out this morning. You've got minor head trauma. He wants to touch base before you're released and they may take some blood. Your heart rate is high and ditto your blood pressure."

"Used to it by now," she said. "Panic attacks are a way of life."

"I didn't realize you had them."

"I don't make a habit of telling people." Her brow

wrinkled. "Why give anyone another reason to think I'm abnormal?"

"You're not," he said.

"Right," Melanie said. "Once you hit forty and you're unmarried, people start treating you like damaged goods. You get those unconscious looks from them wondering why you're still single. As if that's the only way to measure one's normalcy. I just want to move on. This...*hell* is never going to stop, is it?"

Brady couldn't take another helpless woman tonight. Not after Missy. Desperation accented Melanie's face. His urge was to comfort her and there were other thoughts as well, but he ignored those. Instead, he tapped the edge of the bed in a pointless gesture.

"I know he got Maylam," she said. "I'm sorry, Nate."

"I am too. He was a good man."

"He was there you know..."

"Who?"

"Cyrus Hoyt," she said with a voice like broken glass.

"You know it wasn't him," Brady said. "Even if he were alive, that animal wouldn't have the good sense to wear a ski mask, nor would he have a use for it. Our killer is someone who needs to hide his identity."

"Someone else might've killed Steve and attacked me. But Hoyt was there. When I went inside, I heard someone that wasn't Desiree. Footsteps that were heavier and healthier than hers... running. While Maylam was getting killed outside, Hoyt was in there...coming for me."

Brady wasn't going to tell her that Desiree Rosemott was dead too. Not now. He wanted to contest her claims about Hoyt, but that wouldn't do any good. Her mind was made up and he understood why. The only way to change it was by proving that Hoyt had been dead for twenty-five years. At least maybe then, she could move on.

Forest Grove had a killer, yes, but it was someone who lived among them.

"I want to help," Brady said. Sending Melanie home with peace of mind would do that. If he could ease her tortured thoughts, he wouldn't be an abject failure. Not to everyone, at least.

"How are you going to do that?" Melanie said with a doubt of his ability that was close to a scoff.

"I'm going to prove once and for all that your boogeyman is nothing but a pile of bones."

Sleighton sipped piping hot coffee. It steamed up from the center slice in his thermos, fogging the windshield of his pickup.

He'd been sitting outside his daughter's house for the better part of an hour, glancing occasionally at the .44 Magnum resting on the passenger's seat.

It was almost impossible to know who had called him earlier, but something like that had happened once before. Four or five years after the incident at camp. A wealthy family from New York City had stumbled across their little berg, deciding they were going to make the grove their picturesque home.

Only they weren't crazy about living somewhere that was so *anti-culture* (their words). To them, the arts weren't simply disrespected, but contempted. They couldn't appreciate the still-fresh scars on the community then, and were agitated to discover that Sunday booze was off limits. It was worse still when they had to explain to their kids why there was no homecoming dance, no winter formal, and certainly no prom.

Because the grove had decided those were the kinds of circumstances that invited the tragedy they were trying so hard to escape.

This family—it had been so long that he couldn't remember their surname—complained of harassment. They were money, and because of it, they thought they could sprinkle a little around and buy themselves a say in Forest Grove's affairs.

To them, the grove's way of life didn't make much sense. They spoke out against the "old fashioned" thinking they claimed had shuttled this place back in time. It wasn't surprising that they quickly found themselves the target of threatening phone calls that promised bodily harm. Cars pulled into their driveway and honked the horn at all hours of the night. Once or twice, the women of the family reported that someone had been in their rooms while they slept.

No one in town had been willing to cop to it. And then he got a call, too. It was a throaty whisper, not unlike the voice that had woken him this morning. It didn't have much to say, but after all this time, the words still echoed in high fidelity:

"They're gone."

Sleighton had rushed there—it was probably the same hour it was now—and found the house in tatters. Windows smashed, doors broken down, furniture in pieces. It looked like there had been a siege on the place.

He'd been certain that he was going to find murdered bodies, but there was nothing. A few missing bags made him realize the family had fled in a hurry. It took him a week to track them down after that, and when he did, he discovered they were living in California with some in-laws. They refused to speak about what happened. Wouldn't even acknowledge the damage to their home.

They hired contractors to fix the place while movers came in and boxed up their belongings. The house was sold without them ever setting foot back in it.

That family washed their hands of the grove and there wasn't much he could do, legally speaking. Curiosity had the better of him, though and he was determined to prove that he remained the only law in Forest Grove. That lynch mobs didn't get to make decisions from the shadows.

But no one would talk.

The neighbors swore they hadn't heard anything. Not just that night, but ever. Without any witnesses, Sleighton's hands became tied. The whole thing sat in his gut like a pile of worms. There was no two ways around it—that was the moment he realized he didn't trust anyone in the grove.

Melanie was thankful to Nate for bringing the change of clothes. A shame he left her make-up back at the bed & breakfast, though. The bottom of her eye looked like an artist's canvas board—a swirling mix of black, green, and blue. It brought more attention than she would've liked during the hospital discharge, with every passing gaze offering the same consolatory frown.

She'd had enough of this place.

The doctor diagnosed her with a mild concussion, ordering her to avoid further stress on the brain. That meant the book was on the backburner. She had to avoid bright lights and loud sounds like she was allergic and that meant the only thing left to do was go home and curl up with Lacey for a few days.

Good enough for me.

She came into the hospital lobby wearing a short jean skirt and a formless dark tee—two articles that didn't exactly come together to create a seamless outfit. Still, Nate had done the best he could. Why the concept of outfitting was lost on most men was one of life's greatest mysteries.

Trish Brady waited for her, leaning against a pillar with her hands stuffed in the pockets of her black pinstriped pants. A meek smile spread across her tiny mouth and she looked like a clown beneath her dark eye and lip liners. How could she expect anyone to take her seriously?

Melanie chided herself for being so judgmental.

"My dad told me you were here," Trish said. "Heard about what happened and I wanted to make sure you were okay."

Melanie was fine—physically speaking—but it was hard to feel any lower about her desire to dip a toe in the Brady marriage pool. She felt as detestable as Jill Woreley at this point—only Professor Woreley never got anybody killed.

"Anyway," Trish said. "I volunteered to come give you a ride to Stu's."

The last thing Melanie wanted was to accept Trish's kindness. Hospital security had already arranged transport to the garage, but to decline this gesture would be insulting. And Melanie thought she needed to relax in the company of a friendly face, even if it was just for a ten-minute car ride.

She told the guards she was all set, but it wasn't until Trish made it known who she was that they relented and allowed her to leave.

They headed for a nondescript sedan in the visitor parking lot and Trish turned to her and said, "I know Steve Maylam's wife. I was going to go see her, but she's already flooded with sympathetic ears. And none of them want to see the one person dedicated to disrupting the norm around here. But you…well, you're the only one that might be less popular than me. So, of course I felt the need to check in."

"You're sweet," Melanie said. "I think."

Trish laughed. "I'm kind of an asshole." She stomped the gas pedal and peeled out, a brazen, *I don't give a shit* move that only a chief's wife could afford to display.

I'm an asshole too, Melanie thought. "I think Maylam might be dead because of me."

"He's dead because someone in Forest Grove is crazy,"

Trish said. "Don't blame yourself."

"Easier said than done."

It wasn't a long ride to the garage. When they pulled into Stu's, Trish shifted into park and let the car idle. "All I'm saying is that you shouldn't quit this. Not yet. You survived some bad shit and that wasn't by accident. You're a survivor. Skipping town now would mean giving into the limp dick who—"

"Who isn't afraid to kill people?"

"I know," Trish said. "I don't mean to sound insensitive. But there are so many cops around here now that it looks like a small army has invaded the grove. They're going to catch Steve's killer before he can do anything else. Trust me."

"That doesn't make me safer."

"Of course you're right," Trish said. "Shit. It's just that I would hate to see you go. While you're around doing your thing, I kind of feel better about my own crusade. You're empowering... as corny as that sounds."

It did sound corny, but Melanie thought it might've been the kindest thing anyone had said to her in forever. She didn't think of herself as an inspiration to anyone, given her greatest accomplishment was not dying during a summer camp killing spree.

She offered Trish a thank you before climbing out of the car. She waved it away, telling Melanie instead to keep at it. "The grove doesn't know what to do with us," she said. "It means we're hitting quite a few nerves." Then she sped off, leaving Melanie to feel even more conflicted. Trish's pep talk confirmed for her what her nagging gut had already known. She couldn't leave town just yet, because the only thing waiting for her back home was failure.

The garage was quiet. Melanie crossed the parking lot and found the door locked. Odd, considering it was past nine. She knocked on it and then peered through the glass. At least one of the mechanics had done an all-nighter to get the LaCrosse up and running, so it was possible that he'd fallen asleep on the job and forgot to open the shop.

There was an old battered pick-up truck through the darkened window.

The office door clicked and swung open. Stu stepped out and squinted up at the sun like it was the first time he'd seen it in years. "I thought that was you, Miss Holden. Come in."

Melanie followed Stu inside and thanked him for his hard work.

He tossed her the car key without acknowledging it. "Right through there." He lifted a thumb toward the doorway behind him. It was wedged open with a block of wood and led into what must've been the garage proper. She had no way of knowing, of course, because the only thing Melanie could see was a solid slab of pitch black. "You'll find your car out back," Stu said. "Ready to go."

She got as far as the jamb and froze as her eyes struggled to adjust to the space beyond. She glanced at Stu, who packed tobacco into his corn pipe almost as if he were here alone— probably because this was forced labor for him. Even if the town reimbursed the garage, she wasn't a regular here. He didn't care about her patronage and could afford to be a prick.

"Could you turn a light on?" Melanie said.

"Blew a fuse," Stu said without looking.

With her question answered, she took an uneasy step into the shadows. Just a few more to reach the back and she'd be out of this dungeon. She was halfway there when the door wedge went skittering across the floor and the door to Stu's office slammed shut, leaving her entombed.

Melanie shuffled forward and thought she heard disembodied laughter coming from somewhere. She refused to focus on that, instead feeling for the door and throwing her shoulder into it.

It swung outward and Melanie's car was there, parked
alongside a chain fence topped with barbwire swirls. She climbed
behind the wheel and started it, rolling around the building. A
chain-linked gate stretched across the small alley, preventing her
from going any further.

Is he joking?

She honked twice, laying it on a few seconds longer than
necessary. When no one came rushing, she got out and tried
pushing it open. Then she noticed the padlock.

In disbelief, she stormed back the way she came and pulled
at the garage door. It wouldn't budge. She slapped an opened
palm across the window in anger, calling Stu's name. Inside, tiny
orange pipe embers burned out the darkness, revealing the faint
outline of a face behind it.

"Stu, what the hell?" she screamed.

A young man in overalls and carrying a toolkit appeared
behind her. Melanie saw him reflected in the window.

"Miss," he said. "There a problem?"

"Only with your boss," she said. "I need that gate
unlocked."

The young guy stared at her.

Melanie glanced through the window and saw the outline
of Stu's craggy face recede into the black. With the next puff,
his nose and lips blazed again, only now there were other men
standing on either side of him. Half faces emblazoned by the
pipe's glow. They watched without expression.

"Just let me get out of here." She was angry and without
patience.

The kid went to the gate and she followed. "Sorry about
this, miss."

She got behind the wheel again.

He leaned into the window, lowering his voice along with
his stance. "Between you and I, they're not exactly fans."

"Great," she said. "Then he won't be bothering me for an autograph."

"Stu thinks you're out to make a name for yourself."

"Perfect."

"Don't worry, miss, I did all the work on your car so you're in good shape."

"Thank you," she said.

He shooed it off with a cocky grin. "I just...wouldn't be spending any more time here than you need to."

Melanie stomped the pedal and left Stu's Garage in the dust. It was the kind of recklessness Trish Brady would've approved of.

She called Nate from the road, curious to know how he was going to go about proving Hoyt's death, but got no answer. The next call was to Forest Grove P.D., where they encouraged her to come by and wait for his return.

That was the safest option, considering every minute here revealed that someone else hated her. But she felt rebellious now. Being someone's inspiration had that effect and Melanie guessed her relationship with Trish was more than a little symbiotic. They fought their own fights, but Melanie suddenly felt compelled to go at hers a little harder. Otherwise, all of this was for nothing.

Concussion be damned.

It was probably a terrible decision, but she headed for Last Mile Gas. If Trish could fly in the face of an entire community, collecting signatures to reverse a ruling that had gone uncontested by the people of Forest Grove for decades, Melanie wasn't going to be the one who got scared off.

Yeah, she thought. *But no one's tried killing Trish Brady.*

She pulled into the parking lot, thinking there was enough daylight to accomplish what she wanted. Hopefully Jed was around to answer a few more questions. The place remained quiet and closed—likely because Jed was gone. It got her thinking about Desiree. She wondered if the old woman had been killed last night. Was Nate trying to mitigate her shock by keeping that news from her?

How chivalrous.

Jed was nowhere to be found. She threw the car into drive, ready to leave, when an eighteen-wheeler pulled off the road and rolled to a stop behind her. She couldn't see the cab's windshield from her rearview, but remembered the old man mentioning a small stream of loyal patrons.

The truck's horn blared and she jumped at the noise. Melanie climbed out of her car and walked toward it on hesitant feet as the horn blasted for a second time.

The cab's power window dropped and a man wearing a salt and pepper beard leaned out. "You're a welcome sight from the rough old grump who usually pumps my gas." The smile fell off his face. "Wait, nothing happened to him, did it?"

"I don't know," Melanie said. "I don't work here. I'm trying to figure out where he is myself."

"Shit," he said. "I've got to be in Stamford by one and I'm not making very good time."

She pointed to the house. "I was just about to see if he didn't run back there for some reason. Kind of in desperate need of a filler up." To drive her motive home she added, "and I'd sort of like to make sure Jed's okay myself."

The driver killed his engine, took off his mesh hat, and tossed it aside. "I've got some time," he said. "Otherwise, I'm headed to town to try to find another pump and I don't know this backwater hole so well. No offense."

"Believe me," she said. "None taken. I'll go check the house if you want to wait here."

"Shouldn't I come with you? If something's wrong and the guy broke a hip, who's going to help him? You?"

His sexism was charming. Melanie decided she didn't need

the pleasure of his company and instead suggested he check the garage. "I'll shout if I need you."

He shrugged. "Works for me."

Melanie headed off toward the overgrowth that lead up to the house. It was too easy to picture Hoyt lying in wait somewhere around here. She turned and called out for the trucker.

He came hurrying around the corner and lit a cigarette.

"Be careful," she said.

"Sure you don't want an escort?"

"No," she said. "Just…well, don't lose sight of me, okay?"

"Easy enough," he laughed as he wielded his permission to leer. "You'll never leave my sight."

Great.

Melanie hurried off, thinking it was good having him here in case there was a repeat of yesterday. She was dumb for doing this and wouldn't have bothered at all if not for the arrival of his company. There was a driving need to know what happened to Jed—to know what he was talking about before Sam's interruption—and she was going to find out.

Nobody came to the door. She circled the house and peeked through whatever windows she could reach. The place was lifeless. The backyard matched the front and Melanie pushed through neglected overgrowth, forcing her way toward a dilapidated shack at the back of the property.

It sat open-faced and was edged into a cove of Douglas-firs. She peered inside and hoped the old man hadn't suffered a heart attack. The thing was deeper than it looked. Its walls were lined with old and rusted farm implements. Boxes were stacked floor-to-ceiling, each one marked with a year—plenty to pique her curiosity.

She pulled the top box—1979—onto her shoulder and struggled to guide it to the ground without spilling it. Before

opening the flaps, she lifted onto the tips of her toes to make sure
the trucker was still there. A puff of smoke drifted into the sky
overhead where he would've been and she took a deep breath.

The box was stuffed with credit card slips and invoices
from 1979. Last Mile Gas looked like it cleaned up in the days
before downtown development. She thumbed her way through
until finding a familiar name on an invoice: Peter Dugan.

Mr. Dugan had bought the property back in '78 and
worked for nearly a decade on getting the grounds up to snuff.
Spent an entire year landscaping. Then he tackled the cabin
interiors. Then the exteriors. Dugan owned other businesses so
the restoration process had been slow.

She brushed aside the box and looked for an older one. If
anything had happened on the lake once upon a time, the people
it happened to might've visited Last Mile Gas. Probably a goose
chase, but her heart leapt with excitement as she shuffled the
stacks around until the 1969 box was easily retrievable.

"Where you at?" The trucker called from the top of his
lungs.

"Be right down," she shouted.

She yanked the box into the open and a coat of dust kicked
up into her face. She rubbed her eyes and sneezed while leafing
through the landfill of papers inside. This was the closest she'd
come to…anything.

As much as Melanie longed for the idea of sharing a bed
with her cat, and on doctor's orders to cut the stress from her life,
she was tired of being the victim. Hated the way it felt and while
she wanted to run, there was a good book here somewhere—
an untold story. Maybe her lessons during all those years as a
journalism professor had rubbed off. Like a good bloodhound,
she felt compelled to sniff this out. To dig. To find the new career
that suddenly dangled just outside of her reach.

She flipped through every paper, leaving the useless ones in a stack on her left. They were flimsy, yellowed, and mostly faded. Grocery and garage invoices smudged beneath her fingers as she searched.

She was halfway through the pile when she found it: an itemized carbon invoice addressed to Camp Forest Grove. She stared at it as if it were a mirage. A two thousand dollar order consisting of canned items, meats, cheeses, water, bread, and basic medical supplies. Back when this place was apparently called Last Mile Gas & Convenience. The invoice was dated March 16, 1969 and Melanie knew at once that it was exactly what she needed.

The name atop the invoice was Tullus Abblon and it was made out to something called *The Church of the Obviate*.

Her eyes widened as the plot thickened.

Now she had a name.

The Hall of the Arrival

1968

Something was wrong.

Zohra didn't know what, because no woman was allowed to visit the Hall of the Arrival.

That's what they were calling it now that construction was complete. It took a little over one calendar year and the going had been slow. They gathered materials on a shoestring budget and the Elder had to loan brothers and sisters out as weekend labor in order to trade for what they needed.

Those who weren't on loan were not content to wait around and instead took shovels and pickaxes to the earth, loosening and digging out a basement beside the master cabin. They got ten feet deep and fashioned a small makeshift ladder to help with their ascents. Then they used a crude pulley system to remove buckets of rock and soil as they worked. Eventually, contractors from Forest Grove arrived and laid down a proper concrete slab.

Seasons came and went as the men built the framework for an expansion to the existing bunkhouse. In the winter, when the ground froze, they stayed warm and grew their numbers.

Zohra went on a university tour with Brother Peter during the winter semester. Instead of using the church's transportation, they hitchhiked all the way to up New Haven and made the collective rounds. She and Peter were on the younger side, so they could infiltrate campuses as students. They convinced two teenage boys and a twenty-something girl to repent and submit, hitchhiking back with them after nearly two months away.

She spent the rest of the winter cobbling thicker tunics for the coldest months as the Elder worked hard to convert their latest devotees.

All men were required to work toward the completion of the Hall of the Arrival. As such, their usual responsibilities were handed off to the women. Zohra trekked into town for the essential supplies. It was a task she came to dread, because that kind-eyed officer that had thrown her and Jessica out of town was sometimes there. On more than one occasion, she ran into him gassing up his car or enjoying coffee and donuts.

It was not her place to complain, however, considering the Elder once wrangled edible garbage from restaurant dumpsters as their only source of sustenance. He finally acquiesced, realizing that his devout soldiers deserved better and allowed for the purchase of basic goods and supplies.

While Zohra's double duty was shopping, Jessica led the parish in nightly prayer, taking on a teacher's responsibility. If the girl remained conflicted after a shaky first year, she kept all misgivings to herself.

At first thaw, the men went back to work, drilling and chiseling around the clock. The main cabin bunk became a housing quarters divided into five rooms with two gigantic living areas—one for men and the other for women. There was a much smaller hideaway for the three children living with them and the building offered a spacious area dedicated to nightly prayer and assembly. The home had been outfitted with an indoor dining area for the harshest weather, complete with a small storage room off of it.

The Elder would not answer questions about the Hall of the Arrival. One night at dinner, Jessica asked when the women might have an opportunity to see the fruits of their labors. The Elder's eyes, usually empathetic, were glassy orbs of indifference.

"When we are all strong enough to resist."

The women exchanged glances and it was Zohra who dared taking the question one step further. "To…resist? What are you resisting, Elder? Do we not face mortal challenges together?"

"Even now we are tested," he said. "Your flesh tempts us all."

The Elder dined with his assembly every night, but the conversation—once so jovial and inviting—was now segmented and uncomfortable. The women attempted to reflect upon the day's hardships, but the men had no interest in contributing. They ate in silence, steel silverware scraping ceramic plates. When finished, they disappeared back beneath the earth and were gone for the night.

Occasionally, the Elder would surface for nightly lecture, even though his punctuality was sporadic. It fell to Jessica to take his place much more often than not. When he did show, his sermons were nothing more than tired reiterations of frequent bible passages. The passion was gone from his voice, leaving a tired monotone to fill the preaching space.

After one of Jessica's sermons, she took Zohra by the arm while the rest of the assembly shuffled back to their bunks in quiet confusion. Her eyes were distressed. "Something troubles me, sister."

Just one thing? Zohra suggested they talk outside.

Once they were clear of prying ears, Jessica said, "You and Peter came back from New Haven with three recruits. Two boys and a girl. We've seen the men sup at night. But where is the girl?"

"Resistant to change, maybe?" Zohra said. "It's not easy

to leave your corrupted life behind. You of all people should understand that."

"So that's it? You think she is simply being reconditioned? For three months?"

"I will admit that it would be a most extreme example," Zohra said. "But what else could have happened to her?"

"Maybe she *tempted* them?"

Zohra would not hear it. Perhaps she did not wish to acknowledge it. Either way, she left Jessica standing on the shore where the girl often stood with her thoughts until all hours of the night.

Zohra went back inside, she overheard some men talking about the Hall of the Arrival. Originally, they had been digging beneath the lake, but found the soil there loose and unworkable. The tunnels they wanted couldn't be sustained so they turned inward and burrowed beneath the forest instead. Work progressed and the men lined the walkways with overhead shoring that supported the earth's weight above them. They ran corrugated steel sheets along the ceiling, supported by 2x12 lumbers.

According to these brothers, they were far enough down to begin widening the tunnels into a subterranean layer of worship when they found it.

Something.

They discussed this in hushed voices. When a woman neared, they moved from earshot. Zohra found this behavior odd and growing stranger with every passing day. They worked in rotating shifts and soon the Elder stopped surfacing entirely. Dinners were drenched in uncomfortable silence. Men wouldn't look at the opposite sex while they ate and when they weren't eating, they only slept or worked.

Women found it difficult to sleep at night. Construction sounds were constant. Breaking rocks, shuffling soil, various grunts, and other ambient signs of toil echoed without end. They did not dare complain, though. Nor did they dare speak about it. Until the fear they shared grew too large to ignore.

Zohra woke one morning to find the men moving new materials into the basement, passing wood and tools hand-to-hand in an effort to get them down through the trapdoor with efficiency.

Their faces were as cold as the Elder's and stained with so much dirt and grime that they couldn't have bathed in days. Hands were blistered and bloodied as if they'd been worked to death and beyond. As they passed wooden beams from one set of hands to the next, Brother Peter packed the supply closet full of shotguns and rifles. Jessica stood against the opposite wall with questioning eyes that knew better than to challenge. The threat of violence was new, but somehow palpable.

And that was the last time any of the men were seen topside.

They weren't even coming up to sleep anymore. Instead, chanting and singing joined the evening chorus of rigorous labor. The women awoke in nightly cold sweats, launching up from beneath their covers in unison. Their hearts pounded so hard they could hear each other's.

Rest was harder to come by. They tossed and turned while insane laugher floated up through the hole in the hallway. Everybody wanted to know what in the hell was happening, but nobody was dumb enough to ask.

Because of this, Zohra's latest resupply trip was a welcome one. She took the van down the road to Last Mile Gas & Convenience, compelled to abandon the Obviate entirely.

And where will you go?

Zohra watched the young cashier pack the water and bread into a large box, spotting Kind Eyes in the parking lot. His patrol car sat at the filling station and he was moseying her way as she pulled open the door, wrestling with the box of groceries in her arms.

"Let me help you with that," he insisted.

"I can manage," she said. "I always do."

"At least they're not making you walk around barefoot anymore."

Zohra didn't appreciate the mockery. Last time she had seen him, it had been all "Hey, is this your van? You're trading up!" She stomped past with a huff and the officer gave chase. They had nothing to talk about, but that did not stop him from grasping at straws.

"I'm sorry if that was rude," he said. "I only thought you could use a hand loading your van."

This kind of interaction—friendly and superfluous—was forbidden. The policeman was being nice, but that was a luxury she didn't need. Or want. "Apology accepted, sir."

"Say, I don't suppose you'd want to tell *me* all about your religion? I, uh, noticed you and yours haven't been around much. Guess you took it to heart when I said you couldn't be running around bothering folks. I feel a little guilty about that."

"You should," she said. "We weren't bothering anyone."

"I'm trying to help you."

"Let me guess, you think we're all a bunch of wackos, right?"

"*You're* not," Kind Eyes said. "I can tell just by looking at you. Maybe you got dealt a bad hand, I don't know. But you're not like the rest of them."

"Your people did not want our help. Just like I don't want yours. Goodbye."

"Okay," he said. "So you don't want my help. What about my ear?"

She shoved the box across the van's seat. "If I believed for a second that you were interested, officer, I would happily speak with you about the Lord."

"But…you don't believe me?"

"Okay then," she said, cocking her eyebrow to challenge. "Why do you wish to repent and submit?"

"Isn't it up to you to convince me?"

"Sounds like you're putting me on, man." She looked at his badge but his name was nowhere to be found.

Somehow, he knew she was looking. "It's Sleighton," he said. "Ron Sleighton. And just think about it. I got the day off tomorrow and you never know." He smiled. "My mind's wide open."

It was the last thing she wanted to do. But if the Elder found out that she had refused someone the chance to repent and submit, it wouldn't end well. Plus, getting out of the compound for a few extra hours wouldn't be the biggest tragedy. The thought of having to go back there now filled her with the kind of dread that fostered resentment.

What happened to the love and acceptance that once made this way of life so great?

Right now, the only acceptance Zohra felt was in the eyes of this hapless police officer. She smiled and agreed to meet him for lunch tomorrow. Then she hurried on her way as storm clouds broke overhead.

She found Brother Joseph standing outside in the rain when she got back. His arms were folded across his chest as he watched her approach. "Elder wants to see you," he said and pushed strings of wet hair from his eyes. "He thinks you are ready to visit the hall."

Zohra felt a cold and uncomfortable feeling in the pit of her stomach. The invitation sounded to her like more of a death sentence. She followed Joseph through the bunkhouse and to the end of the hall. The trap door was ajar and a wobbly rope ladder disappeared into the black. A spastic orange glow skittered across the darkness down there. Her heart beat heavy—no desire to go any further.

I'm afraid they'll kill me if I refuse.

So she climbed down. Joseph followed once she was halfway, pulling the door shut in the wake of his descent.

Once the ladder ended, she dropped the remaining four feet and grabbed the dancing torch off the makeshift sconce. Joseph fell beside her, his bearded face growing more detailed in the orange glow. He shuffled ahead and expected her to follow.

The cellar air was heavy and they moved through the broken slab, into an earthy corridor that sloped down. Deeper. The drafty hallway whispered ominous warnings as she shivered her way through it.

"Careful up ahead," Joseph whispered. They'd been walking in silence for so long that his voice startled her. He extended an arm outward so that she couldn't pass. The corridor opened into a wide and cavernous chamber below.

Zohra edged forward so that she stood at the crumbly ledge looking down. Small bursts of torchlight resembled little pinholes in a sheet of darkness. She must've been fifty feet up and another rope ladder led to the bottom.

Off in the distance, the brightest red light she'd ever seen pulsed like a ball of energy, light and then dark. Almost like deep breaths.

She swallowed and started down. Her feet landed one rung at a time and her thoughts grew cloudy, her eyelids heavy.

The men were down here, lined in rows of five. They knelt with their faces an inch off the ground. A low-level chant hummed from their mouths in perfect unison. Joseph hopped off the ladder and joined his brethren, picking up the prayer as he bowed toward the soil.

They faced the direction of the pulsing red glow, which seeped out from between the spaces in a stacked rock wall.

She was drawn forward with tears streaming down her cheeks suddenly and unexplainably.

The Elder stood in front of it, gesticulating with his hands as if having a conversation no one else could hear. He turned at the sound of her footsteps, his face engulfed in red glow. His features were harsh in the dark cherry light. He looked angrier than she had ever seen.

"You feel it," he said. "Don't you?"

"I'm not sure," she said. But that was a lie. Something was in her head now, touching her thoughts. Reshuffling and rearranging them. What she meant to say was that she couldn't explain the way she felt. Zohra fell aside and suddenly she was back to being Barbara Hoyt. Daughter to George and Alexis. Sister of Martin. Pregnant at 16 and lost in a swarm of excessive drugs and casual sex. She supported these habits by waitressing at whichever local dive would hire her. Until one particularly nasty heroin kick sent her running out back during her shift. A man rummaged through the dumpster there and his interest in the sickly girl—now unconscious in a puddle of her own vomit— was immediate.

He had been trying to feed his brothers and sisters. The Elder. Tullus Abblon.

Then she was back to being Zohra and her thoughts were as narrow as the paths she'd traveled to get down here. She remembered the faces of every Forest Grove heathen who mocked her faith. Thought back to the kids who parked on their property around the lake—horny high schoolers looking to get their rocks off away from prying parents. The same parents who scorned the Obviate and their faith.

Maybe there were other ways to save them.

She searched her thoughts for something better, more positive, but there was only anger.

Act on it.

It wasn't her thought, though it was in her head.

"He is speaking to *us*," The Elder cried. His fingers massaged the glowing cracks of stone with passion.

Zohra's eyes were heavy, but the awe she felt was considerable. Was this a reward for their devotion? Had God truly arrived in their Hall of the Arrival?

The Elder took her arms in his hands. He caressed them up and down as if enjoying the way her skin felt against his fingers. "The time has come to make you a priestess. You will spread His gospel daily. Right here."

"And what of the temptation?" Zohra spoke with courage she did not know she had. "Does my flesh no longer tempt you?"

"We were tested," he said. "We persevered. Mostly. Those who did not were...dealt with." She followed the tip of his finger to a stack of corpses: six men naked and bruised. Their genitals had been removed and their bodies were little more than bloody, shapeless pulp. Beside them was the young freshmen girl from New Haven. Her legs splayed open, a pool of dried blood between them. A single gash drawn across her neck. "She was the test. And those brothers failed. They could not help themselves. And so we saved them the only way possible."

The sight should've repulsed her. That young girl had been trusting. She'd come along in search of a better life. Yet something about the Elder's solution spoke to Zohra. She stepped close to the bodies, unable to focus on anything other than the need to continue toward this kind of salvation.

Maybe there were other ways to save them.

"A priestess," she said, turning the thought over in her head.

"The first daughter of the Obviate." The Elder smiled. "He asked for a daughter. One who understands alternate passages to deliverance."

She thought again of the people of Forest Grove. All the

faces she could not wait to deliver. "This is an honor."

"It seems the hour is later than we thought," he said. "Therefore, we will make them be saved."

The bursting light was hot and blinding as she approached it with arms outstretched.

Save them all.

She fell to her knees as it spoke to her and only her.

"What is He saying to you?" The Elder asked.

She had no intention of answering. In her most private moments, Zohra wondered if she wasn't crazy for trusting in the existence of a higher power. Now this. Finally, some sense of validation—all good things to those who believe. She wiped tears off her cheeks and allowed the invasion of her thoughts.

"The time has come," he said. "To take those in need of saving."

The brothers got to their feet and their chanting rose to a fever pitch.

"Repent and submit."

"Repent and submit."

"Repent and submit."

"This is what we must do," she agreed. "It's what I've always wanted to do." No more talking. The only way to prevent their extinction was to hand deliver the sinners to hell. It's what He wanted.

And what He would have.

 **Eight**

Brady grit his teeth as the backhoe scraped the coffin top.

Caretaker Eddie Rawls shouted some colorful profanity about squirrels fucking. A few stone rows away a mother covered her son's ears and hurried him from the plot they were visiting.

"Keep it PG for the morning crowd, Rawls," Brady said. "I know you and your salty-mouthed drinking buddies aren't usually up before noon, but some people don't speak sailor."

Rawls was an old Coast Guard retiree. He and a group of like-minded veterans spent their nights at the Tankard over on Biscayne, rehashing war stories, comparing scars like that scene in *Jaws*, and talking about the sorry state of affairs the country had apparently fallen into.

"Chief, I don't know why anyone thinks this sucker's alive. Is this how you look for a killer these days? Digging in the ground?"

"Enough," Brady said and watched the caretaker climb off the backhoe and then down into the unearthed grave. Rawls fumbled with the crowbar and Brady chewed his lip while studying the copy of Cyrus Hoyt's death certificate in hand.

The faded and photocopied typeface pronounced Hoyt dead as of 8:48 am on Saturday, July 9, 1988. County physician Samuel Valeri signed the document, along with then-coroner Larry Fraser.

This official proof eased a small part of him—the part that might've gone on wondering. Even if Hoyt wasn't in the ground now (*please be in the ground*), he had stopped breathing long enough to be pronounced dead. He understood Melanie's apprehension, though. After that kind of insurmountable loss, she had every right to feel afraid.

Rawls' face was beat-red with pressure and his forearms bulged as he pushed down on the pry bar. The coffin creaked open and a gigantic cobweb spread wide.

Empty.

Sending Melanie away with a clear conscience had been his only plan. All of this was to ease her mind, though he supposed he also wanted to be able to cross the most obvious suspect off the list.

"Sumbitch," Rawls said with a trace of amusement. "Looks like you might be onto something here, chief."

"First thing you're going to do, Rawls, is assure me this didn't happen on your watch."

The caretaker climbed out of the earth and raised his hands defensively. "Twenty years at this job and nothing happens in this cemetery without me knowing."

"Leave it," Brady said. If Hoyt had ever been in there, he wasn't stolen recently. "I'll have a guy come over as soon as possible with some questions for you. Rope it off for now."

The caretaker tried protesting and Brady shot him a *not now* look before hurrying off to the car. He asked dispatch if they were done at Desiree's place.

"Just about, chief. Sheriff's office sent a detective over a little while ago."

Brady had just come from the sheriff's manhunt HQ. They had established a mobile command center out on CT-341 and the continued search for Cyrus Hoyt was in full swing. They were also tracking Maylam's killer through the woods behind

Desiree's. His own guys were in the thick of it, with only Alex Johnson running interference for the regulars. The town needed to know there was still someone handling their day-to-day affairs. Johnson wasn't much, but he was keeping up appearances.

"Tell Johnson I want to talk to him as soon as he gets a chance."

"Johnson's been offline since last night. He checked in once the sheriff's office set up checkpoint and said he was going to start fielding all the local concerns we had put on hold."

"That's fine," Brady said. "Just get his twenty and tell him that he needs to check in with me. I don't want anyone going this long without an update. And tell Sleighton to meet me at the station. I need to know how the county physician and coroner signed off on the death of a man whose body has apparently been missing for twenty-five years."

Google had never heard of Tullus Abblon. It mistook her query as one for tulips, bringing her to a page for green thumb enthusiasts.

Melanie groaned at the prospect of another dead end as an old man pushed into the police station lobby. He was probably mid-60s and had the grandfather motif down pat: a belt cinched tight around khaki pants with a Hawaiian shirt tucked into the waist. He stopped and smiled.

"Melanie Holden?" he asked. "I was wondering when I was going to get the opportunity to see you."

"Yes."

"Chief Ronald Sleighton," he said. "Retired. We met twenty-five years ago. I was a lot more fit back then."

"Chief Sleighton." She rose to shake his hand. Now he looked slightly familiar, if much, much older.

He had come to her rescue that night, stumbling across a blood-caked and nearly catatonic teenager. His compassion sheltered her from the three-ring circus that broke out around Hoyt's killing spree.

His hug was soft. "I'm glad you're okay. Nate said you were leaving town. We're all worried sick."

"I am leaving," she said. "Soon."

"Okay." He ushered her inside the station proper, his fingertips bristling against her shoulder blade. "Nate won't mind if we wait in his office. You want the truth of it, still feels like mine most days."

The station was silent—a sign of respect for their fallen comrade, no doubt. Melanie knew where Nate's office was, but allowed the old chief to lead the way.

He closed the door behind them and offered her coffee, water, or anything else she wanted.

She wanted Nate to get here.

"I understand that our chief of police is jumping through hoops to ease your mind," he said. "I'm glad he's inherited my chivalry." Sleighton must've seen the offense in her eyes, because he stuttered out some clarification. "Not that you need rescuing, girly, I don't think anyone else your age could've done what you did. Hoyt's face looked like hamburger by the time you were finished with him."

"If only I *had* finished him."

"Hoyt *is* finished," he said. "Nothing but a bad memory now."

Melanie groaned. "That's what I keep hearing." Protesting felt like a waste of time. She respected Ron Sleighton and it was heartbreaking to find him clinging to the same script the rest of the town had doubled down on. Why ignore the possibility that Hoyt lived?

"Ya keep hearin' it 'cause it's the truth. Whoever came

after you last night wasn't Hoyt."

"Okay."

"This a social call, then?"

"No," she said and folded her arms. "I might have found something important and want to see that Nate gets it."

"You can leave…whatever it is with me. I'll make sure he gets it."

Melanie was growing less nostalgic for Sleighton with every passing second.

"Don't feel funny," he smiled. "Nate's my son-in-law."

"I don't feel funny, chief. But this is something that Na… *Brady* and I discussed, so I'd rather put the information in his hands. He can do with it as he chooses."

"My curiosity's piqued," he said. "You haven't been here a week, so I'd love to know what you managed to dig up."

"Just a name."

The chief's eyes flashed annoyance and Melanie decided that she was in no mood for it, firing back her own glare in the percolating silence.

Finally, Brady made his way through the station. He looked worried as his face passed from Sleighton to Melanie.

"Girl's got some news for you," Sleighton said. "Wouldn't give them to me."

Melanie watched the old man hobble out and Brady closed the door.

"You okay?" he asked.

"Fine. I think I have something for you."

She went through the whole story, culminating with today's stop at Last Mile Gas that led to an old invoice with an interesting name on it. Tullus Abblon.

"Never heard of him," Brady said.

"You wouldn't have. From what I can gather, something happened on Lake Forest Grove long before Cyrus Hoyt attacked me and my friends." She pulled a folded invoice from her pocket and dropped it onto his desk. "Something involving Tullus Abblon and the 'Church of the Obviate.'"

Brady studied it. "You think this has something to do with Hoyt?"

"No idea. Jed seemed to think so. And since someone likely killed him, I think it's the only thing we've got to go on."

"Let's say you're onto something. I've got a dead police sergeant on my hands and we're still in the dark as to who killed him. Tullus Abblon might be the key to your book, sure, but I can't worry about this right now."

"I get it." Melanie got up, feeling both energized and confident in the wake of her discovery. "Does that mean you're incapable of proving that my boogeyman is a pile of bones?"

"For now," Brady sighed. "I had Cyrus Hoyt's grave exhumed..."

She didn't have to hear the rest. "Do you believe that he's out there?"

"I wouldn't be surprised if Maylam's killer had that damn corpse stashed somewhere."

"Or Hoyt was never dead…"

"I exhumed him because I thought for sure he'd be there. I wanted to help ease your mind, and now I've got more questions."

"That's one of the nicest things anyone's ever done for me," Melanie said. "Sadly."

He offered a tired breath and said, "You deserve better."

So do you, she wanted to say, but refused the hackneyed sentiment. Instead, she told him that she wasn't leaving town. Not when there were more puzzle pieces on the board than ever before. The trick was figuring out how they all fit and that would take more work. It was almost enough to take her mind off being terrified.

"After everything that's happened, you think it's safe for you here?"

Not really. It was a terrifying prospect to be sure, but running back home to a self-made prison of motion detectors and surveillance cameras wasn't any better. "I've made myself a target. Who's to say that won't follow me home?"

"If you're going to stay, then you're staying with me," Brady said. "That's the deal. I'm not letting you out of my sight."

Fair was fair—though she wondered how literal a deal this was. Would Trish welcome Melanie into her home with open arms on the off chance that Nate got some down time one of these days?

Brady patted her shoulder and left his hand lingering just a moment too long for it to be meaningless.

Dispatch buzzed the office phone and Nate put it on speaker. "Chief, I just got a call from the sheriff's office. Some of the guys crawling the forest stopped off at Henny Yurick's place and found signs of a struggle…some broken furniture and recently dried blood hidden beneath a throw rug."

Brady's jaw tightened.

"Come with me," he said and headed for the parking lot.

"Where are we going?"

"I think I know who our killer is."

She escaped.

Again.

Last night he had waited beneath Melanie's bed, imagining the sound of her peaceful breaths. At some point, she would come back and slip beneath the sheets and he would hear them. He wanted to listen for hours. Until her sleep was deep and danger the furthest thing from her mind.

Only then would it have been time to plunge his blade into her neckline.

The uproar started before Melanie ever got back. A young policeman made his way into her room. He did things to her clothes. Sick things. In his younger days, the one called Elder would've lashed him for even thinking about doing them.

But he never paid those teachings much mind—mainly because he couldn't understand them.

The policeman raided Melanie's belongings, sniffing her underwear while calling her names through gritted teeth. It went on for a while and Hoyt did nothing but watch—fascinated and confused.

When Melanie returned, the unwanted intruder pulled a mask down over his face and put a coat over his uniform before leaving, breathing heavy as he went.

This was a problem. No one else was allowed to take the woman—especially not after all this time. His remaining eye demanded the privilege of watching the life escape from hers.

Hoyt managed brief pursuit, blood coursing through his veins, driving him on. He felt invincible and determined while rushing down those stairs, surprised that invasive feelings of protectiveness were propelling him: she had to live long enough to die by him.

And then that pervert policeman garroted one of his own, slicing his neck wide open. Hoyt saw it from the second story landing and picked up his pace in an effort to kill Melanie before she could get outside. But she was faster than ever and all he could do was watch from the shadows. He felt helpless. A feeling he did not much care for.

It was strange rooting for her to fend off the unwanted competition.

When it was done, there was no choice but to follow the policeman. This kind of thing could never happen again and it

was up to him to prevent it. He followed him through the forest
to his own personal vehicle, slinking into the backseat while
the injured man changed outfits, bandaging his wounds with a
pathetic whimper.

Hoyt hugged the floor and waited for an opportunity to
strike.

An opportunity that took longer to arrive than expected.
The policeman had thrown his bloodied mask into the empty
seat and sped off for home, but he didn't stay there long. Before
Hoyt could seize the moment, the policeman washed and
sprinted out to his patrol car.

Hoyt watched him leave and stayed behind to plan his
murder.

The situation wasn't ideal. Suburbia made him feel out of
his element. The forest afforded more stealth and protection than
these rows of prying neighbors and playful children. There was
no way of knowing if this policeman lived alone, though a quick
check of living conditions said it was probably the case. He just
needed to wait for him to come back.

And he finally did.

He drove his patrol car into the backyard and popped
the trunk. Then he pulled open the basement bulkhead and
dragged a dead body into the basement. The policeman looked
disheveled and desperate.

Then there was a racket beneath Hoyt's boots. He glanced
down at the floor and waited for the fuss to subside.

At long last there were ascending footsteps on the cellar
stairs.

Here was an enemy whose actions were impossible to
predict. Hoyt knew enough to assume the washroom would
be one of his first stops, though. So he had slipped inside the
closet opposite the toilet bowl and pulled the knife from his belt,
rubbing the balled-edge of the hilt as he listened and waited.

Grumbles of *"killing that whore"* came from the hall. What had Melanie done to deserve this? It troubled him the more he thought about it. He was not used to the competition and did not savor the feeling.

Then came the sound of a shower and Hoyt listened for the rip of the curtain to indicate his prey was inside it.

He excused himself from the closet and pushed through the ghostly steam. No need to prolong this because he wasn't enjoying any of it. Killing the helpless was much more fun—especially women. The way they felt and how they died.

He took the curtain in his fist and tore it off the rod. A naked man jumped back, startled, with blood running from his hairline. Hoyt took him by the neck. With a growl, he slammed the policeman against white tiles and buried the knife low in his stomach, slicing upward in anger.

The cop tried to fight, but the more he struggled the worse it got. Jerky movements caused his guts to spill out, plopping into the tub like meat on a cutting board.

Hoyt realized he didn't have to do more than that. It was over.

He didn't even bother to clean up, choosing instead to leave the water running and the lifeless corpse bleeding out in the tub.

Brady slipped the Glock from his holster and started up the incline to Alex Johnson's front lawn.

What an idiot I've been.

He told Melanie to stay in the car and wait for backup, which was en route. Donnelley and Galeberg had come in off the manhunt and were munching crullers in the HQ canteen tent when Brady ordered them back into town.

Dammit, though, he should've seen it. When Melanie was out at the camp, swearing up and down that somebody was in the cabin with her, it must've been Johnson. Johnson, who either before or after had killed the only one who could refute his story: the old hermit and local scavenger, Henny Yurick.

Johnson had claimed he scolded the hoarder for grabbing a few knives out of the cabin. Brady didn't think anything of it, because Johnson had worked under Sleighton for a few years and he assumed the guy, and the rest of his department, were on the up and up.

Now he understood not to make those assumptions.

Johnson lived in a neighborhood of impeccable lawns and cultivated flower gardens. Brady moved across the fresh-clipped glass, hoping he was completely wrong. His boots landed on the doorstep with more of a thud than he would've liked, side-stepping the doorframe in case Johnson had seen him coming.

You never knew what a desperate man would do once he was cornered, and Brady regretted bringing Melanie along for that very reason.

He slipped the gun behind his back and knocked.

No bustle.

Brady stepped onto the lawn and went to the front window, peering into a sparsely decorated living space that looked like a furniture showroom. Johnson never had the guys over, not for Sunday barbecue or an after work beer, and definitely not for poker night. He wondered if any of the guys had ever been here.

Melanie looked on from the car. He wanted to keep her in sight until backup got here, but worried what he'd miss inside. And wasn't there a muffled voice in there calling for help?

It's going in the report that way.

Brady kicked the lock. On the fourth try, the jamb exploded and the door opened.

Johnson's minimalism wasn't confined to the living room.

The kitchen was bare. Only basic appliances—a coffee maker and can opener—sat atop naked counters. Not even a half bag of sandwich bread littered the shelf space. The dining area served as storage. No table or chairs, just boxes stuffed into a corner. Not unusual for a bachelor's pad. The house must've been at least 1200 square feet—more living space than a single guy needed.

Shower steam seeped out from beneath the bathroom door. Brady tensed as he took the knob in his hand, twisted, and pulled. Johnson was draped face down over the tub wall, his guts strewn across the tile floor like spilled pasta.

Brady shouted "officer down" into his two-way and swept the house. In the distance, sirens cut a swath through the last remaining strands of small town tranquility. The grove was coming apart at the seams.

Once the first floor was clear, he found the basement. A smell akin to putrid meat hit him on the way down. Buzzing flies grew louder with every step. A light bulb chain brushed against his shoulder and his hand swatted around in the dark to find it, fingers at last giving it a tug that revealed a stone slab cellar.

A wet trail of blood ran from the outside bulkhead steps into the far corner. A body was splayed on its back at the base of a stainless steel tank. Stacked against the wall were containers of lye.

Brady froze, realizing what this meant.

"Son of a bitch," he said and approached the body with recognition.

One of the men responsible for giving Cyrus Hoyt a clean bill of death: retired county examiner Samuel Valeri. He was a fresh kill, shot six times in the chest, bullet holes that looked like little craters spread across his upper torso. His face was paused in a permanent scream.

Valeri's body was about to be boiled and then dissolved in

lye solution. The gigantic steel tank sat quiet and Brady expected to find the liquefied remains of someone else inside. He guessed the Audi driver and his two friends.

Alex Johnson was the grove's youngest cop. Twenty-six and with four years in the Marine Corps. The guy didn't lack for community contributions, either. Tireless work with local charities, multiple hats at the summer fair and, when he wasn't working on Sundays, he offered the elderly rides to church. But this was the spot of his darkest hobby. Near the bulkhead was a line of implements displayed across rows of hooks. Commonplace tools in any other cellar—hatchets, a pitchfork, and machetes that tied Brady's stomach into knots to look at them here.

The industrial-sized tank sitting beside a surplus of lye troubled him even more. It suggested that Johnson was settling in to do this for the long haul. This chemical vat might've been at home in a mortuary, but it looked positively creepy in a residential cellar. Brady wasn't familiar with the process but knew the gist: the body slides into the tank with some lye solution and nearly a hundred gallons of water. From there the mixture boils, bathing the corpse in increasingly scalding water and chemical mixture. At 300 degrees, chemicals break the body down, reducing it to a dark and oily liquid with remnants of bone fragments.

All you had to do then was pour the sludge down a drain.

Brady headed back upstairs, careful not to disturb the crime scene as he went. Donnelley and Galeberg were walking across the front lawn with Melanie in tow as he stepped into the dusky evening.

"Johnson's dead," he said to no one in particular. "And there's a body in the basement. Possibly more than one."

The officers exchanged confused glances and then went in to see for themselves.

"If I knew what to say at a time like this…" Melanie said.

Brady shook his head. "Didn't know him long enough to be outright shocked, but…the kinds of things he was up to down there…it makes you question everything. Makes me wonder how in the hell I could've missed it."

"He fooled Sleighton too, right?"

"Speaking of that," Brady grabbed for his two-way and called dispatch. "Tell Sleighton to get over to Johnson's place."

He went back inside and allowed Melanie to followed. The officers came up from the cellar wearing pale faces.

"We need to get county forensics here." Brady tapped Donnelley on the shoulder and motioned to the front door. "Get on the horn." Then he gave the rest of the house a once-over. With a gloved hand, he flipped the light switch in the bedroom. Johnson slept on a frameless mattress and the air in here was crisp—like the space was cleaned often and never used. Against the wall, a series of votive candles arced out in a semi-circle to form a makeshift altar around a battered version of the holy bible.

"Church of the Obviate," Melanie said and peered over his shoulder. She spoke like there wasn't a doubt in her mind. Was she right? Or was she connecting dots that didn't exist?

"We don't know what this means." Brady's tone didn't sell his words, because he didn't believe in coincidences. He went into the room and knelt beside the bible. Three Polaroids dropped to the floor when he lifted it.

Brady turned the first one over. It was a picture of Melanie in jogging shorts, taken downtown at some point during the last few days. He grabbed the other two photos and expected the subject to be the same.

They weren't.

The second was of Trish during her hospital stay. She looked peeked—her skin ghostlier than usual, with all kinds of monitoring wires hooked to her. He stared at it, struggling to comprehend why Johnson would have done this. Then he remembered there was one more photo to overturn and hoped it might bring the picture into focus.

The last picture was of him.

There was no processing it. Three people who had very little in common beyond them being outsiders, some ways literal and other ways figurative. Brady felt more lost than ever and Melanie's conclusions weren't helping. Her logic was a stretch, but on some level he knew the connection between her story and this bloodbath was ready to be made.

He went through the rest of the house and found a stack of pre-paid cell phones in the hallway closet, making it fairly easy to discern the identity of Melanie's texter. There was nothing else of interest to be found and a gathering of neighbors had collected at the foot of the driveway where Galeberg ran interference while they waited for support.

"He killed Samuel Valeri to keep something from me," Brady said. "God knows why he took those kids out, but you and Maylam probably would've ended up back here too if you hadn't fought him off."

Melanie's bright blue eyes shimmied. "Johnson attacked me last night. Whoever was upstairs in the bed and breakfast is your second killer. Someone whose body isn't in the ground at Eternal Walk Cemetery."

"Are you smiling?"

"No," she said. But she was. "It's just that this…well, it tells me that I haven't been losing my mind."

"For all we know, Hoyt's body was turned to soup in that basement long ago. I don't know if this is a break or a hard reset."

"What if it's Tullus Abblon?" Melanie said. I find an invoice that references some kind of religious organization and almost right after that you find at least a possible connection."

She was right and that bothered him for a dozen reasons. Johnson had gone right for Valeri, which supported the theory that there was a larger picture to worry about.

But they were at a dead end.

Except for one place.

Brady glanced at Melanie. "You think you're up for a road trip?" he asked.

The sheriff's guys were tearing apart Johnson's house by the time Sleighton got there. The street looked like a circus: groups of spectators lined it, filling in the available gaps between police and fire vehicles.

He knew what this was about and it was hopeless. He'd been trying to discern *their* identities since forever and didn't envy Nate in the slightest. The kid was exactly where he'd been back in the day—nowhere.

Sleighton touched the handgun beside him, realizing this was as far as he could go by truck. No way of knowing how many of *them* stood between here and his destination. Johnson's house wasn't even visible from this distance and the gathering on the street looked like Paul Simon was playing Central Park.

He rolled his truck onto the sidewalk, holstered the gun, and hoofed it a half-mile past the throngs of commotion, leaving his weapon unclipped in case he needed fast access to it.

Brady waited on the sidewalk in front of the house. He threw a pair of rubber gloves at him and asked where he was parked.

"Back there," Sleighton said.

"Let's take a walk."

They talked on the way back and Brady told him

everything they knew, which wasn't much. Once they were inside the cab, Brady had him put on the gloves and then tossed an evidence bag into his lap.

"What's this?" Sleighton asked.

"Johnson's attempt at a journal."

Sleighton struggled to keep his hands steady as he fished the book from the plastic bag. He leafed across mostly empty pages before finding a few scribbles in the very front. It was gibberish, but that didn't stifle his sudden urge to vomit. After all this time, at least one of his guys was part of this.

Sleighton read the scribbles and shrugged. "What's it mean?"

"You don't know?"

He glanced through the pages again, thumbing back and forth between them. It was Johnson's handwriting, no doubt. He'd read enough of the guy's reports to recognize his chicken scratch. But the content was so vague that he doubted anyone could make sense of it. It was proof that Johnson had a few screws loose, but that was a foregone conclusion following tonight's discovery.

No matter what I do, the whispers find me. Inside or outside, they remain. They know me better than I know myself. Used to think I was going crazy. Now I know it's my purpose. Because others hear them, too.

"Ron," Brady said. "With all due respect, you didn't know that your man had flipped his fucking lid?"

"Brady, same respect, did you?"

"Three months, Ron. That's how long this kid was under my command. But he worked under you for what? Four? Five years? And in all that time, you never had so much as an inkling?"

"He wasn't non-functional, though, was he?" Sleighton said. "Yeah, the kid was under my command, but I wasn't looking in his windows at night and you weren't either. He never tripped our triggers, son. That's the bottom line."

"Seems there's only one way to interpret this," Brady said. "Johnson's telling us there are others in Forest Grove just like him."

Another simple conclusion, but Nate wasn't going to get any further than this. They, whoever they were, wouldn't allow it. They felt emboldened now. With the exception of one incident years back, they let the grove live in peace. They had their own beliefs and practiced them in private—without confrontation. But now they were angry with Trish.

He had to get to her, but this required a delicate balance. Nate couldn't know about the threatening phone call because it would set him off in ways that made him uncontrollable. Then he'd start arresting people by the busload. And the grove wasn't ever coming back from that. It was in this town's best interest to handle things quietly.

When Sleighton realized he'd gone silent for too long, he said, "I wouldn't be so eager to take this guy's words literally. Look at this babble…he was cracked."

"Johnson was ours," Brady said. "He'd be dead to rights if he wasn't already hollowed out. He had photos of Trish, that Holden girl, and me in his place. He must've been the one trying to scare her off. But who killed him? At this point, I'm ready to believe Holden when she tells me it was Cyrus Hoyt."

"Forest Grove doesn't need boogeyman bullshit. It needs this to go away, ASAP."

"Did you know that Hoyt's body isn't buried at Eternal Walk?"

Sleighton was never more thankful for his ability to deadpan. He shrugged the question off like it hadn't been asked. "I can't think of a single person who might've disliked Johnson," he said. "That's why this doesn't add up."

"And you're sure you don't know what he's talking about in

those pages?"

"Gibberish."

"What about this?" Brady dropped a folded slip of paper in his lap.

It was a photocopied land deed from a local attorney. It signified the ownership of Camp Forest Grove had been transferred from the Dugan family to Alex Johnson.

"You're shitting me," Sleighton said. He had a sinking feeling as to why Johnson might've wanted that land, but how in the hell could he afford it on his salary? As disturbing as this was, it still wasn't at the top of the list. "Say, the Holden girl told me she found a name for you."

"She did," Brady said. "Pulled it out of thin air over at Jed's Last Mile."

"What was it?"

"Tullus Abblon. Ring any bells?"

"No," Sleighton said. "Never heard of…it's a him, I presume?"

"I think so," Brady said. "I sent Melanie on a road trip. Figured it would be good to get her out of town. One less thing I have to worry about. Ernie Oviedo coughed up Tom Lawson's address out in New Hampshire. She's going to run that name past him to see what he knows."

"A lot of help he'll be." Sleighton's poker face was unable to hide his disdain for former state trooper Tom Lawson.

"That's why I'm sending a pretty face," Brady said. "He wouldn't tell Oviedo anything in all the years they worked together. But someone like Melanie Holden knocks on his door… maybe it'll be a different story."

"He's nothing but an asshole. He won't help her any more than he helped this town."

Brady cracked the door to leave. "Since we're going to be at this all night, I wonder if you wouldn't mind checking in on

Trish."

"Happy to," Sleighton said. If Johnson had pictures of them, they were all in danger. With one woman out of town, he only had his daughter to worry about. She was all he had left.

He started up the pickup and did a three-point turn in the middle of the street. Someone stood on the corner, far removed from the commotion. A guy whose name he couldn't recall, but had seen around plenty. Didn't he work custodial up at the elementary school?

Sleighton drove past him slowly, rolling his window down for a better look. The guy rocked back and forth on the balls of his feet, waving. "See you soon, chief."

Then he disappeared into the crowd.

"Would you slow down, Dad?" Trish watched her father walk around the house, stuffing random things into an open tote bag without reason: mismatched clothes from a freshly folded laundry basket, men's deodorant, and three containers of lipstick from the bathroom. It would've been hilarious if not so disconcerting.

"There isn't any more time," he said. "Grab anything else you need and let's go."

"I'm not going anywhere. I'm calling Nate."

Dad threw the bag onto the oak table where it slid across the pledged surface. "Your…*husband*…let this town go to hell. Just like I said he would. He's trying to pick up the pieces but it's too late."

"I'm calling him," she said.

"Why do you think I'm here?" His pitch was nearly frantic now. "Nate asked me to look after you."

Trish wasn't a jealous person, but was still glad to hear

tonight's business had nothing to do with Melanie. A few of the friendly small town yentas had gossiped to her that Nate spent a lot of his time running around as her own personal concierge. She liked Melanie just fine, but couldn't deny that the news worried her.

Trish felt some unnecessary guilt over mocking her husband's efforts to comfort her a few nights back, realizing now that she might've started his *grass is always greener* train of thought where Melanie was concerned. But wasn't she entitled to a little anger? He was, after all, the fucking reason she was living this nightmare.

Now her father was looting the kitchen, tossing canned goods and bottled water into a second duffel. She'd never seen him this erratic.

If only she could take her mind off Nate and Melanie long enough to think straight.

Does my husband like her more? The problem was that she liked Melanie a lot. Granted, she didn't know her beyond a few conversations, but they were practically sisters in misery where Forest Grove was concerned.

She didn't want to think that the woman was trying to snake her husband out from underneath her. Trish knew she hadn't been the most pleasant person of late—and maybe Melanie was filling that void in Nate's life.

Dammit.

Trish knew she was in trouble, because even she found Melanie kind of sexy. The woman was in her mid 40s, with nice long legs, a curvy waist, and a flatter stomach than most girls in their 20s. There was a near-flawless quality to her milky white skin. And those beautiful blue eyes and wicked eyebrows made her look more seductive than a reclusive trauma victim deserved.

If there were flaws, it had to be her gigantic forehead. She masked it beneath blonde bangs, but it was there. Trish thought their tits were roughly the same size—Nate had a thing for petite frames. Worst of all, it was too easy for her to imagine her husband and new friend discovering common ground in the wake of personal tragedies.

No, Trish wasn't a jealous person, but she was beginning to feel that way.

Dad reappeared with another bag in his hand. "Let's go," he said.

"Not until I talk to Nate—"

"Call him from the road for all I care," he snapped. "Just get your ass outside, girly."

Night fell on Forest Grove. The streetlamps flickered and cone-shaped patches of light lined the road. A cool wind blew the curtains aside and the neighborhood was so quiet that not even that dog with its annoying kennel bark was yelping.

"You said something happened tonight," she said. "Give me details or I'm not going anywhere."

Dad took her in his hands. His face was almost crazed. "Why can't you just trust me?"

"Because you're scaring the shit out of me!" she cried. "What am I supposed to think when you come in here like a man possessed, treating me like your fucking property. How about telling me why you're so spooked?"

"One of our guys went on a killing spree before getting himself clipped," he said. "That's right, turns out Alex Johnson killed Steve Maylam. We don't know who killed Johnson, but… there's reason to suggest the killer might be after you next."

Trish stifled a laugh. Could Nate break *any* news to her? It was Dad who called to tell her about Maylam and now he couldn't even pick up a phone to warn that she was in danger?

"What the fuck did I do?" she asked, knowing full well the answer. Lots of folks around here were unhappy with her rage against the dark ages. She never thought the grove would take it this far, though.

Fuck this place.

Last year, the Bradys were savoring a New York way of life. When Nate got booted from the force, she felt like a leashed dog being yanked away from a meaty bone. Her bartender's income wasn't much where bills were concerned and so they had to be realistic about where they hung their hats. There was a good gig opening up in the grove—one that Nate was suited for and that she could help him get. It offered safety, financial security, and lots of political mobility. She wasn't happy about it, but what choice did they have? It's what Nate wanted, after all.

Trish loved her husband. The beauty of marriage was seeing how well you maneuvered through the nightmares. She agreed to rote suburban life because it was the best thing for her partner. Stepping away from the city was like going cold turkey and there would be no more whiskey sips at the corner bar while talking about whatever indie movie was playing at the IFC in Greenwich.

"You can drink whiskey here…and we've got Netflix," Nate had said. Doing those things in your own home felt—lame, for the lack of a better word.

Trish felt like one of those soccer moms that had fallen headlong into a midlife *"is this all there is?"* crisis. She saw them around town, practicing half-hearted hobbies out of desperation as opposed to desire—something to pass the menial hours of their empty days. More shambling zombie than human being, Trish's greatest fear was becoming one of them.

Across the room, Dad watched her. "Come with me," he said. "Just for tonight. We'll see where we're at tomorrow. Fair enough?"

"Okay," she said. "Just let me get some things." She picked the duffel up off the table and dumped it out, heading upstairs to grab a change of clothes. A pair of comfy sweats hung off her dresser and she stuffed them inside on the off chance that she was able to get some sleep tonight. Then she looted the bathroom for a few exfoliating essentials—anything to help her relax.

Dad was raring to go when she came back, offering to take her bag as she walked past.

She shook her head and hurried out.

The truck's electronic locks snapped down as soon as they were safely in the cab. The headlights flashed on in time to catch a figure push through the trees dividing her yard with the neighbors'.

"You sure you don't want to leave town for a while?" Dad asked as the engine roared.

"If two police chiefs can't protect me, what chance do I have?" Her levity was punctuated by a gulp.

Dad backed out into the street and floored it as three shadows darted forward.

Trish saw the glinting steel from their blades in the streetlight as the figures came into the center of the street to watch their escape.

Major Thomas Lawson had seen better days.

The retired state trooper was wheelchair-bound with an oxygen tube running into his nose. Thick, globular wheezes came from his chest but his face remained hard—even with sunken features. It was easy to picture the militant law enforcement man he'd once been.

Brady had asked Melanie to drive most of the night to get here. She wasn't stupid—he wanted her out of harm's way while he looked for Johnson's killer. If that's what it took to find Cyrus Hoyt, then she was happy to go.

Because they also needed to hear what the old state trooper

had to say.

A liver spotted hand reached up to greet her in the doorway. "You'll excuse me if I don't get up."

"I hope it's you who'll excuse the intrusion," Melanie said. "I drove all night to be here. Chief Brady got your address through state police so that we might have a chat. I know it's impromptu—"

"Horseshit is what it is," he said. "But at least your lawman had the good sense to send a looker. Rather see a face like yours over some asshole's tough-guy stubble any day."

The old man ushered her into a sun-lit room so bright that Melanie's eyes fell into a permanent squint. Cigar odor hung heavy in the air and she felt like gagging.

"Goddamn doctors." Lawson cleared his throat and wheeled in front of the largest window. "For years they demonize the sun. *Stay out of it or you'll get the cancer.* Know how much jib I took for keeping a bottle of sunscreen in my cruiser? Now I'm retired and my doctor starts telling me that sun is *good*. That I need as much Vitamin D as I can get. One of the reasons we built this room. Soaks up the sun like a sponge. I sit here with my cigar and take it all in."

He stopped speaking and broke into a raspy cough, wracking his throat to force a mouthful of phlegm up into his mouth. He grabbed the nearby ashtray and passed a gob of yellow mucus before fishing a cigar out of a bureau drawer.

Melanie looked at the oxygen tank hooked onto the back of his wheelchair.

"I know, I know," he said. "You sound like my wife and you ain't opened your yap yet." Lawson waved the topic away. "Talk to me. I don't know this Brady guy, but Oviedo says he's got a mess on his hands."

"You might say that. I'm staying in Forest Grove and—"

"Tells me all I need to know."

"I guess I'd like to know what makes you say that. For starters."

Lawson blew a puff of smoke overhead and studied her. "You a reporter?"

"I was at Camp Forest Grove the night Cyrus Hoyt killed those people. He tried getting me too, but…I got him first. I went back recently to try to get some thoughts down on paper…for my memoirs. And things started happening."

Lawson gargled up another wad of phlegm and spat it out the corner of his mouth. "Christ, kid," he said. "You sure were dumb to go back. And why doesn't your chief know what's going on in his backyard?"

"That's why I'm here."

"I'll tell you this…I hate that town. Part of the reason I moved as far away as I could. Only you're making me realize I didn't go far enough."

"Major Lawson," Melanie said. "I need information. The only way for things to get better is if I can understand what's happening."

"You'll never figure that out," he said, voice quiet, almost tortured.

It was obvious that Lawson didn't intend to offer anything useful. The only thing left to do was try and bluff it out of him. Make him think she knew more than she did in order to get him talking. "Tell me about Tullus Abblon, sir."

"Who?"

"The Church of the Obviate," she said. Lawson might've been old and sick, but his eyes remained sharp and thoughtful. He wasn't giving up what he knew on a name alone. "You strike me as a man who knew what was going on in his backyard."

"Don't know where you got that name." His laugh carried the sound of inevitable expectation. "We erased that prick off the face of this earth. It's on me that we didn't figure out what he was doing until it was too late."

"How's that?"

"Abblon was like Jim Jones," he said. "Had a ridiculous cult at his beck and call. They followed his orders to the letter."

"Right," Melanie said. Time to volunteer the last of her knowledge in the hope Lawson's story would continue. "They hid out on Lake Forest Grove."

"And no one wanted them there," Lawson said. "But Abblon somehow got his hands on that property. The grove started seeing loads of hippies trekking through. Didn't like those religious wackos flocking to their little Roman Catholic community."

"Culture clash?"

"Wasn't so bad at first," Lawson said. "Kept mostly to themselves. Once in a while, they showed up in town looking to preach, but they were out of sight and out of mind. Until…"

"Please," Melanie said.

The old man drew sharp breath. Memories passed over the whole of his face, tightening his features one-by-one as he fought to reconcile with these buried ghosts. "Abblon and his followers went mad. Started killing anyone who came near…teens necking in the woods, the town drunk, a drifter…enough blood to raise suspicion. Had twelve missing persons in the span of a year. Local law liked Abblon for it right off. One of the grove's own cops saw the depraved shit they were up to…brought it to me. Got our orders off the record…"

Melanie hung on every word like a child at story time. "You mean…"

"Well, just so you don't think we made the decision lightly…I got called into a meeting with the superintendent and the governor…off the books. I have to know you'll respect that, too. Look, I'm giving it to you straight 'cause I remember the hell you went through. And I'm sorry for you, girl, but this ain't the kind of thing you get to regurgitate. I don't give a shit about me... my best years are long gone. But the guys under me were just doing their jobs. What they thought was right. Clear?"

Melanie nodded. The story could be redacted, saying only that *something* had happened out on there. She could frame it as speculation. Maybe people took justice into their own hands. Or perhaps the cult was destroyed by infighting. It was impossible to say now. She wasn't doing this to ruin any lives—especially when this was the case of a community protecting itself from pure evil. At this point, she only wanted to know the truth.

Lawson cleared his throat again in order to continue speaking. "It was decided that if we could make the whole thing go away, the killings, the cult, all of it, we'd be better off. Went out there without the knowledge of local law enforcement. Didn't know who in the grove was involved, so we played it safe. Showed up at dawn and gave them no quarter. Laid siege to their *church* and left none alive. We shot them like dogs."

"Jesus—"

"There were missing persons there," Lawson said. He took a long puff of his cigar. "Bodies stacked high and spread across that campground. Abblon had his people fan out across the state, abducting people for the soul purpose of hacking them to pieces. All to placate the same God you and I probably pray to. Was me who found Abblon, and with just two shots left in my magnum. I put him down and watched the son of a bitch bleed out."

Here's what Jed had tried telling her. Did that mean there were people in town who were Obviate? "Was that the end of it?" Melanie asked.

"Of course it wasn't. We stacked the bodies in the caverns beneath camp and burned them. The town had some idea of what happened, but didn't care enough to ask. They knew it was for their own good. Only we didn't get everyone."

"Some were off killing?"

"Hell if I know," Lawson said. "Beefed up patrols for the next month and watched all roads to town, checking for that very thing. If any of them had left camp before we got there, they never tried coming back. But old Ron Sleighton, your chief's predecessor, he's the reason for the grove's bad juju."

Lawson lapsed into a coughing fit so severe it didn't look like he'd ever get out of it. His chest heaved, ribs cracked, and his eyes went from looking like runny eggs to bloody ones. "You can't kill the status quo. Town's infected now."

"What did Sleighton do?" Melanie said.

"Fell in love, got indoctrinated…whatever. Smuggled a girl out of that place…and took her as a wife."

Melanie gasped and then cupped a palm over her mouth in embarrassment.

"None of us realized until it was too goddamn late," Lawson said. "We were supposed to exterminate the Obviate. For whatever reason, Sleighton saw fit to rescue a girl from that madhouse. And girl with a son…a son we thought had died during our march on Lake Forest Grove."

Melanie felt sick. This son would go on to kill her friends nearly twenty years later. If only Lawson and his men had been more careful, her nightmare wouldn't have happened. "Cyrus Hoyt," she mumbled. "He was a child of the Obviate."

"Bingo," Lawson said. "People reported some wild kid running around in those woods in the years following our deed. There were more disappearances, too, but we never found any bodies. Didn't know who was behind it." Lawson looked at Melanie with eyes that were almost apologetic. "Until you killed him."

"Sleighton is Brady's father-in-law," she said. "I thought he said that Trish's mother died when she was just a girl."

"Not true," Lawson said. "Zohra, I think that was her name, continued Abblon's teachings in secret, behind closed doors. I don't even think Ron knew about it until it was too late. After what happened in '88, we went back to Forest Grove. My last order of business as a trooper was to apprehend that crazy bitch. She lost her mind when she saw it was her boy been killed. And she's been locked up in an insane asylum ever since."

 **The Priestess**

1969

Zohra looked up at the impressive hand-carved crucifix that hung suspended over the pulsating light. She crossed herself and knelt beneath it, looking into the red glow with her heart outstretched. Its hue had changed from bright red to crimson blaze and her eyes watered the longer she looked at it.

Let me out, the whisper hissed. *Break this barrier and free me. If you do it...the things I will show you...*

Zohra was tempted to obey, as was often the urge.

"It is a test," the Elder said each time it was discussed. "He wishes to see which of us will claim the power. Remember, God does not tempt the lost."

Zohra agreed, but there was another explanation that troubled her. The good lord did not tempt his followers at all. She wondered if this beating glow wasn't their version of forbidden fruit. On the occasions where she considered this, a muted whisper always laughed somewhere between her ears.

They had built a nave around the light. The Elder did not want his parishioners having unrestricted access to the ethereal voice, choosing to limit their exposure to infrequent mass inside this makeshift church.

The whisper was too influential and the longer you were

around it, the harder it was to ignore. Her mind often felt fogged and Zohra wondered if her appearance was anything like the Elder's. His green pupils were completely colorless now, milky white, save for tiny black pinholes in the centers. She saw herself only in reflected puddles of cavernous rainwater and never that closely.

They did not allow the whispers to permeate their brothers and sisters. The Elder and the Priestess lied to themselves daily, agreeing that it was in the church's best interest. The reality was that Zohra worried about losing her influence and the Elder admitted the same. They confided in one another only in the private afterglow of their most passionate moments. The Obviate viewed the Elder and his Priestess as conduits to the Word and that's how it needed to stay.

Zohra might have doubted the divinity of the whispers, but she couldn't bear to let them go, either.

Free me and you will never have to let me go. We can come to know each other intimately and forever.

If you need freeing, Zohra thought with a chill. *Then what put you there?* What could be so wicked that it needed to be banished deep inside the earth and forgotten?

Something evil.

Raspy laughter ran across her brain and lingered like the trail of a wet tongue.

The nave's thick doors creaked and the Elder's frame stood in the darkened doorway. He only motioned for her.

Zohra walked barefoot across the rocky floor and found Jessica on her knees in the cavern beyond. Tears streamed down her cheeks. One of their brothers spat at the girl's feet, labeling her a deserter.

Zohra did not much care for the sadism in his voice, but the violence done to her was more troubling. Violence was reserved for the Lost—those who performed wicked actions and needed to be purged.

That was the only way to prevent Him from sweeping the world away in fire and brimstone.

"She is a whore!" Their brother screamed again, as if his point had not yet been made.

"Do not speak to her that way." Zohra knelt beside her friend and sister, thinking of how she'd rather sacrifice his arrogance than hear his grievance. "My dearest Jessica, why has our brother brought such accusations against you?"

The girl managed a slew of hysteric vowels. Quite incoherent.

"*Shhhhhhhhhhhhhhh,*" Zohra whispered. "It's me. It's Zohra. Whatever's happened we will work this out."

"I told you." The brother spat again. "Whore was fleeing in the middle of the night."

"Is that true?" the Elder said, taking a place beside the accuser.

Jessica nodded through her tears. "My mother is still alive. After all this time, the cancer hasn't taken her."

"You do not have a mother," Zohra growled. "You have *us!*" This girl had worn the Obviate face through endless sermons. How many times had she preached their word and encouraged their path to prosperity? All while harboring worry and regret over her mother? One foot in this world only. An insult.

This is an affront! She must die! The whisper was giddy.

Jessica deserved punishment. This much was true. But taking her life for what amounted to a weak moment—a lapse in judgment—was something else. Reconditioning was preferable.

"Bring her inside," the Elder's voice was so cold she expected to see his breath.

They got their sister to her feet and marched her forward. She whimpered as they walked, begging for forgiveness. Zohra tuned it out, giving her old friend a harsh push forward into the nave's seclusion. She slammed the doors and the Elder was already tearing at the girl's tunic, ripping it away with a savage growl.

"You are not suitable to wear this." His voice boomed through the chamber, startling even Zohra.

The deserter, this girl who had once been her friend, covered herself with trembling arms—truly painful to witness. Zohra's shoulders slumped in discouragement while she watched Jessica take backward steps away from the Elder's slow advance, bumping into a row of crudely constructed pews.

Sometimes they tormented the Lost in this way and it brought them genuine pleasure to do so. Rows of enthusiastic Obviate chanted the Elder and his Priestess on as they stabbed their sacrifices with daggers, completing for them their journey toward repentance. They took all ages without discrimination when the work of the devil was on display. This was war and in it all lives were forfeit.

Afterwards, they were allowed to indulge in the pleasures of the flesh, alleviating their pent up urges. Aggression and bloodlust expunged alongside the dirtiest of bodily fluids. It would have never entered their minds if not for the whisper's encouragement.

"Help me, Zohra." Jessica's screams were desperate.

"Shut up," she snarled. A piece of her, deep down, wanted to do as Jessica asked. But Zohra's hands were tied. "We were your family. Not the cancerous thing that brought you into this world. That vile woman allowed you to travel a miserable path. But the Obviate cared for you when no one else would and still you spit in our faces. In *His* face. He finds your actions insulting and without gratitude."

Have her first. Both of you. Defile yourselves in her blood.

The Elder wrapped his hairy arms around her naked torso

and threw her against the shimmering light. It seemed to expand as her body tumbled against it. She landed on her back and scurried in reverse, quickly running out of space to retreat.

"Just let me leave." Jessica's words wobbled. "I want to see my mother. I just want my mom!"

The Elder dropped down on top of her, belting her across the mouth while forcing her thighs apart.

Zohra glanced up at the cross and thought, *is this what you want?*

Oh yes, it purred back.

Jessica writhed as the Elder screamed a flurry of hatred into her face.

Zohra clasped her fingers around her blade's hilt and approached. For a split second—as long as she dared—she threw her old friend a sympathetic look. Their eyes met and held for less than a blink, but Jessica's eyes honed in on the knife as the last bit of fight deserted her.

Zohra dropped to her knees and plunged the blade straight through her eye.

The Elder leapt off the naked girl, wiping spurts of blood from his face as her body twitched on the ground.

"Our sister deserved more than that," she said, throwing the knife to the ground in a gesture of rebellion. "Will you do the same to me if there comes a time when I am weak?"

The Elder said nothing and there was no ceremony that night. Instead, the Priestess climbed from the Hall of the Arrival and walked the long, winding corridors for what felt like the first time in months.

She pushed up from the cellar and found the prayer hall outfitted with a grisly new addition. A decaying corpse had been arranged into a crucifixion pose, dangling above the altar table while a halo of flies swarmed around it.

"Lead us in early morning prayer, Priestess," one of the

sisters begged, dropping to her knees and reaching for Zohra as if her words might help reconcile these insane actions.

The dining room was even more macabre. Corpses of all ages were placed around the table, bound to the armrests and chair legs with chicken wire. A row of brothers stood along the wall, reading bible passages aloud with chaotic urgency, as if to rappel thoughts that threatened to overtake their minds.

All of the Elder's efforts to keep the whisper at bay did not seem to matter. It already had them all.

The realization made her laugh. Nothing about this place, this life, was worth defending.

The compound's grounds were dark and quiet as she stepped outside, sucking at fresh air for what felt like the first time ever. Taking Jessica's life had jostled the whispers from her mind like the aftereffects of a heroin high, even if its echoes remained.

She headed for the water. This place used to be so alive at night. Fires burning on the beach, beautiful hymns sung for as long as the voices would hold, and long talks of enlightenment that had a tendency to spill into morning.

A beautiful sense of community worth believing in.

It was a ghost town now. Abandoned for pleasures of the flesh.

What happened to us? To me?

A question to which she already knew the answer. Everything had fallen apart once they'd found the light. Whispers wormed into her most private thoughts, offering words that fanned the flames of her most repressed urges—stoking them until they were the only option. The thing that horrified her the most was that she had never been forced to do anything—the light did not have that power.

I did it because I liked it. We all did.

When acting on those impulses, it was like watching her actions through a foggy window. This wasn't God, but it was too late to warn anyone. They had embraced the Elder's violence and perversity without much goading, for they heard the whispers, too, and wanted more of them.

"You." Someone stood on the beach where the sand met the trees. "What are you doing here?"

It never occurred to Zohra that this might've been a stranger. This was their compound and those who got too close paid for their curiosity with their lives. She walked toward the familiar voice in disbelief and found the kind-eyed policeman there.

Officer Sleighton stood in the foliage with a shotgun in his arms.

"What am I doing here?" Her laugh was incredulous. "You can't be serious. You need to go before——"

"Save it," he said. "You lunatics don't come out at night. Too busy screwing each other's brains out by the sounds of it."

Zohra heard swirls of ecstasy at her back coming from some of the other cabins. Would any of them care that Jessica had been killed? Probably, but only because they weren't there to witness it. She had robbed them of a public execution today.

Sacrifice, Priestess, the whisper taunted. *Noble sacrifice.*

Execution, she decided.

"Ain't seen you around for a while," Sleighton said.

This was her first time seeing him outside his uniform. He wore an unbuttoned slicker with the hood pulled over his head.

"You've been watching us?"

"I started thinking you must've wised up and took off. That's what I hoped, at least. Now you show up out of the blue."

"I…was…" Her mind was hazy as she struggled to recall just how long she'd been down there. Meals had been brought to her for as long as she could remember, although it was impossible to recall the last time she'd eaten anything. She relieved herself in one of the far-off caves, same as everyone, and bathed daily in a natural spring.

My God, how much time has passed?

She felt weak and tired. Her eyes rolled back in her head and she swayed off-balance.

Sleighton caught her. "Jesus, you must weigh eighty pounds! Were they keeping you prisoner in there?"

There was no explanation for the things she'd done. Best to let Officer Kind Eyes think what he wanted.

"I watched them drag a few people inside unwillingly a few nights ago," he said. "You people were never going to get away with this."

"You can't stop them." Her eyes dropped to his gun. "Not like that."

"I'm not going to stop them," he said.

A rumble grew from the forest and before she had time to sort what her ears were hearing, a S.W.A.T. van smashed the compound's fence, followed by a parade of law enforcement vehicles on its bumper. They spilled onto the property without sirens or lights and bodies began filing out before the transports had fully stopped.

"But they are."

"What have you done?" Zohra said.

"Your people deserve this."

"This is all I have," Zohra said and realized she was pleading. Her thoughts segued to the apocalyptic visions the Elder had cautioned about. "Without us, you're dooming the world. Everyone will die in the purge!"

"We'll take our chances," he said and pulled her closer. "This is your chance for a new start. Let me help you…please."

The offer sounded similar to the one Tullus Abblon had made her. "Guilty conscience?" she asked. "You condemn my whole family to die, see me walking around and you think… what? That saving me is a means to justify yourself?"

"I'm not that deep," he said. "But if they find you, they'll kill you, too. No one gets away from this."

Was his offer the same kind of slavery in a different skin?

Gunfire erupted behind them as some of her brothers burst from one of the bunks and shot at the raiding party. In a second, the bunkhouse filled with smoke and horrible screams followed.

Sleighton eased her deeper into the foliage, out of sight. "This was never you," he said with a trace of desperation. "Don't let Abblon take you down with the others."

She turned back and started to say, *"My son's in there…"* but the words were whispers. She remembered what happened to Jessica when she refused to yield her old life. Cyrus wasn't hers anymore and hadn't been for a long while. He was the Elder's favorite son now, passing his days wandering the caverns and surrounding forest lost in thought.

"He's going to die." She sobbed in his arms as they retreated through the trees. The bunkhouse wall blew open, lighting the night afire with a series of endless muzzle flashes. "I thought I was giving him a better life." She wasn't telling Sleighton so much as justifying her own actions. Maybe mother and son had truly been better off before the Obviate entered their lives. Whatever happened then would have at least been up to her.

Who will prevent the end now?

She didn't know if that thought was hers, or if it was the whisper's continued torment. Either way, the question was valid. The Elder had allowed things to grow out of control, but his message remained. Zohra realized it was something she still believed in.

I will spread it, she thought. *On my terms, I will teach it. The people in town shall listen. Together we can prevent the end.*

The cries of her brothers and sisters were drowned out by

automatic gunfire as they made their escape.

She did not look back.

 **Nine**

Melanie spent most of the day in the car. First, it was a four-hour drive from Connecticut to New Hampshire, and now it was the noontime trek back the other way.

There was a lot of information to share with Nate and her optimism surged. Cyrus Hoyt was out there, no matter what anyone had tried to tell her, and now she understood why. He was just a boy when he saw his family killed and spent the next few years surviving on his own—until he was strong enough to defend his wilderness from invaders.

Hoyt's warped perception made a certain kind of sense, but understanding it didn't make him any less terrifying.

With any luck, the police would have caught a break in Johnson's murder investigation by now, creating an opportunity for her to steal the chief away for some quiet time. The information in her possession was energizing. She could almost feel twenty-five years of uncertainty falling by the wayside. Soon, everyone would know that Hoyt lived and that she'd been right to be afraid all along.

Mayor Cobb wouldn't appreciate the nuclear revelation. Drudging up a long-forgotten massacre would stomp out the town's last chance at a positive reputation, but she couldn't care about that now.

She would have to figure out where Zohra Sleighton was

institutionalized. If there was even a chance of talking to her, it needed to happen.

Something about that woman's fate was disturbing. Sleighton had offered her a clean break, but she *had* to pedal her gospel to whoever would listen. That religious devotion got her locked up. Maybe she deserved worse for unleashing her twisted ideals upon Forest Grove, but Melanie saw it as a kind of warning. Zohra's prison was literal, but they were both women defined entirely by the evils that lived on Lake Forest Grove.

The last few days made Melanie realize how tired she was—and never more scared for her life. But there was more to living than simply existing. She'd been so stubborn about things. Maybe it was because Nate had stirred long-dormant feelings in her, but that was only a part of it. Yes, he made her realize that there was a gigantic void in her life, one she wanted filled, but more importantly, she'd done what nobody had been able to do in decades—break the grove's despicable history wide open. It was incredibly liberating.

Almost empowering, as Trish might say.

Melanie pulled off an exit somewhere in Massachusetts and checked into a hotel just off the highway. No need for anything extravagant, just a room for the better part of the afternoon. Someplace anonymous where being stabbed to death wasn't a concern. The car ride was draining and she felt disgusting after having been confined to it for a majority of the day. The idea of soaking beneath a stream of piping hot water grew into an obsession. Hotel showers, with their consistent lack of water pressure, were usually awful, but this would do in a pinch.

I wish I could just go back to Desiree's.

She knew Desiree was probably dead and felt a surge of sadness for the sweet woman. If she hadn't ventured back to Connecticut, then maybe—no, that was crap. Nothing happening in Forest Grove was her fault. Time to stop lashing herself for things that were well beyond her control.

Melanie took her clothes off, tossed them onto the bed, and cranked the shower dial. It was the hottest, longest shower she could stand. Days of tension unraveled beneath the coursing stream. She stepped dripping from the bathroom and dialed the front desk, asking if they could bring up a toothbrush and a travel-sized toothpaste tube. No sense in getting this clean when her breath stunk of day-old coffee.

She wrapped a towel around her shivering frame and waited for the delivery by putting her clothes to the iron one-by-one until the day's wrinkles were gone.

The bellhop couldn't have been more than eighteen and Melanie traded him a three-dollar tip for the toothpaste. The kid's eyes were anxious, staring at the generous display of bare flesh above and below the towel. Glancing in the full-body mirror beside the door, Melanie realized the towel was much too short, leaving the bottom of her backside bare. When she'd turned to get money from her bag, she'd inadvertently given the kid a full view of the moon.

It would've mortified her if it weren't so funny. Turns out that Riley had been right after all. She had it, so why not use what God had given her? At 42, things weren't going to stay this shapely forever.

Melanie felt refreshed while slipping back into weathered clothes. Not perfect, but a good start. She checked out and sat in the parking lot for a long while, considering her options. Home was close by, but that lifestyle felt antiquated in the light of all this. No choice now but to see it through.

It was a little past six when she got back into Forest Grove. Nate's phone dumped directly into voicemail. She knew he wanted her at the police station so that he wouldn't have to worry, but there was daylight for another hour or two. Enough time for her to move around town without riling the shadows.

Melanie paused in front of City Hall and wondered if the mayor ever put in late hours. Would he have any information to contribute to her book? She would have to find a way to mention the Obviate without gloating, because she didn't want to step on his toes. But it was hard to imagine that he didn't know what had happened out there—at least on some level.

What the hell, she thought. *I'm going to have to get a statement from him at some point anyway.* What she really wanted was to look Cobb in the eye as she told him about Abblon. Wanted to watch his face flinch. Or not.

She parked in one of the downtown spaces and filled the meter with quarters.

The building was well kept. Polished wood lined the interior and recently buffed floor tiles reflected her as she walked. Most of the individual offices appeared closed. Her iPhone was on its last legs as she fished it out of her pocket to check the time. Almost 6:30. No way anyone was working this late.

At the end of the hall, she hopped the steps to the second floor and went to the end. A woman came out of a door marked "Assessor's Office" and bid her goodnight without giving her a second look. Melanie tried asking where she could find Mayor Cobb, but she was already halfway down the stairs and taking a phone call.

The mayor's space wasn't hard to find. Two oversized oak doors at the end of the hall marked the entrance to it. The secretary's workplace was just beyond and led to an abandoned antechamber decorated with glass display cases of Native American art.

Melanie realized she was trespassing and turned to go, but her eye caught a few blood spatters on the beige carpet.

Her feet were frozen to the spot as she eyed the doors that would lead to the mayor. A hard swallow went down her throat like a stone, then she opened them.

The mayor's body was propped against his desk, as if sitting on an invisible stool. His head was missing above the jaw line, leaving his bottom teeth to point up at the ceiling. The rest of his skull sat in his lap, loose hands cupped over his ears.

Something was scribbled across the desk face in browned blood:

He never bothered to hear.

Melanie called the police on 2% battery life as she sprinted for the exit. Dispatch told her that Nate had just left and that she should come to the station and wait for him to return.

Melanie got as far as reporting Mayor Cobb's murder as her phone died. She pushed through the doors and stepped into the sun-blown downtown of Forest Grove, running across the street when a harsh whistle caught her attention.

She turned to see a man in a disheveled raincoat sitting on the curb. His clothes weren't just wrinkled, but covered in blood. The sidewalk was stained red on every side of him and if he wanted to kill her, he made no motion to stand up.

He simply stared.

Melanie couldn't get to the LaCrosse fast enough. The engine started up as someone screamed. People crossed the street toward the commotion now.

The killer never got up off the sidewalk. He barely moved at all. He just continued sitting in place like a statute. Only his eyes moved, even as people encircled him. He didn't care about them. He only wanted to see Melanie.

He was still watching when she stomped the pedal and sped off.

Brady sat in the gloom of his office, phone receiver tucked between his ear and shoulder. He'd been trying to reach Sally

Dugan for the better part of an hour, but she was, of course, unlisted and almost off the grid.

He got the number of Alex Johnson's lawyer off the land deed Xerox from the dead cop's house. A quick explanation of the situation and Johnson's lawyer passed him off to Dugan's guy—who proceeded to put him in touch with her.

Sally Dugan—Pete's daughter and the former owner of Camp Forest Grove—had never been out here as far as Brady knew. She lived in the Florida Keys and his call to that residence had just disturbed the entire household.

A barking dog and crying child serenaded him with irritating sounds while the land baron took her sweet time reaching the phone. It was only a little past seven, but maybe he was interrupting taco night or something.

When she finally got on the line, her tone was marked with annoyance that Brady didn't feel like dealing with. He introduced himself and cut to the chase. "I'm calling about the transfer of land from your possession to Alex Johnson's in the amount of—"

"You don't have to remind me," she said. "I'm not in the habit of selling land. By the way, if you're Forest Grove police, how come you gotta ask me about this? I sold it to one of your boys."

"Officer Johnson was killed last night in his home. We're trying to—"

"I have all kinds of alibis, man. Don't try to put that on me. You know how many times I fended off that lunatic?"

"Meaning what?"

"Meaning I wasn't going to sell that place," she said. "My father died putting his heart and soul into it. I always thought I'd get back up there one of these years and do the same. But man, those New England winters..."

"When you say *fended off*, what are you referring to?"

"Five, maybe six years of phone calls. Wasn't always him...

sometimes it was a woman. Or an old man. Did you have any trouble finding my number?"

"Yes."

"Right," she said. "Well, there's a good goddamn reason for that."

"They harassed you?"

"More than that. Came home one night and found a group of strangers standing on my lawn. Told me to think about selling that land because it deserved more respect than I was giving it. Said that if I didn't change my mind they would return for another chat. Wasn't a threat, but of course, it was."

"Could you identify them?" Brady needed to know who in this town had to be watched.

"Hell no," she said. "Look, that's the reason I gave it up. That and the fair price they offered for those ruins."

But there was no way Johnson could've afforded the seven figure asking price. That meant a group of them must've taken up a collection. Best case scenario was that Brady would find a paper trail around Johnson's bank account, but when had he ever been that lucky?

"Please don't involve me, chief. I sold off my involvement in Forest Grove when I signed over that land."

"The person who bought your land, Alex Johnson, could be mixed up in a series of murders. Did he, or anyone, tell you what was so special about that land?"

"Don't know. Don't care. Sorry, but I don't."

She was scared. And with good reason. This was so far beyond Cyrus Hoyt and Melanie Holden that he was starting to wonder how in the hell it had remained a secret for so long. Could there really be a conspiracy in Forest Grove? There had to be at least one other person involved, but if Sally Dugan reported revolving voices on the phone, there was a lot more than that.

That notion terrified him.

He ended the call as his radio buzzed to life. The crackle was startling. "Chief," Galeberg sounded panicked. "You'd better get over to Sleighton's place."

"What is it?"

"I'm not sure."

Brady was on his way to the car in a second. "I'll be there in five. Talk to me."

"Just got a report of shots fired. Donnelley was a few streets over. He's going to check it out."

Trish hadn't been answering her phone all day and now this. Shots fired at her dad's. He wanted to swing home first, but his gut said she was with her father—just as he'd asked.

Brady's heart was in his throat as he drove—he couldn't lose her. Their marriage hadn't been storybook, but he could never love anyone more than her. All he could think about was getting to her, and then to safety.

He suspected that Ron wasn't being straight with him last night and now it was obvious that he knew more than he was letting on. You didn't serve a town for as long as he did without hearing a few things.

Please let Trish be alive, he thought as the cruiser barreled down one street and then another. The town never felt so big and he never felt more helpless. Not even in New York City.

The fact that Galeberg couldn't tell him if his wife was there brought worried tears to his eyes.

It'll be my fault if she's hurt.

Brady clenched his jaw and pushed the pedal further, as if forcing it through the floor would make it go faster.

Trish watched her father from across the room—a

shotgun in his lap while he rocked in the old creaking chair. He was positioned so he could see between the slats of the drawn window shade.

It was the only source of light coming into the house.

She was a prisoner. Sitting on the floor, her knees pulled close to her face, Trish was long past the onset of cabin fever. When she got up to use the bathroom, it warranted an explanation and an escort—at least to the door. They ate canned food in pitch black while her suggestion to at least use the gas stove to warm the contents went entirely ignored.

"Dad," she tried for the umpteenth time. "I'm not going to stay here if you don't tell me what's happening."

He didn't flinch.

Trish got up to pace the length of the living room. The soles of her feet were cold on the red hardwoods. They had to go barefoot to reduce the noise. As soon as she'd asked who they were hiding from, he went quiet. The people that had been outside of her house with knives probably had a lot to do with it.

Her muscles felt tight as she stretched and thought of Nate. This was the first time since moving back that she could actually say she missed him. It was because she was scared, obviously, but she would give anything to be with him now.

She would've called him to say that if Dad hadn't smashed her phone to pieces while screaming that they couldn't trust anyone.

"I was almost out," she said mournfully.

"Girly?" He rustled in the chair. "You say something?"

"I said you have to talk to me," she said. "This is giving me the creeps. *You* are giving me the creeps."

Dad eyed the window slat, studying the sliver of light like a foreign object. Then he rose and crossed the room with arms outstretched.

Trish met him with reluctant steps and curled her arms

beneath his shoulders. First time in a while he felt like her old man.

"I'm keeping us safe, honey. That's all."

"I know…I just…well, I need to call Nate."

"Trust me, Nate is better off on his own now. We can't help him."

She pounded a fist against his chest in frustration, devastated by his ominous words. Anger bubbled up over everything he'd ever done—from punishing her as a kid, to sending Mom away like a dirty secret. She couldn't stand to see him now, and for a myriad of reasons. His hug wasn't a gesture of love. It was strategy—one last attempt to stem her anxiety.

"Stop that," he said, "I don't need you making noise."

"Why," she said, every syllable getting louder. If he was going to keep her here like a grounded teenager, she was going to rebel the only way she could. "I want to talk to my husband!" She was yelling now.

"Honey, I'm trying to protect you."

"From who?"

"From them."

"Who the fuck is *them*?"

The cellar door swung out as if on cue and someone was suddenly in the room—a woman whose face was obscured by the darkness. She went right for Dad with a butcher's knife just as every window around them exploded. Wiggling hands were inside now, breaking the panes apart, trying to force them open.

Trish screamed but her father was on top of it. He deflected the woman's assault and screamed for Trish to close the basement door. She ran to it and slammed it shut as a second silhouette—this one male—made his way up the steps. She jimmied a chair beneath the knob and hoped it would hold.

The intruder buckled beneath Dad's fist and she dropped to the floor. He didn't waste a second, hoisting the shotgun back into his hands and swinging its barrel toward the assailant, pulling the trigger.

The burst was deafening. Trish convulsed like an electrical current surged through her. The floor was wet and sticky now, but she couldn't look.

"Back off," Dad screamed to no one in particular. Intrusive hands continued flapping around at each window.

"This is on you, chief. All of it." The voice from beyond the glass had no inflection. "You are as lost as your daughter."

Dad's eyes connected with hers and he looked like a man who had aged ten years over the last twenty-four hours. More than just his disheveled hair and wrinkly skin, his eyes were tired and tormented.

One hand managed to unlatch the window, forcing it up. Dad pointed the gun at the glass. "Don't make me do this," he cried. The hand fell off the pane and disappeared back into the night.

"What do they want?" Trish asked.

"Our deaths."

The phone rang and she raced to it, certain that it was Nate. Not a moment too soon.

"Repent and submit," hissed a dry and monotonous voice.

Dad heard it and pulled the receiver from her hands, ripping the wired base from the wall. It smashed across the redwoods.

The back door rattled and a large shape filled the frame. The doorknob jiggled. "Repent," a woman's voice screamed.

Dad didn't want to hear it. He fired off another blast at point-blank range.

The puff of blood shook Trish. She bolted upstairs and clasped her hands over ringing ears. The old hallway hadn't been touched since she'd left for college and her room felt familiar as she slammed the bedroom door, sidling her weight against it to prevent intrusion.

Repent and submit.

Why was the phrase so familiar? It sounded like something that might've passed her mother's lips at one time. Trish had been a girl of only five when mom left, but memories of that night came flooding back. She suddenly remembered it like it was yesterday.

How could I forget?

She had been sleeping, forcibly awakened by a pungent odor that revealed someone standing inside her room. That someone came stumbling out of the shadows and she screamed when she saw his deformed face. His one good eye studied her with confusion.

That bloodied eye socket was all she could stare at as he lurched forward, scraping his rough hand against her cheek. She must've screamed because Dad charged up with Mom in tow, and he didn't waste time unloading his gun on the scary man.

Little Trish had jolted after every one of those thunderous eruptions, his blood dabbing her face as he stumbled back and slumped into the corner.

A knock at the door pulled Trish out of her recollection. "Stay here, girly," Dad said as the sirens approached. "Backup's coming. You find your husband and you leave town. Tonight. Understand?"

"Let them handle this, Dad."

"I thought they'd leave us be," he said. "But I'm the only one who can stop it."

Trish listened to his footsteps and wished she could go with him. Dad shouldn't do this, whatever this was, but she couldn't throw her life away and he wouldn't let her.

I'm too terrified to even move.

She looked at her old bed and touched the stale sheets, remembering Mom's hysterics as she charged the dead body, shouting *"Repent and submit"* in his ear like she was delivering last rites.

He came home that night because he was scared. There was no place left to go. Somehow, she understood that.

She remembered everything now, amazed that she could've ever forgotten.

It was the only time she'd met her brother.

A New Beginning

1988

Ron Sleighton heard his daughter's screams and knew at once what was wrong.

How did he find us?

The revolver was heavy in his hand as he took the stairs two at a time. The hallway had never felt more confined as he moved through it. The door to Trish's room was ajar and the space between was alive with the yellowish glow from her nightlight. He pushed it wide with his boot and leveled the gun.

Zohra was at his back, hands gnarled around his chief's jacket like eagle's talons.

Cyrus Hoyt was here. He hovered over Trish's bed with red hands. Somehow, he'd gotten inside.

Sleighton's heart was exploding, but he acted on pure instinct and with tunnel vision. Needed to get Hoyt away from Trish, no matter what. After everything this maniac had put the town through, it ended now.

Six shots thundered in quick succession. The room lit repeatedly with bursts of white-hot light. Every bullet staggered the behemoth back, his chest exploding in squibs of blood that littered his daughter's neon pink décor. Hoyt slid to the floor as the gun clicked empty.

The Holden kid had sworn up and down that Hoyt wasn't dead. When they scooped his corpse off that muddy shore, nose bitten off and eye gouged, the old dog looked like he'd seen his last day. Sleighton had been glad for it.

Hoyt had been on ice for three days and was finally ready for the ground. Larry Fraser was pulling morgue duty and planned on calling the second Hoyt's transport to Eternal Walk was complete. But that call never came because this madman had somehow climbed off the slab and put a hacksaw to Fraser's neck, cutting through the bone and taking his head off before escaping.

Knowing he was loose, Sleighton came back here to ensure his family stayed safe. He assumed Hoyt would be en route to Camp Forest Grove—what else did this mongoloid know? But there was always an outside chance that he'd come to find his mother.

Turns out, that's what he did.

He looked dead now. Smoke billowed up from freshly blown holes as his wheezing chest fell into stillness.

His mother threw her arms up like an overblown caricature and rushed to his side. Her knees dropped into pooling blood. Their daughter, white as a sheet, might've warranted more attention than the disfigured freak, but Zohra didn't seem to feel that way.

Sleighton went over and pulled her close, her tiny head nuzzled against his chest. He squeezed her, whispered that the monster was gone, and wouldn't hurt her. Her muffled cries were almost loud enough to drown out Zohra's ramblings.

But not quite.

Sleighton eyed her with a glare. She cradled the retard's bloodied head and stroked his limp wrist—like he was going to suddenly snap out of six bullets to the heart. Bloodied tails of spit swayed form the corner of his mouth.

"Repent!" She cried. "You've got to atone for the horrible things you've done, my son. Submit and accept His love before it's too late. Repent and submit! Repent and submit! Please, for the sake of your soul!"

Sleighton tried speaking over her, but his pitch couldn't match her hysterics. He lifted Trish out of bed and hurried across the room, keeping her cradled against his chest. They left Zohra babbling like some drug-addled whore and headed for a quieter part of the house.

He planted her on the downstairs couch. Her sparkling eyes followed him wherever he went. He brought her a glass of water and knelt down, strengthening his grip on her arms.

There wasn't much left to say, but he floated a few more quiet assurances to promise the worst was over. He didn't know if he believed that, but he needed her to.

Trish's sobs became infrequent sniffles after some time. She was doing better than her mother, whose jabber reached a fever pitch that culminated in a scream of anguish overhead.

A part of him hoped she had taken her life, but he caught the nasty thought and chased it away. Zohra Sleighton was the woman he loved. And she remained the mother of his child.

The upstairs floorboards creaked and shifted. Zohra came down and stared at the back of her daughter's head in silence. Sleighton took her arm into his hand and dragged her into the next room. She went without fight.

He couldn't contain himself. Once she opened her mouth to speak, he cracked her across it, slapping whatever words she had back down her throat. She winced, but didn't take her watery eyes from his.

"Did you know about this," he said. "You did, didn't you?"

She flashed a red smile.

"All this time we thought he was a campfire story..."

"*You* thought that."

"And you said nothing."

"It was my words that grew his legend...*Cyrus Hoyt haunts these woods, ready to attack...He comes by firelight but you won't see him... Don't know you're dead until he hacks...His axe through your bone will please him...*" Her expression hovered somewhere in between anguish and delight as she recited it.

"I should've let you die out on that lake," he said.

"I had to redeem Abblon's vision in the years that followed that night. You never understood that, or cared. But what I did for the church does not change the past...I abandoned my child...and I think about that every day..." Tears fell once more.

Ron shushed her for Trish's sake. "Your *child* killed seven people...maybe more. Ruined a teenage girl's life. And you knew he was out there this whole time."

"I had a mother's hope, Ron. Nothing else. I started that campfire tale because I wanted it to be true."

"He's a reminder of the sick things your people did to innocents."

"I am the Obviate now," she said. "And we're not murderers. You know this."

"What I know is that you chose your monstrous son over your terrified daughter back there. You showed your loyalty is to your religion."

"I saw my son again for the first time in twenty years. Just long enough to see you put six bullets into him. What I did up there was so his soul might find the peace in death that his life never had. My last chance to be his mother. If that makes me a monster, I don't care."

Never once had Sleighton considered what this had felt like for Zohra. Her son had been born when she was just sixteen—six or seven years before she got roped into Abblon's nonsense. She had never been a good mother—this by her own admission—and while she didn't speak of Cyrus often, her occasional tortured stares and vacant looks said the boy's uncertain fate haunted her more than she'd ever let on.

Sleighton took a moment to collect himself and allowed Zohra to do the same. In the living room, Trish's sniffles continued.

"Look," he whispered. "You need to put on a brave face. Take her and run down the street to the Hautanen's house. Stay there until I come for you. I've got a lot of cleaning up to do."

Zohra looked reluctant, but did as she was told. After a few minutes, the girls headed for the door.

Sleighton followed them into the mudroom and watched them shuffle into the brown Volare station wagon. The headlights broke the darkness and he demonstrated a half-hearted wave.

Once they were gone, he took the revolver from his holster. The spent casings fell on the floor like loose change as he pushed six more bullets into the swing out cylinder.

Let's get rid of you once and for all, you bastard.

Sleighton climbed the stairs again and found an empty room.

He studied the blood-soaked carpet. The rug was wet with Hoyt's impression, but nothing else. Bloodied footprints led back into the hall, but they were too small to be his. He remembered his wife kneeling in her son's blood and followed the trail anyway. One solitary splotch looked fresher than the rest. It pooled on the stairwell.

Sleighton checked the rest of the upstairs before heading down. The house was empty all over. He followed stains like they were breadcrumbs, but the blood circled back on itself as he swept the rooms—no way of knowing where the killer went after hopping off the steps.

If the legend was to be believed, Hoyt was a skilled woodsman who had gotten by on his own for years. He hunted his prey out of necessity and that need grew into something worse. It was entirely possible that he had intentionally confused the trail.

Sleighton toyed with the idea of calling for backup, but if Hoyt had escaped—again—then he was going to need his guys out there and on the lookout.

The mudroom screen door slammed and he leapt from his skin, bracing as he headed for the noise. If he had to gun down Hoyt on his front lawn, so be it. He'd already killed the boy once tonight.

But the entryway was empty. Spent casings littered the floor where he had thrown them and not even the wood axe was disturbed. It remained tucked into the corner where he had left it.

Another door slammed—this one somewhere in the house.

He turned, looking down the barrel of his gun.

Which one was it?

He decided it was the basement. Hoyt might've been planning to make an escape through there—a less conspicuous strategy than sneaking across the front yard after gunshots had awakened half the neighborhood.

Sleighton opened the door and started down. He was on the second step when he realized his mistake.

Hoyt hadn't gone down.

The knife slashed at his back and Sleighton tried whirling around to face it. He lost his balance on the limited space of the tread and the only place to fall was down.

He slipped from Hoyt's range and tumbled, smashing against the wooded steps as he went.

Hoyt crashed down the stairs in a thunderous declaration of impending death and Sleighton's revolver was lost in the dark. There was no time to search it out. He was barely on his feet when Hoyt's cloudy outline filled his vision. He raked his hand across the shelf of yard tools behind him, his palm closing around something. Anything. Whatever it was would have to do.

Hoyt was close, his angry eye burning with madness. His physique was so imposing that Sleighton wanted to run, feeling as scared and helpless as his little girl must've been.

The knife came for him again and he did the only thing he could. He threw himself at it, grabbing Hoyt's forearm with his free hand and knocking it as far off course as it would go.

The killer's rotted mouth opened in protest and a gust of fetid air slipped out.

Sleighton pushed through the stench and swiveled his arm out, slamming a three-pronged cultivator into Hoyt's face. The killer's scream was inhuman as blades sliced his cheek and ripped away the flesh to reveal his swollen gumline. Sleighton readied another blow, but Hoyt's free hand clasped around his neck and squeezed—stealing his breath away.

Hoyt prepared the killing stab, but Sleighton refused to wait for it. He drove the garden tool into the creature's forehead with every last drop of energy. It cracked his skull and terminated his grasp. Then he scooped his revolver off the floor and cocked the hammer as the giant fell, pressing the barrel against his malformed head.

Sleighton pulled the trigger.

It took another hour to clean up the struggle signs. Then he wrapped Hoyt in their plastic shower curtain, binding his arms and legs in rigging chains for extra safety.

Lugging the monster up to the top of the stairs left him sweaty and tired while his head begged for sleep. A concussion, he knew, but that didn't matter. Sleep was a pipedream.

He dragged the plastic-wrapped corpse to the mudroom, leaving it there while he splashed his face with cold water and cracked the one remaining can of Budweiser in the fridge. His line of sight never abandoned the plastic wrap. He needed to be convinced it was over. Even after splattering Hoyt's brains all over his cellar stairs, he wasn't sure he could believe it.

Sleighton was halfway through the can of Anheuser–Busch when he wondered if he shouldn't take a hit of something stronger. Just to keep the impending effects of head trauma at bay. It might not have been the right thing to do, but it was how he dealt with bodily harm. Drink the pain away.

He fumbled through the cabinet for a bottle of whiskey when the sound of cracking plastic lifted the hairs on the back of his neck. He threw his beer on the floor, leaving it sloshing and spilling as he strode into the mudroom and lifted the axe from the corner. He hacked at the wrap without hesitation, chopping into the maniac's head with a war cry. He brought the blade down again and again, until the plastic ran red.

He hoisted the sheet over his shoulder and brought it dripping out to his car, nearly passing out after sprawling it across the back seat of his cruiser. He slapped his face as he slid behind the wheel. There would be plenty of time to sleep once this creature was put to rest.

Why can't he die?

He considered this as he drove, mulling his own responsibility from behind heavy eyelids. It was his reconnaissance that had alerted the world to Abblon's madness, his report that condemned the Obviate to death. There was no saving those psychos and he never lost a single night's sleep over it.

Cracking the window filled the car with enough fresh air to keep him from shutting down. The turnoff for Camp Forest Grove came fast. He toggled his eyes between the road and the rearview—watching the plastic sheet with careful attention.

The dirt road was long and Sleighton didn't exactly know why he was bringing him out here. Was it because Hoyt's spiritual family had gone to their graves in the same spot? A poetic burial? Or was it because this was the only place in town where bad memories stayed dead and buried?

Do they?

The campground was silent. He rolled onto the grass and climbed out, remembering the Holden girl's claims that Hoyt had infiltrated her barricade through a trap door. That felt like the best place to go. Bury this monster so deep in the earth that he would never get out again.

Sleighton dragged the bloodied plastic through the grass, ducking below the still-hanging yellow police tape. They headed for the counselor's cabin—and the tunnels beneath it. He had corroborated the girl's story a few days ago and was spooked to discover that she'd been right. There were more than just a few tunnels running beneath the camp.

He dropped Hoyt through the hole and climbed the half-ladder into darkness, clicking his flashlight to life once his boots hit the ground. A yellow beam lit a path as they crossed the basement floor, slipping into the earthen corridor beyond it. Eventually, there was another drop that went deeper inside the hollow. This was as far as he dared to come the other day, but the luxury of chickening out no longer existed.

He tossed Hoyt over the edge. The opportunity to throw him around in the same way that Trish treated her Cabbage Patch dolls brought him unexpected catharsis. Once he heard the body's satisfying splat, he attempted to descend.

He was halfway there when the sinking sound of shuffling plastic echoed up from the depths. He froze on the current rung, ears wrinkling with every fold and crack. He plucked the flashlight off his belt and split the dark with a dancing cone of halogen.

When he saw what was making the noise, he took a few breaths to calm his heart. The plastic wrap had wedged between two rock formations and was gradually slipping down toward the ground.

A makeshift building sat on the other side of this cavern: a wooden church, complete with a mini steeple that rose as far as the cave's ceiling allowed. Zohra had never mentioned any of this, though she rarely spoke of her days with Abblon.

She chose to right his wrongs by preaching the Obviate's original message. Sleighton didn't care for her beliefs, but there were others in town who felt she was right. Their sermons were like modern day speakeasies—and probably as well attended. Many were quick to buy into stories about end times because the notion that it could be prevented made powerless people feel powerful.

That was Zohra's line: the Obviate showed the good lord how much they cared by fighting for humankind's survival. Or some horseshit.

The door creaked and sent a booming echo into the air that riled up a colony of bats. They flapped around while Sleighton dragged Hoyt into the shelter.

"This is where you'll stay," he said, trudging toward the altar. "This is where it ends."

Sleighton fished the plastic wrap out from beneath the chains and cast it aside. Before he could leave, he needed to study Hoyt's face for signs of life. To make sure it was finished. He grabbed a seat in the nearest pew and settled against the rough and uneven wood, watching the obliterated face for any kind of movement.

A suspended cross dangled over his stepson's body. The maniacs that called this place their home truly believed they were doing God's work. This was ground zero for some of the sickest shit that had ever happened as far as he was concerned. He tried forgetting about the madness and debauchery that would've swallowed this town whole if it hadn't been stomped out.

Piles of bones lay around Hoyt, nearly ensconcing him. Some were Obviate and others their victims. Almost twenty years on and their slaughterhouse was a grisly memorial to the massacre.

Forest Grove was home to a serial killer now and the irony was that it stemmed from the very thing they had tried covering up. Sleighton facilitated the slaughter of forty people—maybe more—in an attempt to protect his town. But all he'd done was delay the inevitable.

The bloodshed was coming, one way or another.

There was a wave of publicity headed his way and he hated the idea of having to entertain tourists for the rest of his life. Soon the grove would be on a list right next to that Long Island haunted house. Today's kids had no interest in starting families or instilling positive values in future generations. They lived like children themselves, well into their adult years. Fun to them apparently meant driving out to see a place where people died.

Hoyt's face had so many gashes and tears that it looked like road kill. The deformed bastard didn't move any more than he breathed.

It was probably safe to leave, but Sleighton wasn't satisfied yet.

That, or he didn't want to rush back and console Zohra over the loss of her psycho son. He was curious as to how this would impact her sermons. Was this enough of a tragedy for her to resume Abblon's old ways?

He had watched her carefully in the years following the Obviate massacre—like she was a heroin addict suffering one long comedown. There was no way of knowing whether or not she was guilty of anything herself, but he'd already made the (impulsive) decision to give her a second chance. And for the first few years, she refused to speak about any of it.

Forest Grove was never fooled by her, either. They knew full well where she came from. There were a lot of odd looks at first and many folks chose to believe that the Obviate compound had gone up in smoke, which in turn caused the cult to leave town *en masse*. An odd conclusion, given the cabins remained intact, but people believed what they wanted and chose to deny the truth about what had happened out here. There were murmurs concerning the killings, but no one knew anything for sure. And so it was probably easier for them to forget the whole thing while pretending to heal.

Ironically, many of them wound up coming around to Zohra's word.

That didn't happen overnight, though. Her approach was more tactical than Abblon's. She used topical events and headlines to plead her case: terrorism at the Munich games, Ebola outbreaks in the Sudan, and the destruction left by the Tangshan earthquake—anything she could ascribe to the actions of an angry God. This won her the favor of terrified peers. Slowly but surely, they took her words back to their families to spread the paranoia around.

Zohra had assured him it would be different. That there would be no bloodshed this time. Like most women, she was mighty persuasive when she wanted to be.

Maybe she'd like to see this place again…

He froze at the thought, knowing he would never consider anything so irresponsible. His head felt heavy and his mind scattered. Repressed urges were on the tip of his mind suddenly, replacing the desire to get out of here.

What's your rush?

He sprung out of the pew and took the cold steel of the revolver in the palm of his hand. "Leave me alone," he cried, blasting five more shots into Hoyt's brain. The killer's head shattered, breaking into pulpy strands. It brought no relief to the invasive squeeze on his thoughts, though. They tightened further, his mind awash with alien imagery and gruesome considerations.

He fled the catacombs, desperate to shake free of—whatever held him.

The drive home was the longest ride of his life and the pressure was slow to lift from his head. Whatever was down there wanted Zohra back. As he sped away from the campground, he heard something in his ear—an invisible passenger sitting beside him. It said *"priestess"* and then was gone.

Getting the town on board with Hoyt's death wouldn't be easy. Some weren't going to want to take Sleighton's word at face value, but he could smooth it over with persistence. Fraser and Valeri had already signed the death certificate. Valeri would have to be told the truth, but no one else could know. Hoyt's final resting place was best kept secret. He could cover up the killer's official cemetery plot before Forest Grove had its morning coffee and that would go a long way toward burying this nightmare.

When he pulled onto his street, there were several police cruisers blocking the Hautanen's place. He threw the car into park in the middle of the road and ran through the crowd of uniforms.

Major Tom Lawson stood on the sidewalk with Trish cradled in his arms. "Take it slow there, chief," he said with more than a little warning.

Sleighton paid it no mind, pulling his daughter into his arms. Her eyes fluttered open long enough to recognize her father, and then she dropped against his shoulder.

"Where's my wife, Tom?"

"That's why we're here. You probably think you pulled the wool over our eyes, chief. I've been waiting for things to go tits up. Christ, I never should have given you a chance. But I did. And look what happened."

"Tom, Zohra didn't have anything to do—"

"That's enough." Lawson led them off the sidewalk and around the side of the house. "We're taking her, Ron. Locking her up nice and tight."

Sleighton tried to protest, but Lawson wouldn't let him speak.

"Not a discussion I'm open to having. You took her off that lake. You're responsible for this. What happens if she goes blabbing about the things we did? I trusted you to contain this mess and it's clear now that you can't. Know why we're here, Ron? The people in this house called us 'cause Zohra was screaming bloody murder at your girl. *'Repent and submit'* is all she kept saying when we scooped her up."

This couldn't be real. Sleighton felt dizzier with every passing word. He pulled Trish tighter in his arms—afraid Lawson was going to try to take her, too. "Where is she?" he said.

"That's not a good idea, Ron."

"I have to see my wife. Please."

The trooper motioned for Sleighton to follow and they walked back into the commotion. Zohra was cuffed and sitting in the back of a cruiser. Her hoarse screams were crazed and incoherent.

After all this time, this was how it ended.

Her eyes narrowed when he approached. "You don't know what you've done. What any of you have done."

Sleighton wanted to scream back that this wasn't his fault. She had to see that his hands were tied. He wanted to make assurances that the troopers wouldn't get away with this. *Couldn't* get away with this. Snatching someone in the middle of the night and locking them away forever didn't happen in America. He knew the law as well as any, and would use it.

"You can see that she's agitated," Lawson said, leaning into Sleighton's ear. "And don't you think about fighting this. A lot of people rode out to that lake to rescue this town. You think about *that*. And if appreciating them isn't enough, then you think about your little girl. Someone has to be around to raise her."

The gestapo strong-arm tactic would work, because Sleighton was a man without options. Threatening his daughter was the one bluff he could never afford to call. These troopers would do anything to keep the story buried. They slaughtered an entire commune in the name of justice and would not allow their names to be dragged through the mud. So they were taking his wife away before the spotlight fell on the grove for that very reason.

Because if she was here, someone might get around to asking her a fatal question. And then the story could come back around to bite everyone in the ass.

As much as he hated it, he understood.

The cruiser took off down the street and Sleighton felt his soul leaving with it. Lawson stood beside him, eyeing him with contempt.

"Get your affairs in order, Ron. All of them."

He had a feeling that the troopers had just removed the only chance of that happening.

 **Ten**

"Where are we going?"

"To celebrate, stupid."

"Celebrate what?"

Tanya couldn't believe she was dating someone this dense. She rolled her eyes and dropped her mouth until Rafe figured it out.

"You mean the signatures?" he asked.

"Very good." She patted his thigh.

"Not here. My parents are probably watching from the window."

"Please," she said and started to drive away. "They know their son has been trying to tap the Blue Heron's resident flyer. Deep down, your dad is proud of you for landing a cheerleader."

"Yeah, and my mom grounded me for two weeks after finding that condom in my shorts a few months ago."

"I'm worth it." She took his hand and placed it on her inner thigh, pressing his fingers down. He pulled away and glanced over his shoulder like he was expecting to see his mother in the back seat.

Tanya sighed and headed for the grove's outskirts. Rafe glanced out the window as she got her speed on, hitting 80 as soon as downtown was behind them.

"Be careful, babe," he said. "There's a ton of cops out and

about."

"Which means you and I are home free." Tanya reached into the middle pocket between the seats and tossed a baggie into his lap. "Everyone's too busy to bust us on *that*."

Flashing cherries blazed red and blue in between the trees up ahead, indicating a possible barricade on the outskirts. Just around the bend. Whatever was happening in town, the cops meant business.

"Guess we're not getting in the front way," Tanya said.

"We're not getting in at all," Rafe said. "I told you this wasn't a good night."

"Shut up." She was glad it was dark so he couldn't see her eyes rolling. "When I have my heart set on something, I get it." She slowed the car to a crawl and killed the lights. There was an old fire road somewhere around here that would take them all the way to the lake. With all this hubbub painting the town red and blue, no one would be there. They'd have it to themselves.

It would be perfect.

The fire road wasn't more than a cow path and the car bounced them around like this was a moon landing. Her head launched straight up and hit the ceiling. She was instantly mortified at the thought of her hair. She worked hard and long to get rid of those damn split ends and her idiot boyfriend hadn't so much as noticed.

She didn't think they were going to make it to senior year, despite being the hottest couple in school.

Whatever, they were going swimming anyway.

The narrow trail made their trip twice as long as it needed to be. When the clearing finally appeared at the edge of the headlights, she breathed easy and flicked them off again, rolling straight onto the beach and killing the engine.

Tonight was a hot and sticky one and the town was stressing her big time. Collecting those signatures hadn't been easy. They got more glares than smiles. Apparently, the chief's wife had gathered plenty of her own so they knew there were enough people in the grove who were sympathetic to the cause.

It was weird that someone so much older cared about Forest Grove's class of 2014, though. At first, Trish Brady seemed pretty sad—one of those losers who couldn't let her youth go without a fight. But she was actually kinda cool—an adult who gave the finger to authority. Why weren't more of them like that?

Rafe looked around as they got out, worried that the police would catch them—paranoid without taking a single toke.

Tanya slid out of her shorts, taking her panties down with them. Her t-shirt was next, flinging it onto the hood of the car. It landed on top of her iPhone, muffling Krewella's anthem about living for the night. She wasn't wearing a bra, so she crossed her arms over her breasts to prevent Rafe from seeing the whole show without buying a ticket. Her ankles slipped beneath the still water and she felt like she had his full attention at last.

"Don't even think about following me until you're as naked as I am."

She waded in further, her body temperature adjusting in no time. Once she was up to her shoulders, the swim was cool and relaxing. She turned around in time to see her naked boyfriend flopping his way forward in the moonlight. He must've been cold for as small as he looked.

It made her giggle.

They swam out toward the middle of the lake. One of the houses across the way had anchored a dock out there and they weren't likely to mind that it was being co-opted tonight. Tanya reached it first and hoisted herself up onto the wobbly surface. The water rained off her body as she turned to watch Rafe swim the rest of the way, shivering in what had become cold evening air.

He was nowhere to be seen.

Tanya crossed her arms and called his name in a shivery voice. A lot of help that would do if he drowned, but she felt otherwise powerless.

The lake's serenity was suddenly terrifying. As if all of nature had taken notice of her and was now watching to see what would happen next. Nerves attacked her and she quaked from equal parts fear and cold. The beachfront looked small from out here, completely out of reach, and the night was so dark that she couldn't even see the house across the way. Complete isolation.

The water looked closer to oil—an ocean of undisturbed onyx. The only sounds she heard were her pounding heart and chattering teeth.

At some point, she was going to have to swim for it, even if she didn't want to. What if something got Rafe and was waiting for her to do just that?

Something like Cyrus Hoyt?

She considered a running dive, followed by a make-or-break swim. Her toe skimmed the water in a display of reluctance and something breached the surface and grabbed for it. She screamed and lost her balance, tipping back and dropping ass-first onto the raft.

A dark figure hauled up from the depths to join her, throwing his weight atop hers. Familiar kisses on her mouth, a tongue against her lips.

"I can't believe it's finally going to happen." Rafe's laugh was playful while he sucked her earlobe.

Tanya might've been pissed. She wanted to hit the jerk in the face for this little joke, but this was what they'd come for. She'd been ready a few days ago, but their discovery of an unconscious Trish Brady had thrown a wrench into that plan. Since then, it was all she could think about. Tonight was the night. It had to happen. And once her mind was made up—

While Rafe kissed her neck and groped her breasts, her hand clasped around the hammer that she'd stashed here this morning.

It's true that her hormones raged and a part of her wanted nothing more than to feel him inside. He was the hottest guy in school and the only one she had even considered doing it with. It was wrong to surrender to the flesh, but she was a teenager above all else and that compulsion was forever at odds with her morality.

The temptation was strongest now, while he worked her body over, and maybe it wouldn't be so bad if she just let it happen first.

But *they* wouldn't like that. God forbid *they* ever found out. She'd be branded one of the Lost if she ever succumbed. Then she'd be in his place.

No, it had to be like this.

Tanya swung the hammer down and the mallet cracked Rafe's skull with a sound like melons smashing. He squawked and rolled to his side as she hit him again—this time in the face. His jawbone broke and dangled loose, held in place by his skin. His protest was incomprehensible mush.

She couldn't stand to see this. Her eyes stung with tears of conflict, but there was no time to rub them. Tanya straddled him, fighting his arms with one hand while raining the hammer down on his head with the other. Every blow cracked louder, was wetter than the last, but he wouldn't stop struggling.

Soon her grief became annoyance. Why couldn't he give up and die? She needed this to be over for sanity's sake. Her folks promised that the first time was the toughest and that if she were lucky, there wouldn't be another. She only needed to prove that she was committed.

And she was.

His groans sounded less human now. Just bubbly gurgles.

One more crack to his temple and she forced herself to look. He was already swollen, his forehead a misshapen mess. One of his eyes had popped from his socket and dangled off his cheek like an earring. He was breathing still, but consciousness was long gone.

The disgusting sight was enough to make her retch.

She rolled off and sucked at the air for several minutes—until the thought of lying beside her victim grew too much to bear. She kicked at him, sliding his body across the raft, desperate to get him away. There was a momentary sense of sadness when one final shove sent him sinking to his final resting place. Then he was gone and she was ready to move on.

Tanya felt hysterical during the return swim, but she'd been expecting it. Instead of dwelling on what she had done, she considered how valuable of an asset she'd proven herself to be.

Thanks to her, the Obviate had a list of all of those in town who disagreed with them—so many Lost to punish. She lamented the lack of a homecoming dance, but that was just kid stuff. There were more important things to worry about—like the end of the world.

She toweled off when she got back to shore and quickly dressed. She was supposed to go back home and report in so that no one would worry. But she was so very close to the caverns where her brothers and sisters went to hear the whispers. No one was allowed down there without an elder, but a quick peak couldn't hurt.

I earned it.

She wanted to know that tonight meant something. There was only so much you could take on faith.

As she wiggled back into her shorts, her eyes fell on the cabin.

Why not, she thought, and headed for it.

Officer Donnelley found the front door ajar. He stepped inside his old boss' house with his weapon drawn.

Neighbors congregated in the middle of the street speaking in garbled confusion.

"Everybody stay back!" he screamed in his most authoritative voice.

A woman's body was sprawled out on the living room floor, half her head missing. Shattered pieces of a cordless telephone were strewn everywhere. He shone his light and noticed broken windows all around.

He took careful steps to avoid the mess and moved into the kitchen. The back door dangled off one hinge, swaying back and forth in the evening's breeze. The thing was sprayed with buckshot.

A second body lay face down in the grass out back—a hundred yards away. He grabbed for the two-way on his collar and called for an ambulance.

His gun at the ready, he headed for it.

In the distance, approaching sirens.

Cavalry, he thought with a sigh of relief.

And then the axe struck him square in the chest.

Hoyt sunk the axe inside the policeman and felt the blood spray across his visor, every splat a fulfilling tickle in his ears. He didn't dare take more than a second to savor the moment. Most of the satisfaction came from watching the face—the initial surprise that turns to horror. He handcrafted their final moments, a feeling of power unlike any other.

Unlike the killing of yesterday's policeman, there was no pressure here. Only enjoyment.

He wrenched the axe free and swung it over his head in an artful motion as the gaping chest cavity rained blood on his coat. The young officer grimaced and tried raising his gun, somehow an ounce of fight left in him.

The axe sailed back toward him and broke his nose, demolishing his facial structure with a crack. His eyeballs burst into jellied fluid as the blade cleaved them from existence. The policeman dropped dead in the grass, his legs tangled like pretzels. The stench of bodily discharge seeped up and filled the space between his face and visor.

Wailing sirens disrupted the evening and brought a premature finish to the moment. It was instead a reminder that it was time to escape.

Cyrus Hoyt turned without an ounce of worry in his step and headed for the trees.

The one he wanted would be coming.

All he had to do was wait for her.

Ron Sleighton wished they would get it over with.

His face stung from repeated punches and his breath was short because of the hog tie. He was stomach-down, hands and feet tied together and stretched high over his back. His ankles and wrists were knotted to prevent him from moving at all.

He had never bent like this and his arms and legs burned beneath his skin as a result.

It was the only way to get them to leave Trish alone.

"We want to kill you, chief." The voice was somewhere out of his line of sight and belonged to an older man that Sleighton thought he recognized, but couldn't say for certain. "You forced our hand with that bloodshed."

Sleighton guessed he was referring to the two psychos he

shot down in self-defense. Sick bastards didn't get to come after Trish without consequence. She grew up here, same as them. Forest Grove was home to more than just the Obviate and there had always been a truce.

Until tonight.

"You want to kill me?" he wheezed. "Do it. And leave Trish be. It's my fault anyway. I should've told her to stay away… blame me for that." It was the only reason he agreed to go quietly. Back at the house, they had been ready to keep coming, unfazed by their diminishing ranks.

"Your sacrifice is noble and fulfilling," the voice said. "We will not harm the girl. She must leave town of her own accord, but not before she is converted. When she returns to the city, it will be because she has special work to do."

There was no reasoning with them. They ignored his fevered pleas as a pole was jimmied between his hands and legs and then was hoisted off the ground, carried outside, and shoved into the backseat of a car.

"You must move carefully," the voice said. "There are police everywhere and they are already suspicious. Brother Maki was apprehended for what was done at City Hall."

"A necessary sacrifice," another voice said. "Cobb sought to develop the lakefront for hundreds of future housing developments and we must never face an influx of outsiders who are ignorant to our ways."

"Make him repent and submit," the instructing voice said. Sleighton felt the topic of conversation shift back to him. "He pays for the sins of his daughter as well."

And then he knew where they were taking him.

The hood of the police cruiser felt cold on Melanie's legs.

She sat there trembling over the incident at City Hall, wondering how things in the grove had suddenly grown beyond she and Nate.

The sheriff's officers wouldn't let her go past the police cars. The evening breeze was cold and she kicked herself for not getting a change of clothes in addition to taking that shower.

She'd been waiting for Nate at the police station when he called in. He would only say that she needed to drive to Sleighton's place and give him every last bit of information she had. So that's what she did.

Melanie watched him go inside the house and come out twice. The first time he was as white as a sheet. Watching him made her heart race. He looked vulnerable, but it was even worse than that. He looked scared.

What if it's Trish in there?

Twenty minutes passed and the state troopers had shown up. A man she knew could only be Captain Oviedo lead the charge. Nate came out again and noticed her from across the lawn. He gave her the *one-minute* gesture before grabbing Oviedo's shoulder and exchanging a few words. They disappeared back inside for half an hour.

Additional troopers arrived and went to work on crowd control, pushing the spectators further down the street.

At last, Nate came out and motioned for the nearest cop to let her through.

"Trish okay?"

"I dunno where she is." He sounded like he was struggling to maintain his composure. "Got an A.P.B. out, though. She and her father are missing."

"I'm sorry—"

"I should've seen the signs," he said. "Ron's involved. Has to be. Guy was always looking over my shoulder. I couldn't write a traffic ticket without having to explain myself. Always told me this town had to be transitioned into my control—"

"You couldn't have known."

He continued to speak, uninterested in her comfort. "I figured it was a hard thing for the old guy…moving into the next phase of his life, you know? But he kept me in the dark about… whatever the hell happened in there. And now my wife is missing because of it."

"He knows plenty," Melanie said. And then delivered every last word of Tom Lawson's account.

Nate listened to her oration and his face settled on an expression that teetered somewhere between horror and revelation as some of the pieces inevitably clicked into place. "They bought the camp so they could carry on down there in secret. Consecrated ground for crazy bastards."

It was Melanie's turn to be confused.

"Forget it," he said and went running for his car. "I know where they are."

Sleighton lifted his head as far as it could go and recoiled from the red and blue flashes that stormed the interior of the darkened cab.

Up front, driver and passenger exchanged nervous whispers. He didn't hear every word, but caught "no matter what" as a shotgun flew up from the cushion between them.

Outside the car, the police opened fire.

The bodies twitched and jerked as buckshot charged through the front and side windows, tearing them to pieces. Blood rained on the back seat, pelting him with hunks of brain.

"Get me out of here!" he screamed.

Two troopers converged, at last prying one of the doors open. They fished him out with careful precision and cut through the hog binds as soon as he was on the pavement.

Sleighton took a moment to rub his arms in relief.

"Can you stand, sir?" One of the troopers asked.

Sleighton didn't know if he could. That binding had stretched him in ways he didn't think possible. He managed to stand, but his muscles felt like someone had doused them in gasoline and lit a match.

"We're stopping everyone going to and coming from town," the trooper said. "This place is on lockdown until we figure out what's happening."

Good luck with that.

The troopers led him back to their blockade. Two cars faced each other diagonally, forming two sides of a triangle. One of them went to the radio and called this in while the other offered Sleighton a pour of hot coffee from his Thermos.

"In a minute," Sleighton said, moving across the pavement in small circles hoping to get his muscles to stop screaming. And that was just the first battle. After that, he'd focus on relaxing his pounding heart.

Every cop in the state could be here and it wouldn't matter to the Obviate. They wanted him dead. He didn't know how many there were, but had already seen a wider network than he'd ever thought possible.

Things had always been quiet in Forest Grove—until Johnson murdered those college kids. The Obviate could blame whomever they wanted, but this mess was on them. They drew attention to themselves with that slaughter, and suddenly looked to punish those who did not deserve their wrath.

If by some miracle he survived, he was going to find a way to make Zohra talk. She knew who was running the show here, but always refused to answer the question when asked. She cited loyalty to the church above all else and blamed him for her incarceration. He knew this because every one of his visits ended the same exact way: with silent accusations of betrayal stubbing out her eyes as she watched him go.

Still, the Obviate's favorite daughter would not enjoy hearing that her former sect was trying to convert her daughter.

Ingrates.

He hoped that Trish had been smart enough to stay upstairs. All that mattered was that she got out of the grove. For the first time since Abblon, it wasn't a safe place to live.

"I need to call my daughter," he said, but the troopers weren't having it.

"Relax, chief, we've got to straighten this out before doing anything else, okay?"

"There's no need for this," Sleighton said, hoping that they might exhibit a little professional camaraderie. "Those people abducted me and I just want to call my girl and make sure she's okay."

There was a sound outside the circle of cruiser light and the troopers drew their riot shotguns toward it.

"Officers." A teenager came running from the trees. She dropped her hands onto her thighs once she got into the light, bending over and gasping for air while speaking between breaths. "It's just terrible."

Sleighton recognized her. Brook Walker. Her father was local real estate and her mom taught elementary over in Warren. Seemed like a good kid, but he knew better than to buy that line now.

One of the troopers went forward while the other covered him with a cautious weapon.

"Miss—"

The girl lifted her head and in the red and blue flashes, Sleighton gasped at her crazed eyes. She lunged for the trooper with some kind of blade, stabbing him square in the stomach.

His partner rushed to his aide, taking her by the arm and

throwing her to the ground.

She spilled across the pavement and giggled like a mischievous schoolgirl. "You all are Lost," she cried, "Repent and submit."

Then Sleighton saw them.

The two people standing at the forest's edge.

"Get away from him," Sleighton called, but the trooper wasn't listening. He was too busy applying pressure to his partner's stomach in an attempt to keep his guts from spilling out. "Look over there, goddammit!"

There were more of them now. Sleighton counted five before noticing a solitary shadow inching out from behind a tree. He turned and caught two bodies moving into the light.

He remembered the shotgun in the car behind them—no way of getting to that now.

His attention snapped back to the trooper who was at last retreating back his way.

Sleighton needed one of those shotguns or this was over. These maniacs were beyond listening to reason. He was among the Lost in their minds and that meant he needed to be sacrificed.

A circle of shadows closed in around them while Brook crawled on all fours, laughing as she crossed the pavement.

The shotgun was slick with blood as he hoisted it. The girl was close but she went for the trooper instead, burying her box cutter into his thigh and taking him down to her level.

Sleighton shot her point blank. Skull shards rained against the cars like sleet. Her body dropped atop the injured trooper, but there was no time to worry about any of that now. The rest were coming.

He ran toward the tree line and hoped they would follow.

Melanie couldn't help but assume the worst for Trish.

She would never say that to Nate, whose only concern right now was for his wife. It reinforced the idea that he was nothing if not a stand-up guy. Spasms of guilt twisted inside her. Had she really expected him to drop everything for her?

They sped past the Camp Forest Grove sign that had freaked her less than a week ago. What an overreaction that had been, considering everything that happened since.

Nate's breathing was so labored that she heard it over the siren.

"Trish's mother is alive," he said for the second or third time, getting used to the idea.

"If she is, maybe Ron is Obviate. And what about Trish?"

"Trish doesn't know anything about it," he snapped.

Melanie let it slide, but there was no way to know that for sure. "This whole time I thought Cyrus Hoyt was the story," she said. "He's just a byproduct."

They rounded a bend and the familiar sight of red and blues greeted them.

"Thank Christ," Brady muttered. And then, a second later, "What the hell?"

The lights were growing larger. Getting closer.

"Brady," she cried, but he noticed it, too. The approaching cruiser was on their side of the road, hurtling forward at matching speed.

Too fast.

Brady eased the gas and cut the wheel. The driver of the other vehicle seemed to anticipate this, cutting across the yellow line without breaking.

The airbag smashed Melanie's face as glass exploded all around her.

Brady's eyes were sticky with blood. He wiped them, but it continued to trickle over his face like a runny faucet.

The car was overturned and the dashboard of equipment was smashed beyond recognition. He dangled upside-down by his seatbelt. The roof had buckled on impact, curving his head inward and offering him a view of his bloodied chest.

To his left, Melanie lie sprawled out on the crumpled ceiling, clutching her stomach and moaning.

Brady was weak and his motions weightless as he fumbled with the buckle. "Hey," he said, stunned by how faint he sounded. "You okay?"

Melanie looked, but said nothing. Even with his vision obscured, she looked in bad shape. A vertical gash ran the length of her face. It sliced through her forehead and continued through her cheek all the way to her chin. Her eyes were distant and unfocused.

At last, he found the seatbelt release button and dropped onto the folded ceiling. The shotgun had to be near, but there was no time to look. They had to get the hell out of here.

The driver side window was gone. The car had folded down onto itself, taking away his chance to escape through it.

"Can you get out on your side?"

She was looking around the cab like it was her first time on planet earth.

"Melanie, please. We've got to go." He wasn't going to pretend this was an accident. Whoever was driving that car had steered right for them. They got exactly what they wanted. And they'd be coming to finish the job.

Without any time to waste, he grabbed Melanie and pulled her across the cab so that their eyes locked. "Listen to me," he said. "There are people coming to kill us. We can not stay here."

"I-I know," she said. Her speech was slurred, but her eyes were less cloudy than a moment ago. "I blacked out there for a minute, but—"

"Squeeze through that window," he cried. "Get the hell going!"

Brady followed Melanie's bruised and bloodied legs as she pushed past the twisted metal. Once she was free of the wreckage, she grabbed her stomach and rolled onto her back with a groan.

Slipping free wasn't as easy for him. He was larger than her and the window frame was bent. Jagged glass chewed his forearms as he forced himself through.

He rose and grabbed for his Glock. It was still in its holster, thank God. They weren't completely helpless.

Melanie grimaced as he helped her up.

"Let me see," he said and rolled her shirt up over her midriff to examine her stomach. "Nothing's pierced, so it's all internal. A few broken or cracked ribs, most likely. Can you move?"

"I-*argh*, I-think so."

"Alright," he said. "On me." Then he started for the road.

They found the other cruiser a few feet away. Its hood was a U, cleaved down the middle by a gigantic Hemlock stump. The driver had gone through the windshield and lost his head in the process. Crimson glugged from the torn gullet like milk from a jug.

Brady was relieved to see that he was dead and without uniform. It was short-lived respite, though, as he wondered how a civilian had gotten hold of a state police cruiser. "I need to see if the radio in that car is still working," he said.

The road was dark as they hustled up the embankment, neither of them able to stifle their discomfort. Once they hit the tarmac, they shuffled in silence, moving toward the incapacitated vehicle.

Brady went through the opened passenger window, taking the radio in hand. It was dead, completely smashed and bent outward from impact.

Behind him, Melanie screamed.

Six people walked single file down the center of the road, coming at a casual pace as their shoes scraped pavement.

Brady pointed his gun, hoping it'd be enough to discourage their advance.

They showed no hesitation. It was time to run.

"Turn around," he whispered. "I know it hurts, but you've got to run to town."

"Nate, no…"

Brady steadied the firearm. "I'm not going to say this again," he called. "Stop right there or I'll open fire."

"Repent and submit," their voices boomed in unison.

"Jed's store isn't more than a half mile back," he said. "Book it there. Get inside and call for backup."

"Come with me, Nate. Don't be crazy."

"If we both go, they'll follow us."

There was movement on their right—more shadows lurching out from behind the trees. They dragged axes and pitchforks that scuffed the ground behind them.

Melanie turned to run and offered one last reluctant glance before going.

Brady motioned for her to go. Melanie's footfalls faded from earshot as he leveled the Glock toward the nearest target.

They fanned out like a seashell and converged from all angles. He counted fifteen of them, which meant every round in the magazine needed to be a kill shot.

"Repent and submit," they repeated. "We take the Lost to satisfy the whispers." It was less a justification and more of a prayer.

Brady pleaded with them to stop, but they would not.
He brought his gun up in self-defense—
And was grabbed from behind.

Melanie felt like dying but didn't dare stop. Her body
tingled from head to toe and her breaths were pathetic wheezes.
This kind of run was normally a warm down, but tonight it felt
like a 20k.

Her phone was depleted and she cursed herself for not
charging it on the drive from New Hampshire.

Last Mile Gas was up ahead. All she could do was push
forward and hope to get help—and a drink of water.

The slower she moved, the better she felt, and the less she
agonized. The less she agonized, the quieter she moved. No sense
in alerting anyone to her presence. In a really selfish thought, she
hoped that Brady had been able to keep them busy. The psychos
had shown themselves at last and Forest Grove was crawling with
police.

This madness couldn't go on much longer.

The gas station looked like a darkened square block
beneath the pewter sky. Melanie found a rock in the overgrowth
on Jed's property and grabbed it. With an ache, she wound back
and sent it spinning through the air. It crashed through the front
glass of Jed's dying store.

Of course, there was no alarm.

She slipped over the broken windowpane and headed for
the counter, to where the old man hopefully kept a phone. It was
there, behind an old coffee thermos and a stack of magazines.
She brushed them aside and took the rotary handset in her fist.

There was dial tone as she fumbled her finger into the 9
slot, followed by the 1. She was on her way to tag the 1 again

when the line snapped into silence.

Her heart was turning in overdrive with the realization that someone was here with her. Nothing behind the counter could be used for defense, so she went rummaging through the store. The barren shelves seemed to mock her with useless offerings.

In the corner of her eye, something rose up off the ground. Beyond the busted window, it was shifting in the darkness, rising. Standing. A steel faceplate glinted in the drab evening sky and Cyrus Hoyt stepped casually inside.

Melanie's throbbing stomach tightened. With her movement impaired, there was almost nothing to do. She thought fast and threw her shoulder into the nearby shelving. It toppled over, catching the next shelf and then the next.

It was too slow for the killer to be taken by surprise. He sidestepped the dominos and circled around the front main aisle. An axe dangled from his hand and he waved it back and forth like a pendulum as he walked.

This was no way to fight him. She took an involuntary step back and eyed what little clutter was within reach—all of it worthless.

There were old farm implements housed in the shed behind the house, but reaching them was like asking her broken body to run another sixty miles.

Melanie made a break for it anyway and Hoyt followed. She leapt through the opened storefront and the throbbing pain subsided. It was still there, but adrenaline had blunted it.

Her long legs sprinted for the tall grass, spending every last drop of energy to get there. Hoyt swiped the axe through the air at her back. As soon as she reached the waist-deep brush, she knew she was going to have to slow him down, or there wouldn't be enough time to grab anything.

She dropped to the ground on open palms and kicked outward. Her foot connected with the killer, knocking him off balance. He tumbled into the brush and out of sight.

Melanie's breathing was even more labored now, but she plowed on. The rusted machete was where she last saw it and no sooner was it in her hand than Hoyt came charging across the clearing like a runaway train. She swung the flaky, orange blade outward and braced for collision.

The killer skidded to a stop with his arms outstretched. The axe must've fallen during his tumble and he hadn't bothered to look for it for fear of losing her.

The stalemate didn't last more than a second. He ducked into the woods on the left and disappeared, stomping off through the night.

Melanie watched him go in disbelief, taking the opportunity to catch her breath. Clinging to the machete for dear life, she started back the way she came, a half-hearted jog was as much as her body would allow.

Hoyt wasn't quitting—she knew that. He was toying with her. After all this time, this was nothing but a big game. He was savoring the cat and mouse stuff now that it was just the two of them. He retreated for the same reason he had arranged all his victims for her to find twenty-five years ago. He wasn't done tormenting her.

She considered breaking into Jed's house to find a phone, but guessed that's what Hoyt was betting on. Instead, she went back through the tall grass, glancing over her shoulder for no other reason than paranoia.

What she saw made her feel completely hopeless.

Hoyt stood on the steps of the old man's house, a pitchfork by his side like a mockery of American Gothic.

Melanie went running for the road, pushing her body beyond the gentle jog and hoping to give this bastard the slip.

And somewhere behind her, he was running again, too.

"Take it slow, chief." Sleighton pushed the shotgun muzzle into Brady's back. "I don't want to do this, Nate, but there's no other option."

In front of them, the Obviate halted their advance. Brady couldn't see their eyes in the dark, but he felt them. Every gaze trained on him as their bodies swayed silent in the breeze.

"You'll take *him*," Sleighton called. He repeated the words again, only louder. "I know you have not been pleased with the job he's done. He is supposed to protect our way of life. *Your* way of life. But he doesn't, does he? He lets drunk drivers off the hook, fixes to commit adultery…a disgrace to your practice. He is Lost! Take him for your sacrifice!"

"Ron," Brady didn't know where this negotiation should go. He was attempting to reach the rationale of those who had none. He felt his words bounce off closed ears. "You'd do this to Trish?"

"I'm buying her life," he said. "Think I trust *you* to do it?"

"We have guns," Brady said. "They don't." He watched the Obviate before them and thought they looked especially vulnerable now that there were two of them. They could win this. Last thing he wanted was to play *Tombstone*, but there was no other choice.

"This ain't all of them," Sleighton said. "Not by a damn sight. Believe me, son, I wish there was another way."

"Just tell me where she is, Ron. I need to know that she's safe."

"She's not your responsibility anymore, Nate. I'll find her and keep her safe once this is over."

"You'll find her. You don't know where she is and you're doing this? Goddammit—" The gun slammed into the base of his spine and bolts of pain shot up his back. Negotiations were over.

"This one will repent and submit," Sleighton screamed. "Take him while a few of you go back for the Holden girl. They should die together. Do that and let me have my daughter back. She does not want your way of life. She will leave. Quietly and forever. There are police all over town. Let this end now!"

They stepped forward in perfect harmony like the motion was rehearsed. "Repent and submit" traded past their lips, pinballing from one shadow to another. It was maddening to hear.

"The fruits of your wife's labor, Ron?" Brady said.

The insult didn't register with the old chief. He was beyond reason now. "Yes," he screamed. "Go on. Take him. Allow him to repent!"

"Repent and submit," the cultists cried. The nearest one advanced and the veil of shadows fled the face to reveal the nondescript teenager that served him every time he patronized Walt's Pizzeria. He couldn't believe his townspeople were sentencing him to death.

"Walk," was all the boy said.

Brady felt the shotgun muzzle goad him again. "Let's go, son." Sleighton pointed him toward the forest. "Don't make this any more difficult than it has to be."

Brady made for the trees with slow steps. His mind raced to consider all the ways out of this, but he couldn't envision a scenario that didn't end with buckshot to the back.

When they reached the forest's shroud, the Obviate fell in line behind them, humming some kind of psalm beneath their breaths.

Melanie's lead on Hoyt was considerable, but he was still out there.

Hoyt had gone around the far side of Last Mile Gas, essentially blocking the road to town. She considered going back to Nate, but couldn't risk running into the army of cultists.

So she ran straight into the woods across the street, dodging tree limbs and branches as she moved. At last, there was some kind of fire road, one of the many trails that surrounded the camp. It wound in just about every direction, but she knew the ultimate destination.

Hoyt's aggressive pursuit continued, crunching long-wilted leaves in the distance as he searched her out.

There was no way of knowing how much time had passed, but eventually the only noise out here was hers. Every so often, the exploding pain in her gut flared and a grimace would escape her throat. There was no way to ignore it. She hurt all over.

She froze and listened to the silence. If she survived this, it was going to be the last time she ever saw a forest. The idea of being around an overwhelming capacity of people wasn't exactly thrilling, but city living was preferable to *this*. The finest cafes, dollops of culture, endless bustle—it all sounded so good right about now.

Hoyt could be anywhere. These were his woods and had been for a very long time. It might've been a pointless gesture, but she decided to slink off the trail and move in between a thick pair of trees. She made more noise this way, but her location wasn't as obvious. If she could lose him out here, there was a chance to escape.

Her body was long past the brink of exhaustion and dared her to quit. Its pleas were persuasive, calling attention to a pine bed beneath her, urging forty winks. But that would mean the end of everything.

I won't make it easy for him.

Her spontaneous march went on and on, eventually giving way to a familiar clearing. She laughed when she saw it and was prepared to run back when she noticed the car parked at the waterfront.

Melanie stared at it like it was a mirage. After all of this, her luck couldn't be this good. And she was right. All four doors were locked and the driver was nowhere to be found. The keys weren't in the ignition, otherwise, she would've smashed the window with her machete.

"Come on," she cried, but thought better of taking her frustration out on the sedan.

Fate was never going to allow an easy escape. Deep down, she knew that. All roads led to Camp Forest Grove and, as she turned to face the grounds, she remembered how foreboding the cabins looked when displayed in the moonlight.

The blade was heavy in her hand—just holding it was tiring, but it would be put to use. The only way out of here wasn't around Cyrus Hoyt. It had to be straight through him.

Let's do this you son of a bitch. Even her thoughts were exhausted as she shuffled toward the old counselor's cabin. She would have laughed at this cruel twist of fate if she weren't so scared. Twenty-five years later and she was right back where she started.

If she had to die tonight, it wasn't going to be without putting up one hell of a fight.

If I get out of this, I'm burning this fucking place down.

Brady led the human caravan through the trees. He knew the area well after traversing it over and over for the last few days. He could lead them right to the camp.

And that's where they were going.

He also wondered if he could use the cover of night to slip the Glock from his holster without Ron or the Obviate noticing.

He tested the theory by dropping his gun hand within a few inches of the holster.

"Raise 'em up, Nate. Don't insult me." The response was quick, confident, and it said everything he needed to know about the situation. There was no getting out of it.

They filtered out of the forest single file, walking dead center down the familiar dirt road. From the back of the line, the singing was louder now but no more intelligible to his ears.

Certain death was less than a mile away.

Brady saw the beachfront first. The water was a deceiving placard of serenity underneath the clear sky. A car was parked near it, probably belonging to one of these maniacs. The skeleton of Camp Forest Grove was a reminder of the horrors that happened here. A rotted heart pumping tainted blood right to the town's organs.

They reached the cabin where Mel had been snooping a few days earlier and Sleighton pushed the gun against his lower back once again. "Take a step inside, son. And don't do anything stupid."

Brady pulled the door open and stepped in, searching for a way to slip free. He was almost out of options and dying on his own terms was preferable to winding up a ludicrous blood sacrifice.

All he wanted to do was find Trish and get out of here, his anger at Ron Sleighton expanding by the second. Not because he had a gun trained on him, but because he'd allowed his own daughter to come back to this insane asylum.

For that, he wanted to kill the bastard.

Please let me see Trish again.

He couldn't wrap his head around the possibility that he would not. The last time he'd felt anything remotely like this was when he stepped into the hearing room to explain to a counsel why an innocent teenage girl was dead by his gun. He knew he was going down for that and, more importantly, he knew he deserved it—but that had only been a threat to his livelihood.

This was a threat to his existence.

Sleighton followed him into the cabin, as did one of the cultists. The others remained outside, singing.

"We will do it in here," the Obviate said. "Once our brothers and sisters return with the woman, we flay them both. They cannot go into the next life when their flesh is so weak, so it must be removed."

"Then you'll let me go to my daughter?" Sleighton said. "I promise to pack her bags myself."

The Obviate said nothing.

Sleighton aimed the shotgun toward the cabin's living space. "In there, Nate," he said.

Brady did as he was instructed, thinking that his life lasted as long as it took them to locate Melanie. There was always the possibility that she'd made it into town and got Oviedo's attention. But his fantasies were dashed as soon as he passed into the living space proper, because he saw a figure in the corner with something raised overhead.

Sleighton was right on his heels and it was likely that he noticed the shape too. Brady heard the old chief's mouth pop open in surprise as something cut through the air and knocked him to the ground.

Melanie fell against Brady's shoulder with a groan.

The cultist dashed toward them with his axe hoisted, but Brady already had him in the Glock's sights, dead to rights. He double-tapped him in the head, dropping him where he stood and leaving only a cloud of blood to dissipate in the air.

"I heard you coming," she said.

Brady looked between her and Sleighton, relived that she was alive, but dismayed to see she hadn't gotten to Oviedo.

The old chief squirmed around on the floor, a machete

buried deep in his arm.

"How did you get here?" Brady asked.

"Hoyt," she said as if the answer had been obvious. "He's outside."

"Not the only one," Brady said. They had weapons now and that meant keeping the Obviate at bay while they ran back to route twelve. He pointed to the injured ex-chief. "We'll chain him up until Oviedo can get out here."

He handed the shotgun off to Melanie and reached for his cuffs when Sleighton lunged up and knocked him off-balance. The retired cop scurried for the basement hatch, but Melanie was closer. She grabbed for him as he flung open the horizontal door.

"Bitch," he growled, wrapping a hand around the shotgun's stock and yanking it from her grip. It wasn't a very graceful move and he lost his balance on the tug, pulling the gun free but tumbling back through the open hatch.

He dropped through the darkness and there was a thud followed by an immediate whimper.

"Take them," Sleighton said with slurred words. His voice trailed off as he shuffled away in the darkness below, repeating the invitation like a broken record.

"He went in pretty hard," Melanie said. "He can't last much longer."

Brady was no longer concerned with keeping him alive. The old man had dug his grave. Trish was missing, possibly dead, and they were goners too if they stayed any longer.

"We're out of here," he said, and then they were both moving to the exit.

They were almost out when Brady saw someone standing in the still-open doorway. He lifted his gun to the obstacle, but Melanie grabbed his arm and tugged his attention over to the nearest window. Another shape filled the pane, hot breath expanding against the glass.

A woman eyed them from the far side window. They were all over the place.

They're not going to let us leave.

"Repent and submit!" They snarled as if mocking his realization.

Brady remembered his gun and took aim at the door. He wasn't going to ask this time. "Be ready to move," he whispered. "Can you run?"

After some hesitation, Melanie nodded.

He squeezed off a round and the figure in the doorway crumpled against the jamb before sliding to the floor. They took cautious steps, edging closer to freedom. Melanie looked absolutely decrepit—how much further could she go?

They were about to find out.

Two silhouettes stood just beyond the doorway. Behind them, another two. Each of them watched patiently and without further motion. A look around the cabin confirmed that every window was occupied.

"The back door," Melanie said.

He followed her into the kitchen. But the Obviate were there too, waiting outside. At least six of them. Melanie slammed the door in defeat.

"They're trying to keep us here," Brady said. The realization brought him to the floor hatch. "There has to be a way out down there."

"Only thing down there is death."

"That's what's up here." Around them, the Obviate pressed inward on the glass windows, and the panes cracked gently beneath their fingertips.

Christ, how many of them are out there?

He hovered over the hole and swallowed hard. "Come on, Melanie."

She shook her head and backed off.

"It's down there or back through the woods. I can't fight them all off. I need to get out of here and find Trish."

Hands pushed in through every window at once and glass rained all around them. Two bottles smashed across the wooden floors, filling the cabin with alcoholic vapors. Brady didn't have time to get Melanie to duck before the cabin went up in flames.

"No choice now," he said and got to his knees.

Melanie's bright blue eyes met his in mutual fear.

There was chanting outside. "You die to prevent the end. As we have, so shall we always."

"Go," Brady screamed over the frenzied voices. "I'll lower you down and be right behind you."

His thoughts were frantic. There was no other way out. The Obviate guarded each window in overwhelming numbers and the flames licked him from all sides. They were about to be sacrifices, flayed or not.

Melanie sat at the edge of the hole, her legs dangling over uncertain darkness. Brady gave her his arm as he got down on his stomach and lowered her into the cavern below.

Her eyes flashed like a cat in headlights once she landed.

"Okay?" he asked.

"I am," she said. "Hurry."

Brady spun onto his side to position himself for descent when a blade sliced through his hand and pinned him to the floor. He screamed out and tried prying the knife free.

An Obviate knelt beside him, pressing her knee to his throat. He recognized the town librarian even as her normally placid face was twisted into a hideous death mask that complemented her intentions.

"You're dead," she whispered. Her body went up in flames. "If she survives down there, you must be the one to go beyond. I give my life to protect the others..." her throat bubbled and bled as the blaze surged over her in a wave.

The entire cabin was burning and Brady felt his hair singe all at once. He screamed as a ball of flame crawled his flesh, melting his clothes into his skin in a mess of blisters and boils. He screamed as the heat grew with so much intensity that his eyeballs finally burst.

Alone.

Melanie stared up in disbelief as the cabin cracked apart in the fire.

Nate's body sizzled some fifteen feet above, idle fingers dangling down through the hatch.

Her spirit was as broken as her body, completely numb as she shambled through the dank subterranean depths. Blind fingers brushed at the air as she went, careful not to smash headfirst into any obstructions.

Her body couldn't take any more damage.

If Sleighton had survived the fall, there was no sign of him that she could see—but that wasn't much. The walls constricted around her shoulders as the ground sloped and she raked her fingertips along them to keep what few bearings remained.

Drops of water fell into puddles out of sight while unseen rats squeaked displeasure at her arrival. Despite everything trundling through her brain, she managed to shudder at the thought of those things weaving in and out between her legs.

The hole got darker and colder. Something wet and fleshy smacked her forearm and she recoiled instinctively. Whatever it was, it occupied the very limited space she was passing through.

A puff of flame erupted ahead and, somehow, the candles lining the cavern floor were lit. There was no time to question this magic as the newfound light showed what was blocking the way: Sleighton's corpse hung suspended from the cavern wall, a pickaxe embedded in his chest. The blade had torn through him, leaving smashed and broken rib bones angled inward from the blow. He'd been hit so hard, the pickaxe pinned him several inches off the ground. A drawing pool of piss and blood collected at his feet.

Melanie grabbed the tool's hilt and yanked it with all her might. It jiggled but would not dislodge. Shifting her weight, she pried forward with a grunt. Sleighton's innards sloshed around in his chest cavity until it finally popped free.

The chief fell into his own excrement and she left him a twisted heap, taking the nearest candle in her hand while gripping the bloodied pickaxe in the other.

The cave's path was twisty, but the carved passage was the only way to go, meaning there was no danger of getting lost. Abblon and his cult must've chiseled this in whichever direction offered the least resistance. The walk was painful on her feet and even worse on her ribs.

Nate's horrible scream remained constant in her mind. The way it rose and then severed without crescendo. Crisped fingers dangling in defeat—he hadn't deserved that. He was trying to absolve Forest Grove of its long-standing sins—fifty years' worth. Those thankless fools would never know the extent of his sacrifice.

Because now he was gone.

And I'm on my own.

It was impossible to get him out of her mind. After all they'd been through, it just couldn't end this way. She might've known better than to believe in closure since she was going on twenty-five years without it, but this was going to take some grieving. And there was no time for that now. No sense in inflicting emotional pain when the physical endurance was bad enough.

If I get out of here, I'll tell his story.

As if that somehow made his sacrifice better. She already planned to do the same for Bill, Jen, Lindsey, Tyler, Becky and Mr. Dugan. Adding Nate to that list just felt like a continued way of excusing the exploitation. She wouldn't have needed to do this at all if Dennis hadn't forced her hand.

Him and his little Cliff's Notes-addicted fuck doll...

Melanie's hand closed tight around the pickaxe, imaging what Jill Woreley's face would look like after her head had been shattered by it.

Was she smiling at the thought?

A miner's pick could devastate a skull. Taking away Jill Woreley's looks would leave her with nothing and that was more than she deserved.

Then there was Morton—he deserved so much worse. His death would obliterate all her remaining angst and anguish. And wouldn't it be all too easy to slip into his home one night? The sloth bragged often about how his alarm code was still the default because he didn't have the time to change it.

All she had to do was Google the factory setting code and then wait for Morton and his wife to come home, taking them both by surprise. Or pick them off one-by-one. Kill her and stash the fresh body somewhere where he would find it.

What would Dennis Morton look like in his fleeting minutes? She'd kill him slow enough to find out. So slow that it would be an all-night affair.

Melanie was so disturbed by the bellicose thoughts that she shook her head, hoping that would get rid of them. In her angriest moments, she wouldn't consider doing those things. Neither her body nor mind felt like her own.

Maybe Nate's demise provoked these feelings? She thought of Trish and how much she pitied the young widow.

Do I?

A Goth bitch with tweezed eyebrows, black lipstick, and pierced nipples. Melanie didn't know how she knew the girl's tits were pierced—just a ventured guess. All she could think about was paying her a visit and tearing out her innards for the way she failed to appreciate her husband.

Violent thoughts wouldn't stop pouring into her head.

The path ended at a precipice that opened into a wider chasm. Melanie recognized no choice but to descend the rickety ladder all the way down.

At the bottom, a swell of groundwater collected into a mini-lake on the left and the air felt crisp here. Straight ahead, a makeshift church was built into a natural rock formation. Rows of lit candles lined the ground leading to its wooden doors with hand carved crosses etched in them.

Someone was expecting her.

Blackened skulls and broken bones were obstacles and she sidestepped the human remains on her way past the construct. There was another passage that, hopefully, would lead out of this place.

She took a few steps, but halted when the shadows came alive in the ravine's mouth.

Him.

He stepped into the candlelight wearing a dark military coat slick with fresh blood. The gray welder's helmet hung on his face, stained and dented. He lifted his head in acknowledgment—welcoming her after all this time.

I killed you before.

Melanie stepped toward Hoyt and he did the same. She moved another inch and he did too—a perverse mirror image. This was so familiar, not only from twenty-five years ago, but from countless nightmares, too. Whole lives had been lived in between these encounters, and here was the man responsible for creating hers.

That thought was all the motivation Melanie needed. She threw the candle aside and lifted the pickaxe with both arms, ready for battle. Hoyt didn't flinch and she saw her bloodied, half-crazed reflection in the wink of his helmet.

Kill him and you will be free to kill them all.

Another thought that didn't belong to her. She winced at the mounting pressure behind her eyes. It lasted a split second— all the time Hoyt needed to register a killing blow. She braced herself for an impact that never came.

He was gone. Again.

Melanie spun in a circle, but only flickering shadows greeted her. Her head felt like it was about to burst. Hot streaks of white cracked across her vision. She massaged her temples, but that only exacerbated the pain as she went stumbling and caught her balance against the nearby wooden wall.

I need to lie—

Only she couldn't even finish that thought. Wasn't sure what she needed to do, only that she couldn't continue. Or could she? Had she really come this far to die? No. It was time to escape. To return home and make everyone pay.

Melanie could barely see. Curiosity and desperation brought her along the church's wall, the palm of her hand rubbed against the wall for direction as her eyesight waned. She reached the building's corner and hooked around to the front. The doors wobbled open, pushing aside a litter of bones as they parted.

A teenage girl was slumped in the rear pew. Her head was flaccid against the seat's backing, staring at the ceiling with wide, unblinking eyes. Her blonde hair was wet and ratted, her skin dark blue—the result of the chain wrapped twice around her neck.

There was more. Beyond the girl, at the altar across the way, she saw *him* beneath the hanging cross. Chained at the legs, waist, and shoulders. That ragged, green coat was a shred of fabric wrapped around skeletal remains. His mask was gone and his head was in shattered pieces like broken china.

Cyrus Hoyt.

She could only stare. All this time and he'd been down here, rotting. Twenty-five years spent wondering when—not if—Hoyt would show up on her doorstep. But Melanie trusted her gut. As much as she knew someone was trying to kill her, it couldn't have been Cyrus Hoyt.

Because this is him.

An explosion of wood shards flew across her face as an axe head crashed through the outside wall. Melanie spun away from it, but the blade was already lifting.

Cyrus Hoyt appeared in the doorframe a second later, axe in hand and a welder's mask covering his head. He paced the nave, increasing his speed as he neared. With just a few feet left between them, he broke into a sprint.

Melanie slashed down with the pickaxe, catching him off-guard. The blade tore through his shoulder and he grunted.

Only he wasn't Cyrus Hoyt. The voice was female.

This was no time to lay off the aggression. Melanie slammed the blunt edge of her pickaxe against the welder's helmet, but the other woman was fast. She dodged the attack and countered with an upward thrust of her own blade.

The axe caught Melanie's forearm and cleaved a hunk of flesh like chicken off a bone. Both women shrieked and lunged for one another. In the candlelight, Melanie realized how much height she had over her attacker, digging her fingers beneath the welder's plate and lifting the mask from Trish's head. She threw it aside and wrapped her hands around the girl's neck.

Nate's wife was stronger than she looked, brushing off the attack and coming forward with a fist, landing a punch right on Melanie's nose. It dropped her to the ground and left her flailing in a sea of skeletal remains. Trish's dainty hand closed around Melanie's neck like a clamp and lifted her back up. The girl's eyes bulged as strands of drool dangled off her lips.

Both hands closed around Melanie's throat. Every squeeze weakened her oxygen-starved brain. There wasn't much fight left in her to begin with, but now her life spark was nothing more than a birthday candle.

Melanie hung limp, the tips of her toes scraping against a discarded skull. Life slipped away. Eyelids were heavy. Closing them promised relief. Maybe it would be easier if she just gave up. To see what the next life had in store.

Her head fell forward, followed by her entire body. Trish let her drop and Melanie was drowning in bones once more. The killer dropped to her knees to finish the job and Melanie cracked one, a femur, off the girl's mouth, knocking the assailant onto her back.

Melanie could barely stand and Trish was already on sturdier feet, charging again. With nothing left, she threw herself at the killer like a punch-drunk boxer, taking her back down into the bones.

This time it was Melanie who was up first, kicking her face. Trish's nose crunched beneath her sneaker and she slipped beneath the shifting mass of remains. Melanie was on her knees fumbling for the axe hidden beneath the broken skeletons.

Trish bounded to her feet and came forward just as Melanie's hand closed around the weapon. She brought it up and swung it across Trish's face. The girl collapsed against the nave's flimsy structure, sending splintering wood running in every direction.

She was lucky though, because Melanie missed—sort of. Only the flat side of the axe had landed and it was the blunt force that had sent Trish spiraling. Melanie geared for another swing of the axe as the suspended cross high overhead broke from its chain and crashed into the aisle.

Then everything happened at once.

Trish rolled onto her back and saw Melanie coming. She screamed out in horror, attempting to shield herself from the inevitable blow—

Melanie's head tightened as her vision grayed. She lost her footing during the charge and tumbled down, the axe cluttering somewhere beyond her reach.

If this was death, part of her welcomed it.

"Not death." Something slurred.

Her eyes fluttered, but there was nothing to see.

"Not yet, at least," the voice said as if reading her mind. "Not until I say you are ready."

Then let me die, she thought out of pure exhaustion.

"Let you? After everything you went through? Here, look at this…"

Melanie's eyes opened into brilliant sunlight. She squinted and turned her head, finding herself on a beach. The edges of Lake Forest Grove lapped the soles of her naked feet as she stretched out on the sandy towel.

Brady was beside her, dressed in a wet and clingy bathing suit. He was shirtless and Melanie admired his athletic physique every chance she got. He looked at her with a reciprocating smile. "You're not so bad yourself."

This didn't feel right, though it was hard to say why. They hadn't been together this way, despite her deepest desires. So this familiarity was alien and artificial.

And yet, it was natural, too. Wasn't it? They were here just as they spent every Sunday throughout the summer. Lazing on the lake with a picnic basket of turkey sandwiches and Blue Moons. They always drank too much and then went home and screwed like jackrabbits. A perfect way to cap the weekend and always something to look forward to again next week.

"I know this is what you want," the voice said. "There is no reason why it cannot happen. Let me in and it shall be."

In truth, it sounded great. The cool summer breeze in her hair, Brady's wet skin shining in the sunlight, and grains of sand rustling against the palms of her hands—all of it real enough.

"But this is not…"

Nate leans in for a forceful kiss, exploring her lips with intensity that goes beyond what she'd wanted that night at Desiree's. She touches his bulging arms and slides her long legs up and down the sides of his torso. She hasn't done this in years, but feels ready to do it now.

Nate's ready, too. He tugs at her bikini string, pulling it away from her chest as the threads come loose. His hands cup her small breasts. And then he's kissing her everywhere.

"Let me taste you," he says in a voice that isn't exactly his. It sounds hollow and devoid of emotion. "I want to be with you. In you."

Wasn't this man married? In a second, she decides she doesn't care. Nate's tongue makes it harder to concentrate on anything else. Her blood boils all the way up to her brain. Any hotter and her skin would cook right off.

Then she remembers Brady dying. The crackling sound his skin made as the fire took him from this world.

That was real. The pain from that memory was a fresh wound, sensitive to attention and irritated beyond belief. The rest of this—was something else.

She pushes Brady off and gathers her clothes. The façade of Camp Forest Grove falls away like a bathroom towel, leaving only darkness.

Candlelight flickered on all sides, basking the cavern in low light that brought every inanimate object to life through leaping shadows.

Melanie steadied herself on her knees and took a long pull of air while she reclaimed her thoughts. Her head still hurt and there were memories in there that did not belong. But she could think clearly now.

For now.

Trish was out cold. Her jet-black hair was slick with blood from where the axe had landed. She wasn't getting up from that any time soon.

Something grabbed Melanie's hair and yanked it. Lips pressed against her ear, a wet tongue tracing the length of it. A nose sniffed the base of her neck and a coarse hand slipped beneath her shorts and caressed her ass. "I want to be inside you. To crawl across your innards and spread my seed throughout your brain."

Melanie saw something—or the outline of something—as she turned. There was an occasional flicker of negative space that moved. A yellow light grew from nothing, flickering at eye level. She squinted while it widened into an orb, but couldn't look away. Every so often, she saw its form. It was indescribable and far from human.

"You understand nothing." Hot breath blew across her lips. "I know you think terrible things, Melanie Holden. And I know you'd like to do them even more."

She wanted to writhe free, but convulsions of white-hot pain shot off to every neuron in her body. The presence tugged her hair with so much force that she was sure it was about to tear off her scalp.

It purred soft approval. "The darkness within you is tremendous. Decades of despair and resentment have corroded you. Tell me…when you are not plagued by remembrances of your past, how often do you sit awake, obsessing over those who have the lives you want? Happy families. Loving husbands. Beautiful and healthy children. You pretend not to want these things, but only because they are so far out of your grasp. Would you kill those with better lives than yours?"

There was no way to know whether it spoke aloud or existed solely inside her head. Either way, the words weren't true. At least, she didn't think so. Everyone suffered a little envy. A good friend gets a better job than you, or lands a better-looking husband. Buys a better house. Whatever. Colleagues talked often about dates, proposals, engagements and weddings. Once Riley was able to marry, well—she'd been happy for him, but jealous too.

She didn't feel as bad when she had him to revel in the misery. A foolish sentiment, considering Riley had a lover while Melanie had a cat. But without marriage, it hadn't been official. And for some reason, that mattered.

"It doesn't have to be miserable," the voice said. "We can kill Dennis Morton and his whore. And what about that self-hating wife beater you once called husband. Imagine the ways in which we could make him suffer. Let me inside of you and we can do so much more than that."

The offer sounded like an invitation to freedom—to a life without confinement. What could be better than that? Let everyone envy her for a change. This thing wanted companionship. It promised something that her life had been devoid of: satisfaction.

"That's right, my dear," it snarled. "No more being the victim. Can you begin to imagine?"

Oh, I can...

Brady popped a can of beer and thrust it forward.

She took it and glanced at Desiree's Bed & Breakfast. "Am I supposed to be drinking with the chief of police?"

"The great thing about being chief," Brady said with a smirk. "Abuse of power is a-ok, provided it's used to bend the whims of a beautiful woman."

"Ohhhhh," she laughed. "Aren't you a little forward tonight?"

"Liquid courage."

"So is that all this is," she asked with more confidence than she'd ever had. "Just a fling? A tawdry one night stand?"

He threw his beer to the ground and hoisted her onto the hood of his patrol car. "Not even close, Miss Holden."

"Not here, Nate! Someone will see us."

"Doesn't that make it more exciting?" he laughed, sliding her shorts down past her thighs and kissing her legs.

It definitely did.

It was all a lie and she knew it. But wasn't it oh so much more preferable to dying at the bottom of a cave beside the chief of police's widow?

It definitely was.

 **The Intruder**

I have no name, girl.

You struggle with this, as if suddenly knowing what I was once called would permit you to understand me.

You can never.

We're taking a step forward, you and I, and it is frustrating that I cannot get you to move as I wish. I try to take you one way and you fight me to go another. This—process would be smoother if you simply rescinded control.

Of course, I have no excuse. I used to be much better at this.

Prowling the corners of your mind proves a fascinating exercise. There is so much pain in you and your knowledge is extensive—far beyond the last human I occupied, though that was a long time ago, when beliefs were primitive and the world was coliseums and tunics. Unbridled faith, then. Hilarious superstition.

Yes, the last time I was here, things were different. The world wagered its hard-earned bronze on the outcomes of gladiatorial slaughter. On the bloodiest arena days, when the city stunk of spilt entrails and excrement, I savored carnage that was set to the enthusiastic roars of an entire city. That should have been enough to sate me, right? Thousands of people's bloodlust reaching hysteric heights, the more brutal the demise, the more satisfied the cheer. But mutually agreed upon slaughter grows surprisingly boring and uneventful.

For you, I suppose it would be like suffering through…Sunday football.

That is the most appropriate comparison that I can find in your head.

Anyway, if I was going to stay, I needed things to get worse.

Even then, there were men who refused to fear me. Men for whom it was not enough to interpret the word of their Gods, they had to enforce it as well. They roved the world, battling heretical beliefs wherever they surfaced. At that time, the heretics were a barbarian tribe—pests, really, and more primitive than the primitives. I was delighted to watch the blood spill—both sides dying in equal measure. While those lives were discarded like pawns on a chessboard, I cast my watchful eye on their mourning families—succulent grief that was a welcome ripple effect of the skirmish.

The sweetest death is innocent collateral. I enjoyed crawling the minds of those wives and children, feasting off their final, most terrified seconds. In troubled times, it is all too easy to blend in among the lost, though my chameleon ways were not enough.

Despite the enduring war of ideologies, the men, those…believers, sensed my hand in the mayhem and hunted me still. And it was because of one particularly careless evening that they got me.

It's what led me here.

I had been enjoying my time on the inside of a pestilent beggar. His body was sick and rotted from so many diseases that he should have been dead several times over. He would have gone silently from the world had I not slipped behind his eyes one evening. I have seen lots, but the hardships suffered by this creature were…delightful. Can you begin to imagine a life where you knew not a single instance of kindness? You have suffered some, girl, but nothing compared to this mongrel.

I caressed his mind and came to realize this man could not grasp the concept of happiness. No opportunity, no friendship, and certainly not love.

His thoughts were corrosive even before I arrived. He fantasized about raping the women who happened past. He hardened at thoughts of killing their men and taking what he wanted. He had never known a female's embrace and that withdrawal grew to muted aggression. It occupied his every thought. His desolation was so severe that he could not recall his own name. Understand then, that all he needed was a simple nudge.

So we followed a shop owner, a plebeian girl, one evening. I was along for the ride, yes, an intruder in my vessel's thoughts. But, unlike you, he was determined to do all the work. He only needed a little assurance, which is what I offered.

Only we were not going to get away with it.

My vessel was fucking and murdering the shop girl when the believers caught up. She rattled around on the floor in a death spasm. You would have thought that it would have been enough to slow the leper down. But his thoughts...the perversion, he found it all so very exciting. It made him want to thrust his diseased sex into her harder, while hacking her head from her neck with a jagged stone blade.

Every atrocity this man had suffered in his life was channeled into this act of bloody depravity. And he would have just been getting started if not for the interruption.

They jammed a spear through his back. A blade blessed with the words and water of their holiest. His flesh wilted in the most painful allergic reaction you can imagine.

Before I could understand the severity of this, robed men descended, hacking with daggers, broadswords, and spears. Each blade was embossed with more than just purified water. The incantation was sworn into every piece of hungry metal.

They knew whom they'd been seeking.

The violence did not harm me, but my vessel was as good as dead from a thousand injuries. In his fleeting seconds, he wondered why he had ever believed in my whispers, but perhaps I should not tell you that.

The sanctified weapons had a different effect on me. I cannot find the right word in your modern tongue, although I suppose 'tranquilizer' works well enough. Sure, the blades had a tranquilizing effect, forcing me into manifest submission. All I could do was dwell in the thoughts of the dying—a man who held no remorse for his actions. As his body failed, he admitted to me that he wanted more. Begged for it.

If my own situation had not been so...uncertain, I might have been touched.

The weapons seared me to that body while sprays of holy water repressed my abilities.

Right now, you theorize that it has been two thousand years since those days. Can that be true? It explains why I can barely get you to put a foot forward. Let's try that again, by the way. One foot, and then the other. Very good. I only want to get you out of here.

To help you take revenge.

This helplessness you feel, I felt it then. When the believers wrapped the leper head-to-toe in a linen shroud that was damp with the Holy One's words. It burned so much, even for a non-corporeal such as myself. But I never felt as defeated as when the Holy One knelt beside me and pressed an opened palm to the leper's head.

When I heard his words, harsh and jagged on his tongue, I knew that I had lost.

It was a dialect not of that time or place and he navigated it with familiarity. As soon as he was finished, that diseased pile of flesh became my prison.

They took me then on a tiresome journey by sea. All I could do was settle into the vessel's bones and pour through his depressing memories, one by one.

It was sustenance enough, but just barely.

Months passed before the body was completely rotted. Rats and bugs tried feasting on the gray and purple flesh, but the believers always shooed them off. Had they known that they were relieving me of such an unpleasant sensation, they surely would have left the creatures to their devices.

Horses dragged me across rugged terrain for several weeks and my powers waned with each mile. The believers knew what they were doing and once the caravan ceased, incessant digging filled my ears. When they were not burrowing, they prayed over me—their effort to smite me with love, I suppose.

Yes, they called me 'demon' in the language of the day, but only because they felt compelled to define me. I will tell you that I do not care for that word and it does not describe me.

I already said there is no way to do that.

They tied rope around what remained of the leper's body, lowering us into the earthen tunnel. I assumed that would be the end of it, but there were men down there with us—entombing us so that the world would never hear from me again.

Over time, I was able to reclaim traces of my influence and ability—even if the bones served as my prison bars. The problem was that in the deepest, darkest pit on earth, I was powerless to do anything other than simply exist.

Yes, it was Tullus Abblon who stumbled across my grave. As misguided as he was, the fool believed he could circumvent the end times through acts of kindness and civility. He was weak-willed, however, and I was able to twist his thoughts into something else.

He heard my whispers. There was never any doubt that it was his vengeful God speaking and he convinced his followers to commit atrocities in 'my' name. Just like the leper, every killing increased their hatred and madness and the more they did it, the more they loved it.

Would you believe that I could not use this sway to influence my freedom? So close to it after all this time, only to be foiled by misplaced loyalty.

I promised them rewards, but their refusal was swift. Abblon's Priestess might have been smarter, for at least she recognized what I was. That is to say, she knew enough to consider me a demon, even though she enjoyed having me in her thoughts.

What happened next made me temporarily forget about my terrible fortune. My senses were aroused by a violent onslaught. Modern day weaponry is capable of such devastation, and it produced chaos so rich that I devoured every bit of it.

Once it was over, the victors stacked the corpses of Abblon and his followers down here. Explosives entombed me once more, although vibrations shook the very stones used to detain me, and my prison's most brittle bones ground to dust beneath the weight of sliding rocks.

I was free. Or I should have been…if not for the cross suspended directly overhead.

The Christian symbol somehow supplemented the binding incantation—a stroke of unfortunate luck that left me with no choice but to be amused. Freedom was in the air and I was perpetually tormented by an obstruction.

I put my faith in a young survivor. A boy who did not take part in the battle. Who instead wandered the caverns, fantasizing about his earlier murder of a stray dog. A child whose mind was so scrambled and detached that I could not influence it—no matter how hard I tried.

If I were paranoid, I would have wondered if this was not yet another extension of the Holy One's incantation. The cruelest part, perhaps.

But the boy, wow, you are very curious about him, was black-hearted. He was fixated on the slaughter of innocents. Nothing provoked or created it. His Obviate brothers showed him how liberating it could be to murder the unsuspecting, but the desire was always there.

He used every ounce of energy to clear a path out of his would-be tomb. Then he went after any one he could get his hands on, motivated by a fear that the same brutal fate of his family would befall him as well should anyone else trespass on his property. The child honed his skills gradually for over a decade and always returned here for shelter. Eventually, he forged multiple entrances and made this place his home. During that time, I might have filled his ears with whispers that encouraged more violence. I do not think it had any effect, but how could I not at least try?

Cyrus Hoyt was bloodthirsty and the screams of his victims were music to my ears.

Until he got himself killed.

Twice.

A lawman found his way down next, carrying the poor, stupid boy all wrapped and bound. Reminded me of what they'd done to my vessel all those ages ago. When I touched his thoughts, I learned that the boy had a half-sister. If she could come within my grasp, I could find a way to make things interesting again.

She came many times, but it was recently, on a nostalgic afternoon hike in the forest, that she finally got close enough for me to do something. Not much, mind you, but I plucked the boy's consciousness out of the void and stuffed it inside of her—a little sibling trick from the old world, used long ago by selfish souls who were so desperate to keep their lives that they thought nothing of stomping out the ones belonging to their children.

It wasn't perfect, but it was the only way left to keep him alive. I could not bear to see this community bury its dark past. Why should they be afforded an end to such tragedy? This was the only way to keep me entertained. It would've worked better if he had been more than a half-brother, but sister is such a mess of confusion and doubt now that I'm starting to believe it worked perfectly.

Sure, I would have tried to sit inside her brain had she gotten closer. But it is so rare for me to receive visitors down here. Besides, does not Trish look cute when dressed up like big bad brother?

Now stop fighting me. Your skin fits me like a sword fits a sheath and yet you have the audacity to struggle. You are reluctant when all I want to do is leave this place. These surroundings are sickening. A few more steps and we will be on our way. Just keep going.

You know Nate Brady is never coming back. That is beyond even my ability and perhaps I was wrong to lie to you about it. If we are going to have a relationship, you and I, I need to make you trust me. If it were not for those thoughts of perfect days and lusty nights, you might not have allowed me inside. See, you have to agree to my 'intrusion.' And, in turn, I can help with all of that rage and resentment. Oh, please let me help you with that.

No. Do not try hiding your most secretive moments. If there are things you have never admitted to yourself, then we will explore them together.

No. Do not scream, you insolent bitch. I will not allow it. As we come to know one another intimately, understand that I am not content to guide you like cattle. It will be much more interesting to allow you to discover the darkness inside yourself. I know your body is hurt, but you will not die with me deep inside you.

There. See? We've cleared the cavern and now, as I inhale through your nostrils, I realize this is the first time in two thousand years that I smell fresh air. So tell me: what shall we do first?

I see the answer in images and it is all very interesting.
You want revenge.

We are walking through the forest and I am getting used to controlling a vessel again. Your brain is so much more interesting than the last one and I pick and choose information like books on a shelf.

So much to learn.

It's a brave new world out here. And it is ripe for the taking.

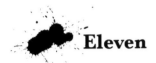 **Eleven**

Trish's eyes and nostrils were runny when she came to. Pulling the slicked coat off her body revealed hairs standing on end. Her head hurt like hell, but for the first time in days, her mind was incredibly clear.

Her cheeks were slathered in what felt like goopy face paint. She rubbed a palm over her forehead and tried to understand what had happened. Where she was.

The last thing she remembered was freaking out in her childhood bedroom. Another headache set in as soon as Dad had gone—a preface to the inevitable blackout.

A bloodied axe lay on top of what she hoped was a collection of animal's bones. As her eyes adjusted to the low levels of light, she counted half a dozen human skulls and promptly vomited all over them.

This was worse than any heroin comedown, but the symptoms were remarkably similar.

I'm beneath the camp. That had to be it.

There was always chatter about some kind of cavern beneath the forest in high school, but no one had ever managed to confirm its reality. It wasn't for the lack of looking, either, because if a secret place to smoke up and fuck existed, then her classmates would've pioneered its discovery.

It was dark and she inched her way out of the structure,

thrashing her arms around to refrain from smashing headfirst into anything. The human refuse was up to her ankles and she kicked a path straight through it, spotting the outline of something in the pew closest to the doors. She quickened her pace to get there.

"Oh God."

Tanya was dead, the life strangled from her. Her face was pocked with dark splotches of post-mortem straining and her tongue was poised between her lips like she was blowing a permanent raspberry. In a quick flash, Trish remembered the chain in her own hands, lassoing it around the girl's neck and tugging with a hideous growl.

That couldn't be right.

She hurried on through the cold and unwelcoming cave, guided by unconscious intuition. Déjà vu hit her hard as she recalled being down here before—several times, actually. That recollection spread as she stepped along the narrow pathway that ascended into the forest.

She had been chasing someone last night, right? No, that wasn't it. It was her brother who gave chase. He was after a battered blonde woman and could think only of killing her.

Trish couldn't understand how she knew that Cyrus Hoyt had gone after Melanie. An especially blurry memory came into focus, strengthening her confusion. Melanie was nude and almost completely submerged beneath a mountain of bubbles, resting after a recent jog. But Trish was inside the room already, in hiding and waiting for her return. Only it wasn't her. She would've had no reason to do that. But *he* would.

My brother's long dead.

He wasn't, though, and now she knew it. Cyrus had been all set to kill Melanie while she stretched out in that tub, her long and smooth legs dangling over the edge—taunting him to come get her. He thought he was ready for it, too. Until he had stalked past the room's mirror, knife in hand, and saw something reflected in it that he could not process—the reflection of Trish Brady staring back.

Last night, Cyrus had been enraged to see *them* set fire to the cabin. For the second time, he had almost lost Melanie to unwanted competition. They surrounded the building, preparing her for sacrifice while he went around back—the very opening that Trish now squeezed through. It was a last-ditch effort to beat them to the kill. After everything, he was not willing to lose her at the end.

Dad had been down here, injured and close to death when Cyrus found him. No, her brother couldn't let him go out like that—not when there was so much unfinished business between them. It's what drove him to bury the pickaxe deep inside his chest with enough hatred to lift him off the ground.

So Dad was dead and it made her feel sick all over again. She stopped to puke before crawling up through the forest floor. All she wanted to do now was go to Nate and beg him to leave this place. Mom had been right all along—they could never be happy here.

She remembered something else about last night that got her heart pounding.

Melanie hadn't been alone in that cabin.

Nate had been there, too.

"Oh God," she said as the tears came. Trish hurried for the camp, despite the feeling that it was already too late.

I can't fight this.

It was akin to riding shotgun in your own head. You saw the road, but had no control over which direction was taken. Melanie tried stepping one way and her feet fell another. Wanted to look around, but glared straight ahead. She couldn't even control her own voice.

"Do not be scared," it said. "I told you that I mean you no harm."

Fight this.

"But why fight? Is it my invasiveness? You will have your lovely body back, believe me. Melanie, you are so much more interesting when left to your own devices."

Then go now, she screamed without screaming.

"I know why you came here...to the grove." She tried stopping herself from talking, but it was no use. Her own words had turned against her. "And I would love to see you leave fulfilled."

You want to help so much that you let that crazy bitch try to kill me.

"Do not go blaming Trish. She is a victim, same as you. When her brother took over, he was in complete control. Yes, some of their thoughts might have mixed together, but that could not be avoided. I am more interested in you now...because you chose to remain here, despite the attempts on your life. You risked it rather than tucking your tail between your legs and going home a failure. To you, that is scarier than death."

Death is only scary when you have something to lose.

"Do not pretend with me. You have done nothing but fight. And you expect me to believe you have nothing to live for?"

I don't fear death anymore. That doesn't mean I want it. I have nothing waiting for me back home.

The intruder considered these thoughts as they moved. Its mind was wide open and peering into it was like looking through a two-way mirror. She suddenly recalled the old tongue as though she always had known it. There was a world of winged creatures larger than jumbo jets and monsters the size of skyscrapers. Others battled them—both through words and actions. An unfamiliar time and place beyond her own.

That didn't interest her. Not now. All that mattered was getting the intruder out of her head. It was quite experienced at hiding its vulnerabilities and each time she searched for one, its attention shifted elsewhere—the thought lost like ashes on the wind.

"You are a fighter," her voice beamed. "Good. I know that I made the right choice. All that is left is to make sure that you have it in you."

"Have WHAT?" The words that came past her lips were for once hers. That surprised the intruder.

"Do not question me. Be grateful that I have not stripped you nude and splayed you between these trees, inviting every creature in this woods to have its way with what sits between your legs."

Melanie didn't respond. If she was going to survive, she was going to have to be smart.

"Correct." Her voice was strange again, singed with cruelty. "Know your place. Start thinking about how you intend to prove your worth. I must admit, I was upset to see the Obviate take our lawman out of the equation. How I would have relished the look on his face when he saw that it was you coming to take his life."

Melanie stopped moving. The intruder moved her eyes back the way they came. Its mind flashed with excitement. "Brady may be dead…but his wife is not."

But Hoyt is still inside her.

"*Was*. His resurrection was a display of my power. Now that I am free, I require all of my energy. We can do better than him and I tire of this place."

Melanie wondered if the Obviate would hear the whispers with the intruder gone. Could they keep on sacrificing to a god that would no longer speak to them?

"It will be fun to find out, will it not?"

All she could think about was killing Trish Brady. A girl she now despised, but also pitied. Nate's wife had become a blunt instrument against her own will—a fate no one deserved.

Would it really be so bad? Killing that ungrateful bitch?

The intruder laughed and clapped her hands together at the cerebral mention of murder.

Melanie liked the idea the more it marinated. Trish Brady was nothing more than a thirty-year-old teenager. She willingly turned her marriage into a sham because she couldn't maintain a nightly routine of martini parties and pretentious art blather. She never deserved Nate. It was appalling to see a person who refused to appreciate the things they had when others would've killed for them.

I will kill for them.

It was easy to find the remnants of Camp Forest Grove. The wooded air was heavy with the smell of charred cabin embers. All that remained of the counselor's bunk was the stone chimney and a few ankle-high sections of wall that the fire hadn't managed to nibble away just yet.

Melanie moved softly through the smoldering debris. Trish was on her knees at the ruins' edge, stroking Nate's blackened skeleton as tears dribbled down her bloodied face. If she noticed that she had company, she didn't seem to care.

She wondered how the girl had recognized the body of her husband before the chief's burnt badge caught her eye in the morning sun.

As much as Melanie wanted to kill this woman, she was much too weak for a straight-on attack. All weapons were underground, meaning she was going to have to find another. She crept toward Pete Dugan's old cabin, leaving the grieving widow lost in her own misery. Breaths were harder to get as her stomach rose in painful bursts, but it was almost unnoticeable thanks to her intruder.

The cabin was a ruddy mess. Melanie fished a rusted butcher's knife out of a puddle of rainwater that filled a broken drawer in the kitchen. Heart racing, she headed toward her prey, hobbling through crab grass with clenched fists.

Trish hadn't moved. Her shoulders trembled with distress while cradling Nate's remains.

Melanie inched forward, blade raised.

At the back of her mind, the visitor spoke: *Very good. I want you to have a better life, Melanie. Believe me.*

I do, she thought. *Watch me gut her like a fish.*

Melanie rushed ahead while the intruder whispered final words of encouragement that failed to resonate. She was in control of her actions here and imagined throwing the girl on her back and carving through that opaque skin. As bad as she wanted the girl's husband, she wanted this bitch's life more.

Trish was within stabbing distance now.

With her teeth gnashed, Melanie raised the blade and then slammed it down with a shriek. It tore through her own belly and she twisted it with such violence that a full-bodied scream escaped her lips in spite of the intruder's lockdown.

It was angry now, demanding to know why she gave it all up. *Your enemies were going to know what it was like to suffer at your hands. And your students...all those impressionable minds. You threw everything away.*

The intruder lamented this lost opportunity and Melanie screamed over its whispers. "Trish, pick up the blade and kill me. Please. It's in me!"

Trish's confused eyes locked onto the knife.

"Grab it, Trish. Hurry. Before it takes you!"

Blood spilled through Melanie's fingers like a broken damn. No point in putting pressure on the wound. It was time to go, taking this monster with her.

I can keep you alive for as long as I want, you fool. This accomplishes nothing. Last time they stopped me, those weapons were blessed. Blessed!

Trish scooped the knife but kept her distance as a terrified spectator, Melanie's pleas for murder lost on her. That, or she was unwilling to help.

Her inhibitions may not be as…interesting as yours, but they will do. I can grow them into something wonderful. We shall start by taking the life of the woman who tried stealing her husband away. While she is killing you, remember all the things you could have had, but elected to give up. Its taunts continued in a foreign tongue that berated her further.

The old tongue.

That was when she caught it. Just as the intruder could snatch her own thoughts, she found what she had been looking for inside its ancient memories.

The prayer.

It was what the Holy One had used to bind him—the language of long ago. Just like that, the incantation was in her head. A split second later, it was on her lips, a long-forgotten tongue that she now spoke with fluidity.

She repeated the harsh sounds and clicking syllables as spilling blood softened the ground around her. This was the end and the least she could do was keep the intruder inside—a temporary conclusion to this nightmare would have to do. She was willing to die for that.

As soon as Melanie made peace with her passing, Trish fell to her knees in tears, screaming, "YES, YES, YES!" in response to an unspoken offer.

And then, the intruder was gone.

Melanie spouted the words again, quickly and before the memories faded. The evil had to be contained somewhere and now it was going to have to be in Trish.

A short-lived but mischievous grin flashed across Trish's mouth as the bloody face charged, dropping onto Melanie and striking in frenzy.

The knife shot down and Melanie lifted a palm to her eyes—her last remaining line of defense. The blade ripped through it, halting the implement an inch away from her gaze. She yanked her impaled hand away, taking the knife with it as ropes of blood swung wide.

Trish's eyes glowed yellow for a second as she shifted her weight onto Melanie's self-inflicted stomach wound. Then they flecked back to hazel-green as the younger woman's assault continued undeterred. The intruder's influence waned following the incantation, but not fast enough.

Melanie couldn't survive much more of this. "I wanted to save you."

Trish leaned in so their noses scraped together. "I'm going to kill you," she growled.

Melanie slapped her bladed palm down at the base of Trish's neck and the protruding tip tore into the younger woman's flesh with a slow squish. Melanie grunted and closed her free hand around the knife's jutting hilt, shoving it further through her hand so that it sailed deeper into Trish.

Trish's hands came for her throat, but Melanie forced the blade to dig further, even as the attack kept coming—hands wrenched around Melanie's neck, squeezing.

The girl on top of Melanie was no longer recognizable as her short-lived friend. She snarled like an animal.

Melanie was desperate to get this *thing* off her and it had to be now if she wanted to breathe again. She lifted her head as far as it could go, using the only weapon at her disposal: her teeth. She bit the deranged face and caught the tip of Trish's nose between her teeth. Then it was her turn to growl, crunching through it with a clenched jaw. The nose severed and dropped onto Melanie's tongue as her teeth scraped together. Melanie spat the detached tip into the dirt as the girl convulsed and then slumped to one side with alarming quickness.

In a second, she was dead.

Melanie stared at the body in disbelief, her hand still attached to the blade that had killed her. It was finally over.

At last.

In the distance, an approaching siren.

Saved again, she thought.

And then slept.

Four days in the hospital.

Recovery had been touch and go for a while, according to the doctor. Blood loss was staggering. By the time the troopers brought Melanie in, her already pale complexion was paper white.

The police were dying to get at her with their questions and the sheriff's office had stationed men outside her room around the clock. No one was allowed to come or go without clearing it with them. They watched every doctor and nurse with extreme scrutiny.

Melanie was grateful for this—the safest she'd felt in years. It was only awkward when she had to use the bathroom.

From the hall, nurses and doctors spoke casually, drowned out by the constant *blip, blip, blip* of her heart monitor. Her nose wrinkled at the unpleasant odor of antiseptics as she faded in and out of consciousness.

At one point, she awoke to find Officer Jamie Galeberg in the room, standing at the windows with his hands folded at the small of his back. She sneezed and he turned around.

"Miss Holden," he said.

Melanie greeted him but found nothing more to say. He pulled a chair bedside all the same.

They were similar in some ways—sole survivors. Melanie's

was the only account of what had happened on the lake, while
he was the only surviving member of Forest Grove P.D.

"I, uh, don't know that we'll ever understand why things
happened the way they did," he said. "Forensic evidence from
Officer Donnelley's murder gives us Trish…looks like she pinned
her father to a wall beneath the camp and killed a teenage
girl down there, too. God only knows why she snapped, but it
happens. Especially considering that insanity runs in her family."

Melanie remembered the girl's yellow eyes in those final
moments. What had the intruder offered that made her so willing
to accept? She remembered how convincing the illusion of
her picnic on the lake had been and assumed it was something
similar. An offer of life with her husband once more, most likely.
No way to know for sure, but that expression of madness would
haunt her forever.

"I thought you should know that Captain Oviedo and his
guys made some arrests in town," Galeberg said. "The night
everything went bad. People who live here. I still don't know
what to think."

"They're dangerous," she said and couldn't figure out how
to say anything more without sounding like a lunatic. "If you saw
the look on their faces as they set the cabin on fire…one of them
willingly burned alive to make sure—"

"I know," he said. "Take it easy. We're aware of what
happened. I didn't know Chief Brady as well as I might've liked,
but I knew him enough to say he was a good man."

Better than that.

"When you're ready, miss, the sheriff's office is going to
have some questions for you. After that, I suppose you might
want to say goodbye to Forest Grove for good."

Melanie agreed to see the sheriff and he arrived a few
hours later. An obese man with a receding hairline, he threw
a catalog of questions at her. She fielded them with honesty,

leaving only the ancient intruder out of her responses. Even now, she couldn't reconcile what had happened and there was no reason to make anyone suggest that her mental health had receded in the wake of her concussion.

Once that was finished, she met Galeberg in the hospital parking lot. He'd collected her things from Desiree's and loaded the LaCrosse with a full tank of gas. She was packed and ready to go when he put an arm on her shoulder and gave her a surprisingly violent tug.

"Don't come back," he said. "Say everything you have to say in your book, but don't you ever come back here."

Melanie didn't know how to take that and it didn't matter. She was planning to follow his advice to the letter.

The drive home was three hours, but it felt like six. Coming home always felt that way. She missed Lacey more than anything else and couldn't wait to get her hands on the little gray kitty. The only thing she could think about was wrapping her arms around her and listening to soothing purrs all night long.

Riley and Aaron wouldn't be such a horrible sight for sore eyes, either.

Aaron answered the door and hugged her immediately.

"I can't even imagine, hun," he said. "We pushed you into it, I'm so sorry."

"Don't be crazy," she offered an unconvincing laugh. "I ran as far away from that night as I could. I had to go back eventually."

"And now?"

"Now I don't know." If the intruder ever got out of its prison, there would be plenty to fear. That was a possibility she would worry about every day for the rest of her life. But anxiety wasn't going to control her anymore. Life was too short for that.

They ate grilled chicken marinated in lemon pepper with asparagus on the side while drinking Belgian ale that reminded her of Nate. How badly she wished things might've been different.

Eventually, they talked about Forest Grove. Melanie kept most of the details close to the vest. There was the temptation to talk more about the intruder, but these friends—as good as they were—wouldn't have believed her any more than the sheriff's office.

That was her burden to bear.

According to the news, a small group of disgruntled residents were about to take the heat for every Connecticut cold case that could be leveled against them. The press was having a field day with headlines, everything from *Connecticult*, to *ConnectiCUT* had already been leveraged during reporting. The state was trying to spin the negative publicity into something positive by boosting their solved statistics—and why not? Many of those cases probably had a lot to do with the Obviate.

After dinner, Riley packed Lacey up in her kitty transport and asked what she was planning to do about school in the fall.

Melanie hadn't yet considered it and only shrugged. "Dunno. Quit, maybe?"

"You're kidding," he gasped.

"Why not? There are other ways of sticking it to Dennis Morton."

"Sounds like the best decision you've ever made," he said. "But don't listen to me, I'm the guy who told you to go back and face your fears."

"Oh, I'm never listening to you again," she said. "But you weren't wrong. And I'm still going to write that book. I already owed Bill and Jen that much. There's just more people to add to that list now." Nate, Desiree, and even Trish. In the end, she must've loved Brady more than anything for as readily as she had accepted that demon. And wasn't it her fearlessness most of all that enabled Melanie to find courage in her own actions?

She hated that she couldn't blame the woman. In those final, horrible hours, it was obvious that the Bradys were in love. Till death did they part.

Riley handed the cat to Melanie. Between the plastic bars, Lacey purred a little welcome home song for her. She hugged the cat's babysitters and wiped allergic tears from Aaron's eyes. Then she brought the kitty out to the car and headed home, surprised by how relaxed she felt.

True, there were things in this world worse than Cyrus Hoyt. But the intruder was bound to Trish's body and would likely stay that way for years. And the Obviate were still out there, but she guessed they were in hiding and would wither on the vine as soon as they realized the whispers had gone silent.

She swung into the driveway and sat there for a long and quiet moment. In the kitty crate beside her, Lacey whined with impatience—sensing they were close to home, perhaps.

Home, Melanie thought, as if this were the first time she had truly returned from Forest Grove. Once she quit her job tomorrow, she'd get started on the book. She'd also look around to see if any nearby schools might be more appreciative of her talents.

Or maybe I'll sell my house and make for the city instead.

Any city.

Her options were wide open and she contemplated them all with a smile.

For the first time in her adult life, she felt free.

Whispered Voices

The whisper never truly faded.

After all this time and mileage, Zohra heard it. Its hissing tongue was little more than an echo most days. Harmless reverberations that reminded her of a life once lived. Every so often, its influence came in faint whispers, just as it had come over the grove's treetops in the years following Abblon's death.

But today it was especially loud.

The courtyard view, a perimeter of freshly clipped hedges and an expansive, bubbling fountain, was calming. Zohra shifted in her wheelchair while staring at it, remembering a time long ago when she was more than just an invalid.

The Priestess was gone, but today the whisper demanded her return.

"Zohra…it's time." Doctor Van Dyce stood in the doorway, checking his watch. "May I escort you down?"

She'd been dreading this ever since receiving the news: her husband and daughter had both been taken from her in the span of one cruel evening.

Never would have happened if they hadn't forced me into this place.

It's true that she was older now—frail and arthritic—but the Obviate needed their Priestess more than ever. They were a serpent with a severed head, writhing without direction, just as they had for the last two decades. She did not fully know what had happened in the grove, but it was their carelessness that had almost ruined everything.

It was hard to believe it even took this long.

"Zohra, I know this is difficult. If you are not up to the task—"

"We can go now, doctor." She swallowed the words with grim resolve. This was the day she hoped would never come.

Ron, you fool. Why did you let her go back?

Pride had always been her husband's greatest sin. Leave it to him to believe he was in control of a situation so far beyond him. He thought he could protect his little girl from anything. But why? He certainly hadn't protected his wife.

Doctor Van Dyce took the wheelchair and guided her through a hall of pale and desolate faces, weaving around the less sentient patients. At the end of the corridor, an orderly thrust an oversized key into an elevator interface and unlocked thick sliding doors. Once inside, the metal slipped shut amidst a blood-curdling scream from the treatment room down the hall.

"I'm alone," Zohra said, the thought dawning on her for the first time.

"I am sorry for your loss," the doctor said. "But you have to know that is not true. The grieving process will take time, but it's not something you will endure alone. The friends you have made here care about you very much. They will help if you let them."

Her first reaction was to laugh, but Doctor Van Dyce didn't need to see her emotions fall out of check. That would lead to more sessions than she could stand. How many times was she supposed to take responsibility for her failings when it was the whisper that was accountable for her past?

It was closer now, crawling around in her head the way it used to.

The doors re-opened in a part of the hospital she hadn't

seen once in her twenty-five years here: a clinically white hallway with dirty brown floor tiles. Her chair bumped over the grouted rivets as they pushed through double doors that lead into a spacious morgue.

Her eyes went to the small white sheet resting on the center slab.

"Can you identify this body, ma'am?" the morgue attendant asked. He pulled the sheet down without waiting for a response.

It was Trish. And she was peaceful, at least at first glance. Slipshod work had been done to mask the entry wound on her neck and there was some kind of rubbery protuberance on the tip of her nose. The make-up was unconvincing, like it had been attempted on the ride from Connecticut to New York.

But Zohra angled her head and was able to catch the body in exactly the right light. Trish appeared as her sleeping beauty once more. Suddenly, Zohra remembered how she used to peer into her bedroom in the middle of the night just to make sure all was well.

What happened to you, my little tulip?

She wanted to cry, but felt only anger.

Zohra asked to know what happened in Forest Grove, but the doctors wouldn't say much, only what they felt she could handle—which was almost nothing. Even now, Doctor Van Dyce stood at the edge of the room, stroking his salt and pepper goatee while observing her reaction. It didn't matter what she did, she was going to answer for it in their next session. Didn't cry enough. Cried too much. Everything was indicative of failing mental health and he would use that in his quest to keep her committed until her dying days.

So she shook her head and spoke. "She hadn't visited in a while. But this is her. This is my Trish."

The last time she'd seen her was right before the move

back to Forest Grove. Zohra was appalled by the news—especially after finding out that relocating had been Nathan's request. She didn't know if Nathan was dead, but the news couldn't have been good if they hauled her body to upstate New York for identification.

Ugly words had been exchanged the last time mother and daughter spoke—the kind often reserved for bitter enemies. Before storming out, Zohra screamed that Trish was getting what she deserved by going back to that hellhole.

I should have been honest with her. Told her about the Priestess. She never would've gone back then.

That regret echoed through her mind as she looked at the colorless body laid out on the slab. She never wanted Trish to think of her as a freak, but the looks her daughter gave during her visitations were painful—like she pitied her mother more than loved her. She would often ask Trish to bring Nathan on the next visit, but her daughter would barely acknowledge the request and certainly never fulfilled it.

The morgue attendant pulled the sheet back over her. "She's going to be buried in Forest Grove with her father, unless you have any objection."

"New York was her home," Zohra said. "I know we are far from the city, but she would have wanted to be put to rest here."

The attendant shuffled over to the doctor and they spoke out of earshot.

While they were occupied, she rolled forward and pulled the sheet back far enough to glimpse Trish one last time before throwing her head into her palms and weeping.

Doctor Van Dyce came over and put gentle hands on her shoulders. "Let's go," he said, sounding almost glad for this display of emotion. "This is good, you need to acknowledge this so that you can deal with it."

"No," Zohra screamed. The thought of this being the

final goodbye was too much. "Please," she said. "Just one more moment. This is the last time I will ever see my daughter."

It doesn't have to be, the voice whispered. It had so much clarity that she thought she was back in the Hall of the Arrival.

Then there was unrequited joy. It spread throughout her, pulsing like a familiar red light. She wasn't alone after all and never would be again.

Welcome, Priestess.

"She always wanted to be put to rest here," Zohra said. "But she never wanted to be buried…only cremated."

"That we can do," the attendant said.

The whisper was here, somehow. Inside her daughter.

Zohra's friends would listen to her when she was ready to lecture about the end times—and what needed to be done in order to prevent them.

They would follow her lead and do as they were told.

She grinned ear-to-ear on the trip back to the elevator, not caring if the doctor noticed. There was nothing he could do to thwart her now.

Zohra asked to go back to her room.

"Of course," the doctor said. "You should get some rest."

"Rest," she agreed without really hearing him. Her thoughts were of the whisper. There was a lot of work to be done. She was about to be reunited with an old friend and had to look her best for the occasion.

Afterword & Acknowledgements

Maybe I bit off more than I can chew this time.

I remember thinking that every couple of hours as I worked to construct the mystery of *Under the Blade*. For a while there, every plot twist I came up with managed to break chains of logic from earlier in the story. And each time that would happen, I'd go back into my notes and examine the history of Forest Grove until I found a way forward that didn't sacrifice any of my preexisting story beats.

Of the seven novels I've written (three of which sit in various stages of completion), this was the toughest nut to crack. But once I did it, once those puzzle pieces started clicking into place, so satisfying was the experience that I knew I was going to be at this game for the duration.

In preparing *Under the Blade* for this release, I was reminded of how much my life has changed, both personally and professionally, in the five years between its original completion and the publication of this second edition. Writing is an ongoing learning experience, but I think there's always one project that gives a fledgling author the confidence to continue. The reaction to this book somehow made all those late night story struggles even more fulfilling, because I think that work paid off.

With this edition, I hope a broader audience discovers *Under the Blade* and I'm asking for your help to make that happen. Every review, no matter how brief, is invaluable. If you enjoyed this book, even a two-sentence Amazon critique would mean the world. And if you want to tell the story of Cyrus Hoyt while huddled with your friends around the campfire, well, I'm not going to stop you. But if you say his name above a whisper, I won't be held responsible.

Of the millions of books out in the world, thanks so much for trying this one.

See you at camp,

Matt
June 2018

A good chunk of my youth was spent prowling video store shelves for horror content, and I have to thank my father for his lax attitude when it came to letting me rent anything I wanted. Just as responsible for cultivating my love of the macabre, however, and she may be surprised to hear this, is my mother. She nurtured my literary proclivities with a stream of genre paperbacks from yard sale tables and book swaps all over town. No better way to invest a child in reading than by giving him access to the things that entice him. My parents ensured that I carried writer's tools into my adult life, and this novel was built using them.

An equally large "thank you" goes out to my early readers. Without their honesty and input, this book wouldn't have been possible. From my great friend Shaun Boutwell, who is never afraid to tell me when something I've written isn't working, to my colleague Adam Cesare, whose lead pipe feedback makes me a better writer, you gentlemen are rock stars. Last, but not least, there's my amazing wife Michelle, who spends most of her life listening to me hash out plot points and character beats. Without her, Melanie might have read like a man in a woman's skin, and that would've been creepy on a whole different level.

There are a lot of amazing people in my life. Without these folks and their support for my first novel, *Feral*, I'm not sure I would've been able to write a second one. Special thanks goes out to Mark Sieber at *Horror Drive-In*, not only for spreading the word about my little werewolf novel, but for more than a decade's worth of friendship and camaraderie. The same goes for Brian Collins at *Horror Movie a Day*, who pimped my work on social media more than anyone should have. This is also true of Steve Barton at *Dread Central*. You gave me a place to talk about all things horror, and I'm eternally grateful for that, and also your tireless coverage of my work. Finally, thanks to Evan Dickson of *Bloody Disgusting* for being kind enough to include *Feral* on the site's year-end holiday shopping guide in addition to covering its release. It's tough out there for all writers, let alone first timers. Because of you folks, *Feral* found an audience, and I'll always be grateful for that.

Which brings me at last to the readers—everyone who bought or borrowed *Feral*. Those who posted a review, told a friend, or dropped me an email. Whether you liked that book or hated it, you gave it a shot. Can't ask for anything more than that.

Thank you all.

Matt
May 2014

About the Author

Matt Serafini is the author of *Feral, Devil's Row*, and *Island Red*. He also co-authored a collection of short stories with Adam Cesare called *All-Night Terror*.

He has written extensively on the subjects of film and literature for numerous websites including *Dread Central* and *Shock Till You Drop*. His nonfiction has also appeared in *Fangoria* and *Horror-Hound*. He spends a significant portion of his free time tracking down obscure slasher films, and hopes one day to parlay that knowledge into a definitive history book on the subject.

His novels are available in ebook and paperback from Amazon, Barnes & Noble, and all other fine retailers.

Matt lives in Massachusetts with his wife and children.

Please visit mattserafini.com to learn more.

Made in the
USA
Middletown, DE